The Dark Apostle
by E. C. Ambrose

ELISHA BARBER

ELISHA MAGUS

ELISHA REX

ELISHA MANCER

ELISHA DAEMON

ELISHA DAEMON

BOOK FIVE OF

The Dark Apostle

E. C. AMBROSE

DAW BOOKS, INC.
DONALD A. WOLLHEIM, FOUNDER
375 Hudson Street, New York, NY 10014

ELIZABETH R. WOLLHEIM
SHEILA E. GILBERT
PUBLISHERS
www.dawbooks.com

First Printing, February 2018
1 2 3 4 5 6 7 8 9

DAW TRADEMARK REGISTERED
U.S. PAT. AND TM. OFF. AND FOREIGN COUNTRIES
—MARCA REGISTRADA
HECHO EN U.S.A.

PRINTED IN THE U.S.A.

ELISHA DAEMON

*"You need not hope that you will ever see heaven,
I have come to take you to the other side,
into eternal darkness, fire and ice."*

—Dante, *Inferno*

Chapter 1

❦

Elisha's eyes flared open in the night as another death suffused him with strength. He lay in a narrow vale of the mountains north of Venice, his breath blowing out into chill clouds, snow gleaming on the peaks all around him and dusting his fur-lined cloak. The mancers had chosen this vale for its desolation and utter lack of habitation, seeking a place where no one had died, and thus, Elisha's power was at its weakest. All of that had changed with the advent of the pestilence that now assailed the little enclave, pilgrims brought there by the mancers' promise of miracles, and held there by the grip of winter and the inevitability of death. The sky overhead wheeled with bright stars, and the Valley of the Shadow flickered, accepting the transit of the dead. For days now, the Valley had never closed, but pulsed around him like an aching wound, anchored by the constant stream of the dying. Jittery with power, Elisha rose and shook the snow from his cloak, wrapping it around him as he stalked among the sleeping and the dead. Even when no one spoke, he heard a windy whisper all around him, the distant chorus of the dying, the growing rumble of death triumphant.

Braziers of glowing coals and fire circles radiated feeble warmth in the huddled camp. Hundreds of pilgrims

lay in the mountain vale, packed beneath rooftops hast-
ily constructed from the lumber carried there by the
mancers who discovered the place. The mancers meant
to build a convent of the Blessed Mother: the young and
beautiful sleeper who gave birth to a miraculous child
and awakened at last from her holy rest. Brigit. Queen of
England, ruthless witch, the woman Elisha once believed
he loved, and now they called her "blessed". After he
had defeated the mancers who brought her to the vale
and wrested away the baby they hoped to use against
him, her handmaiden, Gretchen, had taken her away
down the mountains. Now, Elisha alone of all the witches
remained with the pilgrims as they fell ill and died. The
pilgrims' tales told him how far this sickness spread and
how fast. Did the dying that spread throughout Europe
keep Brigit awake as well? Did it stir her to remember
what she had been and return the bright and dangerous
light to those vacant green eyes?

Prayers and weeping echoed from either side as he
stepped carefully between the bundled forms. A cup of
wine might settle his spirit and allow him to sleep.

"Sir! Doctor!" called a broken voice, and Elisha
turned. "Please, sir, it's my daughter." A man knelt not
far from the chapel where Brigit's child had been born.
He held up his clasped hands, pleading, and Elisha recognized the father he had met on his journey here, a wiry
tradesman from the heart of Italy. Another man whose
child was dying. Elisha's throat constricted, dreading
what he must see, but he worked his way closer, taking
up a lantern on the way, a shaky pool of light that carried
him through the darkness.

The man's daughter lay shivering, her forehead glossy
with sweat, her thick blond hair matted to coils by her
restless tossing. Elisha set down the lantern and knelt
beside them. At his touch, she jerked convulsively, barely
aware of their presence. The chill shadow of death lin-

gered over her, the maelstrom of the Valley waiting to take her away.

"Can you help her?"

Smoothing back her hair, Elisha unstoppered the waterskin that always hung at his side and gave her a few sips. When he first met this family, he had used his power to extend the heat of a campfire, sharing the warmth with the pilgrims around him. This little girl had woken talking about a beautiful dream of sunlight and joy. Now, on this darkest of nights, he sent her the comfort of his hands, grateful, at last, for the cold that his power gave him, the cold power to soothe a fever. She sighed and drank a little more. A dark bulge marked the side of her throat.

The father took her hand in his, clutching her, his head bowed as he spoke. "I know the Lord would tell us not to beg for miracles, sir, but, if you could—I know that you have the healing touch." His voice broke again, and the man crumpled over his child, shrinking from his audacity.

One more time, Elisha sent his awareness deep, fusing his medical knowledge with his magical strength, that too-eager surging of chilly death. Fever shook her limbs—that, he understood. The nodes swelled up at her groin and armpits into these black masses, dark and ugly against her pale skin, her body ached, and her stomach churned with nausea. Any single symptom he might have thought to treat, but the tangle of them together was an evil he had never known. Elisha, too, hung his head. "This is not for me to heal." Bitterness stung his throat and nostrils.

"But all of the priests have left us."

"They were not priests," Elisha said, weary of explaining.

The father flicked him a glance. "Not even one? And the nuns, too?"

"Charlatans, here to take advantage of you and all the pilgrims." Necromancers, here to witness the birth of the child they hoped to use for their own purposes, here to celebrate the chaos and suffering of the sickness they knew was coming.

"I have been a sinner, of course, but she's only a child. Why would God take her from me? Why would He take any of them?" He lifted his head.

Why indeed? In the week since the mancers' departure, hundreds had already died: men, women, children lay buried in snow at the far end of the vale and a beaten track showed where they had been carried to their graves. The deaths started slowly, then spread quickly throughout the camp as Elisha and the other doctors expended their stores of herbs and poultices and tried every remedy they knew. Nothing worked.

"Perhaps the Holy Father at Avignon can intercede for us, do you think? Surely, the Pope himself must have the ear of God."

Twenty years ago, Elisha had become convinced that God wasn't listening. God did not hear the prayers of mothers in childbirth, of husbands, brothers, wives. He ignored the pleas of soldiers on the battlefield and those of prisoners who longed to be set free. This father prayed for hope, and his prayer, too, would go unanswered. "I wish I knew," Elisha said at last.

"But you have power!" The father's eyes flashed in the lamplight. "You have gifts, you have strengths that other people do not have—I have seen it. If God has given this to you, then why? If not to save the children, why do you have it at all?"

The fury in the father's voice stung him, his own questions lashing back at him in his helplessness. Elisha recoiled from the anger that spilled into the night and rippled along the fevered body of the child they both knelt over and worried for. He knelt there as a soldier on the battlefield, confronting this disease, but the man was right in his own way: the other doctors could do nearly as much as Elisha could to ease the suffering. His gifts, his strengths must be for more than this. His power must be put to use in other ways. He was a soldier no longer, and he must take this battle to the generals if he was to have any effect at all. He could not save this girl, but if he found the right weakness, if he tracked this disease to its source and stopped it spreading, he might save a thousand others.

He had to take this fight to the mancers, but how? He had a number of hints and clues, but little to connect them. Lady Katherine, the reformed mancer, spoke of a delivery from Kaffa that the German mancers had been expecting, while Count Vertuollo, the master of Rome, mentioned a man from Salerno who had acted rashly. Renart, the French mancer and architect of their attempt to claim Brigit's child, had sneered at Elisha and gloated over the devastation to come. All of them agreed on one thing: that Elisha could not stop it. In these last few days of fighting, Elisha almost agreed. Almost. If he had not the knowledge to attack the disease headlong, could he attack its masters?

"I'm sorry. I wish I could help her." Elisha lifted his hand and started to rise, but the girl sobbed in pain, and her father caught his wrist, tears streaking his face.

"Please, doctor." His lips trembled. "Please, don't be angry. I shouldn't—I didn't mean." He swallowed. "She is better with you here. Will you stay?"

Elisha swayed on his feet. How much longer? An hour or two? He sank down opposite her father and rested his hand on her brow. He sent her dreams and breezes, and sensed her drifting. Again, he thought of Katherine, this time reaching toward her. She had said she would conceal her sons and return to fight the mancers she once joined with. Had she learned anything that could help him to engage the mancers and stop this pestilence before it killed them all? Through all they had shared, he sought her now, letting the warmth of that relationship wash into his contact with the dying girl. For a time, they dreamed together and she rode a dappled horse whose dark mane flickered against her face until she laughed, and laughing, breathed her last. The Valley swirled to envelope her as she soared away, with the slightest smile on her face.

Elisha lay her hand across her chest and withdrew, leaving her father to his grief, the cold gripping his own heart as his breath misted the air. Then, from the Valley's awful chorus of despair, he heard the echo of his own name and he stopped where he stood. The sensation washed through him, his breath dying in his throat. The last time that happened, his friends had died. Now, again, the Valley was calling his name.

Elisha ran through the camp, leaping the pilgrims and dodging their fires, his senses extended and searching. Urgency pulsed at his heart, but he would not abandon these people as the mancer-priests and their false virgin had done. There! He located that particular blend of knowledge, confidence, and helplessness that must ring from his own presence. Beneath an awning of blankets slung up against the snow, he found Imelda, the woman doctor who led their efforts against the pestilence. Elisha dropped down beside her, but the force of his need had already woken her. She rubbed the sleep from her eyes. "Si, Dottore. What is it?" Her voice came out on a sigh.

"Imelda, I'm sorry, but I have to go. Will you stay and minister to the pilgrims?"

She stared up at him, and her hollow cheeks and shadowed eyes suggested she wished she, too, could escape. "I do not know what there is to be done, but I will do it."

He gave her shoulder a squeeze, sending gratitude

and comfort, then hurried from the heart of camp to a sheltered boulder where none would see him go. Guilt stabbed at him—these people depended upon him—but they were not the only ones.

Elisha opened himself to the call that sang through the Valley, stepping from the cradle of death into the void. It embraced him with fire.

"*Elisha, thank God,*" Katherine whispered through him, beside him, all around him, the heat of her living presence warping the flicker of the Valley. Glints of silver showed in her dark hair, and longing in her eyes, a handsome woman a few years older than himself.

He caught her hands, the voices of the dead pounding against his ears and thrumming in his heart.

"*Then you heard my call.*"

"*How could I not?*"

Her face lit, her silvered hair flickering and cheeks aglow beneath her gleaming eyes. "*You are never far from my thoughts. I hoped the same was true for you.*"

At that, he faltered, almost releasing her, and the current of her disappointment washed over him. "*I know,*" she said. "*I know that you are not for me, but still—*" She lost her smile and her grip strengthened. "*You must tell me what you need, but first, I have need of you—we all do.*"

"*Of course. Where are we going?*"

"*To Sinsheim, there's a riot.*"

He slid from the Valley beside her, his fingers entwined with hers, and stepped into a chaos of anger and an echo of steel. The rafters of a gloomy chapel rose up around them, the walls pierced with narrow windows, the stonework red and German in the glow of a single candle. With a streak of darkness, the Valley flared again nearby, a man screaming as he died. Others wailed in pain and panic. Somewhere a child cried. Instinct tugged him in that direction but Katherine clung to his hand.

"This is a chapel in a town two days' ride from

Heidelberg. We've been fighting, tracking the mancers, Daniel and Harald and I, but they know about us and they are working against our allies."

It took a moment for Elisha to place the names: Daniel, a foreman at Katherine's salt mine, had aided Elisha and Katherine in freeing her sons from the mancers; and Harald, who worked as Queen Margaret's assassin, supported Elisha in the fight that followed.

"The flagellants are back, and in force. Elisha—" She shook her head. Her muscles trembled with the strain, her eyes rimmed with shadows. "You know about the pestilence? There's rumors, terrible things, if it were just the mancers, I'd know what to do." Breaking off, she pressed her free hand to her chest and leaned into him. "We have to stop them, before they slaughter everyone."

"What—"

The door crashed open and a trio of men staggered inside. "Are there any here?" The leader shouted. "You!" he brandished a bloody sword at Elisha. "Recite the Lord's prayer."

Elisha's left eye traced the spirals of death that coiled around the man's blade. "Pater Noster qui et in caelis—" It came out in Latin, Thomas's voice echoing in Elisha's memory. Thomas, the king who prayed over him.

The man blinked, then gave a sharp nod. "Good— you're one of us. Come on, then, the Jews are getting away!"

Chapter 2

———————— ❖ ————————

Elisha marched forward and gripped the man's shoulder. His presence was hot with anger, his arm stiff with tension, but he was no mancer. "I've been in seclusion," Elisha told him. "What's the fighting about?"

"It's the wells. The Jews've been poisoning wells to the south, that's why this pestilence is spreading. If we can stop them now, it won't spread to us."

"You know this for certain?"

One of the man's companions ducked back out the door into a street thronged with fighters. The other growled, "We've no time to explain, just get a weapon."

Projecting calm, Elisha let his hands take on a slight glow, highlighting the scars at his palms. "The righteous do not need weapons."

The man he held glanced down and startled. "Who are you?"

"The Jews're the ones who call themselves righteous," said the other man, swinging about with two hands on his axe haft.

"Our Lord Jesus Christ was born a Jew," Katherine said. "Queen Margaret said—"

"Doesn't matter what she says now that we've got a new emperor." The second man blocked the door.

"Judaizers, that's what they are. That's why they're hiding here while we're out there taking care of things."

"But his hands," said the first man.

The second man turned toward the open doors. "Here!" he called to someone outside. "Drive 'em in! We've found some of their friends."

The shouting on the streets grew louder, and all of them tumbled back into the chapel as a group of people shoved inside, stumbling, still running. They burst between Elisha and Katherine, running for the back of the little chapel, two dozen men and women with children in their arms, some of them bleeding, carrying canes and cudgels.

"Fire it!" shouted someone outside, and the armed pursuit stumbled to a halt, ringing the steps of the chapel. A few of the men held torches, lighting their eyes with fire.

"Neighbors, do not take this madness on yourselves." A man separated himself from the group of refugees, a tall man with a thick white beard. The rabbi of Heidelberg. He raised his hands in a calming gesture. "Let these people shelter and listen to the words of your leaders and priests."

"Shut up!" A ceramic jug flew through the air and struck the floor just past the rabbi, but he did not move.

"We share the commandments of ha-shem, and the first of these—"

A second missile slammed into his chest and staggered him. Elisha caught his elbow, then the man with the ax stepped up, already swinging, his face twisted with hatred. The axe swung downward, and Elisha channeled that mad power of the dying. As the ax slid past him on the way to claim the rabbi's head, he put out his hand, still glowing, and brushed the weapon with his fingertips. It flew apart into puffs of old wood and ancient rust. Elisha put the thunder of death into his voice as he said, "Thou shalt not kill."

The ax-man drew back, and his hand began the automatic gesture of crossing himself. He glanced at the Jews, then back to Elisha, and his ax rose, pointing. "They're stealing the Bible, the holy words! Using their black arts against us!"

The man who had tried to recruit Elisha grabbed his companion's arm and tugged him out, the two of them stumbling down the steps as the doors swung shut. The wooden doors rattled and groaned, and one of the narrow windows showed murky figures barricading it from the outside.

"They're going to burn it, to burn all of these people." Katherine fought through the crowd. Their eyes met. They had a way out through the Valley, but how many others could be brought that way, and to where?

At his side, the rabbi straightened with a groan. A streak of blood marked his scalp, his head bare of its usual cap. His presence warmed when his dark eyes lifted to Elisha's face. "A surprise to see you, and yet, it is not. For what other reason are you among us, but this, to be here at our time of need." The rabbi raised his eyebrows, glancing at Katherine, then giving a little bow. "Margravine," he acknowledged her, using her title.

"You've met before?" Katherine asked, then she brushed this away. "Never mind—what are we going to do?"

Fire crackled outside and already the door at his back grew warm. The crowd outside roared along with the soaring flames. Inside, the Jewish families huddled together toward the center of the chapel.

"We can get you to freedom by folding the way," Elisha said. "Katherine, where can we go?"

"There is no place we are safe from madness and ignorance," said the rabbi. "We are not afraid to die for our faith." Then the corner of his mouth lifted. "Though we might wish it were not so soon for some of us." He gestured toward the gathering.

Katherine touched Elisha's arm. "*I have a few relics—the Church of the Holy Ghost, the royal chapel at Aachen, but he's right, the attacks are spreading faster than the pestilence.*"

Elisha's fur-lined cloak grew uncomfortably hot against his back as the flames licked up the building. "*It has to be stopped, all of this. You said Queen Margaret spoke against the violence—will she help?*"

"*She might. She is resting at my house in Bad Stollhein, but I can't bring so many people.*"

The restless power of death still pounded in Elisha's veins. Would it be enough? The alternative was to stay there and burn. "*I think I can get us to her.*"

"*All of these people? I've never brought more than two, and that was exhausting.*"

"*What choice do we have?*" To the rabbi he said, "We'll need everyone close together, holding on to each other."

"Should we pray?"

"If it comforts you, rabbi. You've taken this path before, you know what it's like."

The rabbi combed his fingers through his beard, betraying the slightest tremor, then he raised his arms and stepped in close to his small flock and spoke to them in a different tongue, that language that sounded like German, but wasn't.

"What about the rest of the Jews in town?" Elisha asked Katherine in a whisper. "This can't be all of them."

She wiped the back of her hand across her forehead. "Yes, Elisha, it very well could be."

The rabbi held out his hand, his face grown still and serious. Last time they met, Elisha had taken him to Jerusalem to show him the truth of his own power and win his aid in the fight against the mancers. Had that very alliance been the event that caused all of this? No—suspicion of the Jews lingered in the hearts and churches of every Christian, waiting for some terrible event to flare up into hatred but rarely into such open violence. Elisha took the rabbi's strong and aged hand in his own while Katherine circled the crowd and took a place opposite, holding hands with a young boy, her other arm circling the shoulders of a mother who carried a baby close against her breast. Did Katherine think of her own children, the daughter the mancers had tortured to death and the sons they had bled to punish Katherine's disobedience?

No matter, her eyes met his. "To the queen?"

Elisha nodded. Twenty-seven lives, to be drawn through the Valley of the Shadow of Death. He focused on Queen Margaret, the weight of the cloak she had given him draping his shoulders, the death of the child she had hoped for and wept for, the one he had arrived just too late to save. The baby's death was a slender thread, a life too young to leave an impact, except upon the heart of its mother. He marshalled his power, the near overwhelming whorls of death and dying that had spread through him these last few terrible days, and opened the Valley. Katherine's own power, small but clear, echoed his, sent to support him, surrounding these people with what comfort she could. For a long moment, they hovered between living and dying, between the chapel that roared with a sudden, ferocious light, and the snarling darkness of the Valley, then he found the thread of the child's death, like a silver gleam, a pin fixed in the fabric of Margaret's life.

The shades of the dead gathered round them, stronger and more numerous than ever before, stroking through his awareness. The rabbi's hand felt slick with sweat and frigid tendrils slid between, trying to drive them apart. The strain of holding the passage for so long shook through Elisha's muscles and throbbed in his skull. He focused on Queen Margaret, but the forces around him built into a frenzy. The rabbi's hand slipped, then the deep tenor of his voice stirred the madness, drawing them together again in the unmistakable rhythm of prayer. *"Baruch aso Adonoi, Eloheinu melech ha'olum, go'er baSatan umoshel beAshmodoi . . ."*

Across the circle, Elisha felt Katherine's cry of elation, then he pitched into a tumble of limbs and a sudden quiet broken by a woman's startled cry.

Chapter 3

❖

Elisha pushed to his knees in a velvety darkness, a single candle burning, the queen's pale, round face staring back at him from a gap between the bed curtains. He knew the room at once, the fine chamber in Katherine's manor house that she prepared for her queen when they came to the salt baths of Bad Stollhein in the late autumn. Likely, the queen's entourage had been caught there by winter after the emperor's death. The broad bedchamber between them held the little crowd of Jews, many of them, like Elisha himself, fallen to their knees with the jolt of their arrival.

The children started crying then, their mothers soothing, their fathers bewildered as the rabbi found his feet and regained his voice, calm and commanding.

The queen shook her head as if to clear it of sleep. "What on earth is all of this commotion? Can that possibly be you, the English doctor?" Margaret pushed back the curtains and rose up, snatching a robe from a hook at the bedside.

"Your Majesty?" Another woman emerged from beyond the larger bed: Lady Agnes, the queen's companion. "My goodness! Who are all of these people?"

"Please forgive us, Your Majesty." Katherine struggled to extricate herself from the group, gently peeling away from the grip of the boy beside her. "These people are in need of refuge. We hoped you would help them."

Agnes and Margaret both lit lanterns, then Agnes took over the lighting as the queen arrayed herself better for company. In spite of her sleeping clothes, within a moment she assumed the regal air and stern intelligence Elisha had come to associate with her. "They are Jews? From where?"

"From a village outside Heidelberg, Your Majesty." The rabbi gave a bow. "I heard there might be trouble, and I travelled there to see what might be done about the danger."

"What indeed? I abhor violence, of course, but I cannot be seen to be harboring Jews, not when my own position is far from secure. At any moment, the emperor"—she gave a little sniff—"the new emperor might withdraw my every rank and privilege."

"There is no need for us to stay, Your Majesty. We are merely in transit to a destination where we might breathe a little while in peace. Again, forgive us for this intrusion." The rabbi bowed again and raised his hands to his people, encouraging them to rise, to move toward the door as Agnes hurried to open it.

Katherine curtsied and darted a glance to Elisha, but he found himself watching the queen, arrayed in the remnants of her royalty, so diminished after her husband's death. Margaret, in her capacity as Queen Consort, had once told him she would look after the Germans—he need not trouble himself. After all, he was not royalty and had no duty to defend his realm. But he had been. If only for a little while, he had held the power of a nation. He knew the strain of balancing the factions, the needs of the peasantry against the demands of the barons, the fear of war against the scarcity of the resources needed to fight it. Would he have turned away two dozen supplicants with no place else to go? Would

Thomas? If they would win this war against the mancers and confront the spreading evil of the pestilence, how could those with power deny it to those who had none?

She stared back at him, her face as lovely and impervious as marble, still pale with the grief of her losses. Elisha gave a bow and stalked from the room, yanking the door shut behind him. In the torchlit corridor, tapestries gleamed with golden threads, and the little crowd bunched together, sooty and bleeding.

"Some of you are injured." Agnes waved them along. "Come to the hall—I'll fetch Klaus and find you some provisions before you go."

Who was Klaus? The name brought a brief smile to Katherine's lips as she moved ahead with Agnes, heads close as they whispered, then Agnes hurried on and they entered a broad hall with a fire banked in its great hearth. A pair of servants roused to stir the fire back to life, but the new flames lit their narrowed eyes and down-turned lips as they examined the Jews. The rabbi moved among his people, settling them on benches. Now that their fear and confusion ebbed, spikes of pain infused their disordered presence, and Elisha became aware of the individuals: the mother and baby, exhausted and worried as she searched among those rescued for someone she could not find; a youth with a torn shirt, a bloody arm clasped to his chest; two men who gripped their weapons, glancing around them, still vigilant.

Elisha trembled, the power of the Valley departing him. He possessed the power to aid, to heal—but if he spent it now, on these injuries, would he be ready for the next battle, and the next? Agnes returned, a tall man following after with the hesitant tread of one newly wakened. The man lifted his head, then his hand, waving a little greeting, and Elisha recognized Doctor Emerick, the queen's physician.

"If you need to tend them, Elisha, then tell me how to

help," Katherine said, coming up beside him. She rested her hand on his back, casual and warm, as if it were the most natural thing in the world, and so it might be, for those who had been lovers.

"Emerick can handle the injuries I've noticed." Elisha wet his lips as he glanced at Katherine, the heat of her presence drawing him, her relief and comfort in his own presence just as attractive, perhaps even more so. "I need to know what's been happening here."

She nodded, then called out, "Klaus, we're going to the armory, if you should need us."

Across the hall, where he leaned over the young man's injury, Doctor Emerick gave a nod.

"Klaus?" Elisha asked softly.

"He and Agnes are quite smitten with each other." Again, that slender smile, then her hand encouraged him onward, down a corridor at the back of the hall. "Why were you seeking me, Elisha?"

He briefly sketched for her the scene in the mancers' vale, with its forlorn and dying pilgrims. "I did all I could for them, but it's not enough. I haven't the knowledge to fight this pestilence victim by victim—and I shouldn't be. For all that I am a doctor, I am wasted trying to treat any single patient." It cut against his instincts, but he knew it for the truth. "I must look deeper, toward the root causes. The mancers intend to profit by this, no doubt. Someone needs to stop them."

Katherine nodded and started walking again, drawing him with her. "When you left, you sent Harald to me for aid against the mancers." He felt regret ripple through her presence, perhaps, for her own prior involvement with the enemy. "Even I hadn't known all of Harald's talents before—even now, I am not sure that I do. For a man who seems so open, he keeps a wide variety of secrets."

"It's what makes him so good at his job," Elisha said.

"Daniel Stoyan, the Jewish salt mine foreman, is our weapons-master. Knowing that the salt inhibits magic, he's started making all sorts of things that even *desolati* can wield against them. We have continued what you began, stalking the mancers themselves." She produced a key and unlocked a narrow door, locking it again behind them when they had passed through. The stairs beyond led down into a musty, salty chamber carved from the salt deposits on which Katherine's fortune rested. The candles she lit, in their recesses of salt, glowed pink against the vaulted ceiling of what had once been a cellar. Even with the deadening effect of the salt that reduced his magical senses, the cold of an unnatural death seeped into Elisha's skin, stinging his face and hands. Katherine busied herself with more candles, her movements jerky. She shook back her hair, then tugged it impatiently into a queue that revealed the curve of her cheek and the span of her throat.

Elisha's raised hand stilled her even before they touched. "Who died here?"

"My husband." She walked to a high table littered with rusty tools. "It is deep, it is salty, it is secure. None have been allowed to come here for many years." With a broad gesture, she displayed an array of knives with slender, crystalline inlays along their blades, then stroked a finger along the crystal in one of the blades. "Rock salt. Steel carries the salt into the mancer's flesh, stopping the flow of magic like a cork in a bottle. If the blade is well-placed, it can kill on its own. The salt inlays degrade the steel faster than we'd like, so they rarely last more than a single use. Only someone willing and able to get very close, like Harald, can use these, but we have arrows as well, with salt embedded in the tips, and even brining our clothing makes us harder to catch."

"Very clever."

"You have given me very capable allies." She flashed

a smile in the direction of the table. "But we have slain most of our targets, the mancers I knew, and those we have since discovered, and of course Harald and Daniel and the others cannot act without me to recognize the enemy." Her fingers stroked the length of a salt-enhanced blade. "But now that you are here, you can aid us."

Elisha, too, traced the weapons they had made, her longing stroking over him, too powerful to be contained by the salt around them. "Do you think your work has roused the mancers against the Jews?"

"God forbid!" She crossed herself. "Since the pestilence began to spread—even since we first heard rumors of its approach, of how many were dying—there have been rumors against the Jews. People are saying it's not enough for them to take our money, now they want everything, they want us to die. According to the rumors, they've been poisoning the wells and stealing communion wafers to use them for black magic. People think if they kill the Jews, then the pestilence won't reach us." Her eyes met his across the table and all the blades between them. "Sometimes, where the riots are, the mancers are as well, feeding off the anger and the death. When I heard about the assault outside Heidelberg, I went a-hunting. I found no one; at least, no one who was not merely furious and brutal—no one magic. The mancers may have begun this, Elisha, but it does not need their aid to crush us all."

From the top of the stairs, a soft knock sounded. "Margravine?" called a woman's voice. "It's Agnes. And the rabbi."

"How much does he know?" Katherine asked.

"About me? Almost everything." Almost. Elisha did things in Rome that he had spoken of to no one, but it was the things he had not done that haunted him at night, the face of the priest he allowed to die, the weeping of children overcome by the plague.

Mounting the stairs, holding up her skirts just enough, Katherine unlocked the door to let them in, but Agnes demurred, hurrying back to aid the doctor. The rabbi descended slowly, some of the solemnity of his position returned to him since their desperate flight, hands folded at his back. "I should thank you both for our deliverance, and for the refuge of your home, Margravine, if only for the night."

"I am sorry I cannot offer more. We hoped the queen might do so, but with her entourage still snowed in here, I don't know—"

The rabbi spread his hands and acknowledged her. "There are only so many unexpected guests that even such a fine manor may support I am sure. No, we can move on."

"Back to Heidelberg?" Elisha asked. "Will you be safe there?"

The old man regarded him gently. "For now. This madness spreads before the pestilence. It is hard to know which will be the more deadly."

"Are they holding services at the Church of the Holy Ghost?"

With a little shrug, the rabbi said, "It has ceased construction for the winter, but I don't believe it is ready for services."

"I can bring you there." Inside the chamber of salt, the jittery sense of the dying had faded, leaving him hollow and relieved.

Katherine stepped before him. "It is still the marketplace, Elisha, bound to be full of people after dawn. Is that wise?"

"Better at night, then," the rabbi observed. "Your Doctor Emerick has seen to the injured. We could be ready for travel."

"*Can you?*" Katherine said through Elisha's flesh, settling her fingers on his arm.

"How are your people taking it?" Elisha asked the rabbi.

"We are resolute. The violence scared them, of course it would, but you coming, taking us to safety ... I have always said such things are superstition, and now it seems an article of faith that such a man exists, that he might be called upon in time of need, and he might come. Their bodies quake with fear, and yet, their hearts are strong." The rabbi gazed at him as if from a great distance. "Their faith is affirmed. With you here, they feel worthy."

Elisha suppressed his incredulous laughter. These last few days, more than ever before, helplessness bound him. Neither his medical knowledge, nor his magical skill gave him any advantage against the plague, this greatest weapon of his enemies. And yet his presence made these people feel worthy. What could he do but strive to be worthy of them in turn? "I can be ready in a moment."

The rabbi gave a nod and ascended the stairs to prepare his followers.

Katherine turned on Elisha, raising her hand to his face, gazing at him. "*Can you do this? I feel so weary already that I may faint on the spot.*"

He caught her hand in his and lowered it, but did not let go, not yet. "*This room contains a single death, Katherine*"—she flinched, fear, anger, guilt flashing through beneath her skin as she recalled her husband's death, but he went on—"*but here, it is the only one. Out there, I can feel them. I can feel the tide approaching, roaring like the ocean, a tide of death that those people can only imagine. It sustains me.*"

"I wish it could be me, sustaining you," she whispered aloud.

Elisha squeezed her hand and let her go. "It's not enough." He moved beyond her dismay toward the stairs.

"What isn't, Elisha?" she called after him. "I'm not

enough? Is it love that can't sustain you, or is it life itself? Have you redeemed me, only to succumb to death yourself?"

Elisha could not answer. As he ascended, leaving the dulling effect of the salt behind, the rush returned, suffusing him flesh and bone. Death rose upon the wind in an icy stroke that left him alert, and terribly alive.

Chapter 4

❖

$\mathcal{J}$n the hall where the refugees gathered and readied themselves for another journey through wonder, Elisha found Agnes and Doctor Emerick—Klaus—cleaning up at a basin, leaning together. At his approach, they parted, looking guilty, Agnes glancing behind him, but Katherine was slow to follow. Either she needed some time to recover from her weariness, or Elisha had finally said too much.

"Where did you take your medical training, Emerick?"

The young physician dried his hands briskly on a towel. "At Bologna. Why do you ask?"

Elisha sighed. No help there. "Our enemies have linked the sickness that approaches to Salerno."

Emerick gave a snort. "As well they might. Salerno used to be the finest school, a hundred years ago. Nowadays, it has fallen off in both attendance and quality. The University at Heidelberg has its own program of study, but it has not yet attracted the best faculty—they're all at Paris or Bologna. Where did you study?"

"The streets of London. And the brothels." Then he took in the refugees around them, bravely preparing for another transition. "For a time, I had a Jewish master-surgeon." A Jew who had decided to burn himself rather than be used by the mancers.

"I paid a visit to the medical library at Salerno once, to copy the manuscript of Matteo Silvaticum's *Opus Pandectarum Medicinae*, a long and tedious task but the gardens there are lovely, even now the medical school has fallen a bit behind. The entire city is built up the sides of mountains, with only a little flat ground in between. No river barges to reach Salerno, it's either a boat or a donkey."

Elisha let his fingers rest on Emerick's arm as the man spoke, gathering snatches of his memories of the place, in case he needed that knowledge later. "Do they have a patron saint?"

Emerick's brow furrowed. "The cathedral is dedicated to San Matteo—it is a beautiful church. But he is not as San Gennaro is to Naples, for example." The doctor took a breath as if to proceed, but Elisha broke in.

"Thanks for your help."

"It is the least I could do, I am sure." He plucked a heavy robe from a nearby bench and slipped it back on. "Do you really think this pestilence is as dreadful as they say? Ships of the dead and so forth? The tales we've heard make it seem, well, positively Biblical."

"It is as bad and worse. I've seen it. It starts with a fever and chills, nausea and vomiting. The victims have dark swellings on the thighs, neck and underarms." He indicated his armpits. "They get disoriented and clumsy. But after a couple of days, they can't walk in any case. Sometimes their fingers and lips turn black. Necrotic."

Emerick's throat bobbed as he swallowed, his long face unnaturally still. "What is the treatment?"

"If I find one, I'll be sure to let you know."

Emerick gave a slight nod of his head, as if they two shared a secret knowledge. "Well, the climate of Italy is hot and moist, quite the opposite of ours, and likely the miasma that carries the disease cannot assail us to the same extent. God willing, the winter's snow shall keep it on the far side of the mountains and give it a chance to die out."

The vibration of the plague's approach thrummed in Elisha's bones like an on-coming cavalry. "God willing, at least it may slow the spread of the disease." God seemed willing enough for them all to die, starting, apparently, with the Jews.

"We are prepared," the rabbi announced, his congregation gathered close, holding hands or arm in arm, all of their shining eyes focused on Elisha. "And there is someone in Heidelberg who shall be pleased to meet you again."

Elisha stepped into the circle of their warmth and faith, and Katherine's steps pattered behind him. She touched the hand of the man beside him and broke their grasp to stand between them, holding a relic that linked them with the Church of the Holy Ghost. She knotted her fingers into Elisha's, saying nothing at all, her touch as cold as a mancer's, her presence concealed with the aid of the bone talisman now pressed between their palms. The second journey, the destination both closer and more familiar, passed quickly, especially without worrying about the chapel bursting into flames around them.

The vast space of the empty church echoed around them, winter's blast pushing through the cloth-draped window frames. The Jews separated into their families, murmuring their thanks to Katherine and Elisha. Turning to Elisha, the rabbi said, "I will guide them from here. Some have family in the city, but we will find a place for everyone. As for you . . ." he gave a sigh. "I do not expect we can look for your help at every danger. I think there are more dangers mounting at every moment. When all is done, and I am once more in my study by the fire, I will be reading and writing of this, you can be sure. You have become mishra, a part of our story." Not giving Elisha time to respond to this, or perhaps expecting he would not, the rabbi continued, "My home will be filled with these people tonight, but there is a small abbey on the hillside, with a very fine guest lodge where you will find a welcome." With that, he turned and brought his people out into the night.

Elisha felt tired from spell-casting, and restless at the same time. He hoped for sleep, but doubted it would come with ease. Not speaking, not letting go, Katherine accompanied him into the dark and silent streets. Snow sifted lightly down over them, the delicate flakes resting on Elisha's hands. They walked up the hill between orderly houses of stone and brick to where a lantern burned at the abbey gate. The gatekeeper smothered a yawn and escorted them to a moderate but well-appointed hall with thick tapestries and cushioned couches. A man sat slumped into one of these, close to the blazing fire, a book clutched in one hand, a quill in the other, though he neither wrote nor drew. At the sound of their approach, he stirred and looked up, his dark, haunted eyes meeting Elisha's. Pleasure flared and died in his presence, and he said, "Then it is true. The end times are upon us."

Chapter 5

❖

After this dire pronouncement, Isaac the goldsmith put down his things and held out his hands to Elisha, meeting him with a clasped hand and shoulder, almost an embrace. His customary velvet and brocade clothing looked mussed and spotted, his curly hair gone limp, as if he had lost concern for his appearance, but he still wore the granulated cross that showed his skill, and his adopted faith.

"I'm glad to see you well," Elisha said.

Isaac's hand trembled, though some of his pleasure returned. "Friar Gilles is here, but he's sleeping. He is either sleeping or eating—or drinking, when he can get the ale." A hint of the acid tone Elisha remembered so well crept into his voice then, a welcome echo of the ordinary, as if the world were not coming to an end. "Queen Margaret asked us to continue our work, to make a fine reliquary in her husband's name. It worries her that he died apostate."

"As well it might. Isaac Burghussen, goldsmith, this is Katherine, the Margravine of Tirol."

"You look familiar from Margaret's court." Katherine covered a yawn, her shoulders drooping, and Elisha slid an arm around her.

Isaac gave a short bow, his curly hair bobbing. "An honor, Margravine."

"Katherine has been working against my enemies."
He could feel the exhaustion that flowed beneath her
skin, her defenses fading away with the long night. *"You
should take your rest."*

"And you," she echoed. Her gaze flicking over him.

"I'll try."

"The novices can prepare a light supper, my lady,"
said the monk who had accompanied them. "We also
have a private chamber to offer you, my lady. We have
only two other guests, and not like to have more this
time of year."

"To bed, then," she told him. "And my thanks."

The monk spread his hand toward an archway in invitation. With a gentle squeeze of Elisha's fingers, she followed the monk away to her rest. Between the two of
them, she and Elisha had slain the mancers of Heidelberg, and he prayed she would be safe through the night.
Isaac beckoned Elisha to sit by him at the fire, moving
his open book, a page full of sketches—arms, faces,
heads, beautifully drawn. "The Margravine is attached to
you," Isaac observed.

"She wants me to stay here, to help her fight the
mancers."

"Will you?" The goldsmith cocked his head, watching
Elisha sidelong.

"She and her assistants need me. I've seen dozens
more mancers since last we met. I can identify them and
track them down. Some of them will be here, following
the pestilence or—" He studied Isaac's face. "Hounding
the Jews."

Isaac's eyes turned glossy. "I need to go home," he
breathed, tracing the images of a pair of children drawn
in ink on the pages of his book. "I am Christian now. My
wife is Christian-born, and my children." He shook his
head. "But if anyone discovers their heritage." He let the
book slide, pressing the heels of his hands against his

eyes. "I am meant to be working in gold, to be crafting a vessel for the body of a saint, for the glory of God and the emperor's soul, and I can't sleep for fear of what may happen. I can't think in gold and metal now—I can barely manage my tools." His voice fell to a whisper, nearly a moan. "I keep seeing my parents die, my brothers— hearing my sister's screams. It's happening all over again. Will it never end?"

Between one heartbeat and the next, the competent goldsmith had collapsed into the child he had been, spattered with his brother's blood, pleading for mercy in the name of someone else's god. Elisha clasped his hand on Isaac's shoulder, sending comfort. "I can take you home," Elisha whispered. "I can bring you there in an instant."

"Folding the way." Isaac's hands fell, his eyes gleaming, caught between terror and hope. "Will we be safe there—or are they safer without me?"

"We'll bring them back here; the gatekeeper said they've got plenty of room."

"Where can a Jew be safer than in an abbey?" Isaac's lip curled.

"That's settled, then." Elisha drew back, smothering a yawn. The weariness of so much magic finally caught him, dispelling that jittery sense of ever-present death. His arrival had saved the lives of those Jews, and here was a way he could aid the man who had risked himself for Elisha in the past. Knowing the good that came from his magic helped to reconcile his own fears with his power. Katherine offered him a chance to use his power in the service of the right, stalking the mancers with weapons she had developed. If enough of them could be killed, the pestilence must die, without the black magic that sustained it.

"Not tonight—even I can see that you're in no condition for that, and you've not even told me what you've been doing." Isaac closed his sketchbook and stood up.

"Come, I can show you to a room. I've taken one over as my workshop, for a fee, of course. No need to wonder how they pay for all of this." He waved his hand to indicate their rich surroundings, then lowered it for Elisha. "Come."

At the end of a short corridor, next to the workshop Isaac had claimed, Elisha tumbled into a soft bed, tugging his fur cloak around him. Katherine lay in the chamber above, already sleeping, and he needed no magic to sense the snoring of Friar Gilles, keeping company with his crate full of relics, a slithery tangle of sensations of death and pain and reverence. To sense their familiar presences gave him comfort against the dread that crept up from beyond the walls. When Isaac, too, had gone to bed, his agitated presence calming at last, then Elisha let himself rest.

He woke to an argument, another familiar event when Isaac was involved, but this argument flowed in clipped whispers, meant to let him sleep. No matter how softly they spoke, he knew the combatants all too well for their rising emotions to escape his awareness. Dim sunlight glowed at the shuttered window, and Elisha pushed aside his cape and rose stiffly. For a moment, he worked at attunement, drawing together everything he saw and knew and sensed about this place. A dozen monks occupied another wing, deep in prayer at this hour, while his three fractious comrades sat in the hall at the end of the corridor. Down the hillside, the city woke, carters hauling their wares, market stalls opening and fishmongers pushing barrels up from the riverside. Yet, if Elisha stretched a little further, the shadow of death stretched back toward him, seeping up from the south and the east as if the darkness would steal the sun. He started down the corridor, the voices growing louder with his approach.

In the hall, Katherine rapped her knife down across

her plate. "You saw how distant and distracted he was—
he must conserve his power and use it to the greatest
good. He cannot simply hare off at any task his friends
would ask of him."

Isaac said, "I would not have asked it of him, Margravine, but it is a boon I will not reject."

"Of course, he is welcome to the nourishment of any
relic in my collection," Friar Gilles offered. "I have many
fine saints who would bless his endeavors, even if they
must be in the service of the Jews."

Isaac's voice growled across the table. "Even the Pope
does not condone such violence as has been done against
the Jews, Brother."

"No, certainly not. And the Lord who knows when a
sparrow falls does not prioritize miracles, at least not in
any fashion that you and I can fathom. Perhaps the doctor himself, ah, but here he is." Friar Gilles pushed himself to his feet, arms wide in welcome, his smile seeming
even wider as Elisha entered the room. His rope belt
slung a bit lower around his stomach than it had before,
testifying to Isaac's grumble about the friar and his food.
His skin glowed with health and humor, thick hair edging his tonsure.

Isaac, too, stood up, chin held high, but one hand
clutching the cross he always wore, his thumb worrying
over the granulated gold. "Forgive me if I spoke too
freely last night, Elisha. Certainly I do not expect you to
turn aside from your tasks to worry over my family. I
have a horse; I'll simply ride—"

"Alone through the mountains in the snow?" Elisha
put up his hands as he approached. "I wouldn't let you."
He darted a glance at Katherine, but she focused on her
plate, slicing a wedge of cheese into tiny bits.

"So you'll simply leave us?" she said to her plate. "We
need you here."

"I fully intend to return, and to bring them all with me."

"Yes, an excellent notion." Gilles clapped his hands, his grin fixed. "Here, the goldsmith's family will be welcomed in comfort. I myself can tutor his children, if such should be required."

"You'll do what he wants of you at the risk of so many others?" She let the knife clatter onto her plate. "You know as well as I do that it's harder to travel to an unknown place. Even your power must have limits."

Gilles moved toward Elisha, his tonsure glistening with sweat. "Ah, my lady, he also has recourse to the bounty of the Lord. With prayer and with the right saints—"

Elisha met Katherine's hard gaze. "I'll do what he needs, Katherine, because it sets my own soul to rights. If that is unbearably selfish, so be it."

She shoved back from the table, her chair clattering against the wall. "You really are a—" But she swallowed the word, her glare shifting from him to Isaac and back. "It is selfish," she said in a softer voice. "Of the both of you. Harald and I have risked our lives daily to find the enemy, to spy them out and dispatch them. The goldsmith has no idea what his little boon requires. That same journey might be spent in slaying a necromancer or in saving a dozen more people."

"I can care for my own family, my lady. You are in the right." Isaac turned away, gathering his things into his hands from the side table—quills, book, a roll of parchment, a bottle of ink. The bottle slipped from his grasp and shattered on the floor in a spreading pool of darkness.

Isaac stared down at it, his shoulders so tight that Elisha could feel it. Almost, he reached out to touch the other man, to reassure Isaac he did not need to be alone, as he had been left as a child to face the men who had murdered his family. But Elisha held back, his hands remaining at his sides. A "bugger," that's what Katherine nearly called him. How much of her argument came from need, how much from envy? She did not know whom he loved, merely that it was another man who held his heart. Now she seemed to think it might be Isaac.

"None of you knows what it is for me to step outside the world. Even you, Katherine, who have done it your-self." He looked at each of them in turn, Friar Gilles's wide-eyed wonder, Katherine's bleak withdrawal, Isaac's bowed head and rigid spine. "You would have me stay and make your miracles. I wish I could. I wish I could be there for everyone who needs me." Katherine's face soft-ened, her lips parted as if to speak. "You and Harald have done so well—you need my knowledge, but you don't need me. With Isaac's help, I can share it with you, and with all of those who would serve at your side."

At that, Isaac did turn, pivoting on his heel, frowning. "What can I do to be of use?"

"Your sketches gave me an idea. I need some pictures. After we bring your family here"—he shot a warning glance at Katherine—"will you help me draw them?"

"Of course." Isaac looked wary rather than victorious.

"Let the monks know that your family is on their way, and we shall go out to meet them after breakfast, does that suit you?"

Isaac gave a nod and walked out, smoothing his velvet clothes, head held high.

"And me? What can I do? The fingernails of Saint Lu-cia came in handy for you, didn't they?" Friar Gilles stee-pled his own fingers together. "I have added a few items to the collection which may be of interest to you."

"Later, I am sure your relics will be of use," Elisha told him, and the monk beamed, his fingers tapping on each other.

Katherine stood by the wall to one side of him, Elisha at the archway. After a long moment, Gilles said, "Well, then, perhaps I'll go join the brethren at prayer, shall I?" He pinched up a bit of his habit and shuffled away down the corridor toward the cloister.

The day grew brighter, for the shutters cast slits of shadow across the wall above Katherine's head. Her silvering hair had been carefully braided, her face washed, the darkness beneath her eyes faded with a night of rest. She stood in a pool of deathly power, the talisman of her husband's hand still bound in the bodice against her breast.

The line of her jaw looked hard in the pale light. Her gaze remained on the floor. "Your friend should have cleaned up his ink. They will never be rid of that stain."

"I'm sure it will be taken care of."

She flicked her hands along her skirts, as if she could smooth the wrinkles away. "Am I meant to apologize for looking out for you, or for the fact that we need you here in order to continue our work, the work that you set out for us?"

"You might apologize for your suspicions of my relationship to Isaac. Though I am glad for all our sakes you stopped short of accusation." He stepped up to the table and took the last seat rather than ally himself with Gilles's or Isaac's empty chairs. A platter of bread, cheese and dried grapes filled the center of the table, along with a carafe of wine. Elisha helped himself and sat down to eat, the weight of her silence almost as oppressive as the growing shadow of the plague. "What do you suppose is a more certain way to get him killed, to spread the word about his past, or to spread a rumor of buggery?"

"Oh, for Heaven's sake, Elisha, I did not mean to hurt anyone, least of all the goldsmith." She dropped into her chair across from him and scraped it closer to the table.

"Me, then?" He smeared butter on a slab of bread and bit into it, fresh and white and crisp, a very long distance from anything they had eaten in the vale these last days.

To be true, with the smell of sickness all around them, they barely thought of eating at all.

Katherine reached across the table, spreading her hand. "Never you."

It was a lie, actually. She once wore poison on her nails for the purpose of killing him. Reformed or not, Katherine had been a mancer. He took another bite of the bread. It reminded him of England, eating the king's bread, made from the finest flour. What was Thomas doing now? Elisha washed down the bread with a swallow of the deep red wine, and missed the cider of home. Thomas's golden ring winked on Elisha's little finger, a dangerous temptation to flee to his home.

He set down his cup. "Much greater things are at risk here than you and me, our friends or our feelings." He reached out at last and touched her hand. "*The mancers are spreading this disease over all the nations. I stopped them from claiming Rome when I ruined their relics, but they had already set it in motion. The rabbi said a long while ago that they might topple the kingdoms, but that they would be hard-pressed to break the Church itself. They are trying, and we cannot let them win.*"

With her thumb, she shifted the ring on his finger. "*Forgive me. I must try not to let my feelings intrude. I should be more like you.*"

"*It means so much to know you are fighting with me, even if I'm miles away.*"

"*Harald does most of the work.*" But still, her touch echoed with her remorse and gratitude.

"Where is he? Can you bring him? Or should we go there?"

She shook her head. "*He's only one, and very experienced at this sort of travel. I'll bring him here. Would to God he were a magus himself. He's at the court of Emperor Charles, to spy out the mancers there.*"

The worried hum of Isaac's presence approached, and

Elisha broke his grip, chewing the last of his bread and swallowing his wine. Katherine made ready for her own journey while Elisha and Isaac spoke about his home. From the heart of his attunement, Elisha reached for the Valley, opening himself again to the tides of death.

In moments, they stood together outside a tidy house on a broad street in a distant town, as Isaac broke his embrace with his wife and struggled with the words to explain what must happen next. When they had packed a few things—clothes, tools and supplies for Isaac's work—each took a child by the hand. Elisha rallied his strength to shield them from the worst of the passage, showing them the glow and sharing the song of the peaceful dead while the wails of the shadows swelled around him. At last, they stepped through the Valley back to Heidelberg, to the deserted Church of the Holy Ghost, rather than be seen to appear from nowhere. As Katherine had said, the journey to Isaac's unfamiliar home, even guided by the bits of blood that every craftsman must spill the course of his labors, left Elisha breathless, while the journey back to Heidelberg felt like just a few steps. The two girls stared around them, gazing at their father like a hero, watching Elisha with terrified awe as he escorted them back up the hill to the abbey that would be their home.

He had not gotten one foot past the gate when a woman assailed him, catching his hands in a grip of magic and howling her fury into his flesh.

Chapter 6

❖

"**W**here is my daughter? What have you done with her?"

The assault dropped him to his knees, her demands beating at his ears while her magic shot into his skin, streaking through him, searching for answers. Her power thrust into him, piercing as knives in the desperation of her need. Gretchen's mother, a prosperous innkeeper, bore little resemblance to the woman he had met a few months ago when he first came to Heidelberg. Her round face looked puffy with grief, her cap askew and apron smeared with the mud of the street, but her teeth set like the mask of a demon.

Isaac leapt between the furious witch and his family, hurrying them through the abbey gate before he turned to Elisha. He unslung his satchel of tools and swung it at the woman's back, but she blew out a breath, turning it to a roaring wind that knocked the goldsmith from his feet and scattered his things all around him. He struck the stone with a grunt of pain.

Snatching for the power of the Valley, Elisha shielded himself with death, rejecting her sorcerous probe with an icy pressure. She fought back with the fire of her fury, a mother's fear he could not simply turn aside. The slithering stroke of her power nauseated him, twisting beneath his skin. Elisha cried out.

"Let him go, for God's sake!" Isaac scrambled to his hands and knees, wobbling, blood tangling in his curls.

As she wrapped her hands all the tighter around Elisha's, forging her flesh into steel, Elisha dropped beneath her. He dragged her off balance so she tumbled over his head with a shout, forced to release him or break her own wrists as she fell. Whirling, Elisha drew up the power of death and put out his hands as if inviting her to make contact. He gathered the cold so that his breath frosted into the air. The effort made him shaky, but he forced himself to be still and project strength. "Do not touch me again, woman." His hands spread low, patently empty yet full of menace.

"You bastard, what have you done with her? Have you skinned her alive?"

"That's not my way and never was. Last I saw Gretchen she had taken charge of another magus, a witch who would see all *desolati* burned if it means the witches can thrive. When you see Gretchen, ask her what she did in England, and what happened to the people she met there."

"My Gretchen's never been to England." The tendrils of her presence reached toward him, tingling.

"She went there searching for me and led a dozen of her husband's friends to steal a sleeping witch and kill her keepers." The loss of Mordecai blossomed into the hollow at his heart, and Elisha shed his weakness. He still believed Gretchen herself to be deceived by the mancers—what more could a mother do, but to seek her child and to defend her? It did not change the fact that Mordecai was dead because of Gretchen's aid to the enemy.

The woman's glance flickered over him. "I cannot feel the lie in this—you must be a very accomplished liar."

"Not half as good as your son-in-law. Or it may just be that I'm telling the truth."

Her nostrils flared, then she blew out another blast of wind that seared his face and hands and tossed his hair about him.

Elisha stood firm. "Last I knew, she was in Italy. The shadows there"—he lifted his left hand, indicating the south—"you feel them too, don't you? Something terrible is coming, and Gretchen is a part of it. If you find her, get her home and get her away from the necromancers."

"She is no part of that. You act as if I don't know my own daughter."

"She stole my talismans, and burned most of them. I still have one only because it fell from her grasp." He clenched his fist around Thomas's ring, but his most important talisman, a vial of the earth where his brother bled out his life, remained in mancer hands.

That caused a breach in the woman's fury, an affront at the idea of a magus stealing another's talismans, much less destroying them. "Because you threatened her, you threaten all of us—we can all see what you are."

"She stole my way home, woman. You may all be stuck with me for a very long time."

"Heaven forbid we stand between you and the gates of Hell."

"You know nothing of Hell, but you will learn. Gretchen's friends will deliver it."

Behind her, on the long slope into the city, Katherine strode upward. A slight, quick figure came with her, breaking off and slipping to the side, a shimmering blade already coming to hand. Harald. The innkeeper glanced around, then her presence withdrew, the pressure of her attention against him vanishing. Two steps back, then she dodged down an alley between the other buildings and hurried away.

Elisha turned to the door, to Isaac, on his knees, breathing heavily, a trickle of blood marking his forehead. "You're hurt," Elisha said. "Let me see to it." But he swayed on his feet, and Isaac waved him off.

"Just a cut, nothing serious." He reached out and snagged his satchel, starting to gather his fallen tools back into it.

"Elisha!" Katherine ran the last few yards, her skirts bunched up in her fists. "You look awful. And what was that about stolen talismans?"

Harald slid into the alleyway where the woman had gone, silent and swift.

"Gretchen doesn't trust me. She stripped me of my talismans. I found this one." The gold ring winked on his finger. "Only in the moment of birth or death would it be enough to transport me. Harald's not going to kill her, is he?"

"I don't think so," Katherine replied. "She's not on our list—not yet in any case."

"What sort of place have you brought me to, Isaac?" A voice demanded from the gateway. Isaac's wife emerged from the shadowed arch, her arms at first tightly crossed, clinging to her fear, then spreading as she came beside her husband, gathering his tools. "You claimed we would be safe here, safer because of him." She tipped her head toward Elisha.

"You'll be safer when I'm gone, Frau Burghussen, but first, I do need his help with something."

Isaac rose. "Anything."

"Isaac, really," his wife began, but the goldsmith faced her, cupping her cheek with one hand.

"There are darker days coming. I pray we shall survive them, and the best way to do so is to keep ourselves to the light, even when it hurts."

She kissed him gently and took the satchel from his hands. "Then we best get inside and do what can be done." She slipped her arm through his and brought him along, drawing him in with close comfort.

Elisha and Katherine watched them go.

"When you're gone?" she echoed. "Where are you going, and when?"

"Back to your manor, I assume."

Her presence burst from the chill of deflection like the sun from behind the clouds. "Come inside then— surely a bit of food and a fire will do you good."

Elisha still felt the shivers beneath his skin of Gretchen's mother's invasion. She had been prepared for him, not to kill, but to question, forcing a close contact to judge the truth of what he said. Had his answers satisfied her, in spite of her defiance? He let Katherine bring him in, to join the others in the common room where the fire roared and Isaac's wife stroked away his blood with a clean cloth while their two daughters ran along the corridor opening one door after another and giggling.

The novice at the gate frowned at this behavior, but not seriously, coming after Elisha. "Forgive me, Herr doctor, it was my task to visit the market this morning, and the vendors asked why so much food, had we got visitors, and I said, yes we had, and one from very far away indeed. The innkeeper was shopping there as well, and I did not think to guard my words, but I wouldn't have thought it of her to assault a man at our very door." He lowered his eyes. "I'll bring some mulled wine, then, and a bit of sausage." He shuffled away toward the monk's quarters and the kitchen between.

Elisha sank into one of the chairs, Isaac seated at his right hand, and they shared a look. "Best get on with it, or I fear Liesel won't abide so much excitement," Isaac told him.

"You shut your smart mouth, sir. With all of this travel, you've no idea what excitement I can manage."

His wife pushed back from the table, taking the satchel with her. "What tools? What do you need?"

"Vellum, and drawing things," Elisha said. "Thank you for the loan of your husband."

"You'd best keep him in better shape or you'll not hear the end of it from me, doctor." She breezed away, her long, fair hair swaying along her back.

"She's your wife to be sure," Elisha said, and Isaac laughed, then they grew serious again as Elisha told him, "I'll need to touch you, to maintain contact, is that all right?"

"What's this about?" Isaac asked.

Katherine said nothing, but sat across from them, her eyes on Elisha.

"Katherine and the others need to know who the mancers are. I can show her, and she can show them — but we cannot pass the images along without contact. If you can draw them, then others can see them as well, and know who to watch out for."

The novice returned. "Nourishment, and another visitor." He set down a tall steaming carafe that smelled of wine and spices, and a platter of sausage alongside. At the entrance, Harald kicked a bit of snow off his boots and entered with a bow to Katherine.

"Margravine. It is good to see you well." With his sleek, dark hair and keen gaze, Harald carried the look of the coursing hound, a fierce hunter in the guise of a mere beast. To Elisha, he tipped his head. "Well met. Rome has not agreed with you, it seems."

"Nor I with it. But I'm still alive."

It seemed for a moment they all held their breath, then Liesel returned with a handful of parchment pieces and a leather-wrapped bundle of thin bars of plummet, a soft gray metal for sketching. She set them at her husband's elbow and reached for the wine. "All around, yes?" After pouring it into a series of ceramic cups, she lifted one and drained a long swallow. "There, that should settle me nicely."

Down the hall, the girls' giggles turned to a shriek as Friar Gilles roared out of his chamber and chased them back into the common room, hands raised and fingers spread like grasping claws. The girls fell onto each other on the cushioned settee, pulling a wrap around them, breathless.

Seeing the light in Isaac's face made the morning's exhaustion worthwhile. Elisha took a swallow from his own cup and set it back. Laying his hand on Isaac's arm, he spoke of the mancers, each one he had seen in the vale where they sought to make a saint of Brigit. He described the stout woman from England who wore the guise of a nun, and as he spoke of her, he pictured her in every detail, allowing this image to flow through his touch to Isaac's flesh. The goldsmith's right hand flew busily over a square of vellum, sketching her out in the silvery strokes of plummet. Isaac pinched off a bit of bread, rolled it between his fingers, and used that to erase and adjust his lines as he worked.

Elisha talked his way through thirty others, including Renart, the Frenchman who appeared to be one of the leaders and had been present both in England, at Brigit's attempt to seize the throne, and again in the vale. Liesel drifted away to work on stitchery with her girls while Friar Gilles joined the monks at prayer. Katherine and Harald sat by, listening and watching, Harald's quick hands sliding away a few of the images into another pile while Katherine kept Elisha's cup filled and quietly went for more wine. He made himself hoarse with talking.

"Are we through yet?" Friar Gilles boomed when he returned, and Katherine scowled at him. The girls, restive with so much stillness, had dropped their stitching and begun to play noisily across the floor with a set of chess pieces. "Forgive me." Gilles spread his hands and bowed his head, then he hustled a few steps forward and scooped the two girls from the floor. "Come, and I shall tell you a story."

Isaac smiled briefly in their wake, and Liesel paused in her stitching as Gilles settled on the settee, one child to either side.

"Will it be a spooky one? I love the spooky ones!" one of the girls insisted.

"Very well, then." Gilles drew a hand down over his face, transforming it from foolish to stern. "Do you know what it means to be a revenant?" He waggled his eyebrows and leaned in toward the fire, drawing them along with him. "A revenant is a poor soul who has died but was not properly laid to rest. Instead of lying peaceful in his grave until the judgment day, the revenant rises up from the dirt and stalks the streets of his home, searching for solace." He thrust out his hands as if clawing his way from a grave. Elisha flinched, but the two girls squealed in mock-terror, and Gilles went on, "The only way a revenant can be quieted is if he shall be cut limb from limb and scattered like a criminal!"

"Brother, please," Liesel cut in as the girls shrieked all the louder. "This work requires calm."

Gilles collapsed under her glower, sinking back into the cushions with a sigh. "Very well then, how about a few miracles of the Virgin? Come, take up your stitching, and I will tell you about them." When Liesel subsided, Gilles whispered behind his hand to the girls, "Some of the miracle tales still have a bit of torture before the Blessed Virgin's intercession, eh?" But his voice fell low, and the girls hushed themselves to listen.

Elisha finished a few more descriptions, grateful for the occasional burst of laughter that made their work flow a little more easily. When Elisha fell silent again, Isaac pushed back and shook out his hand, working the fingers for a time while Elisha withdrew his contact for a longer drink and a few bites from the platter.

"I know these." Harald tapped the pile. "Three are at the court of Emperor Charles all the time, and these two are frequent visitors. These ones had been to call on Emperor Ludwig, God rest his surly soul."

"What about him?" Elisha plucked the drawing of Renart, but Harald shook his head. "This man, Renart, is a leader, probably in France. Keep a sharp eye out."

Isaac leaned back wearily, letting his head rest against the wall at his back. "Is there anyone else? Anyone we should watch out for?"

Swallowing a bite of spicy sausage, sucking the grease from his teeth, Elisha considered the question. There was one he had not mentioned, one who had been absent from the vale. "The master of Rome, Count Vertuollo, but he doesn't travel. He keeps to his own ground and lets his son pay calls beyond his own keep. At least he did until his son's death."

"Not a threat, then." Harald popped a bite in his mouth and chewed.

Not a threat. Elisha considered that. Vertuollo was, quite simply, the most controlled and deliberate mancer and the most sensitive magus Elisha had ever met. The thought of having to fight him made Elisha's stomach queasy and his heartbeat stutter. With a drop of blood, the count could siphon the nectar of dying from the gallows of Rome, and with a turn of his hand, slay a living thing that ventured into his shadow. To be sure, Vertuollo had not gone to the vale. Instead, he barred the Valley to ensure Elisha could not escape that way. Vertuollo held the power to stop the passage of the living into the Valley of the dead. But he held Rome with a similar will. It was his city, nay, his kingdom, and Elisha had broken its heart. Just before he killed Vertuollo's son.

Elisha beckoned Isaac back to the table. All of them

leaned closer, watching, as Isaac sketched the long face and high brow, the narrow nose, sharp eyes and exquisitely tidy hair.

A tiny shock of the Valley pricked Elisha's heart, and he broke off, bolting from his chair, stung by the sudden memory of Father Uccello, the Roman priest whose torture he had overseen, whose corpse he had taken from the gallows. He swung about as the Valley slid shut. There before him stood Count Vertuollo, his robes still swirling in the winds of death.

Chapter 7

❖

"**B**rother, you do not look well. Please, don't feel you must stand on my behalf." Vertuollo spoke in the rolling dialect of Rome, spreading his hand in a gesture of invitation. The deep black of his robes set off the silver of his hair and echoed the darkness of his eyes. "What a merry gathering. Do I smell mulled wine?"

Isaac stirred at Elisha's side, but Elisha's own body blocked him from Vertuollo's gaze. Elisha put his hand behind him, holding the goldsmith back, urging him to stay down. Somehow, he kept his feet under him, kept his heart beating. "Brother." Elisha stumbled over the language of Rome. He swallowed hard. What could he say? What could he possibly do? "Please allow me to offer my condolences on the loss of your son." An apology in part, and a reminder of his own power. As Elisha fought back his panic, he gathered his strength.

"It is kind of you to say so. May I take it that you were yourself responsible?" Vertuollo folded his hands together, waiting.

"We had a dispute over the matter of his knife. I found it stuck in my back. I'm sure you understand."

"At least, I do appreciate your candor."

With a whisper of movement, a salt blade struck through Elisha's awareness to one side, feeling more like a gap than an object. Vertuollo flicked his hand in that direction, allowing his sleeve to make contact and force a magical connection. The blade did not change course, and he twisted aside, his civil demeanor slipping just for an instant as the knife brushed past his arm and the salt inlays shattered against the wall behind. The count's eyes flicked back, but Harald had already dropped out of sight—Elisha felt his departure and sensed him lurking among the furnishings.

"I am not impressed with the company you keep, Brother. You should come back to Rome, and I will show you greater hospitality than I did the last time. A single soul is hardly enough to sustain you, even with such a perfect blow as the one you struck last time you came to call. Rome is turned from an empty ruin to a banquet."

"Thanks for the invitation, but I must refuse."

"You are not through playing with the *desolati*? Well. Don't forget my offer." His extended hand seemed to suck the warmth from the room. "I have certainly not forgotten you." In his hand he held a scrap of flesh, a dried sliver of Father Uccello's ear shorn from his head when he would not reveal Elisha's secrets, a slender but powerful link between Elisha and Rome, one perhaps only Vertuollo was sensitive and subtle enough to use. "What price my son's life? What price, my shattered city?" Vertuollo closed his fingers around it, cradling it like a bird in his palm, head slightly cocked. "Can you be killed, my brother, or must you choose to die?"

Reaching through the contact of that death, Elisha snatched back the sad remnant of Uccello's torture and tossed it into the fire.

The count raised his head and took a long, slow breath. "Would that it were the only one. Brother."

Brother. Every time Vertuollo used the word, it stung. Without the death of Elisha's own brother he would never have become the magus he now was. A bitter gift, indeed, that his brother's death had brought Elisha to the place where he might be seen to share a bond like brotherhood with a necromancer. And yet, how many more would suffer without him? "If you had tended your own city, as you had planned, Brother, there would be no need for anger between us." The ear—a talisman—left a cool patch at the center of his sweaty palm, like another scar. "I did what I had to to save the lives of thousands, so that other fathers need not go through what you have."

"What can it mean to save thousands if you lose what matters most?" Vertuollo folded his hands together again, his gaze perfectly level. "I will unravel you like a bit of bad embroidery." He inclined his head toward the woman and girls on the settee, their stitchery still clutched in their hands. "Enjoy your wine." With a breath of cold, the count vanished into the Valley.

Elisha's knees buckled and he dropped into his chair, trying to catch his breath.

Isaac shot from his chair and went to his wife. "That was him—you said he did not travel. I've risked my entire family for this—for what?"

"Was he a wonder-worker, too, Papa?" asked the older girl, still blinking at the spot where Vertuollo had been.

"I'm sorry, Isaac, I am so sorry." Elisha knotted his fingers through his hair. "He needs the contact of the dead to travel that way, and the death he called upon belongs to me. Your family should be safe."

"Should be?" Liesel pushed up from the couch. "We should leave, right away, if men like that can simply come and go and assault us at their will. We were safer at home, Isaac, away from your friends."

"Liesel, please." The goldsmith bent to his wife, and the pair of them began a furious whispered discussion.

"Elisha, what did he say to you?" Katherine asked, coming around to lay her hand on his shoulder.

Elisha prayed that none of them spoke Italian, then Harald, steward to an emperor, assassin for a queen, emerged from the shadow of a tapestry and moved soundlessly toward them, dropping to one knee before Elisha to meet his eyes. "He said he would unravel you," Harald murmured, in serviceable Italian. "What does that mean?"

"It means I have to go. I have to distance myself from the rest of you and hope to God he wouldn't recognize you." Not only had he antagonized the count, he had brought an enemy into the midst of his allies. Elisha had done his best to shield Isaac, and Harald had dodged away as soon as possible, but the others had been in full view the whole time. Vertuollo wouldn't know them well enough to find them magically, but he would certainly know them on sight, and there was no reason he could not do as Elisha had and find himself an artist to spread the images of his enemies.

Through their contact, Katherine gleaned what he said, and her touch felt hot with fear and anger. "*You can't go now, you just told me you would stay and fight with us.*"

"*I'll have to fight a different way. If I am anywhere close to you, he can find us again. Just my focusing on him, conjuring his image, was enough for him to know I was targeting him, at least while he was holding a talisman linked to me.*"

"What about you? He's just proven that he can reach you at any time," Harald pointed out.

Elisha grabbed the nearest cup and drank down the last of its wine, then stood up, withdrawing from Katherine's touch. "The hunting of mancers must be up to you." He shared a glance between the two of them.

"Where will you go?" Worry pinched her brow and hollowed her cheeks.

"It's best you don't know."

"Well, then," said Friar Gilles in a broad voice, "I'll get my things." He rose and dusted off his habit, then gave a smile and a pat on the head to each of the girls. "You shall have to take care of things for your parents. Do you think you can do that?"

"Yes, of course, Brother. I am nine years old," answered the older girl.

His booming laugh did nothing to dispel the foreboding that hung over them.

"Where are you going?" Isaac demanded. "Are you not as much in danger as the rest of us?"

The monk shrugged. "Yet I am of little use. I am no hunting hound, I am no artist. I am, if anything, a purveyor of blood and bone and stories." He lifted one hand, and added a flourish to a deep bow in Elisha's direction. "And I am at your service." He turned to Isaac. "I shall leave the relics you require for the project, master goldsmith, plus a few other items, as I gather we shall be travelling light."

"I can't accept your service," Elisha said, waving away the offer. "Anyone in my company is at risk."

"You need me, Doctor, for the relics I possess if nothing else. I should like to accompany you, the better to reveal your story when the time comes. Besides, a man should be willing to risk his life in the duties of the lord. What is the flesh but an anchor to the soul?" He sidled out from the nook by the fire. "So. I will fetch my things." He shuffled down the corridor to his chamber.

Harald touched a scabbard at his belt. "The margravine would defend you with magic and I with a blade, but we have our own work to do. Perhaps Friar Gilles's faith will serve where we may not. Godspeed, and good luck."

"This is madness," said Katherine. "Surely there is a better way. We are stronger together, are we not? And you've still had no rest, certainly not enough to undertake another—"

"Let him go." Isaac swung away from his wife, arms folded.

"Indeed," Liesel echoed. "The sooner he is gone, the sooner the rest of us can be at peace."

The goldsmith stopped her with a look. Flecks of blood still marked his temple from the morning's first encounter, and Elisha's heart sank. Here they came to it, a return to Isaac's acid demeanor. "No," said Isaac. "There is no peace, not here, nor anywhere in the entire Holy Roman Empire. The pestilence has only just breached the mountains and already the battle is joined. I have done my part, minor though it may be, and he must do his."

Isaac turned to Katherine. "Forgive me, Margravine, but you know I'm right." He gave the slightest incline of his head. "These villains are not of one nation or another, and we cannot afford to act as if they are. Elisha must be allowed to do the work that only he can."

Katherine stood stiff and straight, then pivoted on her heel and walked away. After a moment, a door creaked open and slammed shut, with a breath of crisp air as she let herself into the bleak winter's garden.

Springing lightly up, Harald gathered the rest of the sausage into a napkin and tied it off. "You'll need something to eat." Then he took one of Isaac's dwindling stack of vellum scraps, drew a few quick lines of plummet and turned back. "It's a map, a place in Heidelberg where you can stay the night."

Elisha's eyes flashed up as he prepared to refuse, but Harald went on, "Yes, I'll know where you are, but I'll be gone from here shortly, and I trust you'll not stay there more than a night. The margravine is correct that you need more rest." He tapped the vellum with his finger. "They'll ensure you get it." Next, he slid a knife from his boot, another from his sleeve, and a third from beneath his jerkin and placed them alongside the bundle of meat.

Each had a handle of wood and a sharpened slice of metal inlaid with salt. Each crystalline weapon lay like a hollow in Elisha's awareness, a dull space occupied by a keen blade. Harald gave a grim smile. "Don't worry, I have more."

In the corridor behind him, the broad shape of Friar Gilles appeared, carrying a pair of sacks tied together, ready to be slung over his shoulder. "I am as prepared as may be, doctor."

Elisha finally rose. "Thank you all." He took a breath to say more, but met their eyes one by one, Gilles's alight with passion, Harald's keen and focused, Liesel's frightened, and Isaac's dark with worry.

Elisha held out his hand, but Isaac did not respond. Just as well, he had no comfort to send, not today. "I pray I have not led your family to greater sorrow."

"It is better we are together, to face what may come. The abbey has a rich larder, it may be we shall simply bar the gate and wait until the winds have changed." The goldsmith stepped back among his family.

"You cannot mean to go without at least bidding farewell to the margravine," Liesel said, her daughters nodding their agreement. "That is the sort of parting a lady could not forgive."

"I'll find some other supplies and meet you at the gate," Friar Gilles announced. He scooped Harald's offerings into his hands and shuffled off.

The big wooden door into the inner courtyard stood opposite the warming chamber where the gate warden usually sat copying pages, ready to see to the needs of his guests. Elisha shoved open the door and a flurry of snowflakes curled in around him. He stepped through and pulled it shut again at his back. Katherine stood in the snowy garden near the far wall, tracing a gravestone with her hand. Elisha spread his awareness, building attunement and projecting his presence to let her know he was there. She kept her eyes down as he approached, then lifted her hand to him.

"*It is hard to be good when you are not here,*" she said to the brush of his fingers. "*The killing is like strong ale. It makes my head dance and my heart flutter. It makes me want another draught. Is it so for you?*"

"*I have felt it so, but then, too, I have been so close to death myself that I can never easily deal it to another.*"

"*Not even Vertuollo?*"

"*If he did not stalk me here nor threaten my friends, then yes, not even him.*"

"*You were the hunter on the night we met.*"

She had been kneeling in a church, praying for deliverance. When she took him for the angel of death, she begged him to release her from this terrible craving for the power of death.

Katherine rapped her chest with her free hand, just over the talisman she carried. "*Now I am the hunter, the righteous dealer in death. I slay not the helpless victim on a slab, but the predator who slavers over him. I have become you, in some tiny way. There are moments that it fills me with pride and with delight—and moments that I wish my dark angel would return and tell me, 'No.'*"

He took her by the shoulders, turning her from the grave to meet his eyes. "*You do not have to do this.*"

"*Of course I do. If there is such evil in the world, such evil as I have been, then someone must stand against it.*" She reached up, stroking her fingers through his hair, her hand lingering on the white streak over the scars that marked his skull. "*It is my penance as well as my pride. My sons are recovered, did I tell you? Soon they will be hunting, too.*"

"Oh, Katherine," he said aloud, his breath disturbing the snowflakes that circled between them.

As if that had been all she had been waiting to hear, Katherine's presence soared with joy. She leaned into

him, cupping his cheek, kissing him, then she pulled
away, releasing all contact. "Fly away, my Raphael. And
if we do not meet again, then I will imagine you safe at
home with your beloved, telling him the tales that you
would not share with me."

With that, Elisha took his leave. He felt a lump in his
throat as he walked away. Could he ever go home and
find his comfort there? What if he made his king a target
to the count's revenge? Perhaps it was just as well he
lacked the talisman of his brother's death, the surest
pathway to where he'd begun.

At the gate, Friar Gilles handed over a pair of sacks,
joined like his own for easy carrying, then pointed to the
assortment of salted blades. "You'll want to find places
for those I imagine."

Elisha followed Harald's example, with the longest
blade in his boot and the next in his belt, but unless he
had hours of practice, he doubted he could slide a blade
from his sleeve without trouble, so he added it to his
medical pouch, draping his fur-lined cloak over all. The
golden ram pin Isaac had given him winked in the dim
light as they departed. Harald's map brought them to the
University grounds, to a narrow door in a tilted alley
where the keeper let them in without a word and gave
them a chamber at the back with a separate exit. They
shared a glance, wondering what manner of place they'd
come to, but neither asked. Friar Gilles sat on his bed,
laying out his relics to organize the hurried gathering of
items, giving a little blessing and a kiss from his fingers
for each and every one.

Elisha, too, sat down, feeling the weight of his exhaustion and the light-headed rush of the wine. As he lay
down and wrapped his cloak around him, he attuned
himself to the place and spread his awareness lightly all
about him. He thought of Vertuollo in his lair in the catacombs, a web of death-magic that transmitted every

twitch straight to its master. The thrum of the ever-present Valley rose up inside as he opened himself to it. He needed no catacomb nor thread of murder to sense that place between the world of the living and the mystery of death. At a distance, it pulsed as it drew down the dying, and wailed as it opened for the living, and he sensed the passage as Katherine and Harald departed on their own dangerous road. Once, in the forests of Germany, Elisha slept on graves to conceal himself, now it was as if he were the grave and all the world lay open to him, all the world that lived and breathed and wept and died. Wrapped in such cold comfort, Elisha slept.

Chapter 8

❖

$\mathfrak{T}$he next night, well-rested and hoping the distant church would be empty, Elisha and Gilles stood together to open the Valley. In their joined hands, Gilles held a pair of tiny relics from his collection, a chip of iron from the coffin of Saint Matthew, a parchment tag dangling from its little silken bag, and a bit of bone from Saint Gregory VII, who shared the apostle's resting place. In spite of their holy resonance and air of death, either of these relics could be false. Elisha hoped the two of them together would point the way. He focused on the description he had of Salerno and sent his awareness south, back into the plague-gripped landscape of the Italian peninsula. Just shifting himself in that direction brought the shadows high, the rising tide of darkness swelling, a pot at the simmer about to boil over. He dreaded the return to Italy, but he must allow Katherine and Harald to track the mancers, and he must follow where his knowledge led: to medical school.

Elisha's expanded awareness flickered with dozens of lives around the twin pools of death that were the two saints, and he withdrew, shaking his head at Gilles. He wanted their arrival to be as secret as possible. They tried again, later in the night, to find a few more deaths, a few lives remaining. By dawn, at last, Elisha could wait no longer and they took their chance. Opening the Valley, Elisha called upon the peaceful dead to surround and uphold them, shielding Friar Gilles from the true horror of the place. But the peaceful dead did not attend him. The soaring laughter of Biddy, the spark of joy that was Martin, even the depth of knowledge that was Mordecai defied him. Instead, Elisha's eye spiked with pain in remembrance of the mancer-monk he had slain at Vertuollo's behest. The martyrdom of Father Uccello, who died rather than to reveal the truth of the monk's death, spread in a heavy pool of guilt that sucked at his strength. Elisha' back and lungs seared with cold, the deep and awful death-stroke he used to slay Vertuollo's son.

Elisha cried out as he stumbled from the Valley, dragging Friar Gilles with him in a roar of dead voices.

Gilles trembled and gasped for breath, pushing away Elisha's hand, and blowing on his own fingers as if to warm them. "You did not say it would be like that, so close, so personal." Gilles shuddered and stuffed his hands into opposite sleeves, hugging himself.

"Vertuollo's using it against me." Elisha pulled his cloak all the tighter, blowing out a cloudy breath. "The Valley. It costs him too much to prevent my passage completely, but he can manipulate it to hurt me, just as I tried to use it to protect you. Forgive me."

Friar Gilles bobbed a nod, but his gaze lifted, then he slipped a hand free to cross himself. "It worked! Here we are. Where, exactly, I cannot say." He turned about as Elisha began the process of attunement, centered on the two familiar corpses who lay nearby, the saints whose bones had drawn them here. They stood in a vaulted crypt lit by a pair of enormous candles mounted on waist-high pillars. Frescoes flecked with gold embellished every surface, depicting the ministry of the Apostle, Matthew. One mural to Elisha's left showed the king's attempt to martyr him, by nailing him to the ground, slathering him with pitch, and setting him on fire. The candles' glow enhanced the pale white in the downed man's eyes, fixed, though they remained, on Heaven. Elisha turned away, his throat tightening.

"Glorious, marvelous." Gilles hurried to each of the artworks in turn, barely touching them. "Look at this martyrdom—have you ever seen such workmanship? And the gold in the halos. It is simply magnificent. Our churches in the lowlands are not so fine, but then, we have not been blessed with the presence of the bones of an apostle. Surely that is an inspiration to all."

The broad hall of the crypt, laid out in aisles divided by arches just like a proper church, held a few dozen forms on pallets. A few moved and moaned restlessly, flinging off their blankets. The rest lay still, the air heavy with the acid tang of vomit that turned Elisha's stomach.

"What's all of this? We have not come to the hospital, have we?" Gilles asked.

Elisha had hoped the nearby medical school would have a ready cure, but now that they had arrived, his hopes withered. "The pestilence. Let's go."

"Oh, dear. Surely the priests are tending these poor, suffering souls—" Gilles broke off. One of the corpses closest to the altar wore stained white vestments and a golden cross, his mouth oozing blood, black swellings pressing over the collar at his throat. A spider web of fine red veins tracked the dead priest's face.

Gilles hurried along after Elisha, down the aisle and up the stairs into the quiet sanctuary above. The few windows let in the weak light of dawn, and a handful of early worshippers trudged along the nave, dipping their fingers in holy water or praying in the chapels. Their eyes edged with darkness and faces tracked with grief, they took no notice of the newcomers, barely stepping aside for them to pass by. Elisha's left eye saw the echoes of the dead all around, thick and gray. The living moved among them, equally gray and lifeless. He nearly walked into one old woman, expecting her to dissipate or pass through him, leaving him the chill of death.

Instead, she aimed a scowl at him. "What's the purpose after all?" she said as if they were already having a conversation. "The church can't help us, can they? Or won't they bother? Is God listening, even to them?"

Elisha gave her no answer. Even to a man who long believed that God turned away from His creation, so much suffering felt like an affront.

"What did she say?" Gilles asked in German, coming alongside as they stepped out the doors. "Oh, I am going to have trouble if I cannot even understand the language. I know plenty of at least three languages, aside from the Latin tongue, but I do not think they will aid me here."

The local dialect sounded quite different from the language of Rome, but Elisha's awareness made it intelligible, and he would likely begin to adopt their pronunciation before too long. What, indeed, would Gilles do? "Perhaps we can find you a tutor, a fellow friar who can be your guide."

"It might do, but I hesitate to trust too much in others, knowing we must keep your true purpose secret for now."

"Likely forever." From the steps, Elisha scanned the narrow plaza before them with its colonnade edging and downward slope. Below, the ocean frothed at the jetties that defended a fine harbor empty of ships. Ranks of buildings marched up both sides, their rise and fall indicating where valleys cut grooves down the mountain slopes around. Above the town, terraced gardens carved into the slopes, and a castle marked a towering cliff. The growing day showed near empty streets—none of the bustle there should be to get to market or to haul goods out for delivery. The few people he could see moved quickly, heads down, as if they tried to escape from something.

Not far from the church square stood a similar cluster of buildings, two and three stories tall, with broad shuttered windows and only a bell in an arch rather than the tower associated with most monasteries. The ever-present thrum of the Valley grew deeper in that direction. That would be the hospital. Elisha set out again with Gilles muttering in his wake. The day was cool, but not so cold as Heidelberg, nor did the skies portend snow. Moist and warm, as Doctor Emerick had told him.

The gates of the medical school had not yet opened, so they bought a few rolls warm from the oven of a local baker, an idea Gilles enthusiastically embraced, saying a blessing as they broke bread together. When they returned to the gates a little later, a pair of young men in long robes responded to Elisha's knocking. "I'm seeking the medical school—is this it?"

The two looked him up and down. "And who might you be?" asked the skinny one. "You don't look like a patient." He stared more closely at Elisha's mis-matched eyes and the white patch in his hair and added, "I don't think."

"No, I'm a surgeon lately attached to the Empress Margaret. I'd like to consult your professors on medical matters."

"Really." The other youth, with owlish eyes and a down-turned mouth said, "You'll find them a little busy at present. Come back after the plague." He started to shove the door closed when a sharp voice reprimanded him, and a woman swept into view behind them, her deep-red hair pulled back beneath a cap, her robes of an identical design to theirs with the addition of a long green cowl.

"You wish to consult? We arc not offering consultations at present, although classes continue." She cast a dark look at the young men who hurried off into the courtyard at her back. "But we do welcome any medical practitioners willing to share in both our knowledge, and our work. You say you are a surgeon?"

"Yes, I—"

"You will have read John of Ardene's work on anal fistula. How do you find his technique?"

Startled first by her interruption, then by her question, Elisha frowned. He had not read the work, but he certainly knew the technique. "It's adequate as long as the fistula is near enough to the anus. Look, do you—"

"Do you blend your own theriac?"

"I find simples prove more useful than compounds in most cases of poison."

She folded her arms, staring directly at him, disconcertingly like a lion. "Galen tells students to dissect their own apes, do you agree?"

Galen, the classical doctor a thousand years dead. Mordecai had shared some of his teachings and discarded most of them as irrelevant. "If students don't do their own work, how do they learn?"

She raised an eyebrow. "Weapons ointment—"

"Is a waste of good coin." Elisha leaned in, planting his foot on the threshold. "Are we done yet? People are dying."

"Indeed they are." She stepped back and waved him inside. "And you're now hired to attend them. With me! Your manservant as well, please. I shall find you a chamber. We've a number of vacancies at present."

"I came seeking advice, not employment, mistress."

"Yet, as you say, people are dying, and we are short of staff. You seek the knowledge of Salerno, and we require your assistance for as long as you remain, agreed?"

That was a bargain he could make, even if he could not stay for long. "I'll do what I can," he answered.

They trotted after her as she crossed the broad plaza, not deviating from her course as students in plain robes, and physicians in more decorative ones, turned and dodged to avoid her. "The teaching hospital is near full-up, but a bed or two empties every day. Some for the obvious reason, some because their families come to take them to the church instead, to see if prayer is more efficacious than medicine. It rarely is."

"She thinks you are my manservant," Elisha told Gilles in German, and the monk huffed out a breath, shaking his head.

"So be it. God's will be done."

"On earth as it is in Heaven," the woman added. "I do not speak German, but I do understand a good deal of it. Latin is the primary language here." She swiveled her head. "It may be best to keep your imperial affiliation to yourself. People in the area are of mixed opinions on the subject of the empire in general. Many would prefer imperial authority over that of the church, while others long to return to the fold, as it were." Her lips bent briefly into a smile. "Whichever encourages the school, that is the one I prefer."

"Maestra Christina!" called a voice from across the yard, with a familiar accent.

The woman did not glance away, her dark gaze arresting Elisha's eyes. The other person must be calling for someone else, then, for she made no reply to the shout. "One last question," she said as they reached an arched door in a long wall of stone. "This pestilence: miasma, conjunction of celestial influence, or God's punishment for sin?"

"Too many children are dying for me to think it God's will," Elisha replied, "and they have died in too many places for me to believe it is a miasma."

"Maestra Christina, I must insist—"

The speaker came nearer, and Elisha extended his senses to the stranger's agitated presence to find it familiar, not a stranger at all, but who?

"That leaves celestial conjunction," she snapped just as he was about to turn away toward the newcomer.

"An evil in the stars visited upon us down below? Is that the kind of thing you teach here?"

Her eyes sparkled, a new smile returning. "Not I, but some do, don't they Maestro Lucius?" She switched to Latin, raising her eyes to the breathless fellow who had joined them.

Lucius? For a moment, the name froze Elisha where he stood. He had known a Lucius, a physician back in England who betrayed King Hugh in hopes of winning himself a medical school for London. But he couldn't have come here, could he? Would he?

"Who are these people that they should distract you from your duties, and from concern for your fellow physicians?"

"They have come to consult about the pestilence, both to aid us and to seek our knowledge. That seems worthy of some distraction." She gestured toward Elisha and Gilles, and he had no choice but to turn or to be woefully rude to a woman who seemed ready to accept him.

Lucius Physician stood before him, towering as ever, his pale hair blowing about, the sleeves of his robe cut with so much fabric they buffeted him in the breeze. "Good God!" Lucius shouted. "A distraction? This man is a murderer!"

Chapter 9

❖

"No more so than you are, Lucius." Elisha's experience serving the physician back in England urged him to bow, but he refused. Last time he had seen the physician, Lucius held a crossbow and his assistant, Benedict, lay dying from the bolts. "Or have you forgotten Benedict so readily?"

Lucius went a little pale, his eyes round and dancing as if he suddenly recalled the magic Elisha used to try to defend the fallen youth. "You do not know what you are talking about, Barber. And I fail to see, Maestra Christina, how a barber can be of any use to us. We shall hardly require amputations for the afflicted." He raked his gaze over Elisha's golden pin and fur-lined cloak and the continental-style trim of his beard, then his gaze narrowed. "How did you even survive the battle or escape justice for your black sorcery. Who have you murdered lately to steal the status you so boldly come flaunting?"

Lucius's convoluted style nearly outstripped Elisha's imperfect Latin, but Maestra Christina drew herself up. "This man ably responded to my every query of his medical knowledge, Maestro, so to answer the first charge, I find that he is likely as capable of meeting the demands of the hospital as any student here. As for the second charge, that of murder, the topic has only just now come up. But perhaps you can remind me again what became of your assistant, Benedict de Fleur. I believe you claimed he had taken service with a noble of your own country?"

"He took service with the grave, Maestra." Elisha took a breath to get his anger back in control. "Lucius shot him to cover for his own treason, then fled the country. It was I who tried to save Benedict's life."

By now, the students and faculty crossing the yard had paused, many of them drawn closer to the brewing storm, books and medical tools clutched to their chests. One of the students hurried off, catching the arm of a young woman and pulling her forward, pointing and whispering.

Lucius puffed out his chest. "These allegations are preposterous. This man merely resents my lofty position and superior skill, as he has always done. There is no reason we should suffer such a charlatan to enter our establishment—his presence will sully the entire school."

Christina spoke more softly. "It can hardly have escaped your notice that half the faculty have not returned this season, Lucius. Half. And the students are fleeing with them. If it continues there will be no school nor hospital, save for the patients who lay there dying."

"Nonsense. While the pestilence has had a minor impact upon our environs, its reach will be greatest among the merchants, allied as they are with the Jews, and in regions without recourse to medical expertise. Doubt me as you will, Maestra, but do not allow this craven access to our wisdom, our works, or our patients." He thrust his finger into the air. "You have no authority to unilaterally appoint a new member of faculty or even an assistant to the hospital. For that, we require the council to convene."

"Very well then, convene them! If you can drag Maestro Antonio from his cups and Maestro Fidelis from his chamber, if you are even willing to brave the ward of

Maestro Danek." She flung wide her arms, embracing the entire yard. "Then do it. In the meantime, there are students to be taught and patients to be seen. Come, doctor." She swiveled on her heel and slammed open the door at her back.

"And this is why I have so strongly advised against the admission of women as faculty or students," Lucius drawled, preening as if he'd just won an argument. "They rarely have the strength of character to maintain a rational debate, but simply disintegrate into emotion. It is in the nature of the fairer sex, not merely an attribute of my esteemed colleague."

Christina's spine stiffened, her hand pressed against the door, but she glanced back at Elisha. "Doctor! With me."

Elisha realized that, in Lucius's presence, he had immediately assumed that the word "doctor" referred to someone else. He waved Gilles ahead of him through the door, keeping his eye on Lucius in his final pose of triumph. In English, he said, "Whatever you say, Lucius, and whatever you do, you and I both know the truth. Treason and murder lie heavy on the soul." Elisha himself knew it as well as any. "Good day." He ducked into the arch and shut the door behind them.

The moment he joined her, Christina swept down a long corridor lined with doors on both sides. "At the very least, he does not lie when he says that he knows you."

"No, Maestra. We have had dealings back in England, none of them pleasant." It took an effort to keep his shoulders square and his gaze direct, as it should be when he spoke with his peers.

She gave a snort. "I cannot imagine anyone having had pleasant dealings with him. I was a bit surprised when Benedict agreed to go with him to England, especially given that he had to leave Ariane behind—we rather expected a marriage of those two. But then, Benedict was ambitious without much impetus of his own, if you see what I mean. I am sure Lucius's offer seemed like a great step forward. Here we are." She opened a door at the end of the corridor, at a greater distance from the others, and walked inside, opening the shuttered window to reveal another, smaller yard beyond. The chamber contained two beds with thick mattresses folded on top of their rope framing. A broad table stood between, with a bench and a couple of chairs before the fireplace. "The chest contains some linens, unless you have brought your own. You shall want to provide your own blankets in any case."

Christina turned, her back to the wall and arms folded. She looked determined, if still flustered by Lucius and his accusations. "Meals are served in the refectory in the next yard, and the hospital occupies the western range of buildings."

"Thank you, Maestra." Elisha set down his sacks on the table, and Gilles did likewise, though he did not let go of his cargo of relics. "What do you need of me?" Elisha asked.

She regarded him steadily. "What do I need of you? I cannot even begin to say what is needed. But at Terce you shall accompany me on my hospital visit and show me if your skill is true and your hand is worthy." Her glance flicked away. "These rooms are for our senior students. Young Benedict had one before Lucius swept him away as his assistant."

"Lucius is an ass who cares more for the stars than for his patients."

Christina gave a hiccup of laughter and stifled it with her hand. "Be that as it may, doctor, you do not strike me as university educated."

"There is a great gulf between education and knowledge. In England, Lucius poured boiling oil on my amputees to see if that healed them faster. It only gave them more pain."

"And what was your treatment?"

"A poultice of rose oil and egg. Egg to seal the wound against infection, rose oil for the healthful properties." He spread his hands, half a shrug.

"Then you are a barber."

"He is so much more, lady," Gilles blurted. "He is a healer, both for himself and for others. To call him merely a barber is to deny what a man might become—" Then he broke off, swallowing his words as he tread too near the secrets they must keep. "Forgive me, lady."

"You are passionate on the subject of your—if not 'master,' then what?" She studied Gilles more closely.

"Teacher, lady."

She laughed more brightly. "Are you then a medical student yourself?"

"No, lady, not medical. If you spare some coin, Elisha, I can go to market for our blankets and whatever else we need." He put out his hand, and Elisha dropped a few coins into his palm.

"There is no shame in being a barber," Elisha said, but the persistent slumping of his shoulders and the struggle to lift his gaze from the feet of his betters suggested otherwise. Good God, he had been cast back to the worst days of his service, a peasant once more, before he knew the power of magic or the gratitude of kings.

Gilles gave a short bow and slipped from the room, leaving them alone, the door open into the empty corridor.

"It does explain your understanding of anal fistula, and your evasion on the question of Galen, but not your rejection of both theriac and weapons ointment, two substances most barbers would not do without. Or is that where your sorcery comes in?" Her eyes twinkled with merriment, and Elisha did his best to match her amusement.

"A good doctor is a bit of a wizard, don't you think?"

"I'll send over a student to show you around. Elisha,

is it? Well met." She tipped her head to him and swept away again, leaving him alone and shaky.

To see Lucius again, after all that had happened, nearly made him forget himself, forget who he had become in his instinctive retreat to who he used to be. It seemed a lifetime ago, though it was just short of a year. His old rank returned so quickly, as if his body remembered what it was to be reviled, representing an ill breed, poorly trained, poorly equipped, the healer of last resort to a patient who could afford no better. Ashamed? No, he had never been ashamed of his duty, even when he knew no better himself. Yet the belief persisted, like the miasma of sickness that hovered even now over the world. Claiming the title of "barber" reduced him back into a dogsbody, to be sneered at and ordered about by other men so much greater than himself. When he crossed the channel to the Lowlands, he claimed himself a doctor, and so he had been accepted by everyone from Friar Gilles to the Empress Margaret herself. He pretended at the time that his study with Mordecai had elevated his education, while his experiences had elevated his knowledge. But perhaps Lucius was right in more than Elisha wanted to believe. Perhaps it had been envy that prompted his claiming a title he had not earned, and arrogance that led him to believe he deserved it.

"Pardon me," said a whispery voice, accompanied by a soft rapping on the open door. "Maestra Christina sent me. Are you ready now?"

At the door stood a willowy person whose gender was not readily clear. Male, Elisha thought after a moment, but slight of build with hair of middling length and poorly kept, cheeks pale enough that they made his lips appear more pink. "I'm ready," Elisha said. "Who are you?"

"Leon." Leon stretched a thin hand in invitation, and Elisha joined him in the corridor.

"You're a student here?" Leon looked a bit younger

than the others, but Elisha guessed that poor nutrition had affected his appearance to a great degree. He extended his senses, working for attunement and for understanding of this curious person.

"No." Leon raised his hands to either side. "Student rooms. Empty by day, except when studying." A slender smile spread his lips. "So: mostly empty."

He glided out the door into the inner yard. "Classrooms—" A gesture uphill. "Refectory—" to the front, and "Hospital," down the hill. "Hospital along the wall into the outer yard as well. Mostly full."

Leon's presence shimmered with waves of heat and cold, flickering not with the bound dead of a mancer or of a soldier, but rather as if he were shedding death as he walked.

From a cluster of students waiting to enter a classroom, Elisha sensed the quiet pulse of a magus. He could not identify the individual from the group, but glanced over them all to remember. Another, darker void moved through the hospital, the chill deflection habitual of the mancer. Elisha's skin tingled as he crafted a projection of his own, concealing his magical knowledge beneath his medical skill.

"Hardest first," Leon said, walking at a languorous pace to a set of steps leading down to a door beneath ground level. He knocked, waited, knocked again, but still as softly as if he'd rather not be heard.

"Enter!" called a voice from within. Leon pushed back the door and held it open, his unfocused gaze aimed somewhere across the yard as he stifled a yawn.

"Sorry. Still tired." He leaned against the door, his thin form sagging.

"Hello?" Elisha peered into the gloomy space. It smelled of decaying flesh and of roses, perhaps the second odor in an attempt to cover the first.

"Did Christina send you? Nothing yet—how's the library search?" A stocky man on a tall stool hunched over a table at the far end of the chamber. Between, more tables held a variety of plants, fresh and dried, bodies of fishes, snakes and lizards, and the occasional bird, likewise dried. Incisions marred the bodies, revealing skeletons or missing parts where bits of flesh or organs had been taken for medical uses.

The man leaned back, stretched himself, arching his back, then raising his arms with a groan as he glanced toward the door. A pair of hooded lanterns provided the only light at that end, so the preparation tables between became murky landscapes of feathers, scales and limbs, emerging again into full color only as Elisha approached.

"Oh, no, I don't know you at all." The fellow rose, his features indistinguishable in the dim light. "Maestro Danek." His Latin held a curious inflection Elisha hadn't heard before, not Dutch, German, English, French or any variety of Italian. "You are?"

"Elisha. I'm a surgeon." Elisha put out his hand. "I've just arrived from service with her Majesty, Queen Margaret of Bavaria."

"Ah, the emperor's widow. Pity." Danek shook the offered hand firmly, projecting health and vitality, then revealing a flash of crooked teeth in his grin as they recognized each other through the contact. "Well met. Doctor." A magus, and one who meant what he said, if a little nervously. "I'll look forward to spending more time. Is that Leon giving you any trouble?"

Leon slumped against the door, sun illuminating his thin features.

"Trouble? No, not at all. He's a bit off, but I can't quite diagnose it."

"He's a survivor. The pestilence. His mum wants him for a priest now, but we faculty all got together and asked him to stay, paying her a few pennies to keep him here for the duration of his recovery, at least. He's a chance to learn more."

"A survivor?" Elisha stared at the young man. That would explain his weakness and malnutrition, not to mention his vacant disposition. It must have taken so much for him to overcome the disease that was already killing so many. Danek matched his own spike of interest. Curious, given how much Danek must already know about Leon.

"Doesn't like to come in here, does he? It reminds him of the treatments, or maybe of the thought of dying, but it's just a preparations room, isn't it? I keep trying to talk with him, but he refuses. See if you can lure him with you another time, and maybe we can put our skills together to learn something from his survival, eh?" Danek shook his hand again. In the way of the magi, he sent, *"Welcome. Anything I can do, you let me know."* Another grin, then he sank back down to his stool and prodded the animal before him with a scalpel. "Can't hardly find the liver in this fellow. I need to get them in fresher, that's all."

"Until later." Grateful to have found an ally who shared at least part of his secret, Elisha gave him a wave, which was absently returned, then he joined Leon at the door. The young man grunted with exertion as he hauled the door shut.

"Most faculty have chambers in the big yard," Leon said, slouching back up the steps.

Elisha fell in beside him, close enough that their arms sometimes brushed, offering him contact. "Maestro Danek tells me you survived the plague?"

"Yes." Leon turned abruptly between two buildings into a tiled passage. The odor of death stopped Elisha's throat as Leon said, "Charnel house, for them that aren't claimed." He turned again and plodded back into the yard, then silently brought Elisha down a corridor of classrooms with high ceilings and tapestries of every saint associated with healing: Luke the Apostle, said to be a doctor; the twin Saints Cosmas and Damian, who had transplanted a leg from one man to another—of a different skin color; Lazarus, who rose from the dead; Saint Roch with his sores; and a fresh work depicting Saint Aleydis whose suffering from leprosy was said to give solace to other sufferers. She lay in bed, her piteous face covered with the scars and scabs of her disease, raising her bandaged hands up to the Lord with a beatific smile.

Two hundred years ago, the workmanship and grandeur of the space must have been exquisite, next only to the cathedral in its splendor, but now the carved wooden beams showed labyrinths of worm holes, and fresh wooden props shored up some of the weaker ones. Paint sloughed in flakes from the murals and broken tiles marked the floor, with some of them missing altogether. As Emerick had told him, the university had been the greatest in its day, and now struggled on in faded glory, haunted by the ghost of what it had been.

At the end of the grand building the corridor opened up into a chapel with a towering image of Jesus healing the sick, the blind, and the infirm. For a moment, Elisha wondered if Christ, too, had been a magus. Blasphemy, for certain. They crossed the broad space, moving through sunlight stained red, green and blue from the tall glass windows. A finely carved door led from the chapel into a corridor somewhat better maintained.

"Faculty chambers. For private patients, consulting, studying. That." Leon flapped a hand at the various doors with their carved scrollwork and inlays. Another broad hall opened off of this as well, with a handful of velvet chairs, somewhat threadbare, facing a series of upholstered benches and small desks. "Examination hall." Leon yawned broadly.

"Look, if you need to rest, I understand. There's no need—"

"No." Leon straightened, quickening abruptly. He pushed himself a few steps ahead, but the distance could not conceal his muttering from Elisha's keen awareness: "Not a child. Not a weakling. Not a miracle." Leon pushed open another door, this one into the two-story building that fronted the outer yard and spanned the school's entrance gate. Here, he climbed a set of stairs, hauling himself up with one hand on the metal rail that bent around each corner until they reached the upper story where a door stood open and a clerk sat at a tall desk immediately opposite. Elisha recognized the gawky gate warden who had tried to send them away earlier. The fellow jabbed his quill into his ink pot.

"Good afternoon, Leon. Come in if you'd like. And the foreigner Maestro Lucius told us about." He steepled his hands. "I don't suppose you'll get permission to come here after today. But you can stand there and admire." He spread his hands grandly to take in the vast space full of books.

Leather-bound books, ranging in size from as small as Elisha's palm, to the size of a small table lay stacked in ranks upon the shelves, many of them chained to the shelves for extra security. Bins held scrolls, some fresh and pale, others yellow with age, still others wrapped in linen or silk that shone in the light of the huge windows that cut the inner wall. More books lay open or closed on the scattered lecterns, some with students leaning over them. A few tables closer to the door held students on benches, ink pots set beside them, painstakingly copying words and diagrams from the volumes of knowledge. Had Mordecai surgeon ever been here? By God, he would have been in Heaven. Elisha swallowed hard. He was, in fact, in Heaven, whatever the Jews might conceive that to be.

From that doorway, Elisha beheld more knowledge than he had ever before had access to, more knowledge than he had imagined might be collected in any one place. Galen, John of Arderne, God knew how many others. Wisdom of the Jews? Perhaps. Herbal guides to every plant any healer, midwife or apothecary had ever applied. Diagrams of astrological connections and wound charts showing how to treat any conceivable injury. Treatises on trepanation, on cataract surgery, on pleurisy and apoplexy, conditions of the heart, the lung, the liver. Anything Elisha might ever have wished to know about his art might be here, inside this room. This was exactly why he had come, in search of the knowledge that might cure the mancers' plague.

In teaching him to read, Mordecai had given him the key to all of this knowledge, and, just as surely, Lucius Physician had denied him the lot.

Chapter 10

❖

$\mathfrak{T}$urned away from the library, Elisha decided to focus for now on the Salernitan mancer he had sensed earlier, the man who must be behind this plague. Had he used the knowledge of that library to generate the magic? In a place devoted to healing, the law of opposites suggested that disease must not be far away, but how had the mancer managed contact with so many, and make that contact spread so fast?

Leon deposited him back at his chamber after the tour, accepting with weary resignation his gratitude and his advice to get some rest. As the young man departed, Elisha considered how aggravating it must be to be surrounded by doctors at every moment, every one of them full of good advice or longing for information. When they met again, Elisha vowed, he would focus on Leon's present, instead of on his past.

"And how was the tour, then?" Friar Gilles perched in the window casement with a platter of cheese. The beds now had fresh blankets and a few bundles and carafes occupied the mantel.

"Very useful. There is a mancer here, and a few magi, at least, one of whom has made contact." Elisha snagged a piece of cheese and found it sharp and hard.

"I met a novice from the Abbey church down at

market — and a rather slow market it was, too. He was all too eager to gossip about the goings on. Did you know Queen Giovanna of Naples, who claims this entire coastline, has fled to Avignon to shelter with the Pope? Apparently, she's murdered her husband, or so they say. She's the one who sold Avignon to the Holy Father to begin with, perhaps to try to influence his opinion regarding the crime." Gilles offered a bright smile. "But His Holiness is beyond such earthly concerns, I am sure. In any event, she'll be brought to trial soon. The husband's brother is King Louis of Hungary. He besieged Naples not long ago, but the rumors of plague have driven him off, so that's one good thing, eh?"

One good thing, but the pressure of the Valley had been growing over Elisha since their arrival. The plague so far had been worse near Venice, but he could feel it coming here as well, like the descent of a storm creating a terrible stillness in the air. So the governing queen was a murderess — *"Naples? Really."* A voice from long past echoed in Elisha's memory. Prince Alaric had spoken those words, needling his mancer supporters with the fact that they had not yet taken Naples, brave in the face of their much greater power. Was the queen their pawn, or did they manipulate King Louis, who tried to conquer her city?

The bells of the nearby church called Elisha off his chair to the hospital, where Maestra Christina, an image of irritation, stood at the door. "Let's go."

Elisha unfurled his awareness. "Leon survived the plague. Are there others?"

"Not many. None yet through our interventions." She grimaced.

Along the inner yard, the hospital felt like fear, pain, despair. Someone there pulsed with streaks of hot magic, a magus, in great distress, but Christina turned away toward the grand outer buildings. Elisha thought to steer her back again toward the ailing magus, then the chill absence of the mancer touched his awareness, and he followed along. First, cure the greater ill.

"We have a few private chambers at the front, mostly for consultations and wealthy patients. Let's see who we have, shall we?" She strode down the spacious corridor, eying the doors.

"How about that one?" Elisha pointed to the door behind which a mancer lurked. The jittery strength of the Valley had returned, sending sweat to his palms, making his heart race. He crafted himself a projection of calm and serious intent, imagining himself as a consulting physician, cool, detached, not magical.

Christina regarded him briefly, then rapped on the door and led him inside. "Good afternoon, my lady, I trust your treatment goes well?"

A large woman reclined on a bed stuffed with pillows, one arm extended and the scent of blood pooling in the air along with the blood that oozed from her arm into a pewter bowl. A barber sat on a stool attending the cut, watching the flow, steadying her arm with a short rod propped on the ground.

"Yes, very well. Maestro Lucius checked in on me a moment ago, and he is very pleased with my progress." She smiled graciously, wide blue eyes blinking at them as if they stood in the sun.

"What's the diagnosis?" Elisha asked, but his attention focused on the barber. A humble man, not unlike himself some time ago, the barber kept his fingers on the wrist of the patient, monitoring her pulse as he watched the blood accumulate. He did not turn around—simply following the physician's orders. In spite of the man's practiced air, a chill flickered at the edges of his presence. A mancer-barber. Elisha almost laughed. His profession had so long been reviled as exactly that: bloody and craven. What Elisha was so often taken for, this man truly was.

"Suffers from severe courses, maestro. Humor too moist. Maestro Lucius recommended bleeding twice a month at slack and full moons, given she's born under Cancer." The barber shifted a little as if he had been sitting too long and glanced over his shoulder at them. "New here?" Broad lips dominated his plain face, a visage so ordinary it betrayed nothing of its evil.

"Visiting," Elisha said.

"Can use the extra hands. I'm Silvio. You let me know, you call for any bleedings—I'm your man." He plucked a wad of cloth from a satchel at his feet and pressed it against the small cut at the woman's elbow and raised her hand as he stood, binding the wound with a tight wrapping. "There you are, my lady."

Christina bowed her head slightly in deference to the woman's nobility and swept from the room. "Because of course a woman who bleeds too much should be bled again," she muttered. Then, noticing Elisha beside her, she said, "Lady Grazia's family give generously to support the hospital. We do our best by her."

"If you don't trust Lucius, why is he allowed to practice?"

"You see that we are stretched thin as it is; even before the advent of this new pestilence, the school has been on a decline. Lucius will tell you it is because it allows such decadence as female doctors. He is not the only one to think so, and the others were pleased to accept his return."

"The other masters?"

She gave a nod. "The council of seven. One of whom is dead. Here is a more interesting case." She rapped on another door, which was answered by a maidservant. They entered the darkened room and quickly became involved in the case of a lord's son taken to convulsions but without sign of the usual causes. Seeing the young man's stricken face, Elisha set aside his other concerns for the moment and proceeded with an examination and inquiry that took well over an hour. They emerged in conversation, Elisha wondering if the young man's taste in unusual foods might be at root while Christina peppered him with questions about his own experience with head trauma—both direct and in his patients. He shortly found himself seated on bench while she ran her fingers over the scars of his trepanation, parting his hair to get a better understanding.

"And that resulted in the change in your opposite eye? Interesting. I've not heard of such a result before, but it is worth searching our case studies. I'll set one of my students on the task."

Lucius swept around the corner, flanked by two students of his own. "I insist that you call the council, Maestra." He stared at her fingers as she withdrew them from Elisha's scalp.

"I take it they are not responding to your demands?"

He drew himself up, using his height to stare down at them both. Elisha merely folded his arms and remained seated, flaunting his refusal to be bothered with Lucius at all, though his hands itched to strike the man's imperious face. Lucius said, "While Maestro Antonio has agreed to the meeting, Maestro Fidelis merely offers to send notes via a runner. There are days I am convinced he is not in his right mind, and if he did not occasionally speak, I should imagine he is not even in his room."

"And Maestro Danek?"

"Is amenable to anything, so long as it happens after curfew. I am certain the staff was never so eccentric as this during my previous administration."

"Indeed the entire school has suffered without you."

She kept her own hands unnaturally still, as if she, too, forced herself to inaction.

"Maestro Teodor is the only man among the council worthy of the title, and he is fully invested in consultation with the Pope's physician, as is only fitting, even if the man is a mere surgeon without proper credentials. It is my fervent hope that Teodor's influence shall elevate the man such that his mean intellect is more suited to provide consultations worthy of the Holy Father himself." Lucius flicked his glance down toward Elisha as he addressed Maestra Christina. "I do hope you have not been allowing your new creature to aggravate the recovery conditions of any of my patients. Or indeed, any patients in this hospital."

"The only person he seems to be aggravating is you. Let's go." Christina swept away down the corridor, and Elisha followed after with little grace. So much for mastering himself while Lucius was around: it was all he could do not to strangle the man. "I'm afraid we shall have to join the masters for supper tonight, Elisha; much as I would prefer not to be subject to that odious man, I would like to hear what the papal physician has learned in his visit. Although I suppose you may prefer to dine in your chamber. A student can bring your meal."

"The less I am in evidence, the more chance he has to turn people against me. I like to think I can sway them if they meet me face to face."

"Indeed." They passed through a thick door into an arched outdoor passage where a breeze rifled their clothing before they entered the next ward. The familiar smells of vomit, urine, blood, and sickness assailed Elisha right away, as if he had returned to the hospital in London, or even to the battlefield, but there blood tended to dominate. Fear and despair permeated the hall as well. Beds lay along both sides, each broad surface

occupied by two or three people who writhed and
moaned with their conditions. Clumps of herbs and dried
flowers hung from the ceiling and decked the floor. Tall
windows pierced the walls, giving light and promoting
the exchange of tainted air for fresh, if they were open.
It seemed a better standard of care than the London
hospital, at least.

"Here, we allow the senior students to lead in diagnosis and treatment, under our guidance, of course." She
motioned him forward with her hand, pointing toward a
cluster of students around one of the beds. A lanky long-
bearded fellow in faculty robes leaned both hands on the
foot of the bed, watching and listening as one student
examined the patient.

"What do you find, Bastien?" The teacher demanded,
leaning in.

"Well, these patches of bad skin—"

"Lesions," supplied another student quietly.

"These lesions aren't black, really, not like the victims
of pestilence, but they're not normal skin?" He raised his
face hopefully.

"Fever?" barked the teacher, and the student, Bastien, put out his hand hesitantly. "No! You don't need to
touch her for this. Look at her. Pale, not flushed, dry, not
sweaty. So." He slapped his hand on the wood. "Skin lesions, particularly on the face, no fever nor sweating.
What other questions should we ask?"

The student who had spoken up about the lesions
stepped nearer the bed. "Have you had any change in
sensation?"

The patient dropped her gaze, her hands burrowing
into the sheet before her. "Maybe, it's hard to tell."

"Numbness?"

Slouching more into the sheets, the patient whispered,
"Can't you help me?"

Elisha took half a step nearer but stopped himself.

This was not his patient, nor was this the time to intrude on another doctor's work, especially not if the students were meant to practice diagnosis.

"You, there, give us a hand," the student said, gesturing toward an older woman who was fixing up the next bed. The woman walked over, bobbing a courtesy.

The patient's fear intensified, her hands wrapping tighter into the sheet, her head dropping forward so that her hair swung over her face. "Help me, please, doctors. I don't want to be—like this."

"Nobody wants to be sick, dear," said the old woman. "What do you want of me, Doctor?"

"I need to see her hands. Can you assist her to hold her hand steady?"

"It's not important, numbness, is it? I mean, it could be anything," said the patient.

Elisha intertwined his own fingers together at his back lest he intervene without cause. His shoulders tightened.

"They're just trying to help," said the old woman as she gripped the girl's elbow and tugged her arm, then pulled at the sheet with her other hand until the girl's own hand lay revealed, her fingers knobbed and the dark lesions even more obvious along her arm.

"Is it the pestilence?" the teacher asked. "See for yourselves. No fever, no chills, the lesions aren't swollen, are they? Nor are they just at the throat and arms. What are they?" He shot out his finger toward the new lead student. "What is your diagnosis?"

The student wet his lips, stepping back. "Leprosy."

As one, the old woman and the students spread away from the bed, bumping into each other and the surrounding beds. Two students stumbled into Elisha, forcing him back in their own haste to escape the patient's tainted air.

"Leprosy. Get her out of here. She should never have

been allowed past the gate, never mind into the wards. Go, get out! We don't need that kind of filth." The teacher swept his arm to guide the students away from the bed while a pair of sturdy men came up, setting down the reeking waste buckets they were carrying.

"Do you need us, Maestro?"

"This girl—remove her from the grounds."

"No, please! It's the pestilence, I'm sure of it." She waved a hand at her face. "See? I'm feeling hotter already. I know the fever's coming on."

The men grabbed hold of her arms as she protested, and dragged her toward the nearest door, as she continued to plead and struggle.

"Go to the church," the teacher called after her. "Perhaps they will take pity on your sins and send you to a lazar house. But you've no business mixing with healthy people!"

The door slammed behind them, and Elisha flinched at the finality of the sound. To the old woman, the teacher said, "Bundle up this bedding and have it burned. Don't put anyone in this bed for at least two days."

She bobbed again and went about her labor as the master summoned his students back from the bed. "Good diagnosis. We did not even need to go on to urine or astrology, did we? No. I suggest you be careful about washing up for dinner." The students glanced at their own hands and the student who had spoken the diagnosis lost his smug expression, but the teacher went on, "What treatments exist for leprosy, aside from prayer and the abjuration of whatever sinful behavior has brought it on?"

"Castration," blurted Bastien, then reddened as the others snickered.

The teacher smiled through his beard. "Perhaps not in this case. Others?"

"Pliny suggested snake's venom."

"Snake's venom! Something to try. What else?"

"Paracelsus tells us that lamb's blood might be efficacious."

"The blood of the lamb, very significant. Anything else? What about scouring the lesions? Some physicians have recommended scouring with arsenic or other agents which may remove the lesions themselves. I am not convinced this gets to the root cause, however."

"What does Maestro Danek suggest?" asked the student-leader.

"If you attend his seminar tonight, be sure to ask him. In the meantime, you have patients to see." He clapped his hands twice, and the students separated into little knots moving to this or that bed.

The door opened again, and the two men returned. They took up their buckets and carried them off between the beds as if nothing had happened. "That girl. He's given her a death sentence," Elisha said.

"Do you not have leprosy in England?" Christina asked.

"Of course, but I'd like to think the lazars are treated with greater sympathy."

The other professor stepped up to them. "Ah, Maestra. Good of you to join us."

"It seemed a good class, Antonio."

His eyebrows leapt. "Excellent. I paid off the gate to let in the next leper who came to the door. It helps the students to get a close look. They shall be more cautious about diagnosis in the future. It pays to be aware, even in the presence of a pestilence like the one that grows about us, that the usual afflictions are still about. And now, I need a drink." He waved a hand at Elisha. "Is this the fellow that Lucius is all upset over? He looks well enough to me."

"Elisha recently arrived from the court of Empress Margaret."

Antonio kept his gaze locked to Christina's. "He does not approve of how we handle lazars."

"In allowing her past the gate, you let her believe she might get treatment," Elisha pointed out. "Why elevate her hopes like that, just to dash them? You might at least have had her escorted to the lazar house with a little kindness."

"She *was* treated—exactly as she deserved. She is still gadding about the streets as if she had no illness at all, spreading her sin and wantonness. Until she accepts her fate and submits to God's justice, she shall never find a cure." Antonio shook his head. "No, I really need that drink." He patted his robes and found a flask, taking a long swallow. "That's better. I have to say, you're not convincing me you should be allowed to stay, much less gain access to something as valuable as our library, not to mention our own store of knowledge."

"Very well," Elisha spread his hands toward the beds on either side. "Assign me a patient."

"I had been thinking," Christina began, but Antonio turned his attention to Elisha.

"Ward three, bed twelve," Antonio said. "That way, if nothing comes of it, at least there is no family to care."

"Really, Maestro, I intended to bring him on my rounds before—"

"He wants a patient, I've given him one. See you at dinner." Antonio dipped his head and strolled away, taking another swing from his flask.

"By dinner he shall be drunk again. An unbecoming excess of fluid that fails to complement his bilious nature." Christina's eyes rested on the empty bed.

"The patient in bed twelve," Elisha prompted. "What can you tell me about him? her?"

"Him. Most definitely him." Her cheeks sagged. "Well, come along then, you can hardly do worse than the rest of us." They mounted the stairs to the upper story as she spoke. "Bed twelve was brought to us as experiencing demonic possession. He had been through an exorcism at the church, but it only made him more wild. He fights tooth and nail to escape, and some are inclined to allow him to go and fend for himself, or not, as God wills it. From my own brief examination, I can tell you that he is of good family and noble birth—his teeth are present and in good condition, suggesting a diet of well-ground bread. I should guess he is about ten years old. He is tall with limbs well-formed, suggesting that he has not contended with starvation. His features are regular, not unattractive, aside from the scars and markings of some disease. It may be that the scars are evidence of a sickness and recovery which damaged his mind."

About ten years old and an orphan. The same had happened to Elisha's brother, Nathaniel, when their mother died, an uncomfortable echo. At least Nathaniel had Elisha, until Elisha let him down and he took his own life. This boy, apparently, had no one. Elisha pushed away the memories and focused on Christina. "Have you been able to determine the origin of the scars?"

"Some appear consistent with pox, but he also has areas of rough skin suggesting a more general rash, and his fingers have lumps that imply even leprosy itself, though he shows no sign of active infection, and that has been discounted as an explanation. In another child, I should say that it is the attention of his parents he desires and so the demonic possession was a creative invention to force that attention—except that he was abandoned at the church, and they brought him to us. Whatever family he had has washed their hands of him. Whoever abandoned him left a rather large sum of money that his problems should be dealt with." She nearly smiled. "You know that the church is at a loss when they are willing to give up such a fortune just to be rid of the problem." She pushed through a door into a room filled with shrieking.

"We had him in one of the private chambers," she continued, raising her voice to be heard above the cries, "but there are now sufficient patients requiring those chambers that we've had to move him up here. The bruises you will see are a result of that transition."

The few other beds held patients more still than lively, some holding pillows to their ears, glaring as Christina passed by, but too poor to insist on better accommodations. Ignoring the screams, or perhaps used to the noise, two nuns moved among the patients, distributing bowls of thin soup, sometimes adding a handful of herbs or a dash of something from a bottle.

And the last bed held a horror scene. A boy stood upside down against the wall, gripping the bedposts with his hands, short ropes binding his wrists just below where he grabbed. Thick black hair hung down around his thin, scarred face. He screamed at the top of his voice, a piercing sound that nearly drove Elisha to ask for a pillow to cover his own ears. Instead, Elisha drew back his senses as they approached, allowing Death to creep through him and lessen his response.

A third nun stood at the foot of the bed, soup dripping from her face and habit. "You fiend! We are here of God's mercy—a mercy you don't deserve—and you foul everything!"

The boy beat his heels against the wall and screamed all the louder. His eyes squeezed shut with the force of his madness, his face gone red and blotchy.

"Bleed him again, Maestra," the nun said, wiping a hand over her face as they approached. "Bleed the devil out of him so at least he can be fed."

"Patience, sister. He can't keep this up, not with his head down like that." Christina stood beside the nun.

Blood marked the wall where the boy was kicking, his feet battering the stones as if he could pound his way through, and Elisha could see why some felt they should simply let him go and take his madness with him. Then the feet went still and the body wavered a moment in the air. He went limp, peeling downward and tumbling to the bed, unconscious. In that moment between madness and silence, Elisha felt the shock of recognition. The boy was a magus, and he was terrified out of his mind.

Chapter 11

$\mathfrak{C}$hristina stared down at the collapsed child. "I'll send a student to bind his wounds and leave some food he can eat when he revives."

"If you tell me where to find the bandages, I'll tend him," Elisha said.

"There's no need for you to take this on, truly, Doctor."

"No, indeed," the nun offered. "It is my holy penance to serve in this ward for my own stridency, I am sure." She bustled off to a chest by the wall and returned with a handful of cloth. "My mistake was unbinding his mouth before asking for him to be bled. I should have known better. He had seemed, for the moment, to be calm."

Before she could begin the task, Elisha took the bandages from her hand. "Maestro Antonio has appointed me the boy's physician, and I shall direct his treatment from now on. You said he was calm until you took out the gag?" He sat down on the side of the bed—large enough for three patients, and occupied by only one.

"Indeed, it seemed the smell of the soup was calming him, and I spoke to him as I was taking the gag. Silvio came up, and I asked him to wait, that perhaps the bleeding wasn't needed. That's when the fiend went mad and twisted all about. Such things are common in possessions like this."

Silvio, the mancer. "There's to be no more bleedings. I can't make a proper diagnosis without full awareness of his symptoms—understood?"

"I hardly think a demonic possession can be mistaken for some other ailment. What the boy needs is a priest."

"Nevertheless, that's up to me now." He met the nun's eye until she looked away.

The boy's leg twitched from Elisha as he reached out, and he projected peace and comfort, letting his hand go warm. He remembered Father Uccello on the rack, asking not to be touched, telling him that it was the power of the captors to touch their victim where they would, when they would, how they would. Elisha drew back his hand. He leaned in close.

The skin of the boy's heels was thick and slightly cracked in a few places by his violence so that blood oozed through. Elisha had been about the same age when he saw Brigit's mother burned. Her transformation into an angel had transformed him as well, but his parents wouldn't believe what happened to him, that an angel had stroked his cheek with her outstretched wing as she died upon the stake. Nor would he refrain from insisting it was the truth. Convinced he was touched by the devil, his mother thought to send him to a monastery, and the priest who was to bring him there had bound and gagged him, so that none need hear his madness. Twenty years ago, Elisha had been helpless at the hands of others. Far too often since then, Elisha found himself helpless yet again. This night, Elisha held the power. He had entered the room, thinking of his brother, and instead confronted himself. So many echoes of the past layered the moment as if his own scars overlaid those of his patient.

"I'd rather let him rest a while than risk upsetting him again so soon by firm handling." He set down the bandages the nun had given him and moved toward the

boy's head, framed by his bound arms. The straps at his
wrists were crossed, evidence of his wild attempt to escape, and Elisha imagined him flailing away from the
foot of the bed, twisting himself around, finishing with
his back to the wall, even at such an extraordinary angle.
Did he feel safer that way, with his back to the wall?
Was it only Silvio whose presence disturbed him so
much? But that wouldn't explain his behavior before he
arrived at the medical school. Still, his wild flailing had
left him on his face. Encouraging rest, withdrawing his
presence to a bare minimum of contact, Elisha lifted the
boy and gently turned him, lying him on his back, his
ragged tunic drawn down toward his bare knees. He
wanted to simply throw off the boy's bindings, but with
no sense of what was wrong with him, that might only
place him at greater risk. As Christina had observed,
disease and treatment marked every inch of his flesh—
the pock-marks of hives, the rough patches of old lesions, the bruises of his confinement and his battle
against it, the thin scars of multiple bleedings, the
thicker marks where growths had been removed or
scraped. He might have been a handsome, well-formed
child but for the ravages of disease and doctors.

"At rest like that, he appears almost ordinary," Christina remarked.

"Only because he's exhausted himself. The devil can
only do so much with such a weak vessel," the nun replied. "Even in the night he thrashes about. If he's not
gagged, he howls then, too."

Elisha watched the boy's breathing grow steady, extending his senses to track the boy's racing heart as it
calmed in his collapse. "What is he so afraid of?"

"Afraid? It's we who are afraid of him, and well we
should be. What if the devil should make the leap? If
someone else, someone vulnerable should come by and
the devil departs from this child into another." The nun

patted the cross at her breast. "I've got the Lord to protect me, of course, but not everyone can be so blessed."

A bell began to toll outside. "We're expected at dinner," Christina remarked.

"Are you the night nurse?" Elisha asked the nun, as
he rose from the bed.

"I am."

"I've been given the corner chamber on the first floor
of the student dormitory—come and wake me when his
nightmares begin."

"Very well," she said, but her face suggested that he
was as mad as the child he had just been assigned to heal.

"You are a man of great compassion," Christina said
as they descended the opposite stairs into the rush of
students heading off for meals and visiting family members heading for home.

"It is my deepest flaw, Maestra." His mind had not
yet left the child, the boy who knew a mancer when he
saw one.

"An interesting diagnosis."

"Will Maestro Danek be joining us?" He would like
the chance to ask his fellow magus about his patient. He
did not yet know if Danek were sensitive enough to be
aware the child was a magus without touching him, but
if the teacher monitored this campus at all, he likely had
figured that out by now.

Shaking her head, Christina said, "He works all hours,
staying down in the specimen room preparing medical
simples much of the day, then checking his patients at
night. Even his students must go downstairs to see him
or attend his seminar. He is not a popular assignment as
his interests are in the area of infectious disease, the sort
most commonly spread among the poor and depraved,
hardly the sort of thing our wealthy patrons are likely to
contract. Given the current pestilence, however, more
people have been paying attention to his classes. That's

why the papal physician has come here, but I'm afraid he's found little of use."

A door stood open into a brightly lit space and a servant bowed them into a chamber small but sumptuously dressed with richly carved and painted beams and tapestries on the walls between glass-paned windows. A fire danced in the broad hearth, illuminating the men who gathered before them—all men, aside from Christina and a few serving girls. Antonio stood, a goblet in hand, speaking with a well-dressed student while Lucius huddled with his two acolytes, including the library keeper. A portly man in professorial robes occupied a head chair. That must be Maestro Teodor, the school's director. He engaged in avid conversation with another man at his right, a fellow with pale hair cut a bit short.

"At last, we can eat!" Antonio declared, dropping into a chair held out for him by a servant.

"It seemed fitting I should meet my new patient before dining, Maestro," Elisha said.

"Whereas I do not believe you are fit to dine with us at all." Lucius strode to the table and rapped it with his fist. "I have so many of you as can be gathered, and so I say to you that this man is no better than a barber. Worse, in fact, for he is traitor to the king of England, and a practitioner of the dark arts."

The director steepled his hands on the table before him. "My dear Lucius. Guy has only two more nights among us—his departure is too long delayed already—and I would rather not spoil the occasion with this dispute. Please, let us be seated. Day after tomorrow, we can speak of all of this, after Guy's ship has safely left harbor, and the rest of us have had the opportunity to familiarize ourselves with the situation."

"I do appreciate your consideration, Teodor," said his conversational companion, "but I don't wish my own brief stay to disrupt the school any more than is necessary." He spoke with a French accent, standing out among the Italians. That must be Guy de Chauliac, the papal physician.

"You see, Maestro Teodor, even Guy recognizes the urgency of this situation. Whereas you do not comprehend the insidious danger of having such a person in our midst! Already he is interfering with treatments ordered by other, more qualified practitioners."

"So let him try." Antonio waved his hand, the fingers still wiggling as he spoke. "He can hardly do worse than some of our students." His nose looked red, his eyes blurry.

Christina said, "Elisha has laid allegations of his own, Teodor, regarding the fate of our former student, Benedict de Fleur, who departed here as an assistant to Maestro Lucius and never returned."

"He entered his own practice in England," Lucius insisted. "As one would hope for all of one's assistants—at least, those who do not prefer to teach."

The library keeper gave the slightest bow.

"You accuse me of being a traitor to the crown of England?" Elisha felt under his tunic for the letters, now worn with travel, sweat and blood, that Thomas had given him when he set sail. His hand trembled, the mere presence of his old adversary setting him on edge. "I have here a royal writ, granted for my safe passage by Thomas, by Grace of God, the King of England." He displayed the document, its royal seal dangling for all to see. "Do you wish to examine it?" Elisha held it out to Teodor, the portly man at the head of the table.

"Thank you." Teodor accepted the document and unfolded it to scan the lines.

Guy, regarded Elisha with a frank stare from across the table. "I have heard that you are a surgeon, is this not so? And yet you are in service to the king?" A smile transformed his thick features. "And so am I, but to the

Holy Father himself." He pushed back his chair and extended his hand. "There are few enough of us worthy of such service, I am well-pleased to meet another. I am Guy de Chauliac."

Elisha accepted his grasp and his well-wishes. The man's presence rang with his medical authority and knowledge, his annoyance with the learned physicians around him, and an echo of loss, perhaps anticipating his crossing the water back to France. Not a mancer then, though someone close to the Pope must be. Even discounting the Pope's religious prominence, he held thousands of acres of land, commanded thousands of soldiers, servants and tenants, and through his priests and monks, held sway over hundreds of thousands of parishioners. This position, coupled with his God-given authority, made the Pope the most powerful man in Europe. In order for the mancers to overthrow all nations, they must overthrow the Church as well, and some of their agents must be close to the Pope, to guide and manipulate him—unless the Pope himself was a mancer, a thought that chilled and worried Elisha as he drew back his hand. "Well met, Guy. But I have no wish to disturb your limited time among your colleagues. I can dine in my room."

"Nonsense," said Christina, just as Antonio said, "Do go away, I'm hungry!"

Someone knocked loudly and pushed open the outer door. "Forgive me, masters, an urgent visitor from Rome." The servant bowed and stepped aside to reveal Count Vertuollo, elegant in his mourning garb.

Vertuollo pressed his hands together. "And here I have found him, the villain who slew my son."

Chapter 12

❖

"Now I'll never get my supper," Antonio wailed. He drained his goblet and signaled for a refill.

Elisha forced himself to maintain a calm demeanor, concealing the sweat that broke out on his palms and the tension that rushed to his shoulders at the sight of Vertuollo.

"You are suddenly surrounded by accusers, Doctor," Teodor observed. He pushed back from the table and rose stiffly. "And who might you be, my lord?"

"My name means nothing without a son to carry it on." Vertuollo spread his hands low as if letting go, the air of humility spread over his noble features.

Once again the damnable count got the better of him. Elisha seized back the initiative. "May I present Count Vertuollo of Rome, a man greatly respected, not least of all by myself," Elisha said as graciously as he might, the cold of the count's presence sending shivers over his flesh. "Alas, the count's son assaulted me with intent toward my murder. The politics of Rome are tangled and violent as you must know."

"Because the Pope must return there," Antonio declared, pointing at Guy with his goblet. "You must tell him so." He nodded his wobbly head.

"Oh, do be quiet," Christina cut in.

"You do not deny this fresh murder, then?" Lucius pounced forward. "How many others have died at your hands?"

Ignoring Lucius, Elisha continued, "Had I any other choice, the count's son would be alive today." Trapped between them, Elisha declared, "I have never murdered another man, though I have killed in my own defense and that of others." Elisha stood, slipped the cape from his shoulders, yanked off the layers of his tunics. He turned on his heel to display his bare back to the gathered physicians, facing Vertuollo across a very short distance indeed. The count swept his glance over Elisha's scarred chest, then their eyes locked.

"Here you see, doctors." Elisha reached back to brush his fingers along a lump of scar tissue fresher than the others. "With neither warning nor challenge, the count's son stabbed me from behind, an upward cut between the ribs, toward my heart."

"May I?" Guy asked as footsteps approached, then his diagnostic fingers traced over the scar, and Elisha could feel the thrust of the knife up through his lung. "It seems broad enough that the knife must have gone very deep. How did you survive?"

"By the grace of God. And quick intervention."

"You have more scars than many a battle-veteran, Doctor. These look like lash marks." Guy's fingers fluttered across his spine, tracing the pattern. "You were standing at the time."

Lucius announced, "I had the duty of punishing him as my underling, for his continued insubordination. As you can see, it had no effect upon his intransigence, and now this noble gentleman comes to bear witness to even greater crimes."

Vertuollo's eyes narrowed, his gaze lingering on the scar that branded Elisha's chest. His examination made Elisha feel colder. Elisha's wrists ached, a reminder of being bound, face to the pole, as Lucius cracked the lash against him. "Tell them why you beat me, Maestro Lucius. What insubordination had I committed?"

"You refused my direct order to tend an injured knight upon the battlefield."

A gasp echoed from several places behind him, and Guy's touch went hostile as it withdrew. The count's faint smile hinted at victory.

"Tell them why," Elisha insisted.

Lucius hesitated, and Elisha lowered his hands, looking back over his shoulder. "Tell them, Lucius. What was I doing when I refused you? What did I say when I did so?" His heart pounded with remembered fury, with the urge to fight back at the moment he was taken from the field.

"You were tending another patient, as I recall."

"Who was I tending, Lucius? And what was his injury?"

"None of this has any bearing upon your crime against my son," Vertuollo pointed out, his voice low.

"Which he has said was self-defense, and presented the wound to support his claim, my lord. Allow us to finish one inquiry before we begin the next," Teodor said calmly. "We are physicians—we must have all the information before we can make an accurate diagnosis of this man's character."

"Tell us, Maestro Lucius, who was the doctor's other patient? And what was the patient's condition?" Christina took up the questioning, her hands propped on the back of a chair, clinging there.

Lucius puffed himself up. "He looked like a common foot soldier, a person hardly in need of our skilled—"

"Prince Alaric, the younger son of King Hugh of England, disguised as a messenger to carry his father's word to their allies," Elisha supplied, and Lucius's eyes grew brighter, his lips compressed. "With a gash at his throat. If it was not stitched immediately, he'd've bled out in moments. I'm sure a learned physician like you, Lucius, would recognize that danger."

Lucius shot out his hand, jabbing in Elisha's direction. "Even you didn't know it was the prince!"

"Because it wasn't important—whoever he was, without my help, he was a dead man. And you told me to leave him in a ditch to die." Elisha snatched up his tunics and yanked them on over his head. "I saved a man's life that day, doctors. Would any one among you have done any less?" He swept them with his gaze, letting it linger on Lucius before he faced Vertuollo. "You claim me for a murderer—" He nearly addressed Vertuollo as 'my brother' in their odd accustomed way. "—my lord. I say bring your witnesses. Bring your proof. If you came merely to ruin my reputation among my colleagues, as you can see, I already have Lucius for that."

"And he has failed," Christina said. She moved up beside him, and Maestro Teodor gave a solemn nod.

"We are men of science and knowledge. We cannot accept mere accusation and rumor. We shall be pleased to hear your evidence, or to accept the investigation of the agents of her majesty Giovanna, Queen of Naples, to whom we are pleased to owe our allegiance. In the meantime, I can offer you the hospitality of one of our master suites, if you—"

"Queen Giovanna is herself accused of murder, is she not?" Vertuollo's face furrowed with grief. "It pains me to see an establishment of learning such as this one sullied with such alliances." With an elegant curl of his hand, the count bowed deeply and straightened. "I leave you to your supper then. You dine tonight with Judas." He strode away from the door into the darkness, majestic in his shadows and his pain.

After a moment, the Valley rippled with cold, and Elisha knew that he was gone. The fur of his cloak draped the nearest chair and Elisha gathered it back into his arms. "Thank you for your invitation, but I'll eat in my room."

"Elisha, there's no need," Christina began, but he glanced back at her.

"Please, Maestra." Given the state of his nerves and his stomach he wasn't sure he'd be able to choke down even a bite.

"I'll have someone bring you a tray," she finished.

To Guy, he said, "It was a pleasure to meet you, Doctor. I'm sorry to have spoiled your supper. Masters." He bowed his head, and departed, placing his feet carefully to stop his knees wobbling. From all appearances, he had won that battle, confronting two enemies at once, yet the seeds of doubt would take root in the hearts of the masters. Even Christina would be hard-pressed to defend him if anything more went wrong.

The walk across the yard in the evening's chill helped to settle his agitation. Shortly after he arrived at his chamber a fine meal arrived, and Gilles was only too pleased to partake, while telling Elisha all the gossip he had been hearing, chatter that distracted Elisha however briefly from his own concerns. Was Vertuollo merely displaying his ability to track Elisha anywhere, or had his intrusion into Salerno come for another reason? What had he learned from it?

After blowing out their candles, both men lay on their beds, Elisha on his back thinking over all the people he had met: the young leper girl cast out of the hospital as she had likely been cast out of many places before; Leon, who survived the plague and never spoke of it; the patient in bed 12 who went mad and recognized a mancer when the man drew near—or was that assumption merely Elisha's own prejudice? Many a person, especially a child, would be afraid of the barber come to bleed his vitality away in the name of health. How many adults with knives had hovered over that boy, claiming to be there to help? The boy who reminded him of his brother, and of himself.

He rolled onto his side, pushing that thought away. He came here to learn about the plague. The first step was to gain access to the library, to all the knowledge it might contain, but Lucius's acolyte held sway there. Maestro Danek had an interest in diseases, but focused on preparing medical simples to treat them. The mancer-barber Silvio lurked in the corners of Elisha's thoughts as well. He shut his eyes, cradled by the mattress, and drew back much of his awareness, trying to dull the throbbing sense of the Valley hovering. It felt like a recent wound, sealed over, but suppurating beneath the skin, silently festering. In the hospital, someone died, and Elisha's eyes snapped open.

In his bed on the opposite side of the chamber, Gilles slapped himself and grumbled softly.

"What's the trouble, Brother?" Elisha asked softly.

"These accursed fleas. I tried to be so careful choosing our bedding, but my blanket's infested, that's plain to see. How are they not bothering you?"

Elisha focused on his blanket in the gloom of the pale moonlight. A few shiny black dots popped here and there. They approached his hand where it rested outside the bedding, then paid it no mind, as if his kinship with death made him an unappealing target. When was the last time he had been bitten by a flea? Not since the battle of Dunbury, anyhow. Something to be grateful for in the morass of his magical talent. "We can prepare some herbs in the morning that should help."

"I don't think any of my saints will defend me against fleabites, more's the pity." Ropes groaned and squeaked as Gilles rolled around in his bed and finally went still again. After a little longer, his snoring began, a series of soft catches and gurgles, and finally full-blown sawing.

Elisha reached for a little magic to draw his mind

down deep and allow for rest, then he sensed an agitated presence, and rose quickly, before the steps could reach their door. He popped the door open, surprising the nun on the other side, her fist raised to knock. "Hush, don't wake the friar," he told her. "It's about my patient?"

"I'm surprised you cannot hear him from here, doctor. We moved the other patients off that floor, since you won't let him be gagged, but the patients on other wards still need their rest."

He pulled the door shut behind him and hurried after her across the darkened square. Indeed, as they entered the hospital arch, a muffled cry reached him, along with an undertone of annoyed shouts and pleading. The nun held up her lantern, displaying a series of long scratches across her opposite arm. "I was only trying to shift his blanket, to keep him warm, and he lashed out quick as you think."

Two lanterns stood at either end of the long ward on the floor below, and a pair of students moved among the patients, trying to keep them comfortable, darting glances at Elisha and the ward sister as they moved toward the stairs. On the abandoned ward above, his patient huddled at the far end of the bed, his back pressed to the wall, jerking at his restraints, his eyes glinting.

"I'm your new doctor. My name's Elisha, what's yours?"

"It's no good, he doesn't speak."

Indeed, the boy's wailing erupted even louder, and he kicked against the bed as if he could shove himself through the wall at his back.

Afraid of doctors, then. An excellent start. Elisha sat down on the foot of the bed. "Do we know what language he does speak, if he were to speak?"

The nun sighed and shook her head. "I've just told you, he doesn't."

"What does he respond to, then?"

"Nothing. Just look at him." She waved a hand at the feral child.

"Not true. Earlier, you said he calmed down at the smell of soup. Can you bring some more? He must be hungry by now."

With a prodigious sigh, she moved away down the aisle. Elisha sat cross-legged, regarding his patient who had broken off from wailing to gasp a series of hitching breaths before he began again. He addressed him first in English, then Italian, German, and the little French he knew. The boy showed no change at all, his eyes rolling and his thin chest struggling to get enough breath to scream. He had kicked his blanket all the way down, and Elisha re-arranged the wrinkles as he considered what to try next, short of forcing contact. A few flakes of dried blood from the boy's heels scattered from the blanket. Elisha dabbed a few of them onto his finger, feeling the heat and the terror of the child in front of him.

He addressed the child again, this time in the way of the witches. "*My name's Elisha, what's yours?*"

The boy caught his breath, shoving hard against the wall, staring at Elisha, his eyes wide and green and shimmering with tears.

"*You heard that, I can tell.*" Talking like this, from one soul to another, required no translation.

He shook his head wildly, his tangled hair slapping his face and the wall. "*Don't talk in me!*"

That stung. For a long moment, Elisha sat silent, regarding his patient. How was he to help the boy at all if he had no way to communicate? The swarm of emotions that assailed him when he spoke in the witches' way suggested the boy had experience with it—and that his experience was, like so much of his young life, not pleasant, not a discovery or a thrilling secret, but an invasion. Elisha calmed his own reaction. He maintained contact through the blood, but this time spoke aloud, letting the contact carry his meaning. "The nun's bringing you some soup—just soup, I promise. If you'd like, I'll try it first, just to show you it's safe to eat."

"*Nothing is safe.*" A furtive, inadvertent reply, but Elisha's recognition must have shown.

What would it have meant to Elisha in the confusion and frustration of his own childhood, to have someone who knew even a little of what he was going through? "I don't believe you are mad," Elisha said aloud, then added, silently, "*You're like me.*"

"*Like them.*" And as if that was the thought most terrifying of all, the boy screamed so that his terror echoed off the walls all around.

"People have different skills. It's not a skill that makes you evil, it's what you do with it." Elisha told him, again using his voice first, getting the child used to his presence and to someone speaking calmly, then he offered more. "*Some people like us are evil. They make everything dangerous.*"

The boy panted, then swallowed hard, but Elisha doubted he had enough moisture left in him even to wet his own throat. Elisha rose from the bed and scouted the corners of the room until he found a stand of washing things with an empty basin. Pouring a few inches of water into the heavy ceramic basin, Elisha returned.

"*Dangerous,*" the boy echoed, his voice still distant and small.

"*I'm here to try to make things safe, to make things better for you.*" Elisha held out the basin. "I'd like to put this near you, so you can drink." Even as he moved to set it down, the boy flailed his legs and the basin flew up, splashing Elisha from head to toe. Thankfully, the basin itself landed on the bed without breaking.

The boy's presence flooded with terror, overwhelming any sense of warmth or conscious thought as he writhed against the wall. He howled and shook his head, keeping his eyes on Elisha. When Elisha raised his hand to wipe the water from his face, the child fell abruptly silent, cowering. Elisha lowered his hand and let the water drip—Lord knew, he'd been drenched with worse than that.

Projecting calm, Elisha retrieved the basin, and returned to the pitcher. He refilled the basin and walked slowly back. "You must be thirsty."

Again, the boy flailed and tossed, though Elisha held onto the basin this time, and only received a gout of water that streamed down from his hair. The child collapsed, whimpering, as that terror rushed through him, spiked, this time, with confusion.

If he had not felt the boy's terror as much as seen it in his face, Elisha might have been angry, but he felt, too, the child's anticipation, the new tension that seized his limbs as he waited for an adult's fury. Elisha started singing, very quietly, withdrawing his presence so the boy would have to be quiet in order to hear. He sang a lullaby, in English, for that was what he knew, but a lullaby did not require words to be understood. The boy's shrieking sank low along with Elisha's voice, as if they were singing counterpoint, a duet of fear and peace together. When the shrieking died away completely, leaving the boy's mouth open, empty of his fear, at least for the moment, Elisha reached out again. He knelt down, offering the bowl.

"I will not hit you. I will not hurt you. If it is in my power to prevent it, I will not allow anyone else to do so. Do you understand? I know it's hard for you to believe, even if I do not know why, but you can feel that I'm telling the truth."

Surprise struck the boy's presence and his lashes fluttered. A magus, yes, but utterly untested and untrained. The boy had no idea what he could do or what he might know.

Elisha almost smiled. *"Here, I will tell you a lie, so you'll know what that feels like. I hate singing."*

The boy flinched, but that tension did not leave him, and he made no move toward the basin Elisha set on the bed before him.

"All right then," Elisha continued, encouraged that at least his voice in the child's flesh no longer provoked terror. *"I hate the king of England. I love to eat pigs' feet. I hate dogs. I hate white bread. I hate you."*

Those green eyes wavered, searching Elisha's face, his hands, the basin between them.

"All of those things are lies." Regarding him steadily, Elisha went on, *"Here are some things that are true. I want to help you. An angel touched me once, before she died, that's why I became a healer. I love dogs."* He smiled, gently. *"You don't have to be afraid of me. Did you feel the difference? To me, it feels slippery, like eels."*

"I love doctors." The words slithered through Elisha's skin. *"Priests are better. I love dogs, too. I'm not afraid of anything."*

Elisha laughed, still keeping his voice very low. *"How can anyone not love dogs?"*

"Are you a demon, too?"

"If I am," Elisha told him, *"then we are demons together."*

The boy reached as far as he could with one bound arm and tugged the basin across the linen. Elisha fought the urge to help him, afraid that any quick movement, anything too sharp would break the fragile peace. The boy leaned into the basin and drank his fill.

Chapter 13

───────◆───────

$\mathcal{T}$he moment the nurse reappeared, their fragile rapport shattered, and it took all of Elisha's patience to convince her to simply leave the bowl of soup and leave with him, giving the boy space to eat without feeling threatened by them. Still, this small success left him elated as he walked down the stairs. He spread his attunement over the quiet hospital, sensing the patients both sleeping and restless. With the boy's silence, the tension ebbed from the night. He could ill afford the attention he must give to this one child, but the peace that the child's successful treatment might bring to both patients and doctors alike could earn him the respect of the occupants—and open his path to the knowledge he needed to confront the plague. If he met the challenge Antonio had assigned him, Teodor and the others might override Lucius's denial of the library and bring him into their confidence.

Throughout the hospital, too many patients still lay fevered and twitching. On the lowest level, a comforting presence moved among them, with the focused shifting of intellect and power he'd come to associate with a magus. Danek? He'd been told the man made his rounds after dark, after a long day's work. Elisha pushed through the door into the long, dimly lit ward.

Danek stooped beside a bed, his fingers pinching the

wrist of one of its occupants. Then he poured a draught from a small bottle and helped the patient to swallow. He glanced up at Elisha's approach, his face in shadow, but his eyes glinting. "Welcome," he murmured. He held up the bottle. "A sleeping draught. If we cannot ease the progression of some diseases, we might at least offer a respite. What keeps you up at this hour?"

"I've been assigned a patient. Ward three, bed twelve." He wanted to reach out, to make contact and have the chance to speak freely. "Have you examined him?"

Danek chuckled softly, then rose from the bed. "I've heard he screams at the approach of any doctor. My presence there at night would hardly be appreciated." He cocked his head then, looking up at the ceiling. "I did hear screaming a little while ago. Your doing?"

"I like to think the silence after was more my doing. The boy suffers from nightmares."

"Perhaps we should get him some of this." Danek waggled the little bottle.

Elisha put out his hand, but instead of taking it, he let his fingers rest on Danek's. "*He's a magus, like us. I suspect he has a high degree of sensitivity.*"

Danek twitched at Elisha's touch, his fingers felt rough, like a workman's. "*Really? Well. I guessed at the first part. Pity. Something must have addled his mind at an early age. The sensitive are easily overwhelmed by circumstance. I shouldn't wonder if more of them went mad.*" He drew back his hand and dropped the bottle back into a satchel slung over his shoulder. "It's expensive stuff, that. I don't know how you'd administer it to a madman, in any case."

Danek moved along the aisle, stooping again to listen to a patient's breathing.

"I hoped you would help me to diagnose his illness."

"What are the signs of active contagion?" Danek went to his next patient, removed a dry poultice, and tossed it toward the aisle for the cleaners before replacing it with a fresh one.

Elisha considered. No fever, no sign of recent eruptions of pustules or rash, though clearly he had suffered those in the past. His breathing was clear, and movement, though wild, appeared to be controlled—no fits or convulsions. Neither Christina nor the nuns had mentioned any significance to his urine or feces, though perhaps he got so little to eat or drink that his eliminations would be worthless for diagnostic purposes. "I am not sure there are any signs of active contagion."

"Back to demonic possession then." Danek's grin gleamed faintly as he approached between the beds. Then he clapped Elisha on the shoulder. "*We should be so lucky, eh? Don't know about your experience gaining your skills, mine was anything but pleasant.*"

Just for a moment, Elisha wanted to trust Danek with the truth of his skill. He carried it like a weight in his chest, the hard, cold presence of Death, but he kept his nature carefully shuttered behind the façade of medical interest and magical friendship.

The touch lifted, and Danek proceeded toward the far end of the ward. "You came to study the pestilence, though? Don't let that boy distract you. Pitiful, certes, but just the one." Danek shrugged, then blew out a breath. "This pestilence on the other hand. Have you had a chance to ask Leon about his experience?" They stepped into a room shelved high and stacked with all manner of hospital supplies. "I am very curious to know how he survived."

"I haven't. I assumed you and the other masters have learned what could be learned."

Danek examined a shelf, leaning low beneath the pool of lamplight. "Not much, alas. I'd like to get a blood or urine sample for study, but, he's reticent. And the library is little help either. The Pope's man is gathering pages of notes and advice from every one of us, doing his duty, doubt it will matter. I'll be surprised if he can even keep the Pope alive through all of this."

"I pray you're wrong about that. Apparently, Guy will be leaving day after tomorrow to bring the Pope what he's learned." Was Danek aware of the mancers and their connection with the pestilence? Elisha so wanted to trust him, but they'd only just met. Best to be cautious. He glanced around, but even his awareness found no others within earshot. "Is it true the library contains books of magic?"

"Charms, incantations, and rituals. Nothing true. Half of it is Egyptian or Greek in any case. If you'd like anything in particular, I might be able to bring some things out for you."

Nothing true. This made Elisha feel suddenly weary, and he suppressed a yawn. "A kind offer. I'll think on it."

"Do that. Meantime, I've got more patients." Danek turned away, perusing the shelves and placing items in his satchel. "Good night."

"Good night." Elisha left him there, and walked back toward his own quarters. As he paused in the open air, taking a few deep breaths and seeking calm before trying to sleep, Elisha felt the pressure of the Valley, no longer simply to the south, but north and east as well. The only direction empty of encroaching death was the calm sea that lapped at the feet of the city, and the salt and the water itself would block his senses. He gazed up at the bulk of the library, its windows even now lit by flickering lamps. Guy, still seeking answers? Or some students working late into the night? Either way, he could not simply sneak inside, not tonight—even if he had the strength for a deflection. Guy would shortly be leaving, giving the faculty the freedom to focus on the accusations against Elisha himself. Vertuollo's intrusion and the tension with Lucius left him feeling wrung out, grateful for the challenge of the child, his sole patient, and certainly one who'd keep him occupied with medical as well as magical concerns. What sickness could have caused the marks on his body—and how many were due as much to attempted cures as to sickness itself? Diagnose the child, hopefully cure him, and win the faculty's trust. Elisha focused on that as he curled back into his bed and let Gilles's snoring carry him off for a much-needed rest.

Gilles and Elisha broke bread in their room, Gilles already eager to return to the church and talk with the novices he'd met the day before. Elisha had only one patient and no privileges for the library or anything else. As he crossed the yard toward the hospital, he watched the students scurry toward classes or flock behind Maestro Antonio—looking a little green—for a hospital tour. Lucius strode from the refectory with a few of his acolytes in pursuit, but he paused to aim his finger at Elisha, who had no need to hear the words to know that accusations against him were spreading. Students who looked curious yesterday now dodged his gaze and shifted their steps to be past him. Excellent. What more would be done to damage his already tenuous reputation? By the sharp light of day, pinning his hopes on curing a hopeless child looked like a madness of his own. Leon sat on a bench at the edge of the yard, a book in his hands, though he did not look at it.

Elisha approached, half-expecting the young man to rise and move away as fast as his languorous pace would carry him, but Leon simply blinked at him and watched him approach. Perhaps he hadn't the energy to flee like the rest. No. Elisha couldn't afford to think that way, nor should he make assumptions about Leon's fitness. "May I join you?"

Leon tipped his head toward the bench, and Elisha sat down. "Don't like you any more, do they?"

"If they ever did. I am a curiosity—first for my English origins, and now for the rumors."

Leon huffed a breath that might have been laughter. "A curiosity." His hand brushed over the leather cover of the book in his lap.

"You've been here a few months, right? You must know a lot of people."

The young man tipped his head again, squinting up at Elisha.

"I'm looking for someone. A student called Ariane. She—"

But Leon straightened in his seat, his interest quickened in a way that made him look more alive than he had a moment before. "Senior student. Good scholar."

"I expect so. Can you introduce us, or at least, point her out to me?"

Leon's eyes widened, and his cheeks grew a little more pink. "After nuncheon, best time. She makes rounds." He pulled his book close against his chest, his presence humming with excitement.

"Meet you here?"

Leon bobbed his head. "Not for me, she wouldn't. But you. You're a curiosity." He pronounced the word carefully. Leon pushed to his feet and, by his standards at any rate, hurried away.

The library and the professors were only one source of knowledge about the pestilence. Elisha, too, pushed up and walked swiftly toward the lower yard. At least the gatekeepers had the word to let him come and go as he pleased, so Elisha walked back up to the church, to its crypt filled with victims of the pestilence. As Danek had said, they might not yet have a cure, but they could still relieve the pain. Elisha pushed back his sleeves, and got to work, laying cool, damp compresses on the sufferers, more often than not, laying his own cold hands, submerging himself in the task at hand, the patients at need, studying their symptoms as he worked with them, looking for any signs he might have missed. When the noon bells rang overhead, echoing down through the depths as if in answer to those voices who called out to God, he sprinted back down to the university and arrived, breathless, at the appointed bench.

Leon stood this time, still clutching his book, staring into the distance. At his side sat a tall young woman with lustrous dark hair and red lips—her beauty unsurprising given the young man's earlier reaction. She rose immediately, taking a half-step back, brushing against Leon's side and making him blush all over again. She wore the long robes of any other student, sliding her hands into the opposite sleeves. "Leon said you wished to see me. It is no more than I have wished myself." She drew a sharp breath, then pushed herself forward with a visible effort, and he recognized her from the day of his arrival. She had been at the heart of a cluster of students, at first approaching his confrontation with Lucius, then closing in around her, solicitous of her response. "You knew Lucius in England? And Benedict?"

"I did."

"Benedict was to marry me." She stopped before him. "He is dead, isn't he. He would've written otherwise."

"Aye, he's dead. I'm sorry."

She sniffed, pressing her hands together at her lips as if whispering a prayer. "I had a letter in the summer, but he'd written it in the spring. He was afraid, unhappy, but he hoped to come back soon, to come for me."

Elisha realized the gift she had handed over, more than he had hoped for in asking to meet her. "Do you still have the letter?"

"Of course. I have saved them all, but I don't think the council will expel Maestro Lucius, not without stronger evidence."

"You're right about that, but will you help me? Lucius

is the only one who can allow me into the library—I'm trying to stop this plague, to stop the madness from spreading. With your letter, I might be able to scare him into cooperating."

"Good. I'd like him to be the one scared this time." She leaned a little forward, utterly focused. "Is it true he killed Benedict?"

Elisha nodded. "Lucius tried to talk Benedict into supporting his own treachery against the king. He left here at the request of Prince Alaric who hoped to overthrow his father. When Benedict resisted, Lucius shot him and left evidence to suggest it had been Benedict all along." It had been Elisha's first contact with Alaric's scheming. "I'm so sorry."

"Then he was brave, my Benedict." Lovely in her grief though she held back her tears, she reached out to him, and he took her trembling hands atop his own. "Were you there when he died?"

"I tried to save him, to stop the bleeding. I—" The death haunted him, trapped in the rushing river's stream, the young man pierced by the arrows of someone he trusted. No matter that Benedict himself had inflicted some of Elisha's own punishments, no one deserved to die that way. "I came too late, lady."

She gripped his hands fiercely, then let him go. "I will gain you that library, sir. Come with me." She lifted the hem of her robes to move faster. Leon trailed after, picking up his own pace, almost breaking into a run, but that would put him beside her, and he held back.

In her richly laid chambers, Ariane pulled out a wooden box, inlaid and polished to a high sheen. From this, she took a bundle of pages, and found the one she sought, clutching it in both hands, as precious to her as any talisman or saint's bone. "Now to find his killer."

"In his study," Leon murmured. "Always, after lunch."

"You are very observant, aren't you. Perhaps you

should study medicine," Ariane remarked, not pausing to see the effect her words had upon him. After pursuing her for the afternoon, Leon would likely need a rest, but he showed no sign of flagging as she led the way upstairs and half-way around the yard.

A murmur of voices echoed beyond the door they had reached, and Ariane knocked. The gawky student librarian opened the door promptly, blurting, "Ariane!" then noticing the others. His expression shifted to supercilious in an instant, and he half-closed the door again. "Ariane, you are welcome here, but your companion must go away. Maestro Lucius is in fear of his very life. Haven't you heard?"

"Because he is marked by the stain of murder," Elisha put in. "Or haven't you heard? Did you know Benedict le Fleur? Was he a friend of yours?"

"Of course. And none is prouder than I am to know he's founded his own practice."

Ariane stood her ground. "And why, then, would he not write to me? Why, then, has he not sent for me?"

The student looked flustered, staring down at her feet. "Maybe, he's found someone else? And, gone off you?"

She drew a deep breath and blew it out through her rosy lips. The student's shoulders shrank.

Lucius stalked up behind his gate-keeper, but stayed well back. "You again. I should have expected neither rest nor safety, while your intrusion at this school continues. How dare you push into my private—"

"Did you know that Benedict wrote letters home?" Elisha cut in. Ariane displayed the parchment. "How often did he write?"

"Weekly," she said. "The ships are less regular. Sometimes I have two or three letters at once. I expect there are still a few to come."

Lucius's long face went still and his jaw clenched.

Elisha shifted a little closer to the door, and Lucius

drew his chin back, stiff from head to toe. "Leon was charged yesterday with giving me a tour of the school," Elisha told him. "Alas, the library was not open to us. Might it be open today?"

Lucius gave a snort. "Are you even capable of reading much less comprehending the texts we hold?" He waved a negligent hand. "Go on then, Herve, take the wretch into our treasury—but keep a close eye lest he try to make off with something. He's more likely to profit by the sale of the books than by reading them."

"Yes, Maestro." Herve, the librarian, ruffled himself and brushed past Lucius into the hall.

"Ariane, I should like to," Lucius began, reaching out toward the letter, but Ariane slipped it away again, and walked after Herve, Leon following in her wake.

That left Elisha in the hall by the door. Lucius, behind it, spoke through a narrow gap. "You will not win this," Lucius said. "That Italian count, he'll be back, and between the two of us, we shall make your life a misery—straight up until its well-deserved end."

Vertuollo hardly needed Lucius to aid him in that. "Nothing means so much to you as your reputation, does it, Lucius? Ariane already believes me. For the rest, it is only a matter of time. You are nothing more than a hollow sheaf of titles, and the slightest wind will blow you away." Elisha put a hint of power in that breath, making Lucius's hair and gown flutter. Childish, perhaps, but so satisfying.

The physician jerked back and slammed the door in Elisha's face. With a bounce to his step, Elisha set off to delve into Lucius's own secret realm.

Chapter 14

❖

They began with any works Master Guy had studied, Leon eager to help as long as Ariane stayed around. With Herve dogging his steps, Elisha chose a broad table with plenty of light. Conveniently, the students already there moved away when Elisha arrived, and he sighed but claimed the space for his own. It reminded him so much of the long trestle table in the manor on the Isle of Wight where Mordecai first taught him to read. The memory shook him. The ashes of that table, and all of the books it once held, mingled with Mordecai's ashes. When the mancers came to seize Brigit from Mordecai's care, he set the manor on fire, and his own wounded body with it, to ensure his flesh and bones could never be used against Elisha. Once he'd sent Leon and Ariane off with their instructions, Elisha stood a long moment, his hands braced on the surface of that table. He felt about to begin a difficult operation, as if conjuring Mordecai's memory were an invocation to his own private saint of learning.

Ariane, either sensing his mood, or sharing a bit of it in her own grief, placed a pile of books on the table and quietly departed back into the stacks. Herve perused the works, flipping back the covers, unrolling a scroll and letting it roll back up again.

"Are you just planning to stand there?" Herve asked. "You can't absorb knowledge through the skin, you know."

Elisha turned a hard gaze upon him. "You have no idea."

Herve stepped back, fiddling with his sash, then scouted one of the books for himself and settled on a stool not far away.

Sinking onto a bench, Elisha opened the first volume. "*A Treatise on The Causes of Mortality With Some Commentary upon the Misapprehensions of treating the Poor.*" Mortality sounded like a promising start, but the work itself proved tedious, its convoluted Latin a match for the strained title. Elisha put it aside.

In a translated work from someone called Avicenna, he found pages of detail about the theory of the humors, and how they might relate to disease, but surely the other masters, much more familiar with that theory, had already delved into it. Fools they might be, though none so bad as Lucius himself, but they did know the ideas of the ancients. He read a bit more, initially excited by a section on diseases afflicting more than one member of the body, but this, too, proved futile, and he began to wonder if Danek hadn't been right about the library. His eyes ached, and he stretched his back, amused to find that Herve had fallen asleep with his feet on the table. Tempting to give it a thump and see Lucius's pet tumble to the floor, but he refrained.

The library contained several hundred volumes—a treasure indeed—and Elisha hadn't the time to study them all. Would he really find something the others had overlooked? Unlikely. So, then, what had they not examined?

Leon sat a little ways off, a book in his lap once more now that Ariane had gone to visit her patients. Elisha must visit his own patient before too long, but he knew his access to the library would last only as long as Guy's visit—after that, his own visit would come under scrutiny. At least spending time in the library supported his claim to be here in search of knowledge.

"Leon?"

The young man stirred, and lay down his book.

"I understand that some of the volumes contain forbidden texts. Magic, dark arts." As Leon gaped, Elisha quickly added, "Some believe this pestilence may be a curse, so a deeper understanding of their workings might be of use."

Leon nodded. "Not books, just parts, a quire here or there, bound in with some other texts."

"Can you find them? I gather you've spent many hours here during your stay."

That brought a flicker of humor to the young man's face, and he gave a nod, then set off. A moment later, the large doors opened, and Ariane stepped through, looking weary. Leon hesitated in his stride, then turned toward her, swallowing hard before he spoke. The two of them moved into the stacks together while Elisha stood up and went to a long shelf where chains kept the books from straying. Herbals, simples, compounds. He moved to the next row. Anatomies and wound healing. The books weighed down his hands, and some of them scattered dust and bits of pages as if they had not been disturbed for a hundred years.

Movement caught his eye and he found Herve glowering down the aisle at him. Elisha returned to his table and spent the next while perusing a manuscript of charms. Some of them contained items of magical use—fingernails and hair trimmings of the beloved, or of someone sick or hated—then added lead or antimony, bindweed, sulfur, sweet basil, and any number of things with no healing use at all outside the body, and only moderate use inside of it. Another treatise might have been written by a magus about the doctrine of mystery, but in the same convoluted phrasing as the other scholarly texts. Elisha let it fall shut with a clunk, drawing another sharp look from Herve. He pointedly pushed back from the table and stalked away, letting the librarian follow him, albeit at a distance. Back to the chains, so much useless knowledge held prisoner here for the edification of the students and their masters. He couldn't help but feel he was wasting time.

To dispel his rising irritation, Elisha closed his eyes and reached for attunement. He'd done this before, when he first entered the library, tracking the students as they came and went. Hints of their work or their patients clung to them, if not with the thickening shadow of mancers. Some carried the deaths of their patients as faint wisps around their hands. Others carried nothing but hope or desperation. Surrounded by so many younger people, every one of them reading faster, writing with more assurance than he ever would, contributed to Elisha's frustration. He walked further from the main study area. Two shades, impressions of the dead, moved in the library, one near the windows, one seated on an unoccupied bench, rising up and sitting once more— re-enacting the quiet death of a scholar. The stacks at the back held works little consulted and musty. Around to the front, individual works chained to separate desks made for easy copying, and a few students sat there, diligently working. Beyond the entrance desk, manned by a pair of younger students, a few more comfortable chairs drew up at another table, with a few more books chained beyond it, inconveniently placed for browsing. Elisha swept his awareness through the floors and stacks and walls, wishing his magic senses extended to reading so many books in so little time. Already, the sky outside the windows shaded to twilight. Guy would be having his final dinner with the faculty, Lucius would be reminding them of their promise to investigate Elisha on the morrow. And Vertuollo? Was he marshalling his evidence or counting on his own lordly demeanor to carry weight with these people?

Elisha turned from the sitting area, thinking to resume his table. Then he was stung with cold, a single barb, as if a thorn had gotten under his skin. Elisha flinched and turned in the direction of the sensation, drawing up his defenses and expecting to find Silvio, the barber, or perhaps a reliquary of ill-gotten bones. Nothing but books and scrolls and diagrams and yet more books. One of the books, a slender, leather-bound volume with a tarnished chain, tingled in his awareness. Elisha skirted the table and chairs and plucked the book from its place. Pain shot through his fingers and the book dropped to smack the shelf below.

"Please be careful," Herve snapped. "I could have you expelled for that."

Ignoring him, Elisha lay the book more gently on the examination shelf, his hand lingering on the cover. Leather, indeed, but of a pale, smooth variety, undyed. Human, stripped from a living victim years before. Tanning the hide could not remove the taint of barbarity that had brought it here. The victim's pain still lingered; a scholar himself, a man seeking consultation for a certain affliction of the nerves, and not expecting his nerves to be assaulted so thoroughly. "*On the Movement of Bodily Fluids and their Passage through the Organs, with Recourse to the Flows of Certain Streams*," read the cover in a spidery hand. Elisha's own hands trembled a little, just handling this.

"Doctor?" Ariane's voice. "Maestro Danek's lecture will be starting soon. And I'll need to eat before then."

"Thanks for all of your help." He looked up from the book as she turned to leave. "Ariane? Tomorrow the council will sit in judgement on me, of Lucius's accusations, and the others."

She nodded, sliding her hair back behind her ear. "I will give testimony, of course, and read out Benedict's letter—I can look over them again tonight, to see if he might have said anything in detail."

"Thank you. If you would, can you introduce me to the other maestros, perhaps in the morning? I should have been getting to know them." He sighed and gave a shake of his head. "I don't know if it will matter."

"In the morning, then. I'll take you to the classrooms as they are preparing." She curtsied, as if he were due such honor, then departed, Leon's gaze tracking her until the doors closed behind her.

"Go on, Leon," Elisha said. "You must be hungry, too. I appreciate your help."

Leon scampered for the door with surprising vigor, leaving Elisha with his discovery.

Elisha bent over the book. The author's name meant nothing to him, nor the obligatory remarks about God's aid in both writing and healing. This introduction ended with the exhortation, "*Let he who is in search of knowledge come before the Lord, and give praise to Saint Stephen.*" Most of the other texts invoked Saint Luke, patron of physicians, or one of the various saints said to look out for particular conditions—a litany of the portraits he had seen on Leon's tour. Saint Stephen stood watch over what? Stone masons? In point of fact, the book merely elaborated the same information he'd already read. It centered on a large diagram at the center which unfolded twice the size of the book itself. This purported to be an anatomy of blood flows in and out of the heart and other organs, except that the organs themselves were just as distorted and misplaced as in any of the other works he'd seen, and the heart itself was strangely shaped, badly drawn and more pointed than it should be, embellished with curious anatomical details. Elisha felt disappointed. If he had anything in common with the mancers, it was a stronger understanding of the human form than many university physicians. This mancer, presuming the same person ripped the hide for the cover as penned the text itself, made so much of his metaphor between rivers and veins that he turned the organs into islands with little boats passing between. The whole thing was ridiculous, but it still took him more than an hour to read, constantly referring to the diagram from the little numbers in the text.

Nonsense, yet bound in human skin. How many of the people who came to the library would ever know that? Only the mancers. Elisha drummed his fingers lightly on the closed cover. The chain carried no special weight or influence that he could tell, nor did anything else about the binding seem strange. The parchment inside looked relatively new compared with many of the works he had seen today, but he had no idea what that implied.

Herve cleared his throat. "Are you through? We now must shelve all the works you and your assistants have left lying about, and some of us would like to have dinner some time tonight."

"Sorry," Elisha muttered. Reluctantly, he replaced the book on its shelf, the chain rattling, and let himself be herded out of the library. No doubt, physicians across many lands now worked on their own ideas of the pestilence, its causes and its spread, but their work did him little good. Up slope toward the church and the mountains beyond, the sky glowed with flickering light and shouts echoed from the walls. Elisha crossed into the main courtyard of the school, drawn by the commotion, and nearly collided with a hurrying student.

"Where's Maestro Teodor?" The student cried, searching his face.

"What's going on?"

"Riot at the church! Maestro Guy had best leave right

away, or they're like to lynch him as the Pope's man." So saying, the student ran off into the night.

Elisha continued on toward the gate where two students and a handful of servants clustered around, listening, one of them up on a ladder, peering over the gate into the street beyond. "I told you, we're closed up tonight—you'll have to wait 'til morning," the man explained.

"You're as bad as they are. People are dying out here!"

Projecting authority, from experience if nothing else, Elisha moved through the gathering toward the gate. "Is it not our duty to help those in need of medical care?"

The student on the ladder, a senior fellow by his age and bearing, glanced down. "There's a dozen people with the pestilence out there who won't go to the church—we can't take them on all at once—and there's rioters down by the church already, threatening to burn it down."

"Won't they do the same to us if we don't let them in?" asked one of the others.

"We can't afford to be overrun with this pestilence. There are other illnesses and injuries to be seen to."

Elisha's extended senses felt the fear outside the gate and the tension building by the churchyard. Then a bolt of pain shot through his awareness and someone cried out. The shouting erupted into orders of attack and defense as the riot turned violent.

"I knew it would come to this," said Maestro Danek, his face and figure shadowed. "We can't help them, and they've low expectations of us in any case. When the church turns them away, well, what are they to do?"

"Surely there's something we can do." Elisha held back from reaching for contact, tempted as he was to communicate with the other doctor, magus to magus. Danek felt familiar, his presence rich with intelligence, yet mysterious at the same time.

"We can treat only the symptoms, and likely become infected ourselves as it is passed from man to man. I heard you spent the afternoon at the library. Did you learn anything different?"

A servant nearby crossed her arms tightly, hugging herself. "Maestro Fidelis has the right of it, hiding out 'til God's punishment is passed."

"Maestro Lucius says it is the influence of a malign conjunction of the stars," said the senior student, waving a hand toward the heavens from his lofty perch on the ladder. "When the season turns, the alignment will no longer cause such effects."

"Maestro Antonio says it is a miasma caused by air that lingers over the swampland—the only way to escape it is to go higher in the mountains, and block any windows that face the water," said another student.

In moments, this, too, rose into an argument. Outside the walls, a chill shaft pierced Elisha's awareness as someone died. He caught his breath and heard many footfalls pounding across the yard, accompanied by a glow of torches as a party of men approached, Guy de Chauliac among them, clutching a satchel. "Stand aside," Maestro Teodor commanded, his face weirdly lit by the torch he carried. "We need to get Guy to his ship."

"If any of you go out there, you're liable to be attacked," said the gatekeeper.

"I have no illusions the situation will improve by daylight. In fact, no matter whose theory prevails, none of them project an immediate end to this pestilence." Teodor beckoned the student down from the ladder and handed off his torch to a servant.

Outside, someone screamed, a voice that fell into a death rattle, and a group of others cheered. Teodor hesitated. At his back, Guy clutched his satchel, his professional demeanor faltering in the night. "The Holy Father needs me. This was to be a brief visit only. If this rioting should spread, I need to be at my post by his side."

Danek stepped up. "I've made this for the Holy Father—it's a sachet with some healing herbs and minerals that may have a preventive effect." He held out a small packet, and Guy accepted it with a nod.

"I'll see that he gets it. Thank you for your aid."

"I wish I had greater faith in its utility." Danek withdrew as the pounding outside increased.

"I wish I had faith I'd even reach my ship," said Guy.

"Tell them we'll come out," Elisha said, projecting calm. "Tell them a party of doctors from the school will come outside to see to the sick and the injured. Then Guy and a few others head for the harbor once we've got the crowd a bit more under control."

"But the plague," protested one of the students. "I've done nothing wrong—I don't deserve to get sick like that, vomiting my life out. No!" He backed away, but Danek seized his arm.

"This is what we're here for, isn't it?" he barked into the student's terrified face. "You cannot turn away from the sick, you're a doctor! People need you, both the sick and the dying. The priests are already turning away. Are you just a coward like the rest of them?" He snatched back his hand as if the student disgusted him. "Fine then, Elisha and I are ready. Let's get the Frenchman back where he belongs and see if he and the Pope can't figure a way to save the sorry lot of you."

"I'll go," said another, and "Me, too," came the familiar voice of Ariane.

"And I." Silvio, the mancer, the sinister void of his presence filtering through the crowd of the living. "I wish to see Master Guy safely aboard."

The gatekeeper swept them with his gaze, and gave a bow to Teodor, who nodded back, then faced the gate.

He swung aside a little panel in the wood and spoke through it. "Attention! Everyone listen! I cannot let you in, but some of the doctors will come out to see you—to tend the sick and the wounded. Clear a path. Lay the patients over there." He indicated the uphill side of the street.

"Give us the Pope's man—maybe he can say why my children are dying," a woman shouted.

"If you cannot be civil, then these gates stay closed."

"Come on then," demanded a voice outside. "We've waited long enough for this." With a last blow against the wood, the crowd outside shuffled and shifted.

The gatekeeper let the panel slide shut, then he and a pair of servants raised the bar and opened the gate just wide enough to let one person through at a time. When the others hesitated, Elisha pushed forward and stalked into the street, and they followed, a dozen or so doctors, students and servants. The gate slammed again behind them. "Danek," Elisha said, "will you see to the comfort of the plague victims? It seems you've got the greater knowledge."

They moved toward the cluster of patients, victims, and their families, but Elisha spotted someone lying in the street not far off, her body splayed as if she had been running from the church. "What about her? Can some of you bring her over?"

The shuffling crowd edged even further away. "She's a leper," said one of them. The area around the girl cleared rapidly, and Elisha could feel the chill of her death already, but Danek's ire was roused.

"You can't get sick just by checking to see if she's still alive," Danek snarled. He crossed the street toward her in a storm of tension that stung Elisha's senses. Danek stooped and gathered up the dead girl, but even the plague victims cried out when he tried to place her near the wall. "You're all dying," Danek said, "and she's the lucky one to be already done with this plague of living—especially among craven wretches like you."

As Danek carried her off to one side, Elisha felt Teodor and Guy's party quietly drift away toward the harbor under the cover of Danek's furious display. Yet the magus wasn't play-acting his fury: the girl's death had really affected him. Even as the other man bore her away and lay her gently down again, Elisha felt the swirl of his anger and the edge of a deeper grief, a reflection of Elisha's own dismay when the girl had been expelled from the hospital, but much stronger. In Danek, he seemed to have found his kindred in both magic and compassion.

Elisha dropped to one knee by a man who groaned in pain, cradling his arm. Quickly finding the break, Elisha busied himself setting the bones and wrapping it with scraps one of the servants carried in a satchel strung over his shoulder. As if he had indeed gone back to the Battle of Dunbury, Elisha worked once more among the injured. He moved on to the next, using his other powers a little here and there. He did not need to be a miracle worker here, but a little encouragement to healing could only aid both the victims and the mood of the town. Down the slope, the Valley rippled wide, but the black chill of death lingered low to the ground, and Elisha looked up. The mancer Silvio worked among the victims, mumbling platitudes, bandaging cuts, and apparently nudging the occasional sufferer beyond all suffering. His movements seemed exaggerated—his voice too boisterous, his gestures of comfort too strong, as if he could barely maintain the pretense of practicing his art with the rising tide of horror all around him.

Elisha came near to another team and recognized Danek among them. "Danek." Elisha set his hand on the other magus's shoulder. "*Silvio is a necromancer. He's killing people.*"

"Here, apply this poultice." Danek pressed a damp

bundle into Elisha's palm and rose up, stalking among the fallen toward where Silvio worked, but the mancer moved away, talking with someone from the crowd and disappeared around the corner. Danek looked back at Elisha, glanced at the suffering people around them, and got back to work.

Beneath Elisha's hands, the fevered patient sobbed.

"Will she be all right? I hear some folk do recover," an old man asked, staring down at the stricken woman. "The rest've already gone."

"How long has she been sick?"

"Four, five days?"

Across the way, Danek shook his head.

"You've done well in getting her care." Elisha guided the old man's hand to hold the herbal poultice in place against her burning brow.

"Don't waste yourselves in anger at the church or at the doctors," proclaimed a loud voice. A man parted from the darkness, waving his hands at the air. "We're all doomed, right enough—God's done with us, to be sure. We might as well enjoy our last days!" He reached to his belt and pulled out a bottle, dramatically popping the cork and pouring it down his throat, then wiping his mouth on his sleeve.

In the crowd, a woman giggled then emerged, her hair tangled and face streaked with tears. "He's right. It's why the priests won't see us, they know we're done for. My husband—" She sniffled and wiped her face. "My baby, all done for." She stumbled up, reaching out and the man with the wine bottle cast it aside to clasp her hand. He snatched her close for an embrace, his hand roving over body.

"We're all for the devil, for the devil," he sighed into her hair before he kissed her again.

The presence of the Valley swelled and simmered all around Elisha, like the chanting of a crowd of believers, waiting for a saint to manifest on his holy day, acolytes waving their hands, beseeching and delirious with expectation. Power crackled through his flesh. The wild couple stumbled and swayed together through the torchlight to a darker alley, the man already pressing against the woman in anticipation, when Elisha caught sight of the man's face. Silvio, drunk on the wine, or simply drunk on the power all around him. Even an ordinary necromancer, through his association with the Valley, would sense a little of what Elisha could—that strength flowing, the energy of the fear, and the focus on death as it swelled into an intoxicating brew. Apparently, Silvio had utterly succumbed to its allure. Pity the school's faculty hadn't seen him—but then, any official censure would still leave him free to pursue his vile ways.

Finding another victim of the riot, Elisha brought his charge into the light and painstakingly stitched up his wounded leg. As he arched his back, stretching out, he caught sight of Silvio's leman staggering back down the street, crooning to herself. Letting his presence go cold, Elisha pushed up and strode into the alley where Silvio stood tugging his trews into place and fumbling with his ties, the normal chill of a mancer's suppressed life replaced with a giddy warmth. "Hey, hello." Silvio tipped back against the wall as Elisha approached. "Skilled at projection, aren't you? Didn't realize before what you are."

Elisha gave a nod. "It's hard to know who can be trusted."

"God, this is the best we've ever had it, isn't it?" The mancer grinned and chuckled. "Relax and enjoy." He reached out to shake Elisha's arm.

"It's impressive to be sure. I know it started in Salerno. Your doing?" Elisha braced the mancer against the wall, preventing him from falling, letting him feel the surging strength that flowed from every death. A miasma indeed: the miasma of pain, fear, and misery that mancers thrived on.

"Wish I could claim it." Silvio's round eyes reflected the distant moon. "But the maestro—oh, some of them do earn the title, don't they?" He clasped his hand over Elisha's, and his eyes narrowed. "Wait, that Roman git dropped in. It's you he—"

Elisha slipped the salt-inlaid knife from his belt and slammed it into the other man's throat. The thrust cut a void into Silvio's glee, the salt parting him from his power. He gaped, and his knees buckled. With the last of his magical strength, Silvio pushed back, but his power dissipated into nothing. The mancer's control had fled in his giddy enthusiasm for death. Taking back the knife, Elisha hooked his arm through the dead man's and pulled him a few steps further, to where the land dropped away into the harbor. He wiped his soiled blade on Silvio's clothes and tumbled him over. The body splashed into the sea to be carried on the outgoing tide along with the boat that carried the Pope's doctor. Would to God that Guy's studies and the Pope's faith combined could stop this madness, but Elisha knew that they could not. Tonight had been only a glimpse of the revelry to come with the spreading pestilence.

Silvio was not the Salernitan Vertuollo spoke of, and now Elisha had one less lead in finding that person. Perhaps the mancer behind the pestilence wasn't even at the school, but in the church, or at some other post in town— or already moved on to another place else entirely. He stalked back through the night, finding a gleam of light upon the mountains, the sky in that direction showing a few shades more pale. In the piazza, the medical team clumped together, shifting toward the door, Danek at the lead. "Come on, then, we've done what we could." He briefly squeezed Elisha's shoulder when he caught up. "It's rare to find a man of your skill willing to work in such a fashion."

"I couldn't have done this without your support to get

the students out as well." Elisha followed as Danek hurried the students along into the gates and pressed in behind them, walking quickly. Danek knew so much of what they faced, yet he faced it with both power and passion. Impulsively, Elisha said, "Have a drink with me? My companion's brought back a fine bottle of port from the market."

Danek's shadowed face turned toward him, hesitating, then said, "Come with me—I've got something stronger."

Together, they crossed the yard to the door of Danek's subterranean workshop. "I don't have much time," Danek said apologetically. "Rounds."

"Right. I'd appreciate any time you're willing to give."

Danek led him down the aisle between the preparation tables and gestured toward a bench, then reached into a chest and pulled out a jug. He cast about for a moment, then plucked two jars from a shelf, holding one out to Elisha. "Don't worry, they're clean."

Danek poured into each jar and replaced the jug, then sat on a stool, his back to the hooded lantern, leaving him in silhouette. He raised his jar. "What do we drink to, such as we are? To health? To life?"

"To hope?" Elisha suggested.

"Hope for the hopeless." Danek snorted, swirled the jar, and took a swallow. "Maybe when the mighty have fallen so far they're looking up from the grave then they'll finally understand compassion."

Elisha, too, drank, finding a strong, dark liquor that warmed his mouth and seared down his throat. "The girl's death, the leper. It really bothered you."

Danek thumped down his jar. "It's the same everywhere—doctors, priests, noblemen—everyone with any power, yet they disdain those who need it the most. Their fees come from the rich, so they fawn over a lordling's rash while a leper can't even keep a warm bed, then they blame God for their own heartlessness." His head shook, then he hefted the jar and took a longer drink.

Danek's words resonated with everything Elisha had ever struggled for. "Oh, aye," Elisha replied. "It's why Lucius and I hated each other from the first, back in London. I worked in the streets, and he in the manors, afraid to get his hands dirty."

"I heard about your confrontation at dinner. You really saved the prince, when he would've left the man to die as a common soldier?"

"We do what has to be done," Elisha answered.

"More than anyone knows," Danek agreed. "Yet we're powerless in the face of so much indifference. I've searched for years for a way to show them what it's like, to open their eyes to true suffering. And now, well, here we are, aren't we?" His presence brightened as if he, too, found reason to hope.

"Is that why you became a teacher?"

Danek rumbled with laughter. "In a manner of speaking. But this isn't why you wanted to share a drink."

"It is in part," Elisha told him. "It's been a long time since I met anyone I might . . . think of as a friend."

With a noncommittal grunt, Danek poured himself another draught and held out the jug toward Elisha, who shook his head. He'd gone too far, encroaching on the other magus's well-guarded privacy because of his own need. "The other masters, what can you tell me about them?"

"Haven't you met some of them?"

"I've asked Ariane for introductions in the morning. I've already met Teodor, Antonio, Lucius, and Christina."

"Most of the council, then. There's six others on staff who haven't run, and Fidelis, who's hiding out in his room."

"Any others like us, or like Silvio? Do you know of others in Salerno?"

"Look, Elisha, I keep to myself. I do what I can, but I don't reach out. It's too risky—you must know that." Danek's presence exuded this fear, as if even talking with Elisha were dangerous.

"We can't simply hide and hope for the best, even if we, ourselves survive. You've said it yourself: they need us. There must be something we can do, not just as doctors, but as magi."

Danek's crooked grin glinted faintly in the low light. "Optimist. You sound like a child. Tell me: You've seen the library, you've spoken with Leon, yes? Have you found any cause at all for optimism?" He leaned forward, his presence keen as if the answer truly mattered to him. As well it might—it mattered to any man who cared for others.

So it hurt when Elisha told him about the search, and had to admit he'd found nothing.

"Don't take it ill, Elisha. I'm sure you've done your best—you've hardly rested in your efforts, have you? And do I take it we won't have Silvio's aid with the bleedings anymore?"

Elisha tipped his head.

"Just as well." He pointed at Elisha. "Watch yourself. You already have enemies." Danek drained his jar. "And I have work to do." He stood up, groaning.

"Thanks for this," Elisha said. "It's rare to share something so ordinary as a drink with a colleague."

"Rare indeed." Danek laughed again, but there was little humor in it. "I know precisely what you mean."

Chapter 15

❖

When Elisha reached his room, he found Gilles sitting up. "Were you at the riot, Elisha?"

"It's aftermath, in any case, I'll be glad to get some rest tonight."

"Not yet, I'm afraid. The nun came by and reported that your patient had one of his fits." Gilles sighed. "I shall pray for the lad, of course."

Elisha sagged a bit but it was true, he hadn't visited his patient since the middle of last night. If this was how the boy carried on, no wonder everyone had turned against him. "Thanks for waiting up." He started to leave, then paused at the door as Gilles pulled up his covers. "Gilles? Saint Stephen. Patron saint of stone masons. Martyred by a dozen arrows in the streets of Rome. What else do you know about him?"

"There's more than one. One was born king of Hungary, but he's not a martyr. And of course the founder of the Cistercian order." He chuckled in the darkness. "Most times, people mean the Roman, the first martyr, after all. Why do you ask?"

"I found a book dedicated to him. Nothing about the book made sense, least of all that." He shrugged it off and said, "Pleasant dreams," then shut the door and went in search of his patient. The yard by the hospital stood empty and silent. Curious. Perhaps the boy managed to calm himself this time. More likely, the nun had gagged him again. Elisha extended his senses. On the third floor, he felt a muted well of horror. He lengthened his stride, bounding up the steps, only to find the nun sleeping on a pallet outside the door of Ward Three. She started awake. "Oh."

"Move aside, Sister. I'm here for my patient."

"No need to be brusque, Doctor." She stood up, dusting down her habit. "Not sure it's wise to disturb him. I went to find you at his outburst, as you asked, but by the time I came back, he was much improved—he's been completely silent the rest of the night."

"You didn't gag him?"

She scowled. "I am a sworn sister—I am nothing if not obedient, to the Lord, and then to my mission here." She crossed herself.

He set his hand upon the door, hesitating. "You say he's much improved?"

"When I returned to check on him, he didn't scream at all. He didn't even move."

"Shit." Elisha burst through the door and ran down the aisle, fearing the worst. Silent and unmoving? Surely, he would have sensed if the boy were dead, surely. What if the boy's unknown malady had caught up with him at last, while Elisha wasted time with books and a pestilence he couldn't cure. That thought pierced him. He'd come here not to tend the sick as individuals, but to learn how the plague came to be and how it afflicted so many, so quickly. He meant to rise above the care of a single soul to the stewardship of all *desolati* against the mounting terror of the plague and its mancer masters. Earlier, in the library and when he took the lead in treating the riot victims, he felt himself drawing closer to that objective goal: he had access to the stored medical knowledge of centuries, and was gaining the respect of those with more experience than he. Then the idea of losing his patient overcame all intention. So much for becoming the general he must be, overseeing the movement of armies—all it took was a single patient depending upon him, and he found himself right back on the battlefield.

Still, in the dead of night, with the sole mancer he'd found here having professed his ignorance and died shortly after, Elisha could hardly pursue his larger goals. All day, he worked among the plague victims, read a dozen tedious tomes and drew himself closer to the school's community. Now, surely, he could indulge his heart and serve a single child. The nun followed more hesitantly as he dropped beside the bed. She carried the lantern that had hung by the door and held it aloft.

His patient sat with his back to the wall, knees curled up tight, his arms pulled across to their bindings. His eyes stared straight ahead. His unruly hair lay tangled around his face, and a trickle of blood worked down his forehead and right cheek. For a long time, he did not breathe, then his chest suddenly hitched and he gasped a breath.

"You see? It is as I said, completely silent. For the sake of the other patients, Doctor, I suggest you don't disturb him. He was so wild earlier that he's torn out his own hair." She pointed toward the trickle of blood from his scalp.

Elisha reached out to the child and gently brushed his shoulder. The boy gave a spasm, then resumed his immobility, his chest jerking with each breath as if in protest. "You call this an improvement? Sister, he's nearly paralyzed. What happened?"

"Nightmares. What else? The demon grips him most strongly at night. He woke me, and I came for you."

Elisha shifted slowly toward the bed, drawing closer to his patient, projecting a calm he did not feel. He stroked the hair back from the boy's face and saw that the nurse was right, a patch of hair as thick as a thumbprint was gone, yanked out by the roots and tearing the skin. Elisha let his senses unfurl, spreading over the child and his disordered bed, damp with sweat and urine. From his medical kit, he drew a scrap of linen bandage and wiped the blood from the child's face. He tucked the cloth back into his kit to be burned at the next opportunity. "What's happened to your hair?"

"I told you, he's torn it out in his frenzy."

"Then where did it go? It's plain his bedding hasn't been changed for at least a day."

Placing the lantern on the floor, she stomped around to the other side of the bed and pulled the bedding off the next one. "Forgive me, Doctor. You are not alone in feeling the strain of these dark days. I will take care of it right away, if you can take care of him."

Braced for a return to screaming, which might be better after all, Elisha leaned down and gathered the boy into his arms, lifting him just high enough for the task at hand lest he tug the child's bound wrists. The thin frame strained away from him, and the boy issued a pained cry, so low Elisha only felt the vibration of despair in the child's chest. Elisha started singing his lullaby, very softly, as much into the contact as aloud.

The nun efficiently stripped off the soiled bedding and replaced the straw mattress with another over the rope supports below. She placed a blanket over this. Through it all, Elisha saw no sign of the tuft of the boy's hair, torn from his head with such violence. He replaced the child and retrieved the nun's lantern from the floor, holding it up to shed light on the boy's face, blotched with evidence of sickness and cures, bruised by his own terrors. Elisha sat on the bed. With his off-hand he touched the boy's chin, turning him toward the light. Again, the body resisted, and Elisha released him immediately. Over the boy's mouth, faint, but plain enough to Elisha's sight, lay the imprint of a large hand.

"Who came here before you? Who was here when you woke?" Elisha demanded.

"Nobody. I woke to the screaming and came for you, that's an end of it. I noticed his hair when I got back."

"So, in fact, you don't know." Elisha shot a look at her. "Anyone could have been here."

She held the bundle of soiled bedding at arm's length. "Who could've got by me to come in? Who would've wanted to?"

A magus, for one thing. Any magus skilled enough to cast a projection, which was all of them Elisha had ever met. Or a mancer who missed taunting a favorite victim? Silvio. Elisha could picture him gliding over the sleeping nun, letting the boy sense his approach to build his terror, then shutting him up while he yanked a talisman from the boy's own head. Had he meant to kill him, then, only to be interrupted by the nun's return? Or would that spoil some vicious mancer game?

"You can take care of that, sister. I'll call if I have need of you." He did not take his eyes off the boy, but heard and felt her retreat until the door shut behind her. Elisha returned the lantern to the floor. He reached out and lay his hand very lightly on the boy's knee. *"This man who hurt you,"* he said into the contact, sending an image of Silvio that made the boy's flesh squirm and his knees draw up even tighter. *"This man will never hurt anyone again, do you understand?"*

"Demon," the boy's flesh answered, barely a whisper even then.

"Him, or me?"

The boy's eyes flickered. *"Killer."*

"Yes. Would you rather that I lied to you?" Elisha tried to turn the hard edge of his words, the anger he felt toward those who inflicted such suffering, and ensure he did not visit his anger on the victim instead. *"Very well then."* He added a smile. *"Bream is my favorite meal.*

Maestro Lucius was my dear friend in London. Tomorrow's going to be a wonderful day."

The boy blinked, and his next breath sounded more even.

"Go on—lie to me. Tell me anything. Tell me your name."

"I wish my father were here." A lie that slithered hard, like the crack of a whip. *"This is my home. He called me 'runt.'"*

Two lies, painful and hard given, and one truth, small, and just as hard. Runt: like the smallest piglet in a litter, bound to die and not worth feeding. *"You deserve a better name."*

"Lie."

"No," said Elisha out loud. *"Even if you don't believe me."*

The boy's chin dipped, his body slowly releasing his fear, shivering. Elisha reached down for the blanket and drew it up while the boy's eyes searched his face. He lifted his elbow, letting Elisha tuck the blanket under his arm. Softly, Elisha started singing, watching the boy's breathing grow ever more regular. From the wary flitting of those eyes, he knew the child would not go to sleep while he stayed. Elisha rose and backed away, those eyes following him as he collected the lantern and walked back to the door. He hung the lantern there and stepped out onto the landing. The nun stirred on her pallet, and Elisha bent down. He set his hand on her shoulder. "Thank you, Sister. I do appreciate you keeping a watchful eye. It's only my worry for my patient that makes me harsh with you."

"I understand," she said, gazing up into his face as he sent her an image of watchfulness, a sentry on duty against the depredations of evil. She sat up taller against the wall, fingering the cross she wore at her neck as Elisha took his leave. She would sleep no more that night, but knowing this would allow him, and maybe his patient, to rest.

On the way back to his room, in spite of his weariness, Elisha itched to learn what he needed to know—to find the mancer-maestro responsible for the plague. His mind kept returning to the flesh-bound book in the library and its strange diagram, but he tried to set aside that obsession. Only a magus would suspect anything about the work, only a sensitive or a mancer would recognize the skin for what it was. The blasted thing had a purpose, he was sure of it. Or was it merely the jittery power of Silvio's death, combined with the ever-present thrum of the spreading Valley that made him suspicious? Salerno, like Heidelberg, began to feel like a city of ghosts where the dead and the living freely mingled; like the map of Rome, its streets of the living overlaid with the shadowy passages of the dead.

Streets of the living, and a map of the dead. Elisha's eyes snapped open. No wonder the diagrams looked all wrong—it wasn't meant to be anatomical at all—it was a map! The rivers presented as a metaphor for the passage of the humors weren't metaphorical at all. He scrambled out of bed, hurriedly casting a deflection so as not to wake Gilles, and pulled on his robe. He ran back to the library, breathless, pleased to see the windows still flickering with at least a single light. Elisha bounded up the steps to the door. "You can't—" began the student at the desk, another of Lucius's acolytes.

"Ask Lucius in the morning. Better yet, ask him now." Elisha pushed through the chairs toward the shelf where the flesh-bound book resided, but there was no sense of chill, nothing at all. He spun about, extending his senses, searching.

"Look," the student began again, but Elisha cut him off.

"There was a book here, a thin one bound in pale leather and chained. Where has it gone?"

"If it was chained, it hasn't gone anywhere." The student sighed heavily and went to the shelf where Elisha had been looking. He triumphantly plucked out a slender, chained volume just as Elisha had described. "See?" He presented the cover, but Elisha shook his head.

"That's not the same book." Damn it all, someone had gotten here first. Half the students and all the professors knew he wanted to get into the library. Whoever knew about the book had taken it back. "Do you have any maps? Or anything about Kaffa?"

"What the blazes is Kaffa?" The student replaced the book.

"It's a trading port. Genoese, I think, or Venetian?"

"Oh, for goodness sake. If it's a trading port, and it's not heathen, then it would be Genoese or Venetian, wouldn't it?" The student flounced over to another section, to a large chart on the wall, the only one that wasn't medical. He waved his hand over it. "Maps and trade are hardly our line of interest, but this one shows the origin of a number of medicinal spices. Good enough?" Without waiting for an answer, he resumed his post by the door.

Elisha leaned in close. Fine lines traced all over the chart and names of herbs, minerals, spices both rich and ordinary. He was so tired that he swayed on his feet. Damnation. He took a few steps back, perching on a study carrel, his eyes growing unfocused as he looked at the map. One of the seas looked like a kidney. Another shape . . . yes, he was right.

He was right! There. Elisha stalked back to the map, letting his gaze remain addled and pressed his finger upon the "heart," a spit of land where so many of the lines began. Kaffa. The mancers bound a book in flesh, to guide their fellows to the place where the pestilence began, seeking knowledge. So, was Salerno just a false trail? It, too, appeared on the map, no doubt thanks to school pride. But Vertuollo himself mentioned a Salernitan, and showed up here, for what? Not just to hound Elisha with accusations, but to distract him, to join with Lucius to try to keep Elisha away from the library. What other clues had he missed in his distraction? What had that strange invocation said? "*Give praise to Saint Stephen.*" The martyr of Rome? The founder of the Cistercian order, or the one-time king of Hungary?

The mancers began their plot years ago, and they had been laying the groundwork all this time. Binding books, disseminating the knowledge, pointing to where to find them and providing a map, to what, exactly? More slowly, Elisha descended once more to his chamber, his senses still unfurled.

Several of the plague victims outside the gate died during the night, while a few others now writhed with the fever and swellings that started the disease. Elisha let them be—he hadn't the strength right now. At last, he tumbled into bed and buried his senses, save that ever-present net of awareness that would warn him if anyone came near.

Morning came all too soon, with the weight of its delayed reckoning. He felt so much closer to an answer, yet he knew he was out of time. He needed to visit his patient as well, to see how he had passed the night. That thought gave him a moment's pause as he washed his face and prepared for the day. When he found what he needed, what would become of the boy? Perhaps Danek would consent to serve as his physician when Elisha moved on to track down the mancers, leaving behind another who trusted him, another who needed him. As he had left behind Katherine and Isaac. As he had left behind the rabbi and his people. As he had left behind Thomas and Alfleda, and his own infant boy.

His eyes slid shut against a sudden stinging.

"Come on, then, you're not the only one with places to go!" Friar Gilles bumped him with an elbow. "The prior up at San Matteo is interested in some new relics. I won't divest of anything you think you'll need, of course."

"Let me know how the church is faring—the riot last night was caused when they shut the doors against some plague sufferers."

Gilles crossed himself, his fleshy face turning to an unaccustomed frown. "Why'd they do a thing like that? Still plenty of room, and it's now more than ever that folk need to come to the Lord."

"Folk are starting to say the Lord has abandoned us."

"Surely not! Well. I shall see what I can do, and perhaps the idea of a new shrine will kindle the faithful." Gilles swung about, patting his head as he considered his stash of relics, then he was probing his scalp a little more closely. "Say, you've got a razor, yes? My tonsure's growing in. Would you be willing to take care of it?"

Dropping his towel, Elisha pointed to a chair. "Let's get you fit to meet the prior." It had been a long time since Elisha last carved a tonsure; most of the monasteries had their own brothers trained to do so. Still, he worked carefully, and cleaned up a pink circle with a few reddish flea bites standing out. "Sorry about the fleas. I'll ask Danek for some rosemary to rub on the bedding."

"They really don't bother you," Gilles mused. "When the Lord touched you, He gave you gifts both large and small."

"Just stop." Elisha prodded him out of the chair. "I'll see you later." He strapped on his belt and medical kit, then hesitated. "There was a young woman, a leper, chased from the hospital yesterday. She died during the riot. Will you see she's properly buried?"

Gilles met his eye and nodded. "I'll make it part of my price. Go with God."

"And you as well."

Elisha ate a quick meal in the refectory and found Ariane waiting for him by the door. Her robes were of fine cloth that brought to mind Vertuollo's mourning garb, so plain in color, yet so clearly expensive in weave.

"If your tour is to be complete, we might as well begin with the lair of the enemy," Ariane said. She led him efficiently toward the northern range of the yard where the ground floor held the classrooms. "Maestro Lucius teaches Galen and the other masters, so his room is at the end nearest the library, and his students take all of those duties. Here." She conducted him into a theater with ranks of benches and a cluster of students milling about, but no sign of Lucius.

Elisha's restless energy, gathered for the fight, held in a hard knot at his breast. Just then, Herve the library keeper entered, descending the stairs toward the center of the room and waving the students to their seats. "Come, come. I shall begin, and Maestro Lucius can assume the class when he is available to do so."

The physician's absence instantly roused Elisha's interest. Was he mustering evidence for his accusations, or had he, after yesterday's confrontation, quit the battlefield altogether? Elisha trotted down the steps two at a time as the student prepared at a lectern. "Where is Lucius?"

"I do not believe that is any of your concern. Doctor. If that's what you would have us believe." Herve tried a smile, which did not sit well on his angular features.

"When do you expect him?"

"I believe he was called out last night to aid the victims of the riot, as such, he is due some rest."

"No, he wasn't," Elisha said. "I was the one who led the team. Lucius was nowhere in sight."

Herve looked briefly disconcerted. "I am certain

that's what the messenger said who came for him, that he was needed. No doubt he simply avoided wherever you were . . . working."

"Where is he then? In his chambers?" Ariane demanded.

"Not there either, as we customarily dine together with some of his other advanced pupils and we did not find him this morning. He may be in consultation, or he may simply have sought a moment of solitude from his recent trials." Herve aimed a pinched look at Elisha. "Now, if you will excuse me, I have a lecture to deliver." He brushed them away from the lectern with one hand.

Ariane glided back up the steps into the corridor. "We might as well carry on, I suppose. Maestro Cenci teaches a concentration in the relations of the humors, here." They stood at the door of another lecture hall, this one with a level floor and a cluster of desks. Maestro Cenci, a thin man with a sharp mustache, oversaw a group of students, heads bent over vellum sheets, painstakingly copying a chart from the wall. He glanced up at them and gave Ariane a nod, before resuming his inspection. Elisha sensed only the focus of a man intent upon his work, with little apparent imbalance in his own humors. Not the mancer he sought. They continued along the corridor.

The next room exuded a distinct chill, and Elisha drew his power up beneath his skin, honing his projection of merely academic interest. Ariane knocked to enter, revealing a chamber dominated by a large table with a skeleton on top. Other bones occupied the perimeter, most of them broken, and the instructor, Maestro Carel, discussed the various breaks, how they might occur, and how they might present in an injured patient. Carel glared at the open door until Ariane shut it again, leaving Elisha with an impression of annoyance and possibly even violence—not the sort of projection a mancer would allow. That deflated his excitement at sensing the chill of death. Somewhere his enemy was hiding.

"This one is Maestro Danek's, but he won't be there until evening, of course." Ariane started to walk by.

"May we look in any case? I am curious about how the lecturers arrange their classes and materials," Elisha explained, a plausible reason if he were seeking to be hired as Maestra Christina had suggested.

With a shrug, she opened the door on a room with long tables and benches, the walls decorated with a series of hideous paintings: lepers with thick faces and stumpy hands and feet; Saint Roche with his open sores; scabious faces, rough and red; limbs distorted by one ailment or another; views inside of infected mouths; an enormous eye blotched with darkness. It made him think of his patient who bore so many different signs. Not of a single disease, but of several? How could a boy so young have been afflicted with and survived all of that? He stepped further into the room, studying the diagrams.

"Maestro Danek knows more about disease than anyone else at the school," Ariane said. "He is so devoted to his work that he insists on lecturing only in the evening, giving his greater focus to his patients and to his research. I had little interest in the field when I arrived here, but he has inspired me to consider a specialization." Her cheeks flushed and she slid back into the corridor, drawing the door shut behind them. "Benedict did not approve. He felt the work was unseemly."

"For a woman?"

She smiled faintly. "For anyone. Disease is the sign of God's disfavor, after all. Should we be trying to fight God's will in sickening these people?"

"You don't agree?"

"Not all of the sufferers have led unholy lives. Even the

priests will send people to us for treatment. After all, if we cure them, then that, too, was God's will, was it not?"

The next room reeked of urine, and Ariane wrinkled her nose. "They must be doing a practicum today with Maestro Elazar." She pinched her nostrils together and opened the door, letting Elisha see the room where students clustered around a broad table covered with clear glass bottles in varying shades of yellow. A chart covered one wall showing an array of such bottles from clear to greenish, red, and even purple, with suggested diagnoses written under each. Maestro Elazar wore a black cap, and something in his features reminded Elisha of his own mentor, Mordecai.

"I know it is vital to examine the urine," Ariane said, her voice distorted by her pinched nostrils, "but it is better on cold days when the smell does not travel so far."

They departed in a hurry. "What can you tell me about Maestro Fidelis?" Elisha asked.

"He is a coward. When the first rumors of a pestilence began to reach us, he took to his chamber and hasn't come out. His specialty is complaints of the mind in any case. He works closely with Maestro Lucius on the astrological implications of the patient's birth and time of complaint, then recommends bleedings, poultices and simples." She pointed him toward a door on the outer wall. "That's his classroom, but there's nothing to see. Sometimes, Maestro Garamus, the surgeon, performs a trepanation there, if Maestro Fidelis orders it."

"So he still sees patients?"

"Oh, he doesn't see them, but he is still prescribing, based on all of those other signs." She waved her fingers. "You took on the patient in bed twelve? He was Maestro Fidelis's patient when we first took him in. Whatever the Maestro learned of his nightmares gave him nightmares of his own." Ariane shook her head.

"You don't think much of him."

"A doctor terrified by the visions of a mad child can hardly be counted on to deliver good care. Here we come to Maestra Christina's theater. She is beginning a new anatomy today, the last of the season before it gets too warm."

As Ariane moved into the chamber, Elisha thought she and the tall, pale Benedict would have made a handsome couple, and Benedict would have been led by her just as he was by Lucius.

"Careful, there—careful!" Christina lunged across the room to hold open a door at the back as two brawny fellows wrestled with a cloth-covered corpse on a litter. They jostled the dead man as they bumped through the doorframe. The chill of death reached Elisha, reached out for him, almost, the dark shade lingering from a recent passing. It seeped through him, even at such a distance, with an intimacy that made him feel queasy.

"She is the school's anatomist?" he managed to say. "I did not realize."

"It is one of several reasons for the controversy about her teaching here. Every few months, it seems, the Church changes its dictates about the use of corpses in anatomy. Maestra Christina must be ready at any moment to perform the work, or to teach from illustrations instead."

Christina noticed them, waving them closer to the long table at the center of her students, several of whom already looked a bit more pale. The men lifted the shrouded body onto the table and removed the litter, stomping back out through the other door and shutting it behind them. "Welcome, Elisha. I've asked them to bring us one of the plague victims this morning, so we might learn more about the progress of the disease through the study of the dead. Anyone who does not support this examination is invited to leave now." Her stern gaze swept the dozen students, clad as she was in a long apron, sleeves rolled back and bound with ties. A few glanced toward the door with longing, but no one departed. "Very well, then. Christopher, what should we do first?"

"Prepare our tools?"

"Very good. It helps to have your tools close by." She gestured toward a smaller table with an array of knives and saws. "Next?"

"Uncover the body?" Christopher leaned back from the table, his fingers twisted together behind him.

"Second year students," Ariane whispered, with a hint of amusement.

"Go on, then."

Christopher reached forward, stretching his arm as far as it would go to take a pinch of the fabric near the corpse's feet and gently tug the shroud toward him.

"Oh, for goodness sake. We shall be here all day. Roger, how about you?"

Roger, a heavy, dark-haired youth, stepped up and grasped the shroud with both hands to peel it back. The wet sound set Elisha's teeth on edge. Christopher's eyes rolled back and he tumbled to the floor while other students gasped and some covered their mouths. The corpse glistened with the red striations of bare muscles, yellow globs of fat clinging here and there, white ligaments and cartilage visible around the joints.

"Is it common practice to skin the cadavers, Maestra?" Roger inquired, inspecting the body before him.

Christina wet her lips and swallowed hard, her eyes flaring at the sight, then contracting as she retained control. "The face, quickly."

Roger moved up toward the head, blocking Elisha's view of the body, but not of Christina's own face as she gasped and her eyes flew wide again, staring straight at him. One of the students shrieked, staggering back from the table, and fainted, clearing a space. On the anatomist's table, stripped bare of dignity and clothes and skin itself lay Maestro Lucius, his eyes vacant, mouth gaping over a gash that carved through his neck nearly to the bone.

Chapter 16

❧

Elisha clamped a hand over his mouth as the bile rose from his churning stomach.

Roger crossed himself quickly. "Shall I cover him, Maestra?"

"We need to finish a gross examination at the least," she said, wiping trembling hands on her apron. "Pray attend me, Roger. Giovanni, please find Maestro Teodor and tell him what has happened. Ariane, perhaps you can revive the students who have collapsed and see to their treatment if necessary."

Ariane brought her gaze back to Elisha. "Yes, Maestra." She marshalled two of the other students, those who looked most pale, to carry Christopher out into the corridor and follow with the other student.

"Maestro Lucius's students should be told," someone else offered, and Christina gave a nod of assent, sending him out on the task.

"Ariane and I went to his classroom this morning." Elisha closed the last few steps to the table and steeled himself to examine the body. "His senior student told us they usually had breakfast together, but that Lucius wasn't in his chamber. He thought Lucius went out last night to aid with the riot."

"And did he?"

"Not while Danek and I were present, certainly, and the gates were closed after we came back in."

Lucius retained the skin of his hands and feet, his ankles showing ligature marks. Someone bound him before he died. His cause of death gaped across his throat for anyone to see—one swift, powerful blow from what Elisha could tell, the edges smooth of any notching caused by multiple attempts. The knife had been very sharp. A few slender cuts at his chest showed where the flensing blade dug a little too deep, but only a little. The process had been brutally efficient. And somewhere, a necromancer had a new trophy. Had Silvio done this, before Elisha killed him on the street? Surely, Elisha would have sensed the familiar dead among Silvio's talismans. Count Vertuollo appeared the night before at the dining hall, witness to Lucius and Elisha's fraught history, and that had been before Lucius had allowed Elisha access to the library with its secret volume. The calculating and precise master of Rome might well have done it. Where? How? The why of it was all too clear as Maestro Teodor strode into the room.

"Doctor—your rival lies dead. I command you to tell me what has happened."

"I wish I knew, Maestro. I attended the riot victims, as you know. I visited my patient, stopped in at the library to confirm some information, then went to bed. I woke this morning to meet with Ariane and see the rest of the faculty. We had already convinced Lucius to allow me access to the library as I said."

"Convinced? Coerced, perhaps? Given his low opinion of you, he was hardly likely to grant access so readily, and if it were appropriate for him to do so, I should have been consulted first. With the testimony we've heard from the Roman gentleman, and this latest discovery, it seems his concerns were fully justified." Teodor's eyes bored into him, his presence hard and cold. "I have sent to the castle for aid in arresting you, Doctor—if I should even call you that."

Four solidly built men, groundskeepers, Elisha guessed, waited at Teodor's back, fidgeting uncertainly, one of them holding an ax, the others armed with knives at their belts and nothing more. If he wanted to escape, they were no match for him, and they seemed to know it. He alone carried the scars of battle. They dodged his gaze.

Elisha tried to speak calmly, to win them over as he had before. "Lucius plotted to kill the king of England, and he killed Benedict de Fleur in the hopes of framing him for his own treachery—Ariane has letters from Benedict suggesting he was afraid and suspicious of Lucius. Yes, I hated him, but I had nothing to do with his death. I came here seeking a cure for the plague, just like the rest of you. I suspect one of my enemies slew him, hoping to cast the blame on me."

"Come, gentlemen," Teodor insisted. "We need to take him into custody and secure his person."

"You don't need to do anything—I have no desire to leave." Elisha spread his hands, pleading. "I haven't learned what I came for. Why should I ruin my chances here by killing someone?"

"I cannot claim insight into villainy. Perhaps Maestro Fidelis could do so. In the meantime, come with us." Teodor gestured him out into the corridor.

Stewing inside, but unwilling to push the director too far, Elisha followed, two of the makeshift guards in front of him and two behind with Maestro Teodor. As they exited into the sunlight, Elisha heard a familiar wail and his head rose, not sure if he should be disappointed or relieved at this return to his accustomed behavior. "Maestro, that is my patient. May I please go to him?"

"We cannot have you at liberty in this school." Teodor folded his arms, but he winced a little at the sound.

"Neither has my patient any liberty, Maestro." Elisha put out his hands, wrists close together. "Bind me in chains if you must, but please let me attend him. It'll be better for all of us."

Their eyes met, and Teodor's calculating gaze softened. "You are a doctor, aren't you. Very well. Giuseppe, run and fetch a set of the restraints we use on the mad. Meet us in the upper ward." He tipped his head, indicating that they should keep moving while one of the men trotted off in another direction.

As they mounted the stairs, they met the ward sister on her way down, scowling fiercely. She stopped short when she saw him. "Maestro, your patient is in need—and is aggravating everyone else in the hospital. I can understand that you would not have me gag a child, but really—"

"I'm coming." Elisha pushed between his guards and pounded up the stairs. If he had only a few minutes of freedom, he'd best use them carefully. He ran along the aisle and dropped to his knees at the child's bedside. When he reached out, the child, initially calming at the sight of him, jerked back and began to shriek all the louder, scrambling onto the headboard. Elisha put up his hands for peace. "Don't, please don't." He anticipated the child would twist himself about again, wrenching his arms and bloodying his heels—but the blood he used for contact yesterday had vanished in the course of sleep and cleaning. Except where it stained the wall above the patient's head. Elisha slapped his palm to the wall and searched for contact. There! Tenuous, but more clear as he focused on it.

"*I'm here, please, please, you must calm down.*"

The boy's cries fell into a series of jagged, whimpering breaths.

"*You can only hear me if I can touch you in some way. Your blood is on the wall, and that gives me contact, as if*

I were touching you. Do you understand?" He searched the boy's haunted eyes. The boy glanced up and back. Was that a tiny nod?

"A demon thing."

"A demon thing, or a witch's thing." He took a long breath and forced himself to be gentle. *"We call ourselves the magi, and you are one of us."* He could hear the echo of Brigit's voice as he spoke, telling him the same thing when he had discovered his own magic.

The boy's bound hands twisted together, over and over, his fingers itching at his skin, though Elisha could see no sign of rash or bite. *"Is that why?"*

"I don't understand," Elisha replied. *"Do you mean, why you are scared?"*

"Why I am mad, why they do this to me, why he did it."

Elisha caught his breath. He set aside his own worries, ignoring the men who stomped up to wait at the foot of the bed, ignoring the jangle of chains. *"Your father, is that who you mean?"*

But the boy could not ignore the others. He cried out and struggled, pushing himself into a tiny ball at the top of his bed.

"Please talk to me—I haven't much time."

"But you can see the boy is better when he's here. I can't say why, perhaps they've got the same madness inside, Maestro," the nun was saying, her scowling demeanor transformed as she pleaded. "We must find a way to keep the peace of this hospital."

"Doctor, come. Come away."

Elisha's head slumped against the wall, eyes squeezed shut. The cold power of the Valley burned at his chest and thrummed in his ears, and if he used even a trace of magic here and now, he doomed them both.

"They hate you, too."

"They fear me, just as they fear you." He blinked his eyes open, the boy staring back at him along the wall.

"Give us your hands, Doctor. You have so far cooperated with us. If you maintain that attitude, things will go better for you," Teodor said.

"*They are right to fear you,*" the boy said, his inner voice grown very soft indeed.

"*Yes, they are, but not for the reasons they believe.*" Elisha pushed off from the wall and rose, meeting Teodor half-way along the bedside.

Maestro Teodor held out a set of padded manacles with a longer chain dangling at one side, meant to lock to a wall in some stinking cave. "I hereby arrest you in the name of Queen Giovanna of Naples, and of her agents, for the murder of Maestro Lucius, a physician of this school." He locked the manacles about Elisha's wrists, checking that they were neither too tight nor too loose.

"Please find Friar Gilles, the monk who accompanied me here. He's volunteering at the church, with the plague victims, and he can support my story."

Holding the free end of the chain in his hand, Teodor regarded Elisha. "I had the duty of checking on the survivors of the riot this morning. You did some fine work for those people. Stitching and bone-setting in the dark. It could not have been easy."

"Thank you, Maestro."

"Lucius told us that he beat you for insubordination, but I find it hard to imagine, given that you do not fight my authority now, that you were so contentious at that time."

A thousand things had changed since then, and Elisha most of all. "Lucius demanded obedience because he could not command respect."

"You could." Teodor tipped his head. "Pity. Under other circumstances, I expect you would have made a fine addition to our faculty."

The shackles weighed down his hands, but Elisha found a smile. "Maestro, I appreciate the compliment. If your good will can extend so far, then would you ask Maestro Danek to see me during my captivity?"

Behind him, the boy's rough breathing and whimpers broke into a low, sustained wail.

"Should we resume the bleedings, Maestro?" the nun asked. "If the English doctor is to be relieved of his duty? We need to keep that boy under control."

"Silvio never returned from the riot," said Teodor. "I'll have to find someone among the students to do it." He gave a heavy sigh, that pained look returning to his face.

One of the other men reached out to take the chain, and Teodor stepped aside as the man asked, "Where should we take him? The dark chamber? It's got only one door." He had to raise his voice to be heard over the boy.

Then Teodor's beard broke in a smile. "And so has this. Chain him to this empty bed, would you? And two of you can keep watch at the far end. That should be sufficient. We've all the facilities here to maintain a prisoner, after all."

The man shrugged and rounded the spare bed, looping the chain around a post and sliding a lock into the links to hold it there. Elisha had about four feet of liberty, plus the length of chain between his hands. He could reach to the boy's bedside. He met Teodor's smile and bowed his head as he had never done for Lucius. "Thank you, Maestro."

"It is no favor to you, but to the other patients who deserve a better rest. Come." Teodor turned on his heel and led his party back along the aisle toward the stairs.

Elisha sat on the bed and raised his right hand to the wall. *"Did you start up just for me? That's hardly a sign of madness."*

The boy shuddered with each breath as he shrieked and did not open his eyes.

Very softly, Elisha started to sing. After a long

moment, the wailing slowed and fell away to a whisper. The nun shuffled up the aisle with the basin Elisha had used the day before. "Brought you some water. He's sure to be thirsty after all of that." She looked Elisha up and down. "Not sure how I feel about using a murderer to soothe a demon, but there you are. As the Maestro said, 'tis better for the other patients not to put up with his caterwauling." She set down the basin on a little stool between them. "There you go. Also a visitor on the way for you."

"Maestro Danek? But it's still light out."

The boy gave a sharp howl, and the nun raised her hand as if to strike. Elisha thrust his own chained hands between them, her hand striking the metal. "Don't, Sister, please don't."

She drew back her hand. "Then you see to it he stops with all of that racket. It's why you're here, and if they see it's no help, then I've no need to have a murderer on my ward, you see?"

An icy wind preceded his visitor, and Elisha pulled back, his hands clenching into fists, his back to the wall.

"I hardly expected to find you in such circumstances," Count Vertuollo said, staring down at him. "A good bed? Fresh water? Thanks to you, my son has no bed except the grave."

Vertuollo's presence soared with a sinister majesty, the nun and door guards shrinking back, bowing as Elisha searched for his lost composure.

The count's voice sank very low. "Nobility is so hard to defeat, even in such dark days as these. They will grow darker, Brother, mark my words." He made a slow pushing gesture with his palm, as if leaning upon a door.

The frigid power of the Valley exploded in Elisha's chest, and he screamed.

"Oh, don't you start," groaned the nun, but Elisha barely heard her.

Pain shot through him, a wrenching sensation as if he were being torn apart from the inside out. Vertuollo twisted his hand.

Elisha snatched for strength, pushing back, driving the count from his heart, chasing him from the Valley that they shared. The searing cold raced through his limbs and mind and spirit, and he fought it with his will alone. He would not die, not today, not like this, shackled and condemned. He couldn't breathe. His teeth chattered together, his hands shaking. Then a slender heat wrapped his fist, a grasping hand that clung to his.

"*Demons!*" cried the boy's voice against his skin.

Shaking off his panic, Elisha lifted his chin and stared at Vertuollo. "No." With an effort, Elisha forced back the Valley, not sealing it—these days, it never wholly vanished, but he narrowed its touch to a slender gap like the mouth of a cave, opening into the endless darkness.

Vertuollo finished his gesture, drawing back his hand to cross himself, his gaze resting on the boy, then lifting to Elisha. "Not today, Brother? Soon, you will meet your justice." Vertuollo inclined his head and swept away out the door. Moments later Elisha felt the Valley shiver as the count took his leave.

Trembling, Elisha huddled on his bed, the boy's hand wrapped in both of his.

"*Even grown-ups get scared,*" the boy said.

"*Especially grown-ups.*" He swallowed over and over, wet his lips, brought the boy's hand up to his forehead, letting it warm him. Vertuollo had stretched out through the Valley to clutch at his heart, but that had not been his full strength, just a test, a thrust against his armor.

The tremor of someone else approaching rippled through Elisha's awareness, and he reflexively seized at his own power, but the voice allayed his fear.

"Elisha, I came when I heard! My goodness, what has been happening? And was that the Roman count I saw upon the stairs? He gave me such a smile that I thought I might well be struck dead by it." Friar Gilles hustled up the aisle. The friar's fleshy face streamed with sweat as if he had been running all day, not merely from the church to the hospital. "Oh, thoughtless of me, you hardly wish to be reminded of untimely death." He finished at Elisha's bedside and dropped onto the foot of the bed, panting for breath and patting his freshly shaven tonsure with a folded bit of cloth. "My goodness," he said again, blinking at Elisha's chains. "You do look in a bad way."

Elisha stared back at his companion; he wasn't the only one who looked in a bad way. Gilles's face was red and blotchy as he patted his tonsure and forehead. Then he tugged at the collar of his habit, tipping back his head to blot the sweat beneath his chin. A patch of darkness marked his jaw, a small, dark swelling. The unmistakable sign of the plague.

Gilles smoothed the cloth back into place, glancing at Elisha, his eyebrows edging up, then glancing away as both of their eyes clouded with tears.

Chapter 17

❖

Elisha should have known. By God, he should have known! How could he have so much power, so much strength and knowledge and be unable to stop this pestilence from claiming his friends? Because he did not know enough but to bring them into danger. Elisha squeezed away the tears, rubbing his eyes with one thumb.

"*Your friend is sick.*" The boy's presence, withdrawn and frightened at Gilles's entry, strengthened and he let his hand remain.

"I shouldn't have come. You do not need my burdens atop your own." Gilles rose heavily, but Elisha stopped him with a gesture that made his chains clank ominously.

He found his breath and tried to control his emotions. Self-recrimination did no good. Gilles willingly came with him into danger; Elisha could not let him suffer the consequences alone. "No. Please stay. You couldn't have known all the rest of this. It's not your fault."

"Is that so?" Gilles stared at the kerchief in his hands. "Is it not the will of God, the punishment for my sins?"

"What sins can you possibly have that deserve this?"

Gilles flinched at his tone, and the boy's tension rose. Elisha took a deep breath, and tried to calm himself, but Gilles spoke again, very softly, "The relics I carry have not defended me. The saints are angry about their translation. We have always maintained that relics would not allow their translation if the saints did not condone it, and perhaps they do not. Is my mission over? Is it time for God to call me home? I have prayed it was not so. I have never even seen Rome, but I don't want to defy the will of the Lord." His shoulders trembled, then he sank down to the bed, elbows on knees, his head in his hands. Sweat beaded on his tonsure and the exposed back of his neck. "But I don't want to die." He broke into gut-wrenching sobs.

Elisha glanced back at his patient, then gently extricated his hand from that desperate grip. He slid toward Gilles, lifted the chain over his friend's shoulders and wrapped the friar in his arms, Gilles's fevered head nestled against his chest. He allowed his flesh to go cold, radiating such cold comfort as only he could offer. Waves of sorrow crossed the friar's body, accompanied by the guilt of denying his fate, and the fear of death itself. Had he been worthy enough to pass into Heaven? Or was this growing corruption of the body merely the sign of the corruption of his soul?

The boy on the other bed made a little sound of inquiry, the most gentle and speech-like sound Elisha had yet heard from him. His patient uncoiled himself from the top of the bed and crept closer, then stretched out his skinny, scarred legs until his toes touched Elisha's knee. "*Don't leave me.*"

For the second time the boy had reached out to him, quite possibly the only times he had ever reached out to anyone. Elisha's throat, already aching from Gilles's grief, threatened to close up completely. "*I won't.*" Then he drew a deeper breath. Gilles's appearance, both the fact of his presence, and the clear signs of his sickness, had cut through Elisha's fear, but it had not been Vertuollo's appearance that set off his patient's terror, as it had his own. As Elisha mastered himself again, he traced back the moment to the name he had spoken, twice in the boy's presence, the man who knew everything about sickness, whose presence felt so familiar — because it felt like the boy's. *"There's another man here, a doctor and a master of the school. I've spoken of him twice, and both times—"*

Before he even finished forming the thought, he felt the rush of panic that welled up in the boy, and he sent comfort, calm.

"It's all right—I won't bring him here, I won't make you face him." He took a moment to consider how to approach what he must do, what he must know. *"He's your father, isn't he? This isn't your home because he moved you to Salerno. He left you at the church, but they turned you away to the hospital."*

The boy's sending throbbed with pain, and a burst of images: cuttings, bleedings, piercings, needles, and welts, cupping and herbs, emetics, his skin scraped raw or coming up in boils. Strong hands gripped and turned him, held him down, cut him and cured him, prodded and pinched him, fed him and forced open his mouth to check for symptoms.

"Oh, dear God," Elisha sighed, and Gilles stifled his tears to raise his head. Elisha kept his skin cool even as he felt his blood must boil. *"He did all that to you. And you weren't the first one."* The runt, the smallest of a litter, and not worthy of feeding.

"My father had sons before me." The boy shrank back from his knowledge, bound up in confusion, as if he did not know what the words meant.

Elisha thought of his own father, a farmer, strong and capable, rough when he had to be, loving when he could be, and he thought of his own son cradled in Thomas's powerful arms, defended with all the love of the man and the strength of the crown. *"That's not what a father should be. You deserve so much more, so much better."*

"*How can you be sure?*"

"*Because you're a child—because you're alive. Because you depended on him on this earth, and he made you live in Hell. If you're a demon, he made you so.*" At the boy's fear, Elisha drew back his anger, binding it deep within, forging it into a blade. "*This is no lie.*"

Tears sparked in the boy's eyes as he shook his head in mute denial.

"What's happening, Elisha? It is as if the two of you speak, but I hear nothing." Gilles lifted Elisha's arms away, slipping back a little, his eyes red and weary.

"Gilles, you know a number of languages from your travels. Do you speak Hungarian?"

Gilles blinked at this apparent change of subject, then said, "A little. *Jo nap. Hogy vargy*?" He shrugged, but the child froze, staring.

"*Bocsass meg,*" the boy whispered, the first words Elisha had ever heard him speak. *Forgive me.*

One of the men called Saint Stephen had been the king of Hungary: invoked in a skin-bound volume of false medicine—in truth, a map to the heart of Kaffa, the source of the pestilence itself. "I know where the plague came from—it's not from God, not for a moment. There's a man I have to see."

"A mancer?"

"A magus." *Indivisi*, unless Elisha missed his guess. A magus who devoted his life and his talent to a single course of knowledge, a single understanding from which he derived all of his power, making himself indivisible from it. The Salernitan: the *indivisi* of plague.

"*Don't leave me! Don't go to him, please.*" The boy shook so hard his tears scattered, and his toes barely kept contact.

Elisha sank to his knees before his patient, tugging his chain as far as it would go to close the distance between them, and took the child's hand. "*I need to stop him, to*

*stop them all, so that there need be no more demons, do
you understand?"*

"*He will kill you.*"

"*He doesn't have that power.*" Not unless Elisha chose
to give it to him. Would he die for this, if his death-magic
could make it stop? Their eyes met over their bound and
clasped hands. Gilles stumbled to his feet, shuffled a few
steps to find a bucket, and vomited into it, the stench
quickly suffusing the room, turning Elisha's own stomach, but he chilled it with the echoes of death, even as his
chest burned with anger.

"*While I am gone, you must keep silent, no matter what.
I can send the guards to sleep, I don't want them to wake
and find me gone.*" He regarded the child seriously, the
child whose welfare he had made so important to his own.
"*You must learn control if I am ever to teach you magic.*"

For a long moment, the boy sat and trembled, ideas
forming and breaking apart before Elisha could even
grasp them. Finally he said, "*How will you get free?*" The
boy looked down at their hands, both bound.

Elisha breathed in the death of metal. He pinched
each lock in the fingers of the opposite hand and let the
rust disintegrate their hasps, then slid his wrists from the
shackles and left them on the bed, in case he might need
the illusion of captivity.

The boy's eyes grew wide. "*Is that a demon power?*"

"*Aye, and one that you will learn, then no man shall
ever keep you prisoner.*" He was already working his deflection as Gilles returned. The friar walked along the
other side of the bed and lay down, his breathing ragged
with pain and exhaustion.

"Gilles, there's something I need to do—I'll be back
as soon as may be."

The friar gave a weary wave of his hand in acknowl-
edgement. After a moment, Gilles rolled over to look at
the other bed. "The boy, what is his name?"

"His father called him 'runt.'"

Gilles's soft face crumpled into a frown. "I will pray that the wickedness leave that man's soul. And we will find a better name, a true name."

"You'd better pray fast, friar, he's going to need it." Elisha burned, just looking at Gilles, his flesh already sallow with sickness. "*Watch over my friend?*"

The boy squared his narrow shoulders and gave a solemn nod.

Elisha silenced his steps, his breathing, his very heartbeat, as he extended his senses. He rose and stalked down the ward. The two guards sat with their backs toward the beds, talking softly. Elisha prepared his suggestion, and let his hand sink to the fringe of the man's hair, a contact he would not even feel. The guard started yawning, and when his friend reached out to cuff his shoulder, he, too, blinked his eyes sleepily. In a moment, the men leaned against each other, snoring softly. Elisha passed by like a ghost, silencing the door at the top of the stairs stepping over the ward sister where she lay on her pallet. Last night, he had forced her to stay away, keeping watch, and now that inducement had caught up with her. Very well, she had earned her rest.

Where would he find Danek now? Daylight would not defend the Salernitan from Elisha's discovery or his wrath. But even a nocturnal magus needed sleep sometime. At this hour, most students were in class, the yard abandoned. The door to the basement preparation room stood locked until Elisha got there, then it opened to his command, the metal latch withering at his touch, the bar inside tumbling to the floor with a dull thud.

Whispers of death twined from the dead animals on the benches and tables, but the smell no longer bothered him. At the far end of the hall stood another door that would not remain sealed against him. He pushed through into a round chamber at the base of the school's bell tower. Lit by a guttering night candle, it contained a single chair and table, basin stand and a chest pushed against the walls. In the center, a barrel stood beneath the high ceiling where a bare hook held a chain that should have supported the chandelier resting near another chest. The barrel reeked of blood. Lucius's blood. A magus to suggest he should sleep, a doctor to send him deeper with a few herbs, a strong man to chain his ankles and haul him up, a preparator to bleed him out, making it easy for someone to skin him, someone who liked things tidy. What would Danek say if the other maestri inspected his chambers? Or would he simply place the barrel outside with the other results of his preparations, another resource to be studied in the quest for healing, or roll it away to be discarded with the results of other bleedings. No hospital could ever be free of blood.

At the opposite side of the chamber, curtains concealed an alcove where a single presence lay sleeping. Elisha shut the door behind him and crossed the room, cloaked in his deflection. He thrust his hand beyond the curtain and seized the throat of the sleeping man. He hauled Danek from his bed with the strength of his fury and of the Valley that throbbed all around him. As the magus jolted awake, grappling with his hand, Elisha dragged him across the chamber and thrust him to his knees, shoving his head into the barrel of blood. *"You made the plague, you fucking arrogant unbelievable shit."*

Chapter 18

❖

"*J* didn't make it—*I made it better.*" Danek flailed and struggled against him, kicking and scratching. "*Let me up—let me up or you learn nothing.*"

Elisha wrenched him from the barrel and tossed him across the floor, blood splashing the room. Danek struck the wall hard and pulled himself up, whirling to face Elisha, wiping some of the blood from his face. Elisha stalked across and caught him again, this time from the front, staring into his blood-streaked face. Never in his life had he been so enraged. Everything he had ever struggled for and fought against was refuted by this one man. "*Tell me how to stop it.*"

"*You can't. Nobody can.*" Danek grinned through the streaks of blood, already recovering. "*Not even me.*"

Elisha rapped his prisoner's head against the wall. "*Bullshit—you made this, you know it better than any man. By Christ, you sired children just so you could torture them with sickness after sickness until you made this one—how did my patient even survive it if you can't cure it?*"

The grin slipped a little, the presence pulsing with a shot of concern. "*I am ashamed to say I do not know. A few people do survive—what would be the point otherwise? The runt appears to be one of them. Leon is an-*

other, but he will not consent to my examination. How can I further my understanding without their cooperation?"

"And the boy screams his head off at the sound of your name, never mind at your presence if you should enter the room."

"I gave him to the church with a sum of money that should have ensured that they kept him."

"Because you couldn't get what you want from him."

"You understand nothing. Disease maintains a sliver of mystery, even for me. No matter how much you know about anything, knowledge can take you only so far, after that, the mystery remains. You are a magus, at least, surely you have learned about mystery and knowledge? We who focus on knowledge tend to neglect our understanding of mystery."

Lucius's blood froze upon his fingers and flaked away as Elisha's power, his knowledge, swirled through his grip. *"How could you do this? How could you forge a pestilence to kill everyone?"*

"Not everyone." Danek's teeth chattered. *"Nothing is learned when the patient dies."*

The patient? As if all of humanity were his patient, and he the doctor developing his cure. *"What are you learning, then? How to kill better? How to serve the necromancers—how to serve them up the rest of mankind on a platter for their lunch?"*

"What am I learning? Rather ask what they are learning, all of those the pestilence assails." Danek's skin flared with a sudden fever that cracked at Elisha's cold, and Elisha snatched back his hand, bracing for the fight, but Danek did not attack, his hand rubbing at the marks of Elisha's fingers against his throat. "Humility, doctor. They learn to tremble. They learn that their lives are not safe, secure, or worthy. They learn that God doesn't care about any of them, not the churchmen, not the kings, not

the children. The Pope himself is powerless as are his priests and his physician. They are subject, every single one of them, not to some great and powerful God, but to the power of the powerless. They're subject to me, Elisha, to me." His finger tapped at his breast, leaving a mark of blood on his pale nightshirt.

"Are you so in love with power that you would let so many people die?"

"Not in the least. I am a doctor, and a teacher." Danek, still shaking from the assault, took two steps to his table and perched upon its edge, for all the world as if he and Elisha were in a lecture hall, his face streaked with another man's blood, regarding his pupil. "What I told you before is true. I want everyone to learn what I have learned, to know what I have been forced to understand." He laced his fingers together.

"To know the plague?"

"To know what it is to be sick unto death and yet to find no rest, to be turned away from church and hospital and home, to be outcast even from charity. There is no love in this world and no compassion. They seek it from God, and they are deluded. They demand compassion from each other and then lie to each other about offering it." He flicked his fingers as if to cast away every man, woman and child of the earth.

"Because you are a cynic, you want everyone else to be, is that it? You sired a child without love and tortured him without remorse to teach the world to suffer?"

"I am no cynic! No close-minded philosopher, not merely an abstract physician devoted to the great masters of an ancient time. Elisha, I am like you—a man of the world, a man who has suffered himself, and hoped to learn and to teach by his experience."

"You're nothing like me." Elisha took a step back, shaking his head, utterly mystified. "You're a madman, a monster."

Danek surged out of his chair and jabbed his finger in Elisha's face. "There it comes! You claim compassion, you even sought to be my friend, but you're just like all the rest, a hypocrite who dares call me a monster, who would smother me in my sleep rather than to look me in the eye."

Fetching up against the table by the alcove, Elisha grabbed the candleholder and urged the flame higher. Light swelled between them, flickering and fair, and he saw Danek's face plainly for the first time. Pits marked his uneven features, swellings hid beneath his hair, and dry patches of skin marred his cheeks. His fingers looked fat and blotchy, one fingertip missing and badly healed.

"Go on, Doctor, what's your diagnosis? What would you say of a man in my condition?" He brought his hand over his face and down his body, indicating every sign of his disease, putting himself on display.

Elisha's instincts, his years of training urged him away, but he forced himself to be still. "Leprosy," he whispered.

"Leprosy," Danek repeated. "A leper, a lazar." He stepped back from the light, calling out, "Leper! Unclean!" His hands balled into fists. "Throw me from the hospital, cast me from your sight. Send me out in the streets to beg for my life. To beg for my death. Give me a bell to warn them of my coming." He swung his hand to and fro as if ringing the absent bell, and Elisha could almost hear its chime. "Leper. Unclean. You claim compassion, you claim knowledge." His head swung back and forth in rhythm with the missing bell. "You know nothing, and neither did they. Until now."

Danek stopped dead still, hands clenched, eyes locked to Elisha's. Then Danek's voice came low and insistent. "Are they learning their lesson, Doctor? They do not learn from books, not when they cannot even read. They do not learn from listening, not to homilies on Sundays nor to the beggars in the streets. They do not learn from the Bible, not even to turn the other cheek. Oh, no, but they are learning now. Humility and hopelessness. That there is nothing on this earth as precious as life—not gold, not faith, not friendship, not fatherhood. Nothing, nothing, nothing. And they learn that lesson only when everything they have is gone. Men are despicable, deceitful, disgusting creatures. They did not honor the word of their Lord. Perhaps they will honor the word of their new masters. They will finally have the saints that they deserve."

Folding his arms, Danek breathed out in a satisfied sigh. "Thank you for attending my lecture today. Have you any questions?"

"How do I stop it?" Elisha repeated.

Danek groaned and shook his head. "Dear Lord, don't be so thick. Ask me one I've not already answered."

"How did you make the plague?"

"I told you, I did not: I found and improved upon it. I made it more virulent, easier to transmit. The boy was the warmth upon which the yeast of death was grown. His own magic potential made it easier to maintain contact." Danek spread his hands. "Ask me another."

Danek could not be spreading the disease on his own, not with the variety of people who had already contracted it. Even if a hundred mancers followed the map in the flesh-bound book, they could not spread it so far and so fast. Elisha demanded, "How is it spread?"

"In small ways. Ask me another." Danek lounged on his desk, casual in his nightshirt and bloodstains, as if he cared for nothing and no one, giving Elisha answers that were none at all.

"You think I know nothing," Elisha said, pushing off from the wall and stalking forward once more, "but I know this." Danek dodged to one side, but Elisha had contact through Lucius's blood, and he pulled the magus back again. Danek flailed his arms, his feet skidding across the floor and his face twisting with helpless rage until they came once more face to face.

Elisha seized his arm and launched them into the Valley. Even in the few days since Elisha travelled to Salerno, the Valley had grown deeper, stronger, a torrent of death and power that rushed through him. He plunged through to his destination, dragging Danek with him. They stumbled in the candlelit basement of the church of San Matteo. Elisha pulled him up the aisle between the victims, dead and dying, their deaths gathering in shadowed rivers around him. "I know Death, Maestro. I know how it comes and when. I feel it stalking, like a shadow that clings at the heels of the dying. My friend Gilles volunteered here among the sick, and now he'll die because of them."

"Ah, is that what this is about? Your friend is dying, so now you care?"

Elisha shoved him to his knees at a bedside where the darkness lay most thickly, a young woman round with child, her face glossy with sweat, her eyes shot through with red streaks as they searched the heavens. Elisha caught her hand and opened them both to her dying, the child within her already dead. Pain wracked her limbs and fever torched her throat. The swellings at her neck, arms and legs ached and distorted her flesh, a wrongness palpable in their contact. Her parched mouth worked, cracked lips praying, "*Not for me, Lord, for the baby, please Lord, for the baby . . .*" Her frail chest hitched up and sank down, expelling a breath of heat, the dark chill of her dying swirling into Elisha's touch, the slender shade of the baby lingering at her side.

"This is what the world becomes, because of you."

Danek met his gaze. "Did you draw down that woman's death, into yourself? I did not know a mancer could do that."

"I am no mancer."

The other man blinked at him and said nothing.

Elisha hauled him up again and tore open the Valley, stepping into the maelstrom. Danek's doubt still stung his hand, Danek's utter disregard for the suffering all around them stoked the fires of Elisha's fury. Ever since he slew Vertuollo's son, the Valley turned against him, the shades of his friends and those he had honored vanished into the howling madness of all the rest: Those he had killed, those he had failed to save, and those who died now all around him, while he stumbled helplessly from place to place, desperate to stop the dying, and utterly unable to do so. The dead mobbed him now, a thousand shades that flickered and shrieked with all the hurt, the fear and the despair of living. Elisha let them come. He let them slash through him and shared every sensation through the contact he forced on Danek. The maestro's eyes flared, and he twisted in Elisha's grip, then he struck back with his own dread knowledge.

The heat of fever, the rash of disease spread along his arm, but Elisha refused them, rejecting Danek's assault with his own cold callousness. "*This serves no purpose, Doctor—give up and let me go*," Danek insisted.

For a moment, their eyes met in the queer wavering light of the Valley, then Elisha did as Danek asked. He flung Danek into the Valley and let go, sealing the void with the Maestro on the inside.

Chapter 19

Gasping for breath, Elisha stood once more in Danek's basement study, staring at the blood-spattered walls. What would happen to a living man left in the Valley? He had no idea. It was not a place like other places, but rather a between, a portal through which the dead must pass, leaving behind their earthly cares. He sank into Danek's abandoned chair. The *indivisi* of plague himself suffered from leprosy, a disease that had spoiled his body, but also left him bitter and closed. At any other time, Elisha would have sympathized with the man, suffering first from his sickness, then from the disdain showed to him by other men. It was that suffering and the medical skill that grew from it which had drawn him to Danek—to a man who might be so much like himself. His chest tightened. He reached back, re-opening the Valley through Lucius's blood, using it to search for the man he had left behind. The swirls among the shadows showed the signs of other travelers, trails of absence in the same way that death left marks upon the earth, but Danek was gone. Elisha returned, once more empty-handed.

Then he remembered his patient's hair, torn from his scalp to be used—for what? A talisman? Danek hardly needed a talisman of disease, he carried it within him. A charm, then—not a blessing, but a curse. Elisha pictured the night of Guy's departure, Danek's parting gesture to present him with a sachet to ward off the pestilence. To be given to the Pope. Good God: he had sent his gift to the heart of the Church itself.

Back in the Maestro's study, Elisha searched Danek's few belongings, looking for any clues: writing perhaps, a journal of his accomplishments, or a treatise on his methods; any hint at all of how the plague might be fought, but he found nothing. True to his fears, he found no trace of the boy's hair either. Facing his ignorance, Elisha considered what to do next—what could possibly be done next. Had Danek given him any lead to pursue? Any course at all to lead him to his next steps? Danek claimed the plague could not be stopped, not by him nor by Elisha. Could it be true? The idea chilled Elisha more than any single death had ever done. The thickening of the Valley and the way it remained so near the surface made passing through it easier than ever, and could be an end unto itself for the mancers who commanded Danek's terrible design. Thousands were dying, all around Elisha, all the time, his distorted sight barely discerning any more between the living and the dying, and mancers like Silvio became drunk on the power, no longer able to control their dark desires, or no longer caring to conceal them. Danek drained Lucius of his blood to be sure, but he had not the skill to skin him so well.

For a moment, Elisha sat stunned by the recognition that he could distinguish between expert and amateur flensing, and Elisha's denial that he was a mancer felt hollow indeed. Vertuollo must have conspired with Danek, on the murder, another trap for Elisha. Vertuollo could no longer keep Elisha out of the Valley, now that the dead swelled it nearly beyond all recognition, but the count would be sensitive enough to know when Danek, likewise stained by Lucius's death, might have need of him. Vertuollo came for Danek in the Valley, and took him where? Back to Rome. Where the devout Friar Gilles longed to go before he died.

Cleaning the blood off as best he could, Elisha left the chamber, letting the door stand open just a bit. In moments, he'd be gone. His absence would make him look guilty for Lucius's slaying, but anyone visiting Danek's room would have to wonder what had happened there, and perhaps Danek's own absence would suggest the real culprit, even if they never understood why. Casting a deflection of death and of darkness, Elisha returned to his own chamber. His things were gone, removed by his accusers no doubt, but Gilles's carefully labelled and lovingly displayed relics remained; no need to confiscate the possessions of Elisha's apparently innocent, if misguided, companion. Good. Elisha gathered them up and returned to the hospital, treading carefully, watchful for the ward sisters. The nun on his own ward lay where she had been, snoring softly. Given the boy's restlessness and wailing, this might be the first good sleep she'd had in weeks. Let her rest.

At the far end of the ward, Friar Gilles sat on the bed facing Elisha's patient, speaking softly, the boy sitting before him, silent. Elisha shed his deflection when he drew close, and Gilles managed a smile. "I'm feeling much better, and I do wonder if I might have overreacted earlier." He searched Elisha's face, but the black pall of his dying had not departed, and Elisha's face must have shown it, too, for Gilles lost his smile and looked away, smothering a cough.

Feeling better. The boy rested his bound hands on the friar's knee, his young face solemn, his presence radiating need. When Elisha opened his medical kit, the boy jerked back, but Elisha settled on the floor beside him, looking up into his eyes, and offered his hand to make contact. *"I'd like to cut you free, so you can come with me."*

"To Hell, with the other demons?"

"Through Hell, in any case. There will be demons, and not all of them will be our friends."

The boy held out his hands, and Elisha drew his short knife, cutting through the leather bonds, though the child flinched at the nearness of the knife, as much because of its medical nature as because of the blade, Elisha guessed. Replacing the knife in his medical kit, he drew out another blade, a short, sharp knife with an inlay of salt, and offered it to the boy. *"This blade is proof against demons, if you are fast enough to use it. It has to plunge into soft flesh, but if it does, it can cut through magic."*

The boy accepted it solemnly, running his finger down the flat of the shimmering crystal.

From the sack, Elisha drew a spare tunic, too large by half, but better than the rags the boy currently wore. His patient accepted this as well, drawing it on over his own torn garment. Elisha took up the leather straps that had bound the child to the bed and made a belt of them—blood and terror stained the bonds. They would serve him as a talisman when he knew how to use it. The boy tucked his blade through the belt, pressing it close.

"What shall we do? You stand accused of murder and sorcery," Gilles pointed out.

"There's nothing more we can learn here." Elisha stood up. "We're going to Rome."

"That is the home of your enemy, Elisha, which I have not forgotten even if you have. What about England?"

"Gretchen stole the talisman that could have brought us there, unless you have a relic that can forge such a connection." Elisha tried not to let the bitterness seep into his voice but could not hold it back. He should have been searching for a way home aside from the talisman of earth tainted with his brother's blood, and now it was too late—they must move on. "Besides, I have a duty to try to stop this plague and the men who are spreading it—I cannot simply run away. If there is another destination that will serve us both, then tell me, Brother Gilles, where would you like to die?"

Gilles swallowed, his face pale and slick with sweat. "Rome will do," he said softly.

The hollow voice, once so boisterous, sank into Elisha's heart. He touched his friend's shoulder sending comfort. "Forgive me my brusqueness, it's only—I would have given anything to be able to save your life, and I can't. I don't know how."

"Then perhaps my death will show you. What about your patient?"

"He's coming, too. I can't leave him behind, not here. Besides, he may know more than almost anyone about this plague. He was the first to suffer it."

"I'd no idea." Gilles raised his eyebrows. "He told me that you both are demons, but I find nothing demonic in him. And of course, I have seen the truth about you." He crossed himself. "Do you know, it had a different meaning before? An older term. Daemon," he pronounced carefully. "In pagan times, such a being stood between the human and the divine, an instrument of God among His creations."

Elisha opened his mouth to protest, but Gilles waved it away as if he would suffer no more protestations of Elisha's angelic nature. "We were speaking of the problem of his name before you returned. I think he has settled on Jude."

"The patron saint of hopeless causes. Your idea?"

"It may have come up in conversation, or in my prayers." Gilles took up the bundle of his relics. "Rome, you say." He stared down at his hands where he clutched the sack. "Is that where you, too, would like to die?"

"They can't kill me, Gilles. It's not that easy."

"No, I imagine not. But this Vertuollo . . . I have not seen you scared before, not like that. To think that someone like you could feel such terror. Is Rome where these villains will have their feast?"

"I don't think so, not anymore. But Count Vertuollo has taken the best source of knowledge away with him."

"You are not giving up." The light in Gilles's eyes was not merely from the fever. "Perhaps not so hopeless after all, then. I have faith in you, that you will find a way to conquer your enemy in spite of everything. Are we going to any church in particular?"

Elisha considered the question. Several of the churches had been destroyed, in part or in whole, and most of them were controlled by one faction or another of the dueling families who controlled Rome, save one, where the archpriest held his own and maintained his allegiance to the Pope above all else, and to the Lord beyond. "San Giovanni."

Gilles rooted through his sack and came up with a silk-wrapped parcel. "San Giovanni." He nodded, and started to rise, only to stagger, clamping his hand to his mouth. Elisha caught him around the waist and supported him, holding him close even as he retched into the bucket.

Jude scrambled over and stared, his mouth twisted. Cautiously, he touched Elisha's arm. "*He has the gift. My father's gift.*"

"*He doesn't deserve it, nor does anyone.*"

"*Did you kill my father?*"

"*Not yet.*" Then Elisha cursed himself. In his anger, he failed to consider his words. He should have simply said "no." Instead, he'd made a promise or a threat. "*He still knows more about this disease than anyone else; I'd like to question him again before he dies.*"

"*Does he deserve it?*"

"*I am not one to judge for all I've done, but you haven't seen the results of his work. What he's done to you was only the beginning.*" If the plague was Danek's gift to mankind, then what was Elisha's?

Gilles shook against him, and Elisha pressed the relic between their hands. San Giovanni was the church overseen by Pierre Roger, an even-handed priest of Rome and, perhaps, the son of the man who had become the Pope himself. Even better, Elisha himself had visited the church a few months ago—creating both knowledge and contact to draw him there again, assuming the church had survived the earthquakes caused when Elisha stripped away the false relics the mancers had planted. Aside from sending Jude and Gilles his own compassion, he could do nothing to shield them from the horror of the Valley, the boy clinging to one side, the monk cowering at the other, but his knowledge of the church made the passage brief, like a nightmare they woke from in an instant.

Jude wailed in echo of the Valley, but Gilles crumpled to the floor, and Elisha went with him, bearing him gently down, cradling his head.

Elisha caught Jude's hand, making contact and sending him comfort. "*Jude, you're safe now.*" The boy shrieked all the louder, twisting against Elisha's grip. "*Please, Jude, he's dying.*" Torn between the anguish of the ailing friar and that of the living boy, Elisha felt himself more stretched than ever.

Jude beat at his back and shoulders, shouting, his presence so infused with fear, he could not even hear Elisha's words of comfort. Elisha let him go, and Jude stumbled back, his cacophony briefly interrupted, then he fled into the darkness.

"Come back! Jude!"

"Go after him," Gilles breathed. "I'll be all right." His body heaved, and he rolled on his side, retching and gasping.

They knelt in the darkened church of San Giovanni, a few small windows supplying the only light, just enough to gleam upon the gilt and silver canopy at the heart of the church. When Gilles collapsed again into panting,

Elisha gathered him up and carried him to lie beneath the canopy, the monk's flesh lying loose and quivering. Elisha wiped his friend's face and laid a cool hand upon his forehead. "Go after him," said Gilles again. "The living need you more."

Elisha blinked back tears. "Gilles, I hardly know who is living any more. We seem, every one of us, to be bound in the shadow of death." Already, the friar's features carried a shadowy echo. He faded faster than any plague victim Elisha had yet encountered, and Elisha could not help but feel that travelling through the Valley explained the difference. It was wrong, unnatural, for any living man to enter into that passage of the dead. It had to leave its mark. Just as the pilgrimage left the pilgrim more holy on his return, travelling the Valley stripped a little of a man's life or his humanity. Gilles had no strength for such things, and Elisha could see the change in his glassy eyes.

"Who's there? Who calls like the enemy in the night?" A clear, strong voice echoed in the empty church, counterpoint to Jude's piteous wails. The speaker approached, carrying a lantern. "If you've come to steal from the church, I say to you that the Lord who sees the sparrow's fall sees your perfidy. San Giovanni survived the earthquake, and it shall survive this as well." Father Pierre Roger walked closer, his handsome young face revealed in the lantern's glow. Elisha remembered him well, first from the compassion he showed during Father Uccello's so-called trial, then when Elisha came to visit San Giovanni before departing Rome. Father Pierre's face revealed his own recognition. "It's you. I little expected to see you returned to Rome, much less to find you here. I take it there was no pass through the mountains?"

"Forgive me, Father, but my friend dearly wished to see Rome before he is called back to the Lord." The phrase felt empty on his lips. He knew too much of death to feel it as any kind of homecoming. But then, he had not gone beyond the Valley, not even when it opened for him with the soft warmth of springtime and beckoned with the voices of his friends who had gone before. Some of them entered the void with joyous hearts, and he recognized that he did not know everything, even about this. There were some mysteries only open to the dead, the sliver of mystery that a man with knowledge so often forgot.

Danek's words. Elisha's teeth tasted sour, his stomach aching.

Father Pierre stood over them, lantern held high. "We have many hospitals in the city, Doctor, to which your friend might be admitted, and many monasteries where they tend their brethren."

"I wanted to find a place where I knew we would be welcomed." With the city's former leader, Cola di Rienzi, gone and the barons resuming control—or resuming their own battles—Elisha had no idea who could be trusted any more, with the exception of Father Pierre.

"You are fortunate to find me here, on the last night of my vigil before I sail to the Holy Father at Avignon, to consult with him and to seek his intercession for . . . for those who are not his children." Father Pierre's brow furrowed, and he flicked a gaze over Elisha's face as if uncertain whether the trust might be mutual.

"The Jews," Elisha guessed.

The dark eyes blinked, and Father Pierre gave a short nod. "The Jews of Rome live in fear and in hiding."

"Would that I could aid in your mission, Father. God bless you for undertaking it."

The priest's face softened. "And what of he who wails in the night? Is he, too, your friend?"

"Indeed he is, and more in need of one than any."

"Well, perhaps you can coax him to worship more silently in the house of the Lord. And I shall bring blankets and water." Father Pierre made the sign of blessing over Gilles's chest. "Do not fear, my son. You will be well-cared for."

Elisha strode into the blackness, searching by the scrap of bloody cloth he still carried in his medical kit. Jude's howling sent eerie echoes through the church, making it hard to know where to look for him. "Jude," he called, "remember control. I know you can do it. You have every right to be afraid, but now you need to be brave. Can you do that?"

Jude's cry sank low, and Elisha heard his breathing. "Yes, yes, that's it."

"What if I cannot learn it?" Jude's touch whispered back.

"You can; you already are."

Elisha walked toward the door, his senses mapping out the dim interior where Jude waited for him. Then a chill wind cut through the church and silence devoured all sound. Into the darkness, a high, childish voice cried out his name, and Elisha ran.

Chapter 20

❖

The voice cut short, but the heat of a new presence flared in Elisha's awareness, and he was already preparing his armor, drawing up the strength of death within himself, drawing it down from the Valley. He ran down the aisle of the church toward a widening gap of evening light, a pinkish hue interrupted by a hurrying figure, its silhouette distorted by the thrashing form it carried: someone had seized Jude and hauled him out the door. Elisha ran even faster and plunged into the day, blinking at the sudden light.

Jude's terror touched him from the left, and he swung about, glimpsing the running figure as it rounded the corner of the church's colonnade and gained the freedom of the street. The shades of the dead massed in Rome, the shades of ancient soldiers joined by a throng of new victims, not fighting in ghostly battles or succumbing to ghostly crimes, but merely gliding from doorways, standing in windows, lying in the streets, their freshly dead corpses lying there still. The reek of death suffused the air, a combination of vomit and rotting flesh. The corners of the piazzas held low mounds of the dead and those barely living lined the wider streets. It was easier to discern the living from the dead here—the living held cloths over their faces and ran, furtive as rats

as they dodged among bodies. A handbill on the wall
opposite the church offered a rich price for anyone willing to haul the dead or dig their graves. A line drawn
through the price raised it twice already since the notice
had been posted. Elisha thought of the mancer-
gravedigger of Rome, who had died in a distant valley
trying to conceal Brigit from Elisha. The gravediggers
had never been so vital to a city's health. If there had
been no miasma of sickness before, there surely was now.

Fending off the odor, dulling the senses of his mouth
and nose, Elisha turned, tracking his quarry. There!

Elisha leapt a broad crack that cut the street and split
a nearby house. All around him, the crumbling structure
of Rome frayed even more, the piles of rubble larger
than he remembered, the buildings more tilted and roofs
leaning at precarious angles as a result of the earthquake. A few buildings collapsed completely, lying in
heaps among their fragile neighbors. Cracks and fissures
marred the streets and the standing houses, with slabs of
stone thrusting up here and there. Paving stones scattered the ground. Beneath the facades of the numerous
churches, patches of colored plaster and bright bits of
mosaics twinkled in the growing day. And among them
all, the dead.

A girl with bright hair and pale, vacant eyes lay beneath the Virgin's statue near a shattered chapel. Two
men side by side, faces distorted by black swellings and
reddened eyes. Others lay wrapped in anonymous cloth,
their lingering shades rising up and lying down in endless repetition of their final moment. The rhythm of
these shadows, slow and dreadful, gave the impression
that the city breathed in death and breathed it out again.
Before, Elisha had felt the jittery surges of death as the
plague advanced. Now, it seeped through him in a constant rain, sending strength to his limbs and turning his
breath to a misty shroud of ice crystals. Never before,

even in the act of killing, had he felt so powerful or so helpless.

Sealing in his emotions, Elisha allowed himself to grow cold, his divided sight showing him the gray tracks of death, his extended senses reaching for the child. If he could do nothing else, save no one else, surely he could at least do this.

He flung himself around a corner and found the vast, ruined bowl of the Colosseum towering before him, his quarry vanishing into its shadow. "Jude!" He cried out.

The figure ahead of him stumbled, the thrashing of his captive gone wild, and Elisha gained a few steps, enough to see the flash of the other man's eyes. Danek held Jude's wrists clamped in one hand, a band of leather in the other, wrapped through the boy's mouth to stop his voice, though he still moaned.

"He is my son, Doctor. By right and law, he belongs to me."

"No man who would treat him so deserves a son." Elisha stalked closer.

Jude flailed and twisted, his legs dangling, so that Danek carried him at arm's length, like a cat about to be drowned.

"You are a doctor, you understand the need for greater knowledge. It is vital that I study him. The similarity of his flesh to my own makes it clear that I am the only one who can do so effectively. What if, by doing so, I discover the reason he survived? Surely, that would be a discovery that you would support."

"If you would learn from him, then earn his trust and make him your ally, not your victim." Elisha took another step, hands spread as if in conciliation, the power of death lurking just beneath his skin, his muscles trembling with the urge to use it.

"Stay back." Pulling Jude against his chest, Danek shifted his grip on the leather, giving it a pull that turned the boy's head. "A broken neck is not an injury to trifle with."

"Kill him and you die."

Danek claimed he wanted to learn from the boy, but he was just as willing to kill him. In both body and mind, Jude contained so much knowledge about the plague he had survived, knowledge Danek had not intended to share. In bringing Jude to Rome, Elisha gave Danek the chance to steal back that knowledge. Elisha could not afford to lose both father and son, but Jude's trust was hard won, and his life was worth fighting for.

The shadows at Danek's side resolved into a blanket-draped mound with a few limbs poking out, the lingering shades of the dead rising and falling from beneath. The Valley whispered all around and through him, and Elisha reached out along it, stretching his senses, drawing up the insubstantial shadows of a family, father, mother, three children, cold and frightened. Elisha drew upon their terror and their grief and pulled them forth in a frigid blast.

Danek yelped at the touch and spun away, stumbling into a column. His elbow hit hard, and he lost his grip on Jude's hands.

Elisha snapped himself through the Valley to Danek's side as Jude grappled with his father. Then Jude's hand came up with something that shimmered pink. The salt blade plunged into his father's stomach, jerked free and stabbed again, blood streaming from the wounds.

Cursing in a language Elisha did not know, Danek slammed Jude's face into the column, then flung him aside as Elisha caught Danek's arm, blasting him with cold. Through the contact, Danek's confusion swirled, his knowledge disintegrating, the diseases that had always defended him now slipping away from him, blocked by the stabbing pain that cut his belly, and by the sharper slice of the salt through his awareness. Screaming, Danek dropped to his knees, trying to reach the blade. Elisha grabbed his wrists and shoved him to his back, looming over him.

"I can heal you—tell me how to stop the plague."

"Told you, you can't."

"But you're still alive, so's Vertuollo, so am I. You must have a way, even just to save a single life."

Danek's mouth gaped, blood seeping between his teeth. *"One at a time, Doctor. Not enough for you. You're greedy for life."*

"Why did you help them?"

"They helped me." He worked his mouth into a bloody grin. *"We travelled the world to get this far, to share the gift of humility."*

To get this far—not yet so far as England. The black pall of death coalesced around the pinned man. *"Immunity, for one, how do you cast it?"*

"Fuck off." Danek's rough skin twitched, pain spreading from the wound, his presence still flaring with the attempt to reach his magic, his panic spreading as he could not.

"You sent a gift with Guy to the Pope, it was tainted with the plague, wasn't it?"

Danek had lost the will or power to reply. Digging in his fingers, Elisha pushed himself deeper, his awareness invading Danek's wounds, tracing his knowledge, grasping for every fleeting thought. Immunity, a charm, a talisman. Survival rates at half or less, charts of calculations in an orderly script. An image of Jude lying bound upon a cot, flea-bitten and weeping. Mice, rats, larger furred creatures and smaller ones. The boy's little friends. A startling, tender moment of Danek combing his son's hair.

Danek struggled against him, that sickening wrongness flooding Elisha's own senses, as he remembered how Gretchen's mother tried to do the same to him, to force herself inside and tear out his knowledge, doing anything to strip from him what she needed. Danek thrashed, his features warped with an overwhelming horror.

Stomach roiling, Elisha pulled back as the salted blade slid free to shatter on the ground in the pool of blood. Elisha shifted his awareness, out and away, focusing his left eye on all the pathways of the dead, the family that lay beneath their blanket, the surging presence of the Valley and the slick cold spark as victim after victim died in the city all around them. Here and there, the Valley thrilled with a wicked glee as the mancers reveled in their conquest, drunk on the power all around them. "*There's your gift. You didn't give humility to the* desolati, *you gave power to their oppressors. To the mancers we are all lepers, worthless, weak, disgusting.*"

He reached again for power, this time to heal, but Danek jerked his arm away, dodging Elisha's touch. Danek's eyes rolled, and he coughed up blood in a racking wave that finished on an exhalation of cold.

Did he understand what he had done before he died? Elisha felt the unfurling breath as his spirit passed, coiling toward the Valley, then gone, as if, indeed, he had sworn his soul to someone. The barely felt shift of Vertuollo's presence rose from behind him and vanished again as quickly beneath deflection. The salted blade prevented even that most powerful of magicks, conjured by the death of a magus.

Abandoning his attachment to the dead, Elisha searched for the living. Jude lay crumpled at the base of the column, his arms over his head, his breath coming in sharp gasps, as if he prepared to scream, but no sound passed his lips.

The horror of all that had happened sank into Elisha, flesh and bone, his throat seared with bile, his heart sore with—what? Regret? Over what he had done and how? Or over the fact that he learned so little from his brutal invasion of another man's secrets?

"Jude, are you hurt?" He crept closer, holding out his hand, not touching, not yet.

Jude twitched one elbow, peering up at Elisha, then he gave a sob, and flung himself into Elisha's arms. Blood streaked his hair from where his head had struck stone. He curled into a tight ball, shaking, and Elisha gathered him close. *"I'm sorry. I'm so sorry."*

"I killed him."

"To defend yourself and me—a witch's greatest power is at the moment of his death, and you stopped even that."

"I'm bad, a demon. I didn't listen to you. I never listen." Jude's miserable words stung Elisha's skin.

"You are what he made you, Jude, but you don't have to be. From now on, it's all up to you. You have a choice— you can choose to do the right thing."

"I'm nothing."

Friar Gilles wrestled with his purpose, wondering if he had finished all that God had in mind for him, but Jude lived beneath the sway of a vicious creator, one who forged him as an instrument of suffering. Elisha hugged him fiercely, flooding him with comfort. *"That's a lie. Don't believe that, don't ever believe it. Your father gave you much better gifts than that. You can learn to use them. I'll teach you whatever I can."* He still had a lot to learn himself, and he prayed that Jude could teach him in turn, but now was not the time. He gently parted the boy's hair, probing with his medical knowledge and his secret senses to judge the depth of his injury and found it painful and jarring, but not desperate. He urged the skin to knit and lifted the pain away, feeling it throb against his own skull, reminding him a little too much of his own near-death.

Jude's thin arm slipped around his neck, pulling him even closer.

Unsteadily, Elisha rose, leaning briefly against the column to catch his breath. His legs trembled, too much magic, too quickly in bringing them here, then in pursuing Danek. He stumbled as he walked, but he did not try to set the child down, nor did Jude make any move to escape his arms.

In spite of withdrawing his contact from the Valley, Elisha still sensed its rising hum as they approached San Giovanni. His weary limbs could move no faster, but a lump formed at his throat. The great door still stood open. Across the shattered city, a few church bells rang to acknowledge the hour, but their voices sounded hollow and discordant, as if too many notes were missing to make the joyous noise, as if the bell pulls hung limp without the hands to sound them. Inside, Father Pierre bent over Friar Gilles, anointing his head with oil. Gilles's breath rasped in and out over swollen lips, but his eyes flickered open at Elisha's approach.

Sinking down beside him, Elisha at last released his grip on Jude, both of them staring down at their companion.

"I will miss seeing you in your glory," Gilles breathed, and Elisha had not the heart to deny his fervor. "For it will come, and you will rise to vanquish the enemy." The friar nearly smiled, a tremor of his lips and the slightest lifting of his cheeks. *And there shall be no curse, rather the throne of God, and of the Lamb upon it...*" He coughed harshly, and whispered, *"And there shall be no night, and they need no candle, for the light..."* But he spoke no more of the light, nor of anything at all. His shade rose up in brightness, released from the corruption of the flesh, and Elisha felt the flash of joy and sorrow and let him go.

Chapter 21

———— ✦ ————

Father Pierre spoke a soft prayer in Latin, then said, "So many have been quoting from Revelations lately. I have heard rumors that the woman clothed with the sun was seen in the mountains, and gave birth there to the child of the prophecies, the one who shall be hounded by the dragon."

"The end times," Elisha said, watching as Father Pierre closed Gilles's sightless eyes.

"Just so." The priest sat back on his heels. "The miraculous mother is on her way to see the Holy Father at Avignon. It is another reason I am going."

Brigit on the move to visit the Pope? The idea was too strange for words.

Father Pierre gave a deep sigh, sounding too weary for a man so young. Elisha knew how he felt. The priest stoppered his vial of oil, holding it in his palm. "There is a shortage of gravediggers, I fear. I do not know when or how we can properly tend his earthly remains." He glanced over his shoulder at the daylight stretching toward them across the floor.

"And you have a voyage to make." Over the salt sea toward the Pope, the most powerful man under Heaven. If the Pope himself were already under mancer control, the world was truly doomed. Elisha tried to shake off his despair; it reminded him of his last sojourn in Rome, making his confession to Father Uccello, confessing his despair before the priest's own execution redoubled it.

"I take it he has neither family nor brethren in the city. What about his visitor? Would he have the means to see to the burial?"

"He had a visitor? Who?"

"I did not see clearly—the man departed as I was returning with the things I needed to tend him and offer his last rites. Forgive me, I assumed you would know." The priest spread his hands in a slight shrug. "There is always the catacombs, of course."

Then Elisha remembered what he had sensed, that Vertuollo himself had moved through the Valley. But why come to visit Gilles? What did the mancer want? He had done nothing to hasten the friar's death, nor had he left any sign of his coming as a warning to Elisha himself or to siphon away the power of that death. The church floor felt too hard beneath his knees, and Elisha longed to sink down at the friar's side and rest, but he could not do so, not in the city of his enemy, especially when he did not understand what his enemy was doing. He could, of course, always ask him. The mancers had been busy: Vertuollo coming to see Gilles, Brigit traveling to visit the Pope, and God only knew what the rest of them were up to while Elisha chased the plague. It was time for the two quests—stopping the mancers, and stopping the plague—to become one. What did Brigit want with the Pope? If the Pope stood already under mancer sway, then why had Danek bothered to send him a charm already infected with the plague? And if the Pope still gave allegiance to God alone, then could his earthly influence be harnessed against the mancers who sought to claim the world?

"I think that Friar Gilles would be grateful to lie among the martyrs of the past. Father, may we join you on your voyage to Avignon? It might be best if we could manage a private cabin on board ship."

Father Pierre's warm glance flicked to the silent child and back, and he gave a nod. "I cannot say when we will return here." Or if, but he need not say that either. "The Jews are already at the port. I will take a boat down the river, and we sail with the evening tide."

"Then we'll be there. Thank you for everything, Father." As the priest moved away, Elisha draped the blanket over the friar's body, then he turned to Jude, touching his knee. "*I need your help, Jude, but it will mean showing me what happened, with your father. This voyage . . . You will need to try to trust, or, if not to trust, at least to hold back your fear. Can you do that?*"

Jude's chin quivered, but he resolutely clamped his jaw and gave a nod. "*May I have another knife?*"

Elisha took the salted blade from his boot and handed it over. Jude clutched the hilt a long moment before he tucked it through the belt made of his bonds. "*On the boat, I can begin to teach you. We will be surrounded by strangers, and you will need to be very brave.*"

Another nod. "*What's the secret? The thing you didn't say to the priest.*"

Just how sensitive was Jude? Without any training at all, it was hard to know what the boy was capable of. "*Before I go to the boat, I need to pay a call on my enemy.*" His hands felt clammy and his chest tight.

"*Another demon.*"

"*A lord among demons. It would be better if you did not come with me. I don't want him to hurt you.*"

"*I will hurt him back. I still have my friends and my father's gift.*" These words tangled with pain and fear in the boy's touch. "*And yours.*" He touched the hilt of the knife.

He had recovered from the plague his father made, and Elisha had no idea what to make of the reference to his friends. No matter what happened, Jude had already been hurt: his life, his heart, his presence twisted to his father's will. He might not be possessed by a demon, but he would never be an ordinary child. They had little time to pay their visit and escape again to the sea. Elisha gathered Friar Gilles's body to his chest and staggered as he lifted him. How he longed for rest, but when would he ever find it? Travel by sea served as a barrier in both directions—it would give him the peace to recover, but it would also prevent him from reaching his enemies without extraordinary effort. And he remained acutely aware of Jude's presence at his side. He had taken on responsibility for the child's safety and for his training as a magus, a responsibility that could all too easily turn against him.

They walked out into the sunlight and made their way between the dead toward the Porto San Sebastiano and the catacombs beyond. Last time he was in Rome, the shuttered houses displayed the tension of their owners, uncertain which baron to trust and whether the Tribune Cola di Rienzi would maintain his grip on power. Now more dead than living occupied the streets, and some shutters bore the black marks of plague houses. Elisha's left eye caught glimmers of the Valley all around. They passed along a quiet street and suddenly entered a riotous piazza where a makeshift stand of minstrels played a wild dance tune barely keeping time with one another, a shawm bleating over a lute, a drum beating for attention. Couples flung themselves about, linking arms and changing partners, men and women dressed in rich gowns and gold while tears streamed down their faces. A pile of barrels stood to one side, each of them tapped and flowing into mugs and goblets.

A man clambered up on a standing barrel, swaying until he found his balance. He wore no clothes but a gold-woven shawl stitched with gems in the shape of crosses and likely stolen from one of the churches. "Here we stand in God's own city, celebrating our lives amidst the shadow of death!" He thrust up his hand toward the heavens, greeted by cheers from those who bothered to stop their carousing and listen. "We have pledged ourselves to the Lord, to no avail! Now, I ask you, pledge yourselves to me—the Lord of liquor and of living!" He raised up the glass in his other hand, and a roar of approval met his demand.

The irony of this declaration struck Elisha with the void of the man's presence: he was a mancer, the natural warmth of humanity concealed by his intimate association with killing. Jude pushed against Elisha's side, clamping a hand over his mouth though the howl of his fear echoed through their contact. Most definitely Jude knew a mancer when he saw one.

"You've met him before? Stay close, keep your head down." Elisha cast a deflection of his own, woven from the death of Gilles and from his sadness. If they were noticed at all, let them be merely another family mourning their loss. Jude was more than an experiment; his father had wanted him back and hesitated to kill him. If he could bring Jude together with Isaac, how many mancers could they sketch then? But the mancers avoided knowing too many of the others. They worked in their little rings, barely linking with one another, like chainmail as Katherine had once described it. Just like the magi, they sought to maintain their secrets, even from each other. The Salernitan, Danek, linked many of them, at least through the flesh-bound book of directions, which had probably not been the only copy. Now he was dead without ever giving up his own secrets. Vertuollo said Danek had been too hasty in releasing his gift upon the world. The other mancers did not seem to agree. Was the count still at odds with his comrades, and could that work to Elisha's advantage? Vertuollo called him "brother," and they shared a curious kind of respect. They two might

have reached a truce, if not for the fact of Elisha's having killed his son.

As Elisha walked, Gilles's body weighing down his arms, he allowed the dying to reach him, breathing in that black power, letting it sustain him and lift him from both despair and weariness. For this, he must be strong, as formidable as the count himself. At every step, Elisha steadied, the jittery power welling up in him, leaving him eager for confrontation.

Slipping around the edge of the revelry, they reached the gate at last, and the open air of the lands beyond the city. Even there, ruins marked the fields, old columns thrusting up from grasses just barely greening for the spring. Broken halls from ancient palaces formed the walls of farmers' hovels and richly carved sarcophagi emerged from rubble and earth, their honored dead long vanished. Ahead he saw the first of a few small chapels that gave access to the catacombs below, Vertuollo's special domain. The first time he came here, he avoided entering those low portals marked by the count to monitor who came. This time, Elisha stepped through into the gloom, feeling the tingle of interest against his awareness. He let his eyes adjust along with his extended senses. A few old candles rested in an empty basin near the entrance. "Will you light us a candle?"

Jude separated from him barely long enough to comply, clutching the candle in one hand and Elisha's elbow in the other. The candle's flame danced as its shaft tremored in his grip.

The shadows of death lay thickly here, guiding him down a set of stairs between shelves of old bones, some draped with shrouds of spider web or scraps of ancient cloth. Jude whimpered as he followed slightly behind. The passageway opened out into a chamber decorated with crosses and carvings of wings. Here, one of the shelves lay empty, and Elisha lay down his burden, resting Friar Gilles among the other Christians, his arms as heavy as if he still bore the weight. He slipped his hand down to grip Jude's.

His left eye showed the continuous shiver of shadows along the floor, like dust disturbed by the slightest current of a breeze, and they walked on into the tunnels, taking with them their small circle of light. Carved grave markers loomed out of the darkness, skulls made in stone and those of bone leering back from their places. Here and there brass bowls, jugs of wine, rusted swords and other offerings marked the dead. These old bones had a serenity that might one day reach the dead lying above them, when all those who still mourned and fought for life had passed away.

"I thought it could not possibly be, that my dear brother should come here, in search of me." Vertuollo's voice echoed around them, the drift of shadows changing direction, swirling and eddying as if they could no longer find their master.

Elisha called out, "Your city is sunk in misery and ruin, Brother. Is it all that you hoped for? Were you not already master here without punishing Rome yet more?"

Something rumbled, and a force of air knocked into Elisha, but he stood his ground, rooted in death like a tree into the earth. Jude gave a low moan, and Elisha divided his focus, sending courage to his companion, shielding him from the worst of the dread.

"Do not taunt me with ruins, Barber, I am not the only one who has not found what he sought in this."

The candle blew out with the next shock of wind, a twirling storm that lifted the bones all around them, battering Elisha not only with the hard matter of the corpse, but with the painful stabs of knowledge as the dead revealed their paths: a woman who died in labor, a man who died on the battlefield in agony, an old woman with hands so crippled she could not feed herself, a man torn

apart by lions for other men's sport. Armoring himself
with death, save for his left hand, where Jude hung on,
Elisha pushed back, forcing away the contact, loose
bones clattering. Vertuollo's own sensitivity allowed him
to spark these reminders of the dead when they were
living, a distraction Elisha could not afford. If he could
reach the count, touch him and break his hold upon the
power here, then Elisha might force contact beyond Vertuollo's defenses and learn the truth.

A child's corpse rose up before him, head dangling,
flesh oozing from the skull, but still marked with the
black swellings and streaked with the blood of the plague.
Elisha turned, pivoting between Jude and the dead child,
but another bone struck him hard at the knee and he
staggered, Jude's hand slipping from his grasp.

The dead child swept forward with the unnatural
wind, brushing by Elisha with a streak of terror and grief.
Elisha seized that contact and stole it for his own, using
his knowledge of the way that Gilles died. The corpse
collapsed as the wind cracked around it, but Jude was
gone, shrieking into the darkness, stumbling and crying
out. Elisha fell with the dead child, pushing it aside with
a breath of sympathy.

Jude's screams echoed all around him, beating at his
ears and at his heart. He pushed himself to his knees,
searching. Shreds of old cloth and withered skin slapped
his shoulders and stroked his head. Lovers slain together
in her husband's bed; a young man who threw himself
from a tower, another who drowned in the river,
weighted down by armor. Already exhausted from the
last few days, Elisha tried to ward himself against the
assault, to find Jude. He had entered the count's domain
of his own accord, bringing the child with him, pretending he could protect him. Every bone and scrap and lashing hair struck him with the crippling pity of the dying.
If he drew down Death and made himself go cold, he

could stop feeling them all, Jude along with them. "Jude! Where are you?"

Vertuollo spoke again, a commanding voice using a language Elisha did not understand. The scream broke into a series of panting cries, then Jude's voice, answering. The first time Jude had spoken in Elisha's presence was to call his name, summoning his aid against Danek. Now, he spoke in words Elisha did not know, halting and soft. The wind died back, bones thumping to the floor, as if their master were distracted. Vertuollo spoke again, silky and soothing, and Jude answered, his voice shaking with tears. They were ahead of him—both of them. Elisha crept forward, reaching, opening himself to search through the shadows.

Someone shifted in the darkness, with a scent of dust and decay. Passages lay to the left and right, lined with the dead.

Elisha reached for his power, letting it swell through his flesh and spread to his fingertips. "Do not touch him, Brother. He is not for you."

"I thought of seeking out your baby, Brother." Vertuollo's voice, from the left, much nearer.

"Why? Because you think I don't know loss? It was my brother's death that started me down this road. It was my mad wish to bring back his dead son that taught me anything of this power." Elisha listened for movement in the darkness. "Why do you think it's so hard for me to kill? Every life is joined to so many others. Every time someone is killed, there is another who feels a pain like yours."

"No!" the count roared, his denial echoing in the caverns. "No one can feel pain like this, Brother."

"For any other two men, Brother, that would be true," said Elisha softly, "But not for us—your pain lies all around you."

Vertuollo's presence felt chill and brittle as new ice.

"No," said the count a second time, and Elisha could feel his power gathering.

He'd gone too far, and for what—Vertuollo was a sensitive, yes, but a mancer still. Another's pain meant nothing to him, and the idea that someone might share his pain only made him angry. The count's voice resumed its cold, conversational tone. "The baby is not yours alone. This child is different. Not your son, but very like you. Perhaps your younger brother."

Elisha lunged toward the voice, hands outstretched, surging with power. Light blinded him, searing to life in the darkness with Vertuollo's power. It blazoned the count's sharp features in Elisha's shocked vision.

"You went to Gilles to trap me, to lure me here. But not for Jude, his father was meant to take him." Elisha focused his vision, away from the world of the living, to the shadows of the dead. The light went soft, Vertuollo's living form flickering before him, outlined in the shades of those he had killed, Lucius now prominent among them. "What will you do with me, Brother, now that you've got me?" Elisha concentrated the crackling cold into his palms, as if he could wield hammers of ice.

"As if you were at bay in the caverns of the dead. I said it to you once, Brother, and now I say again: Go home. England is not yet fallen to the plague, and you could save it. Go home and leave the ruins of Europe to the men who have cultivated these fields and will reap their harvest."

Elisha pictured London, a soft rain parting, the sun gleaming on the grand White Tower, Princess Alfleda's joy and his baby's fresh, wrinkled face as he tried to make sense of the world. He thought of Martin, dying that his city could live, and Allyson, mourning her husband Count Randall, defending her land; Sundrop, Madoc, Pernel, and all the rest. Just for a moment, he once again met Thomas's keen blue gaze, always seeing the truth, seeing the things Elisha wished he could hide. Go home to England, to save his country—let the rest of the world burn, and let the mancers win. Even if Thomas survived, Elisha could never again meet those eyes.

He stared into the darkness, staring down the enemy, and said, "No."

Chapter 22

◆

The next blow of the count's power knocked Elisha against the wall, fighting for breath, the bones clattering all around him, and he could not even reach Vertuollo. What had the count said to Jude? Could the boy be won over by the count's grace and command of Jude's language? Elisha came here to confront the count, to learn the truth, and by God he would try. But how to reach a man who hid in the darkness, among his own familiar dead?

Elisha focused instead on his old enemy, Lucius Physician, the sneering charlatan who had dragged him into this war to begin with. Elisha pictured Lucius's haughty features, his arched brows, his over-long sleeves indicating that the physician planned to do no work whatsoever. Then he imagined Lucius's body stripped bare, down to the muscles, leaving his face intact, a great gash nearly parting his head from his neck, and he imagined the hand that had flayed the corpse.

That death linked him to Vertuollo, a single, shifting tendril in the chaos that surrounded him. Elisha opened the Valley and sprang through. Rather, he sprang in, readying himself for the attack, and met a wall, a sheer, cold surface forged of the suffering of thousands. In the spiraling madness of the Valley itself, lit by the flicker of passing souls, Vertuollo stared back at him and shot out his hand straight for Elisha's chest.

With a stretch of his presence, Vertuollo conjured the Valley, that private passage of Elisha's own death, the death that he refused when he returned to this world. But no matter that he had refused it, it had never left him, lighting his left eye with the vision of shadows, binding him to the Valley and all the shadows it contained.

The count vanished, and Elisha felt the impact against his chest. His breath shocked out of him, his limbs jerked taut, as if he stood bound against the mouth of a bombard that fired through him. Agony shot from the center of his being, searing up into his skull, as if streaks of flame would burst from the scars of his surgery. Elisha's mouth gaped but he made no sound, all breath stolen in an instant. His fingers and toes went numb, his throat working without purpose.

All strength left him, yet he could not fall. Death poured through him, scouring him from the inside out. Vertuollo's power was tearing him wide open.

Vertuollo's voice, smooth and cultured, echoed through him. "*Perhaps you cannot die, Brother, but I can make you, every moment, wish that you had.*"

Elisha's flesh shuddered with cold, his skin slick as if it were stripped from him again and again.

"*Choose, Brother. Choose death now and be at peace.*"

Choose. The choice remained to him, just as he had told Jude who cowered alone in the dark. Alone, but for the thousands across the world who cowered just like him.

"*Lie down among the martyrs and let them build a shrine to you,*" Vertuollo whispered.

Elisha let go of the Valley, rejecting it, with his last ounce of wit flinging himself out of the passage between the worlds and staggering into darkness. It made no difference: the hollow, horrible rush continued, pinning him against the wall, as if half his being tumbled back to the

Valley with the shades that swirled within. Choose. To die. What a blessed relief it would be to simply let himself go. Elisha's heart hesitated.

A sharp and singular pain pierced his left side, like a consuming mouth that sucked back the Valley into a hard pearl buried in his flesh. Elisha gasped a single breath, tumbling as if he'd been shot. His awareness fled, his every secret, magic sense bound up with that pain. His fumbling fingers touched a hilt, a blade thrust between his ribs at a low angle, stopping his blood even as it stung his flesh with salt. "Jude," he breathed.

A trembling hand touched his face, his hand, his chest. "I *killed you, like him. Dead demons.*" The words came and went, broken with Elisha's senses.

"Get out, leave," he panted, not knowing what language he spoke, knowing it didn't matter.

Then two small hands wrapped his arm above his elbow and dragged him forward on unsteady feet. Bones clattered around him, grinding into him, blessedly silent of their history. Elisha shoved against the wall and fell forward, managing his feet, any progress simply a matter of falling in the right direction but failing to hit the ground. Jude hauled him along the corridor, silent. The pearl of death throbbed at his chest, but could not devour him, not so long as the salted blade skewered his side. God, but it hurt. Elisha wept without tears.

Jude hesitated with a whimper, and Elisha crashed into him, the two of them scraping the wall. "Gilles," he said. "Can you, find his body. The exit." They swayed around a corner and stumbled onward, the tunnels clammy against his skin, the boy's hands burrowing into his muscle. Elisha pressed his other palm around the blade, keeping it in place as they fled through the darkness.

Jude cried out, with that particular wail he used when a mancer came near. Hunched around the salted blade that kept Vertuollo from reaching into him, Elisha was blind to the Valley as Jude was not.

They ran on, then the boy suddenly rose, his hands hauling upward, and Elisha shouted, thinking Jude had been grabbed. Instead, Elisha's toes struck stone and he was falling again, up the steps, floundering into the overwhelming day. Sunlight spilled into the chapel at the top of the stairs. Once again, the pearl pulsed with Vertuollo's strength, then they tumbled out past the threshold, beyond the count's dark domain.

Elisha rolled onto his back, arched and sobbing. Blood streamed around the shifting blade. "Wine, water, something."

Jude's hands slid along his arm, down to his spasming fingers and finally released him. Shadows passed his vision — clouds, crows, dying children. Then the mouth of a bottle pressed into his palm, Jude's hands clenching his own around it. With a convulsive grip, Elisha pulled free the salted blade, opening himself to magic, but his flesh remained too thoroughly salted to heal the wound. He kicked onto his side and poured the contents of the bottle, stifling his scream. The ancient wine stung with vinegar, but it swept away the salt, letting it spill forth with his blood. Clenching his shaking fist around the ring he wore, the single talisman he still had that was not linked to death, Elisha forced himself to heal. He had to focus on every nerve and vessel, working slow and clumsy as a barber's poor apprentice, finally sealing the skin and tossing the ancient wine bottle away.

Blinking up at the sky, Elisha found Jude's face, the boy kneeling at his head, staring down at him with wide eyes. "Have to run," Elisha told him. "The river. The boat. Help me."

They clasped hands again, and Elisha struggled to calm his mind enough to send the images: the dock at the river outside of town, the water that would give them some protection, the salt water that would offer more, all in a rush. Then a question, quiet, almost pleading. "*Lend me your strength.*"

Jude gave a high-pitched bark of laughter. "*Too weak, too worthless.*"

"*You have strength enough, and more.*" But even before he found the way to convince him, Jude's barricades fell before him, the boy's fear and power infusing him with the vital strength of life itself. Elisha could not accept the power of death, not now, so he chose its opposite. Between them, they were enough. He let Jude pull him up and they ran on, as fast as they could. Vertuollo knew the Valley through his murders—he was powerful, but even he would feel the strain of such a spell as he had attempted, forcing himself through Elisha's armor. Elisha noticed his own right hand pressed against his heart, as if to reassure himself it still beat. Choose death, the mancer urged, and Elisha had been a heartbeat away from obedience.

They took a dirt track between tilted wooden buildings and the broken columns of pagan temples to fetch up at the riverside. A few boats lay on the shore, and they turned over one of these, dragging it down to the water. Elisha remembered all too acutely Thomas rescuing him from the Thames, hauling him into a boat, Thomas's strong, lean arms stroking the oars to speed them away. His own work was clumsy at best, but the current was with them, pushing them along down the broad river marked with docks of wood and stone, broken houses, and floating corpses, their arms waving with the lapping wake as the boat passed by. Elisha felt raw and vulnerable as he had not for years, perhaps not since he was Jude's age, watching an angel die. The boy huddled before him, watching with haunted eyes.

"I need you to tell me about your father and his gift," Elisha said.

Jude inched a little closer, not understanding the words without contact, and set his hand on Elisha's knee. His presence clouded with worry and confusion as Elisha repeated his need, as gently as he could.

"*My gift*," Jude said within his flesh. "*My pets, my pestilence.*" He trembled on the verge of madness, and Elisha held his gaze, holding himself open.

Then Jude remembered. His father combing his hair, the fleas hopping onto small, furred creatures, the mancers visiting, following the directions in the flesh-bound books, and taking the vermin away in a steady stream. Fleas would not bite Elisha as they did Gilles. They would not bite Vertuollo, either, he'd bet on that—nor any other mancer, so Danek used them to send his gift into the world, spreading it, as he had said, in small ways, and his son was the breeding ground, once he, too, learned to fend off the sickness they carried. Knowledge, but fleas and the animals that carried them, spread faster than even Elisha could stop them. Could there be another way? Charms, Danek implied, a way to protect people one by one. What else? What more could be learned? Jude showed him the suffering, the panic of his closing throat, the pain of the swellings and the taste of vomit that seared the throat with bile and blood. All things Elisha knew from tending his other patients and from watching Gilles die. It was not enough.

"*I need to know the plague, Jude.*"

Jude snatched back his hand and scooted away, shaking violently, his hair flying around him as he denied what Elisha was asking.

Elisha shipped the oars and shifted forward, kneeling in the bottom of the boat even as Jude pulled up his knees, curling into a ball, still shaking his head. Elisha touched his shoulder, sending comfort, confidence and desperation. "*Jude, I have to know all there is to know. You've told me what you can, and you can show me how to survive. You'll be there on the ship with me, to protect me, to help me as your father never helped you. Please, Jude. Your father made you a demon—he made you the carrier to kill the world, you know that. It's not your fault, and I hope to God you know that, too. Please, help me heal it."*

Only now that he had buried his connection with death, with his skin warm and his heart too frail, only now could he hope to have what so many rushed to escape. Elisha opened himself to the plague. Jude knelt before him, the boy's presence alive with fear, with hope, with an unaccustomed duty and an unspoken promise. Elisha embraced him, feeling the prickle of the boy's tears, and the tiny pinch of a flea's small bite.

Chapter 23

❖

When they reached the port, Elisha briefly worried that they might have trouble locating the ship they were to sail on, but they found none of the usual bustle of a port town. At a small market manned by wary stall keepers, they paid inflated prices for the food and herbs they would need on board. The docks were nearly deserted, marked by a proclamation that no boat was to land by order of the barons, co-signed, Elisha noted, by both Orsini and Colonna representatives. Apparently the plague had done some good if it could bring together the warring factions that fought for Rome. A single two-masted vessel at the far jetty showed signs of activity, loading a few dozen passengers while a restless mob lurked at the shoreline.

A woman with a scarf over her head gathered two children close to her as she hurried past the group of citizens.

"Good riddance!" someone shouted. "Let the Holy Father see to your wickedness."

Someone else threw a bottle that struck her on the back. She fell, one of the children tumbling with her. Up ahead, a man in a black cap turned back, but his arms were loaded with bundles. His eyes flared, and he started toward the woman. The mob gave an ominous rumble, pushing up as if to close the gap and make good on their promise of violence.

Projecting peace and confidence, Elisha strode into their midst. They hesitated, glancing from him to the boy at his side. "Come now, they're leaving already—no need for all of this." Elisha smiled at the man who had thrown the bottle. "I'll see to it that they get aboard." He shifted his own sacks to his other shoulder and kept walking, stooping to take the woman's elbow as she tried to rise.

He sensed the throbbing of the bruise at her spine. She darted him a glance and snatched back her arm, stumbling in her long skirts to put some distance between them. Elisha and Jude followed more slowly. "*Scared people,*" Jude observed.

"*Jews,*" Elisha replied. "*Many people hate them and fear them almost as much as lepers.*"

"*Are they sick?*"

"*No, but many of them are learned where others are ignorant, faithful to beliefs that others don't understand. Often they are rich while others are poor. People will speak evil of them, Jude. Don't listen.*"

Jude gave that single nod, then walked up the narrow board onto the boat. Father Pierre Roger greeted them warmly. "There is a cabin, but you will need to pay the crew—have you money?"

Elisha fingered the coins in his purse, the last of his wealth, aside from Thomas's ring and Isaac's pin, and the fur-lined cloak itself. It should be enough. "Aye, Father. I have terrible sea-sickness and am unlikely to be about for the crossing, but Jude will tend me."

"Fare you well, then." Father Pierre turned back to the company of Jews who laid out blankets and found space for themselves on deck. Most of them would spend the several days of the crossing in the open air, hoping for good weather. Elisha thought to give up his own cabin for one of these families, perhaps the mother with

her two small children, but more dangerous to them than
a bit of rain would be the plague he knew he carried.
Best he stay apart and pray for a quick recovery.

A fleet-footed ship's boy led the way, and they were
soon settled in a narrow cabin curved at one wall into the
bow of the boat. By the time the orders echoed from bow
to stern and the ship heaved-to into the sea, Elisha's armpits and groin ached with swelling, and he had trouble
concentrating. Stripping off his outer clothing, he lay
down, keeping Jude's hand for as long as he could, speaking to him of attunement to one's surroundings, the
spreading of that awareness through contact and knowledge, the laws of affinity, polarity, and mystery, the uses of
a talisman to echo the power of a magus. Jude carried his
own talisman about his waist: the leather thongs that
bound his wrists at the hospital, stained with his blood
and marked with his fear.

The rolling of the waves carried them away from Italy,
and Elisha's stomach roiled. Jude placed a bucket beside
him, unflinching. The boy knew sickness, but his father
had never taught him sympathy. For now, it was a relief
not to bear the burden of another person's worries. Elisha's hands and back ached, his pulse leaping, and he
could give no more lessons. He retreated within, burrowing down even as his mind wandered. The fever rose,
heating his face, blazing into his scars. He sucked on
scraps of willow bark, vomiting them back again as often
as not. Jude patiently offered another, sometimes turning Elisha's face with his small, cold hand to push the
medicine between his teeth. Elisha fought him off, but
weakly, sobbing, clenched around his hollow, aching
stomach.

Jude lay his hand on Elisha's cheek, sending images
from his own illness, his small body thrashing off his
sheets—bound, always bound—black swellings bright
against his pale skin, burning with fever, then one day,

cool again. Before he grew distracted with his own suffering, Elisha searched himself. He methodically reviewed his knowledge of anatomy and of every illness he had ever seen or treated. He slid through veins and arteries and experienced the pounding of his heart, the twitching of his limbs, the swelling inside his nodes that pushed forth and blackened the skin. Little things, Danek had said, and Elisha felt them, as if that single flea spawned thousands inside of him, forging a contact with his every vessel and poisoning every one, a seething mass of foreign creatures intent on his destruction.

When the fire raged at its worst across his skin, and he began to lose all sense of himself, Elisha clung to Jude's hand, begging for mercy, begging to be shown the way to live, or the way to die.

The Valley sighed open, vibrant with lost souls. Lost in his own fire, Elisha did not heed it. He remembered that he used to be cold, frigid even, so cold that his hand could bring comfort to the fevered, so cold he could make ice of the Tower moat on a summer's day. But he would die not in ice, but in fire. Like Mordecai.

His mentor's presence rose into his awareness, and they sat again in the dining room of the manor house on the Isle of Wight, Mordecai watching him over a pile of books, the knowledge he loved and used to defend his own sensitivity. Elisha tried to retreat from him. Surely, the plague that ravaged his body would hurt his teacher, but Mordecai showed no pain at all.

"The best way, you think, to gain knowledge?" Mordecai inquired.

"The library taught me nothing." Elisha tapped one of the books before him, a manual on the punishment of witches. Not all books were worthy of reading.

Mordecai smiled gently, his steely hair curling beneath his cap, his moist eyes patient. Then he was standing at the door to the makeshift hospital where Elisha had first met him. At Elisha's back, the injured dragged themselves from the battlefield, shattered by bombards and pierced with arrows. Mordecai ran that hospital, before Lucius imposed himself, adding torturous treatments to the already agonizing injuries of the soldiers. Mordecai the surgeon had been harsh, distant, almost disdainful—terrified of being found out as a Jew, not to mention a magus.

By day they antagonized each other, the arrogant young barber defying authority to his own detriment, the experienced surgeon simply working to heal. By night, they spoke in the river, Elisha learning only much later that the calm voice of Sage, the magus in the stream, belonged to the master-surgeon. "*We are each of us soldiers in our own war,*" Sage once told him, "*All we can do is soldier on until we fall beneath the enemy and do not rise again.*"

And Elisha had answered him, "*Or rise again in a way even we cannot imagine.*"

Elisha had learned all he could of the plague. It was time to rise again. Jude held him, anchoring him in the gloom of the ship's cabin, in the realm of the living. As Elisha tracked this contact back to his own corrupt flesh, he could almost feel Mordecai's rare smile. He returned to the sound of singing, Jude's small voice, crooning the familiar lullaby that Elisha had once sung to him. The English words broke in strange places, merely sounds to the boy, but comforting enough for all of that.

His eyes blinked open. Clammy linens draped his legs. The bucket at his side smelled, but faintly—it must have been emptied regularly.

Lying still and exhausted, Elisha said, "Jude. Thank you."

As if the words released some cork at the boy's emotions, the contact flooded with relief, shame, fear, regret, hope, bombarding Elisha with all that he had been holding back these last few days. How many? Six. The boy slumped against the bedside, as wrung out as Elisha by the ordeal.

Taking sips of water from a leather bottle, Elisha worked to integrate what he had learned by living inside the disease with everything he had witnessed as a doctor and as a magus. Danek was right; there was no way to stop it, not the whole rising tide of plague that swept the land as tainted blood from the sick carried their sickness to those who were well. But the fleas avoided cold; they would not bite a mancer, nor Elisha himself—not until he had to embrace his mortality to escape Vertuollo's terrible onslaught. One by one, he could mark those he would defend. One by one, he might force back the plague in someone already infected, by sending his awareness so deeply within another's flesh that he could defeat those tiny invaders. But the world itself he could not save.

What remained, then, but to stop those who would profit from the world's devastation. The ship groaned around them, still tossing on the waves, but sea-sickness could not compare with what Elisha had just lived through, and he mastered his stomach. Hoping to send comfort, he stroked Jude's hair, but the boy flinched away with a flash of horror and shame. More deliberately, Elisha touched Jude's shoulder. "*If you wish, I can shave your hair and leave them no place to hide. We can kill them all.*"

"*All the demons.*" The boy turned, meeting Elisha's eye.

"*Yes,*" said Elisha. "*Them, too. But I don't yet know how.*"

When he had eaten a little, rested a little more, and finally felt steady enough, Elisha plied his razor, shearing Jude's wild, dark hair and spreading his magic, conjuring just enough of death to kill the fleas. Here upon the sea, it should be safe, and he did not feel the reaching of his enemies looking for an opening to attack. At the last stroke of the razor, Jude withdrew, running his palm over his bare scalp. For the first time since they had met, quite possibly for the first time ever, Jude smiled, a slender glow that pierced the veils of sickness and despair. Too thin, too pale, too scarred, the boy looked like a child-saint, his suffering granting him majesty.

Overhead, orders rang out and ropes groaned, men pattered about in the flurry of duties as they came to port.

Elisha pushed himself up and changed from his sweat-damp clothes while Jude gathered their few possessions back into the sacks and bound them at the ready. With the rising voices outside, Jude's tension grew, spilling over into his presence and making his movements shaky. Elisha tucked his hand into his medical pouch and handed over the last of his salted blades, small, but sharp, perhaps Jude would be able to put this one, too, to good use. Elisha's side still ached from his forced healing, but it was a wound he would always be grateful for. In his vulnerable state, Jude needed even the slight edge of power the blade could offer.

Together, they pushed open the door and blinked into the sunlight. The Jews, too, had packed their things and clustered at the center of the ship, staying out of the way of the scurrying sailors. Fishermen's cabins edged the water, surrounded by the upturned hulls of boats and spread with nets. A stone jetty thrust out from the rocky beach, and a small party of soldiers waited there. One man, richly dressed with golden chains, shouted at the captain, who stood with Father Pierre, gripping the rail and shouting back in Italian. He pointed at the young priest, voice rising. Father Pierre waved off the furor with one hand, and answered in French, his voice calm and commanding.

Finally, the captain shouted again and the sailors sprang into action, bringing the boat about, still pitching with the waves as one sailor tossed a line around a pillar on the jetty. Father Pierre turned about with a grimace and his eyes lit upon Elisha. The French priest offered a purely Roman shrug. "In fear of the plague, they will not allow the sailors to land, and they demand high fees from the Jews. I have claimed you for my retainer so they don't ask the same price. Someone must go ashore to make ready for disembarking."

"I'll do it," said Elisha. "And thanks." Wobbling with the shaky deck, he made his way to the gunwale and watched for a moment. Timing his leap, he jumped down to the jetty and made fast the rope, then accepted another, tying that off as well, though the activity left him weak and panting. Jude scrambled up and followed after, moving more surely on the deck, and helping to lay down the ramp.

"Your son is much improved," Father Pierre remarked as he accepted Elisha's hand to balance on the narrow ramp. "I do believe sea-living agrees with him, if not with you."

"He's chosen his better self," Elisha replied, then he stood ready to help the Jews, accepting the worried looks of the women, and the suspicion of their menfolk as they came down and huddled on the jetty while the priest negotiated their port fees. Purses and sleeves gave up far too many coins, and the harbormaster glared at each and every one—checking their necks for signs of swelling before he allowed them to pass.

After dragging down the plank and casting off the ropes, Elisha tossed them back to the sailors. Weary from his days of sickness, he wondered if he had enough coin left to purchase a horse for them to ride, or perhaps river passage up to Avignon. He could barter with the golden ram pin Isaac had given him, but he would hate to part with it. Once he was on land, the vibrating presence of the Valley rose steadily in Elisha's perception, threatening to topple him with its growing strength. The Valley within him echoed that rhythm, and Elisha's hollow frame, battered by sickness, felt again that horrid rush. Back in Heidelberg, Vertuollo announced would unravel Elisha like a bit of poor embroidery, and by God, he'd nearly done it. Elisha sought balance between the power of death and the urgent need of living.

Taking up their things, Jude and Elisha walked up the jetty, the boy's hand knotted into his, head bowed. As they passed the group of Jewish families who had disembarked from the boat, one of the men leaned over and whispered, "You're the man the rabbi wrote us about? I am Menahem—please tell me if you need any help." He straightened and looked away as if he had said nothing of importance.

Hoofbeats ahead announced the arrival of a new party and the soldiers parted in rough attention as the newcomers approached. Elisha extended his senses, coaching Jude to do the same, squinting at the mounted men. Priests, from what he could see, and one in the rich red cloak and square hat of a cardinal. One long face he recognized right away: Father Osbert, the inquisitor he'd last seen in England, examining the evidence of Elisha's own sorcerous crimes. Before he could identify any others, Jude's fingers dug into his hand. Through the contact, he was screaming.

Chapter 24

❖

Elisha settled his other hand over Jude's, projecting calm. *"That's it, Jude, you are in control. You make the choice. Who is it you fear? Can we face him together, as we faced my enemy?"*

In answer, Jude sent him a blinding flash of red.

The cardinal. *"You have been so brave on the ship and earlier. Can you be brave again?"*

Jude hesitated, but the incoherent terror of his touch had ebbed, and he swallowed hard. Finally, he gave a nod, and Elisha returned his attention to the gathering.

Father Pierre stood before the mounted men, hands spread in greeting. Elisha unfurled his awareness, using his knowledge of the young priest to listen attentively and begin to understand his French. Thankfully, with French often spoken in England, even so long after William the Conqueror, the language was not completely foreign.

"We could not land at Marseilles, Cardinal, and I am sorry for your trouble," Father Pierre said. "Had I known you were waiting, I should have tried to send a message."

The cardinal's head tipped down, his red hat toward the jetty as he listened, but his fingers tapped out impatience upon the pommel of his saddle. "Yes, Pierre. You should have expected some sort of escort, what with all of the messages that have come and gone in recent months. The Holy Father does hold you in some esteem after all."

His voice sounded curiously familiar, and Elisha bristled at the cardinal's tone, addressing the archpriest as if he were a wayward child, as if the Pope's esteem were ill-placed. Then he remembered the rumors of Father Pierre Roger's birth, that some claimed him to be the son of the Pope himself. Did the cardinal imagine that Father Pierre's position was merely a matter of his parentage? Even before the cardinal raised his head, Elisha placed that voice, too sinuous for sincerity: Renart, the French mancer who had orchestrated the ruse in the Alps, bringing Brigit's still body to give birth there to the legend she had apparently become.

Sealing his own skin and raising his defenses, Elisha encouraged Jude to do the same. The boy's presence slammed shut. He learned fast, giving Elisha some reassurance about the next stages of their journey. Already, he had learned to master his fear and to control his presence, and his sensitivity enabled a depth of awareness few could match. With time and patience, Elisha realized, Jude could become one of the greatest of magi. If they had the time. Cardinal Renart's head twitched as if his eyes traveled to the boy, then up to meet Elisha's gaze. He revealed nothing, projecting holiness, arrogance, impatience. Arrogant indeed if he did not care that anyone else would notice his rudeness to his fellow cleric.

"I am sure I do not deserve such esteem, Cardinal. Perhaps you can tell me, what is the best way to arrange transportation for these families?" Father Pierre continued.

"That is hardly your concern, Pierre. Let them make their way as they will. We have a mount for you, it will have to be sufficient."

At the cardinal's side, Father Osbert, the inquisitor,

gazed at Elisha with frank curiosity. "Here is another person I believe the Holy Father shall take notice of, Cardinal." He gestured toward Elisha. "Some months back, I was sent to England with a commission to investigate certain rumors of miracles surrounding this man. He is somewhat changed, but I should recognize that face even were he to lose half his weight."

"Few men have witch's eyes," murmured a voice behind them, a slight figure at ease on a tall horse. Harald.

Elisha's heart leapt to find an ally, but he gave no sign of it. Instead, he found words in English, his own tongue sounding foreign to his ears. "I should be pleased and honored to meet the Holy Father, if that suits him, Father."

Father Osbert stared down at him, then straightened, adopting a tone of authority. "I command, by order of the Holy Office of the Inquisition, that you shall stand before the inquisitors to answer for charges of witchcraft in the recent events of the succession of the crown of England."

The charge jolted Elisha, and he took an involuntary step back while Father Pierre asked in French for an explanation. Father Osbert repeated his charge in French and Latin both, his voice stronger with each repetition — or perhaps it only seemed that way as all other voices fell silent in a spreading wave. Cardinal Renart stared down from his horse, a prim little smile on his lips. Elisha had fought a hundred battles since the one that placed Thomas firmly on the throne in England — he had thought the matter far behind him, and Lord knew, he had the greatest battle yet to come. But he wasn't sure what could be done about it — he had already said he willingly went on to Avignon. How would resisting such a summons, or even flatly denying the charge, reflect on his innocence? His word against the cardinal's here would surely fail, but Father Osbert was a fair man, a good observer. Elisha caught his breath. No matter: Father Osbert was the face of the inquisition. The idea of facing the inquisition, here in France where the Templars had burned and the Cathars before them, chilled Elisha to the very heart.

"I am not at all sure it is wise to bring a foreigner," said Cardinal Renart, "especially a practitioner of the black arts, into the city of the Pope himself, especially in such dark days as this. Guards! Attend him well. We shall find a cart to transport the witch and his familiar."

The soldiers who accompanied the two priests, including Harald, rode up to surround Elisha and Jude, some of them jostling Father Pierre, taking their master's hint about how he should be treated.

Brow furrowing, but only slightly, Father Pierre stepped out from between the soldiers. "Then there is no violence here against the Jews? You believe, Cardinal, that it is safe for them to proceed without escort to Avignon?"

"Why shouldn't it be? I say again, it is not your concern. We have been sent to ease your own passage, and surely their arrival will be eased by speeding your own." Renart turned in his saddle to address a mounted priest behind him. "Arrange for a cart for the prisoners—barred if possible, chains if not."

Elisha checked the magic that rose within. "As I have said, Father, I should be pleased to ride to Avignon and present myself to whatever demands the Holy Father requires of me. There is no need to treat me, and certainly not the boy, as a prisoner or a criminal."

"After all we've heard of you? Surely there is a demonic presence here," Renart said, "in either one or the both of you. The sooner you are submitted to trial, the safer we all shall be." He leaned down, looming over them. "In fact, given how widely traveled you seem to be, sir, I shouldn't wonder if this pestilence itself is linked to your coming." Jude shrank against Elisha's side, his jaw clenched so tightly that Elisha feared for his teeth.

"In the interests of haste, Cardinal," Father Pierre

broke in, "please allow the doctor and his son to take the horse you brought for me. I shall remain to shepherd the Jews to Avignon." He gave a slight bow as if the cardinal had proposed this course and then dismissed him.

Renart's lips pinched at the reference to Jude as Elisha's son, but neither of them corrected the impression. A demonic orphan would be ill-served in any nation, and in an enclave of priests, Elisha could only imagine what would happen to him. Even if Elisha could not protect him, at the least they would not be alone. "Very well," the Cardinal snapped. "See if you cannot shepherd them to the proper obedience to the Lord." He jabbed the sign of the cross over his chest and jerked the reins to swing his horse away.

"Cardinal," said Father Osbert carefully. "I fear that the Holy Father may be displeased if Father Pierre does not accompany us back to the city."

"Then Pierre can explain to His Holiness that he felt it more important to consort with Jews than to answer the summons of God's representative on this earth. Come—we have wasted enough time already, Father Osbert."

"I would request that the inquisition wait for my own presence, Cardinal," Father Pierre called out, plucking up his robe to trot a few steps after the retreating horse. "I have observations of this man from his time in Rome which may be pertinent."

The cardinal's servant brought up the empty horse, richly arrayed with silver on its bridle and saddle, and a velvet blanket decked with the fleur-de-lis. Elisha mounted and put down his arm to swing Jude up behind him. The boy clung about his waist, his every muscle taut, and Elisha almost wished the ship remained in harbor so he could send the child away from anyone who caused him such terror. How would he balance his responsibility to Jude with the problems that faced him now? How could he?

They rode at the center of the gathering, Harald not far off, at ease in soldier's garb, one hand resting at his thigh as he rode, giving no sign at all of their acquaintance. Elisha longed to pepper him with questions. Where was Katherine, and what had brought Harald here, away from the royal court? Clearly, Harald's work required secrecy and so, Elisha ignored him as well. Through the contact of Jude's arms, clenched around his middle, Elisha said, "*The slender guard on our right is a friend. He's the man who gave me those blades. He is here in secret, but he will help us if we need him. Harald is his name.*"

In a long afternoon of riding that made Elisha's legs ache and his empty stomach feel more queasy than ever, they reached Avignon, a walled city at the banks of a broad river, joined by a long bridge to a smaller city dominated by the ramparts of a great castle. The party had stretched out, Cardinal Renart still in the lead, but the inquisitor dropped back, closer to Elisha, watching him. "The land here belongs to the Holy Father, given him by Queen Giovanna of Naples for his private use, but across the river belongs to the king, King Phillip, and he has built this bridge to show the union of heavenly and earthly authority," said Father Osbert.

When they first met, Elisha thought the inquisitor might be a French spy, but his dry words showed it was the Pope he served with all his heart. King Phillip was already a tool of the mancers—it remained to be seen if this "union" joined the Pope in such service as well.

At the city gates, guards pulled bars and unlocked great locks, allowing them to pass. Father Osbert covered his nose and mouth with a kerchief as they entered. A wagon-load of corpses rumbled in the other direction, and the winds carried the scent of sickness and death. At least here, they still had men to carry away the dead.

The papal palace occupied one long side of a vast square, dominated by a series of tall, square towers, marching along a hillside toward the river and its bridge. At the crest of the hill, a group of windmills swooped their long arms into the sunset, gathering rose and golden light and bringing it downward, the unity of Heaven and Earth indeed, but Elisha and Jude were taken aside, toward a thick, rectangular building with narrow windows and too many guards. Inside the soldiers stripped his medical kit and his every relic, eyeing them as if they were the evidence of murder, Elisha suspected his own inquisition would happen all too soon.

Chapter 25

❖

As it happened, Elisha and Jude remained isolated in their prison for four days. The guards spoke little, only delivering meals twice a day through a slot in the door, removing the chamber pot, and locking the door behind them. Elisha and Jude had more space than on the ship and two narrow beds, so they occupied themselves in magic, Elisha aware at every moment of the irony and also the urgency: He was being held for sorcery, and could not stop himself even then from practicing—and from sharing his knowledge with Jude through contact, silent and precise. He introduced Jude to the laws of knowledge and mystery, though the distinctions puzzled the boy. The law of contagion, which governed the connection between a talisman and the thing it represented, Jude already knew intimately. When the tension of the truth intruded, they played at lies, each inventing ever more absurd claims to dispel the doom that seemed to hang over them. Jude practiced finding affinities between unlike things and exploiting them to magical advantage, and each little victory eased Elisha's mind that much more.

Their single narrow window showed a thin slice of the papal palace, shining above its city. When the breeze blew off the river, they could hear the windmills chopping the air, their sails crisp, but when the wind changed, it carried the stench of dying. The pressure of the Valley swelled daily, leaving Elisha restless. His strength slowly recovered, but the meager fare they received from the guards did little to help. The ever-present Valley made it hard to conceal his presence from any local mancers as the passage of the dead breathed straight through him, infusing him with power. At times, it flared so strongly with the dying that it pierced him all over again, evoking Vertuollo's attack so he sat breathless, struggling to keep it away.

On the third evening, the plate shoved through the slot on the door came with the brush of a familiar hand, and a folded bit of paper. In German, it read, "Courage. She comes. Trial tomorrow." He wished Harald could linger long enough to talk with him, but understood why it could not be so. She comes: Katherine. Trial tomorrow. That night, Elisha dreamed of fire, burning again as if with fever, limbs bound, and no one come to save him at all. He woke to Jude's howl of terror, the boy shaking him to make the dream stop. Two sensitives, bound to each other by affection as well as by the lessons they shared; their awareness of each other increased daily. Just as once Elisha and Mordecai had come to know each other, a dangerous intimacy.

A key rattled at the latch and the door groaned inward. "Come!" barked the guard outside, leader of a phalanx of men with Harald among them, straight and silent. Jude took a deep breath, but did not cry out. Instead, he crafted a projection of confidence even as he glanced uncertainly at Elisha. Together, they walked out of the building and across the great plaza to the papal palace. Would the Pope himself oversee such a trial? The heat of early summer gave way immediately to chill and gloom inside the thick stone building. In a large chamber with richly painted walls and carved capitals on every column, an assembly of clergymen already waited with Father Osbert at their head and Cardinal Renart at his right hand. Echoes reached Elisha from several points in the crowd, and he found Guy de Chauliac occupying a bench to one side. Did he still have the tainted sachet Danek made, or did it even now rest with the Pope, infecting him? Then all other thought left him. Right next to Guy sat a pale, red-haired beauty, gazing at Elisha with disinterest. Brigit.

She wore a gown of blue that echoed every portrait of the Virgin ever painted. She must have chosen it for that reason alone; the color did not suit her, yet she glowed with youth and life, and Elisha could easily imagine her at the center of a worshipful cult. Indeed, her handmaiden, Gretchen, stood beside her, glaring at him from across the hall. Brigit idly rested her cheek on her hand, gazing into nothing, as if the proceedings bored her, or as if she remembered the angel's wing on the day her mother had died. He caught his breath, his throat feeling suddenly too dry.

Jude let out a cry, and Elisha turned his gaze from Brigit to find Katherine squeezing past him on the left. "*I thought your true love was a man,*" she said through a fleeting touch.

"*I loved Brigit,*" he told her, "*but she was never true. Thank you for coming.*"

"*Harald said you were pale and overwrought, but you look half-dead. Who's the boy?*"

"Step aside, milady, this is the accused."

"Oh, forgive me, I was simply looking for a seat." Katherine pressed onward, his hand tingling with the sense of her concern. A pair of monks stared up at her, wide-eyed, and moved over on their bench to let her sit, continuing to stare as if at a viper. Katherine had beauty of her own, with her keen gaze and soft lips, despite the traces of silver in her hair, but only a few monks worried for their souls would spare her a glance with Brigit in the room.

"*She is our friend as well,*" Elisha told Jude.

"*But she is one of them.*"

"*Yes, that, too.*"

Two more mancers mingled with the crowd, one in a monk's habit, the other a townsman, both otherwise unremarkable.

Father Osbert motioned the soldiers forward, Elisha and Jude with them, and opened the proceedings with a prayer, then he lay his palms on the table before him and said in Latin, "You are summoned before the Inquisition to answer charges of black magic in the death of the Archbishop of Canterbury, in August of the year of our Lord, 1347. For the benefit of those gathered, allow me to state that I was sent to England on behalf of the Holy Office of the Inquisition last year to investigate the rumor of miracles or magic in regards to the death of King Hugh and subsequent accession of his son, King Thomas. I was therefore present in that land at the time of the events under consideration here." He glanced over at Cardinal Renart who said, "Proceed." The cardinal-mancer added a spike of menace that drew a yelp of fear from Jude.

Every eye turned to the boy as he burrowed closer to Elisha's side.

"Who is this child and why does he have such a strong reaction in the presence of the men of God?" Renart rose from his ornate chair and strode closer, his red robes sweeping the floor.

Jude cried out, then stuffed his hand into his mouth, trying to hide. Elisha sent him strength, pleading with him to stay silent as Elisha explained, "He is my ward, Your Eminence, and I am treating his condition."

"His . . . condition? And what condition would that be?"

Renart was using Jude's fragility to undermine Elisha's confidence and suggest a demonic association to the inquisitors. "It is not relevant to the matter at hand, Your Eminence." Elisha stared him down, in spite of the fact that Renart stood a few inches taller. He projected his power. "Please do not make the plight of a sick child an object of the inquisition."

"I am inclined to agree with the accused, Your Eminence," Father Osbert said. "We are here to examine the accused, not to concern ourselves with his ward."

"Then I suggest his ward should be removed from the chamber so that he and the court may concentrate on the matter at hand." Renart spread his own hands, displaying the patently clear logic of this suggestion.

"I have no objection, Your Eminence," Father Osbert said.

Elisha protested, "He is fearful of being in a foreign place, surrounded by strangers, Your Eminence. For his health, I would rather he stay with me."

Renart gestured then toward Guy. "We have with us the Holy Father's own physician. He can accept your ward until such time as it is appropriate to return him—and he can oversee any necessary treatments for the boy's well-being."

Standing abruptly, Guy gave a heavy sigh and a shake of his head. "Your Eminence, I've met this child before, in the hospital at Salerno."

"You see?" Renart displayed this evidence to the crowd. "Then you are ideally suited to care for him."

Guy's head kept shaking. "No, I'm afraid not. While in hospital, the child displayed an almost total madness, to the extreme of fighting the nuns who tried to feed him, in addition to wild outbursts in the presence of physicians and others who attempted to treat him." His eyes met Elisha's the bushy eyebrows raised. "In fact, it speaks rather well to the medical skill of the accused that the child has shown such marked improvement in the short weeks since I last saw him."

Elisha bowed his head slightly in thanks, but Renart pressed, "What was his diagnosis at that time?"

Again, Guy hesitated. "He was remitted to us when the church was not able to treat him."

"The church? What role could the church have in treating problems like those you describe?"

Guy's throat bobbed, and his mouth worked as if he were chewing something over, then he faced the inquisitor Father Osbert. "Father, the boy was believed to suffer a demonic possession. No attempt at exorcism resulted in improvement."

"Explaining his wild behavior in the presence of priests." The cardinal swept forward, causing Jude to flinch and whimper. "The demon within this child fears the men of God and the Word of God." He jabbed a finger toward Jude. "I would not presume to diagnose illness, Doctor, but it is not medical skill, it is demonic knowledge that bonds these two. The child is quiet in the presence of the accused because they share a passion for the devil, and he howls in the face of clergy to warn the accused of the advance of his enemies."

The murmuring of the crowd rose to a of rumble of shock.

"For Heaven's sake," Elisha shouted over them, "He's just scared. He was raised in misery, a prisoner to his own father, he has a right to his fear when so many priests and doctors have hurt him rather than helping him as they should. Where's Father Pierre Roger who sailed with us from Rome? He can attest that Jude showed him no such fear." He searched the room, and did not find the young priest. "Where is he?"

"You are bold to call upon Heaven, sinner," said the cardinal.

Father Osbert said. "We were indeed asked to stay the trial until Father Pierre could be present. Unfortunately, he was injured during his travel to arrive here, and the decision was made to go on without him."

Elisha stepped forward. "Injured? What happened? Were they attacked?"

Renart stalked nearer to the head table. "Another incident which is not germane to this trial. Why does the accused reject examination when it speaks to the question of demonic possession, then seek to distract the proceedings with irrelevancies of his own?"

This provocation swelled Elisha's fury, but he kept it tightly bound. Renart's purpose could only be served by Elisha's anger escaping in a public forum, especially with the Valley so close to him, the potential for deadly magic hovered in his fingertips—exactly what the inquisition sought to prove. "Father Pierre looked after us in Rome and on the voyage, and I haven't been told of his injury." He cast a dark look at the soldiers positioned around the room. "It seems to me that one of us doctors should be with him, and not in here."

"I have done what could be done," Guy snapped, retreating to his bench. "It is in God's hands."

In God's hands. The physician's way of passing on the blame for injuries he could not heal. Elisha forced down his anger. "Please, Father, is there no way that I can see him?"

"Not while this trial is in session, certainly. And not if you should be found guilty and in need of penance to return to the fold of the Church."

"On with it then, Father," said the Cardinal. "Though perhaps it would be more wise to clear the chamber of any unnecessary persons, to safeguard them from the presence of demons."

"There are no demons here," said Elisha, then offered a grim smile and added, "Your Eminence."

"I think we have, at the least, established that you are

in no position to judge such a thing." The mancer stalked back to his seat, spreading his robes as he sat, hands folded. "Proceed."

Father Osbert took a sip from a goblet, and said, "It is customary at this time to ask if there is any man who bears you a mortal grudge and may have added to the accusations against you in the hopes of personal gain, but in this case—"

"Wait." Elisha seized on this. "A mortal grudge? Indeed there has been."

The inquisitor frowned at the interruption. "Who, then?"

"The Archbishop of Canterbury. He undermined my regency and sought to destabilize the kingdom in the face of a forthcoming invasion from France."

Father Osbert gave a long, slow blink, as if allowing that to sink in, and it occurred to Elisha that bringing up the failed French invasion might not aid his cause when the court, and the inquisitor himself, were French. "You are saying that the deceased—God rest his soul—was, in fact, your mortal enemy."

"Yes, exactly. He was a traitor to the crown of England, and as regent, it was my duty to oppose him."

Renart slapped his palms against his thighs, with a resounding smack, and Elisha wondered if he had enhanced his interruption with magic. "This is absurd!" Renart said. "Many of us knew Jonathan, the Archbishop, from his sojourns here as well as from his eloquent statements on behalf of the Church. The accused will do anything to deflect interest from his own sordid acts, even to casting aspersions at a man who was not only a stalwart of the church, but who has passed beyond the pale and cannot speak in his own defense. How can we judge the truth of what you say when the man you accuse is dead, and by your own hand?"

The third man on the daïs, another cardinal, leaned

forward then and spoke in a voice tinged with the sound of Rome. "In England, the native land of both the accused and the man he accuses likewise, his victim, there is indeed such a method." He blinked dark eyes at Elisha. "Trial by Ordeal. If he would swear to the veracity of what he has said, then heat up the iron. If he can carry the iron for seven steps without suffering the corruption of the flesh, then God shall have given His witness." The man smiled beatifically and crossed himself with simple grace, as if he had not just suggested that Elisha carry a red-hot bar of iron in his naked hands. The dreams of burning shimmered in Elisha's mind.

Chapter 26

❖

$\mathfrak{R}$enart came to his feet at once. "This is barbaric. The Holy Father's predecessors have forbidden it and forbidden clergy from overseeing such a thing."

"We are merely seeking recourse to the man's native justice, and to a method allowing the direct intervention of the Lord—should He deign to do so—in discerning the truth." The other cardinal looked to Father Osbert.

"Then let us go to the Holy Father and ask his council," Renart suggested. "We can always delay the trial and simply retain the accused until such time as we are ready to proceed."

It felt strange to have his enemy arguing for a more lenient approach, but then, his enemy knew he could heal himself, and Elisha hesitated, wondering what course to follow when the mancer rejected the idea of torture.

"Mmm. Perhaps that would be wise," said the other cardinal. "The inquisition rarely moves so quickly as this in any case. Surely a few more months are worth being certain of our course."

A few months in prison, while the mancers carried forward their own plans? "No." Elisha squared his shoulders. "Your Eminences, Father, I have no wish to languish in your prison while you search your conscience. I speak the truth, and I am not afraid to prove it, even if it must be by ordeal." His mouth felt dry as he asked to be burned.

"But think of the very evidence you brought from England, Father," Renart said. "You first arrived there when this man had been buried face-down at a crossroads—clear sign that even the English king believed him to be both traitorous and sorcerous."

"Is this so, Father Osbert?" asked the other cardinal. "I have not heard all of your discoveries."

"He was buried, it is true, and the burial, according to those present, involved a great outpouring of protest and devotion from the common folk, only to be followed by what might best be described as fire and brimstone." Father Osbert drummed his fingers. "The coffin was raised at the behest of the local Church, including the Archbishop of Canterbury, prelate of the nation, and found to be empty, Your Eminence, which some there took to be a sign more angelic than demonic. That very archbishop later proclaimed the accused to be of holy rather than malign influence, due in part to the stigmata he bears. And I myself witnessed his laying on of hands for members of a local congregation, though I cannot say that they were healed, for I was not familiar with their injuries, nor the extent of their recovery."

Cardinal Renart narrowed his eyes. "Yet you are still bringing him to trial, Father, that suggests you are not convinced of any divine status. Is it not more probable that the devil allowed his survival during that earlier trial, fomenting rebellion among the lesser classes, elevating him in the eyes of others in order to bring havoc down upon the church of England? His apparent return from such an ignominious execution won him the trust of the very man he later murdered."

"You say that he rose from the grave?" the surgeon, Guy, asked suddenly. "Did he seem to be more impervious to physical harm thereafter?"

Osbert considered the question and consulted the thick manuscript at his side, the familiar book in which he scratched his notes during his sojourn in England. "Yes, I should say that might be so."

"Then it is also possible that he is a revenant, one who has risen from the dead, still animate, but no longer fully souled." Guy regarded Elisha with sharp speculation. "It is a subject I have been researching to see if there might be any plausibility to the rumors of such individuals."

The other cardinal leaned forward, his silk robes crinkling. "But would the ordeal not also show this, any evidence of unholy or inhuman imperviousness to harm?"

"Has the queen recalled anything of herself which might be of use to us?" Father Osbert gestured toward Brigit.

The cardinal inquired, "What has the lady to do with this proceeding?"

"She was there," Guy explained, "but the events that followed seem to have taken her mind, at least for a time. She came to Avignon in pursuit of aid against this affliction, both in the form of medical expertise and spiritual guidance. Alas, she recalls nothing from England, not even that she, by rights, is its queen."

The cardinal gave a little sigh, his face softening as he crossed himself, his pity for the beautiful, vacant queen shining in his every movement. Brigit looked away, chin raised, as if modestly, yet bravely facing whatever she had lost, a figure of sympathy and virtue.

For a long moment, the room held silent, waiting, until Osbert finally said, "Such an ordeal is not without precedent. In the interests of speeding this trial, especially with the other duties we all neglect for this proceeding, I will allow it. Bring a brazier. We shall carry out the ordeal in the yard."

Cardinal Renart bristled with frustration as he swept by, leading the procession out into the square. Two soldiers carried the brazier between them, a short iron rod already thrust into the coals, then the inquisitor and the other cardinal followed. The remaining soldiers closed ranks about Elisha and Jude, hurrying them along while the crowd gathered at their backs and pushed out the doors into the courtyard at the center of the palace. Curls of smoke and fingers of flame rose from the brazier around the iron rod, hypnotic and horrifying.

"You are cold—you will not burn," Jude said, squeezing Elisha's hand.

Elisha squeezed back, but he said, *"I'll have to burn a little, or they will believe the accusations are true."*

"I'm killing you," Jude said, a quick burst of sorrow that shot up Elisha's arm like the stab of a needle.

"I can't die, remember? Whatever they do to me, it is their fault, not yours—their choice."

"Yours to keep me."

Elisha tried to frame an answer, but he saw Brigit walking with Guy, speaking together in low voices, apparently taking no notice of him at all. The other cardinal approached her, giving a little bend of the knee, a courtesy she accepted as her due. There in the sunlight, she seemed to sparkle. Magic, but not of the sort that summoned the inquisition. He once knew her presence as well as his own, but just as he had changed when he refused the Valley during the surgery to repair his fractured skull, she had changed when she awoke after the birth of their child. If the inquisitor knew that Elisha himself had crushed her spirit so deeply, he would be for the stake without a doubt.

Jude's growing agitation pierced Elisha's reverie, and he seized upon a distraction. *"The other doctor, Guy de*

*Chauliac. Your father gave him a talisman made from
your hair. He meant it to be given to the Pope, so he would
die of the pestilence."*

Jude's touch registered his sense of guilt, but Elisha
rejected it. *"That's a lie, Jude. That's what your father
made you—from now on, it is your choice, remember?
While all this crowd are distracted, can you get close to
Guy? You should be able to sense if he still has the talisman. We need to find it, to prevent it staying close to the
Pope."*

Jude gave a serious nod, tracking the surgeon with his
eyes.

Katherine took up a position at right angles, apprais-
ing Brigit from a distance, then tipping her head to
glance in Elisha's direction. The murmuring crowd gathered into a ring around them, Elisha at one end, with the
soldiers and the heat, Father Osbert and Cardinal Renart at the other. A man wearing a laurel wreath and a
dark tunic overlaid with the columned livery of the Colonna barons of Rome stepped up to the other cardinal
and whispered with him, nodding and taking council.
When he joined the group, the fellow brought out a
bound book and began making notes in it.

Elisha recognized his desire for distraction, but he
quelled it, forcing himself to concentrate on the ordeal
to come. He must carry a hot bar of iron seven steps.
Then his hands would be bandaged, and the inquisitor
would check the burns in three days to determine if they
were healing in accordance with God's beneficence on
an innocent man. When Lucius beat him, Elisha did not
cry out, standing on his pride, nor did he then know how
to heal. This time, he must show himself humble, God-
fearing. He must be wounded, but not so badly that it
could be construed as heavenly disfavor, nor so lightly
that it would show him impervious.

He sank to his knees, drawing Jude down with him,

and let him go, pressing his palms together in prayer as he focused his awareness on his hands. When Elisha was imprisoned for killing his brother, Lucius came to him and expressed dismay over his lack of reverence for God. "*Is there anything you do believe in?*" the physician had demanded, and Elisha held up his own hands, skillful and strong. He could block the pain of the injury when he took the iron, but the idea of his hands being burned filled him with dread. His allies, Jude, Katherine, and Harald, could not intervene without risking everything.

"*Your brother is dead, too,*" Jude said, their elbows brushing as they prayed together.

"*I still miss him.*"

"*You think you killed him. That's a lie.*"

Elisha leaned a little nearer, acknowledging the complicated, painful truth. "*Brothers are meant to be there for each other, to be the one you can always depend on, and I failed him.*"

Tentative and a little clumsy, Jude sent him comfort. "*Now you have a new one. The count is the finest brother a man could have.*"

The lie coiled with sly humor, quick as a ferret, reminding him that this moment was a tiny stitch in the tapestry of troubles that built around them. "*He is certainly powerful enough.*" Elisha felt a burst of affection for the child he had claimed. With Jude beside him, Elisha found his focus again, crafting his defense and burying his fear. When he had warded himself as much as he could without growing impervious, Elisha rose. "I am ready."

Jude whimpered softly, reaching after him, and Elisha touched his forehead. "*Stay strong. I can do this, and so can you. Remember the charge I've given you—see if Guy has the talisman.*"

One of the soldiers hefted a pair of blacksmith's tongs

to lift the red-hot bar from the brazier; shimmering heat rose from its surface. Harald stared straight ahead, but his lips compressed into the slightest wince.

Elisha held out his hands, his bare palms before him, the pale scars showing at their centers. A series of other marks, the brands of his torture, traced up his arm beneath his sleeve and Elisha remembered that moment, all too vividly—the shriveling hair, the piercing pain, the smell of his own burning flesh. Brigit's mother, Rowena, burned at the stake for witchcraft on the order of Thomas's father, King Hugh. None but Elisha tried to save her, and that smell would never leave him. His hands trembled, and he quelled a nervous laugh. After all that he had been through, facing a single bar of iron should be as nothing.

The guard swiveled, balancing the burning thing a bit too far from himself. He fumbled it into Elisha's hands, forcing him to lunge a bit and catch it. Elisha cried out when the hot iron struck his skin. It sizzled into him as he turned, the tremors in his hands spreading up his arms, the longing to preserve his own flesh at odds with his choice to claim the ordeal. He turned, shifting his hands to carry the weight and a bit of skin tore. This second cry brought a sustained echoing wail.

Jude ran toward him, tears streaming, hands outstretched.

"Stop him! Do not allow the ordeal to be disrupted!" Cardinal Renart commanded, but it was Katherine who sprang forward and grabbed Jude's arm.

"Come away, boy," she said sternly, hauling him back a few steps, in spite of his shrieking. He slapped and clawed at her hands, and Elisha sensed the swirl of magic rising as she sought to master him, to strengthen her own resistance and reach the boy within the shield of his panic.

Elisha could not afford the attention or the gratitude

that welled in him. In spite of his wards, his own memories of agony broke his concentration, and the pain shot through him, the stench shocking him into memories of branding and cauterization, of a woman at the stake, and Mordecai accepting the flames to forge his own magic. The Valley moaned all around him then, whistling through his heart and thrumming in his ears, as if reminding him it was still waiting.

Elisha lurched forward, one pace, two, three, a stumble that made him instinctively tighten his grip, but he bit down on his voice, lest it trigger Jude to greater hysterics. "*Go, Jude, go. Remember your charge*," he chanted within himself, letting the boy's distraction be a distraction to him as well. A few tears stung his eyes, and he shook them away, staggering the last few paces to drop to his knees at the feet of the clerics and let the bar fall from his grasp. The bar clattered to the ground taking bits of his flesh along with it, and the cardinals leapt back lest it burn them.

Trembling, Elisha stared at the damage, trying to reclaim his focus and force back the pain. Blood seeped from his palms, outlining the shape of the bar, parallel burns marking both hands. Blackened flesh patched the centers, and Elisha realized his old scars, thickened and nerveless, had protected him there. He sent all his awareness to his hands, the pain intensifying as he did so, but enabling him to identify the worst of the burns and push back, healing just a little, just enough to save himself permanent damage. He hoped.

Behind him, Katherine snapped at someone, "Do you have children, Father? I think not. So let me handle the boy." In a softer voice, she said, "You cannot go to him, not yet, do you understand? You're only making this harder."

Father Osbert stooped nearer, inspecting the burns for himself. "Master de Chauliac? Perhaps you can make an examination, for the sake of comparison."

Guy approached, and the two of them bent over his hands, the priest with his fall of gray hair around his tonsure, the doctor with his hairline receding to nearly the same degree. "The injuries appear both appropriate and relatively superficial. Interesting how the earlier scarring resisted the burn." He indicated the pattern with a movement of his finger over Elisha's palm.

"Fascinating," Brigit murmured at his side. Elisha flinched, but again, she took no notice of him. "I am learning so much from you, Doctor. I do so appreciate your taking me into your confidence."

"I am pleased to be a part of your ministry, my lady." They backed off together, leaving Elisha queasy, but not quite sure why. Gretchen cast him a dark look, but turned to follow Brigit. For a moment, Elisha glimpsed Jude in the wake of the surgeon, following Elisha's commission, his scarred face determined despite the tears that still coursed down his cheeks.

A young man in the rough clothes of a laborer and the apron of a barber came to one knee and efficiently wrapped fresh, unbleached cloth about Elisha's palms. "Be careful with these the next few days, sir. You're not to remove the bandages or seek any other treatment— I'll recognize my knots. Can't give you anything for the pain or any poultice for the healing, but after three days, if there's any trouble, we'll be right there, eh?" He flashed a grin, then stepped away.

"Three days. You shall remain in the blockhouse until then." Father Osbert started to withdraw, and Elisha put out his bandaged hand.

"Wait, Father—what about Father Pierre? May I see him?"

"Of course you may, in three days, if you are found to be innocent." The inquisitor gave a slight bow of dismissal and turned away.

A firm hand gripped Elisha's elbow and drew him to

his feet. "*Lord, Elisha, but that was awful*," said Harald with great focus, into the contact. Katherine must have been training him on how to focus his thoughts so they could communicate in secret while out on their missions. "*Will you be all right*?" He hardly needed to ask—his concern flared through the touch.

"*In a few days. Three, apparently.*" Elisha sent his gratitude, letting himself, ever so briefly, be supported by another.

"Is that truly a tactic they use in England? How barbaric," Katherine remarked in German.

Straightening, Elisha gave her a slight bow. "Thank you for tending to my ward, my lady." Then he glanced around. Guy and his party were gone; Jude was nowhere in sight. Damn it, he should have been more careful about his commission—for Jude to find his own hair should have been the matter of a moment, he never meant for Jude to leave the yard. "Did anyone see where he went?"

"Oh, he was right here the whole time—just silent for once." She turned about, then turned again, hands falling to her sides. Her face drained of color, lips parted, but she could not say all that she might, not in public like this. "Sir, do forgive me. He fell silent, as a result of my speaking to him, I thought. He was right here beside me, at least until you fell." She knotted her fingers together, visibly restraining herself from touching him.

Harald released Elisha's arm. "I'll find your ward and bring him to the blockhouse. What's his name?" He spoke with the brusque efficiency of any soldier, though his eyes hinted at his sympathy.

"Jude. He's Hungarian—he doesn't understand most other languages. He might have gone after the other doctor."

With a sharp nod to the guard commander, Harald sprinted through the crowd.

Elisha nearly dropped all over again. He'd been such a fool, thinking Jude was ready for even such a tiny mission. The boy would never survive on his own in a strange city, not with tensions already so high and his clear scars of sickness. But the other soldiers closed around him, nudging him onward, back to his prison. Alone.

Chapter 27

❖

Elisha sat, legs outstretched on his narrow bed, lean-ing his head back against the wall. He conjured up the cold and divorced himself from the agony of the flesh to concentrate on searching for Jude. Letting his aware-ness stretch, he sought any sign of the boy, and found nothing. A few other chill mancers echoed here and there, their presence made visible by the swirls of death they siphoned from the misery all around them, like stones against the rising tide of the plague. Trouble was, when he had worked with Jude these past days, they fo-cused on deflection, on concealing his presence and avoiding the notice of all those he feared, those who might still wish to use him, or to kill him. Now, that very teaching worked against him, for Elisha could not locate him with magic, though he searched for hours, spreading himself thin, drawing the attention of every mancer in Avignon, and perhaps beyond. It didn't matter; they al-ready knew he had come and had responded by trying to prolong his prison sentence.

Withdrawing back into his aching body, he let his head rap gently on the wall as if he could beat some sense into himself. Foolish, not to take Jude's reactions into account, the powerful combination of his devotion to Elisha along with his fear for him. Even just leaving

him behind in the cell would have been preferable to
losing him completely. Surely, if someone had abducted
him, Elisha would have known even through his agony.
At the very least, Jude's shrieking would have alerted
the crowd. That suggested he had left on his own, his
choice, as Elisha had been at pains to point out, whether
in pursuit of Elisha's commission, or simply in horror at
the ordeal Jude was forced to witness, an ordeal for
which he felt responsible. Elisha's hands throbbed with
every beat of his heart.

A rap sounded on the door, then the key rattled and
the door swung open. Elisha rolled his head to get a better view, and sat up straighter as Harald entered, carrying a tray of bread, raisins and soup. Two other guards
stood just outside.

"Sir, I am allowed to give you a report on the search
for your ward." Harald set down the tray on the table
between the heads of the beds, the room so narrow that
their shoulders nearly brushed. As he touched the items,
as if to assure himself everything was there, he slid a thin
salted blade from his sleeve to rest beneath the lip of the
tray, then turned to Elisha, hands held behind him. His
hawkish face looked pinched and pale, lips compressed.
Finally he said, "He did follow Guy de Chauliac for some
distance, but no one seems to know where he went after
that. I have searched the public areas of the city, and
made inquiries at those places most likely frequented by
children, including churches, poor houses, and gardens.
As of yet, I have not located him. All members of the
guard have been informed and will be on the alert, but
given your ward's proclivities, I don't expect they will be
able to apprehend him. Our best hope is that someone
will see him, and we will at least know where he has gone
to ground."

"And that he's safe," Elisha murmured. And alive. He
sagged.

"You should eat, sir. You'll need to keep up your strength."

"How?" Elisha held up his bandaged hands, the thick cloth inhibiting movement. He could barely bring together his thumb and forefinger.

For a moment, Harald's face froze, and Elisha knew he shouldn't have said it. The situation was strain enough on both of them without his frustration spilling over to his friend. The moment passed, and Harald said, "Also, sir, there is a visitor who wishes to see you. The inquisitor has given his permission. If it suits you to admit him, a guard will remain present to ensure that nothing untoward occurs. I am detailed to remain, but I can send one of the officers if—"

"It's fine," Elisha cut in. "You've done your best to find Jude, and he won't make it easy on you, I know that. Who's the visitor?"

"A poet," said Harald, his lips nearly smiling. He crossed to the door and spoke with the guards outside. After a moment, he returned, taking up a post by the foot of Elisha's bed as the laureled Colonna man entered, his dark sleeves fluttering, his head bowed as if the laurel weighed too much for him just now.

With a sigh, he sank onto the opposite bed and helped himself to a few of Elisha's raisins. "Thank you for seeing me, sir, under such difficult circumstances. But lately all circumstances are difficult, are they not?" His Latin had a particular inflection that reminded Elisha of Rome. That and the laurel wreath triggered his memory, and Elisha turned on the bed, sliding his feet to the floor.

"Are you Petrarch? The friend of Cola di Rienzi?"

"Aye, 'tis true." The poet sighed, drooping all the more. "Though that once-august name now conjures only more pain." He set a hand to his heart, then flicked a gaze at Elisha's own hands, bandaged and curled carefully to guard against further injury, and he let go of the guise. "That is what brings me to you, sir. I heard you had been in Rome during the final hours of Cola's great republic, and I wished to hear of it from you, if you will speak."

Elisha set his fingers around the wide base of the flask of wine and managed to lift it for a sip. "You wear Colonna livery."

"Indeed I do, for I am currently in service to Cardinal Giovanni Colonna, that great figure you saw at the trial, a noble lord and a fine prince of the church." He added a twirl of his hand to indicate his employer's lofty status. "Then you are aware of the difficulties suffered by that family during the recent problems in Rome. We sought only to return Rome to her rightful place in the court of the world, to bring the Eternal City back to its glory, and to bring the Holy Father home to the city of Peter." His eyes gazed into the distance as if picturing that miraculous sight. "Alas, in this, we have not yet succeeded, in spite of the aid of both Heaven and Earth. The Holy Father did give his support for the barons to reclaim the city in the face of Cola's . . ." His brow furrowed as he considered.

"Madness," Elisha supplied. He pinched a slice of thick bread and took a bite, watching Petrarch's reaction to the word. The poet's eyes flared, and he sucked in a breath that swelled his chest for a lecture, only to deflate again a moment later, with a nod of his head. His presentation, from his reactions to his words to his clothes, felt slightly absurd, as if he were eternally on stage, performing the role of "poet."

"Then you were there," Petrarch said drily. "His letters to me grew ever more bold, and it became clear that the great escapade was doomed to failure. I went again to the Holy Father, although I feared he would no longer give me his ear after my schemes had so far come to naught."

Listening keenly, Elisha laid out the pieces. Petrarch had supported Cola in his reclamation of Rome, an attempt to bring the chaotic city to peace prior to the Jubilee Year for which Petrarch himself had campaigned. The glory of Rome, an event planned to be the glory of the mancers as well, as they terrorized the thousands who would come there. With Elisha's destruction of the churches there, would the Jubilee Year even be held? But neither Petrarch, who proposed it, nor his Colonna master, was a mancer. How were they linked to the mancers' plot? "It was your proposal to hold a Jubilee Year early, was it not? As part of the revival of Rome?"

"Indeed. I am somewhat known for my eloquence." He brushed the laurel wreath with his fingertips. "But the proposal was of divine origin, sir—none is more surprised than I that, given such exact instruction, the Heavenly Host then allowed the city itself to be cast to ruin and the Holy Father thus dissuaded from his plan to visit."

The Heavenly Host. Elisha tried to parse this thicket of fancy language. "You had a vision from Heaven to suggest the Jubilee?"

Petrarch darted his glance toward Harald who stood at ease, as if bored by the talk, head tipped back, perhaps trying to avoid falling asleep on his feet. Only someone who knew him as well as Elisha did might recognize disguise in the posture. The poet leaned forward, inviting Elisha to meet him in the middle, their heads so close Elisha could feel the other man's breath and see the grief that edged his eyes. "Sir, I was visited by an angel. In the very church of Saint Agricol not five blocks from where we sit." He crossed himself furtively.

Elisha echoed his gesture, acknowledging the holiness of what he said—and hoping to draw him out even more. "An angel. I have seen one, too, but not since I was a child. What was it like?"

"He was more beautiful than any mortal. Glowing with the glory of the Lord." His fingers spread and swirled, his gestures restricted by his desire for privacy. "With a fall of hair near as bright as my Laura's." His eyes brimmed with tears.

Elisha set his fingertips on the other man's knee in sympathy. "Laura must have been very beautiful."

Nodding eagerly, Petrarch said, "Laura was worthy of a thousand poems, sir. Had you arrived only a few weeks earlier, you might have seen her to judge for yourself. And yet, to be in her presence was to find yourself devoid of judgement, lost in her smile and her eyes."

"I am sorry to have missed that chance. Was it the plague?"

"A plague indeed." Petrarch shook his head, and wiped away his tears. "When shall I again write of her grace, and what words could capture the depth of my sorrow?"

Something in the poet's declarations struck Elisha as staged, already composed for the benefit of an audience, and he wondered how many times Petrarch had used the same phrases. "I'm sure there are no words."

"None." His breath seeped out in waves of sadness, unfeigned, in any case.

After a moment, Elisha said, "You were speaking to me of your angel."

"His presence overwhelmed me, nearly placing me in terror at his greatness, and he spoke to me in a perfect Roman dialect, a master of the languages of man, no doubt."

Through the contact, Elisha caught the vision as Petrarch spoke of it. A beautiful, bright and pale man, with a long fall of hair, appearing in a church and speaking the language of Rome. Lord Vertuollo, the count's son, the family resemblance clear in Petrarch's memory. "He asked your aid in planning a Jubilee Year and convincing the Pope to attend?"

Petrarch brightened. "I wondered why he did not address His Holiness directly, but I think the angel wanted to gather the strength of man as well as of Heaven. A shame his heavenly favor extended only so far, in spite of his visits."

"I saw my angel only once," Elisha told him. "How many times were you favored?"

"Oh, that's not what I mean." Petrarch gave a roll of his hand. "He came three times to entreat my aid, and also to offer a boon, a gift to me in the darkness to come. He gifted me a relic so great it could defend the bearer against all earthly ailment."

Elisha adopted a tone of conspiratorial sympathy. "But it didn't work—Laura still died."

The poet blinked. "It worked perfectly. I gave it to my brother. The other monks of his abbey have succumbed one by one to the pestilence, but he remains, vigilant in his aid of them."

Brothers should depend upon each other, as Elisha had told Jude, but this seemed a step too far. Feeling thick as a board, Elisha said, "The angel gave you a talisman against plague, and you gave it to your brother instead of your wife."

"Laura was never my wife, sir! Oh, no. Laura was my muse, the light of my life, and the beacon to my soul." He leaned back, gazing skyward with a lift of his hand. "And so she remains, in the perfection of her youth, now that she has passed on to Heaven."

The poet had loved her, that much was clear in his every line and aching look, yet Petrarch chose to let her die rather than to let her fade into old age and mere humanity.

Elisha thought he had never heard a thing so revolting. His own brother died by suicide. If Elisha had the chance to save him, or to save his love, what would he have done? Which love was the stronger, which the more worthy? His brother's life bled away into the soil of his workshop, that soil Elisha used to wear in a vial around his neck, invoking the terrible power of that death to draw him home to England—to the one he loved. Was his choice any better? Who was he to disdain another man's use of the dead? "I should like to visit that chapel where the angel came," he said. "To offer my devotions in such a blessed place." And to identify the relic that made it possible for a mancer to arrive.

Petrarch smiled. "When you are free to do so, sir, I should be well-pleased to escort you there." Outside, bells rang the hour, and the poet jumped up. "Ah, I see I have strayed too long, and not even asked you what I should. I shall come again, if it please you, to hear the tragic tale of the death of Rome." He thrust out his hand, then snatched it back and bowed instead. "Thank you for your ear and for your sympathy. I pray to the Lord that he shall grant your innocence." So saying, he swept away into the hall.

Harald tossed back a glance, raising an eyebrow, and Elisha gave a shrug. Would Harald make the connection to the mancers in this strange tale of angels? "The church of Saint Agricol, sir? I will see if the inquisitor will allow it early. He may well grant such a visit as sign of your contrition." Flashing his fierce grin, Harald bowed and was gone, the cell door slamming behind him.

Chapter 28

Elisha slept fitfully, dreaming that he chased Jude through a tangle of streets lined with the corpses of the dead, then that Jude was among them, buried in a heap of bodies Elisha must dig through to find him. When he cleared the mound, he fell into a cave below and found himself surrounded by mancers, including Brigit and Katherine both, blood dripping from their hands as they reached for him. He woke sweating, as if the fever of the plague returned, his hands throbbing. Mancers pretending to be angels to lure *desolati* to their cause. Mancers trying to bend the Church to their will, the last great institution that could survive through the downfall of kings and the dead in the streets. Was the Pope already with them? Danek's attempt to infect him suggested otherwise, but how could Elisha find out? If an accused sorcerer asked for an audience could it conceivably be granted?

Elisha moved the salted blade under his pillow and hoped it might cut these nightmares, but he found no more rest, losing himself instead in the submersion of his thoughts and emotions, a level of awareness that allowed him to imagine he slept. When he finally abandoned his bed, he slid the blade into his boot, a hollow hardness along his ankle.

When the poet came back the next day at lunch,

Elisha interrupted the poet's ramblings to tell Petrarch what he wanted to know about Cola's downfall and the state of Rome. He steered the conversation back to the vision of the angel, but learned nothing more, nor did his probing about the Pope himself reveal anything new.

"Some whisper that the Holy Father is too greatly enamored of the earthly wealth of his position, but it seems to me only his due," the poet declaimed. Elisha, having seen no more of the palace than its courtroom—better appointed than those of the English king or the Holy Roman Emperor Ludwig—could not yet judge on that account.

"Many fear that he is too closely bound with King Phillip," Elisha said. "I think that may be the greater concern."

"Well, they must be neighbors. Without the gift of this land to the Holy See, there is also the question of the Pope being vassal to a king, by virtue of the land he holds. I deem that a matter for lesser minds. The Holy Father answers to a higher lord than a simple crown." He waved off the entire consideration, and asked instead for a description of Elisha's own angel, which Elisha delivered, neglecting to mention that his angel was the mother of the "queen" they revered for her pale beauty and fragile state. The last thing he needed was to start a rumor that Brigit herself was divinely born.

In the midst of this conversation, Harald knocked at the door, rousing the guard who stood in the room, and admitted himself. "Forgive the interruption, sirs, but I have news."

"Have you found Jude?"

Harald's face fell. "Alas, no." His eyes pleaded for Elisha's faith. "But the inquisitor has granted his permission for a visit to the church of Saint Agricol, for the betterment of your soul." At another time, this might have been a jest between them, but the loss of Jude still weighed on both men, and Elisha merely nodded.

"Excellent! I have a few more minutes, only, but allow me to bring you there and show you the place, then perhaps these men can escort you back?" Petrarch bounced up, jostling the laurel wreath upon his head, and the soldiers parted to let them through. A half-dozen men joined ranks to bring them to the church, which lay a few blocks away. Aside from the ringing of church bells, the city loomed near-silent around them, many houses shuttered and barricaded while others lay open, with unbarred doors that suggested the hasty departure of the occupants. While in Rome the streets echoed with weeping, with rage, or with the too-gay celebration of lives too short, Avignon brooded over the dead, resigned to the mounting losses, emotions restrained, perhaps by the nearness of the Holy Father who oversaw the world on behalf of the unresponsive Lord.

Elisha, who had long distanced himself from God, felt the weight of that absence now, surrounded by churches in a city dominated by the massive palace of the chief Shepherd, with the sheep ever-dwindling, ever more anxious, ever more angry. His own anger against God had been indulgent, personal—if all men turned away from God, and from the leaders they could no longer trust, what happened then? The world as they knew it disintegrated into confusion, terrified masses of *desolati* ruled by necromancers who sucked their strength from the dying all around them, and molded the new world into a shape of their choosing. Mancer-lords would become mancer-kings, mancer-cardinals would rise to mancer-popes, exterminating the magi who might defy them and enslaving everyone who remained.

A boy darted across the street, and Elisha froze, resisting the shove of the guard behind him, but the boy had lank blond hair and stopped at the building, coughing blood and breathing too hard. He propped himself up with a hand, revealing the bulge of darkness beneath his arm, then he plunged onward, up the steps of a house, where a woman took him in, already scolding by the time the door shut behind them.

The soldier pushed again. "Get a move on!"

Elisha obeyed, catching Harald's quick glance.

"I see you are still missing your ward," Petrarch said. "Truly, it is a pity. So many parents will be without children, and children without parents. Here I had believed us on the verge of breaking with the darkness of the past, taking with us only its glory, to birth a new age of the dignity of man." He spread his arms, then let them sink. "But it shall have to await our recovery from this great misfortune."

"If recovery there shall be," muttered one of the soldiers.

"Ecco là!" Petrarch announced in Italian. "Here is the church. But I shall have to hurry."

The pale stone building loomed ahead of them, with two great, peaked doors, richly carved and somewhat in contrast to the austere lines of the papal palace itself. The church gave the appearance of a holy space carved out from a fortress. Inside, the ceiling towered over them, with sweeping arches and a glory of stained glass windows in the nave, presiding over a scene of misery. A few people crouched among the pillars, some in attitudes of prayer, some slumped over. A few of these occupied irregular shadows, the blood and fluids that leaked upon dying, their smell mingling badly with the scent of incense and candles. Dark, fresh shades lingered through the gloomy church, so still in their deaths that Elisha longed for the battles of shadow he had witnessed in England, even the tragic suicides, the women lost in childbirth, the murders, beatings and drownings—even those had some sense of the heroic struggle of life. Every person who died should at least be striving toward something worth the struggle, be it the life of a child or the service of a king. This death smothered with indifference, crushing the spirit even as it destroyed the flesh, leaving these silent, standing shades, sentinels to a weary desolation.

"Here, this is the place." Petrarch had brought out a kerchief to cover his nose and mouth as he led the way toward an alcove at one side. A woman knelt there, her presence seething with hope and fear. Katherine. "Ah, Madame, forgive us the intrusion," said Petrarch.

"Not at all, sir. The Lord's house always has room." She shifted over deliberately toward the left, where Elisha stood, so that he must kneel between them.

"It was here," Petrarch whispered, with a glance to see if Katherine objected to the conversation. "I knelt in prayer, and bowed my head, then I was touched with the light—with the wailing as of lost souls crying out unto the Lord, and when I looked up, there he was, beside the altar." He crossed himself reverently, kissed his fingers and touched the altar itself. "Alas, I must go. The cardinal is a demanding master. I shall hope for your acquittal on the morrow. In the meantime, may your soul be lifted by this holy place." With a nod, Petrarch rose and departed, the soldiers shuffling themselves about to maintain their watch over Elisha.

Elisha imitated the poet's gesture, crossing himself and reaching out to the altar, feeling the chill sting of a torturous death. One of the mancers' forged relics resided in this altar, a portal to the Valley. He was about to withdraw, when Katherine's hand joined his, fingers splayed to grip the stone, her smallest finger touching his hand, the exposed flesh above the bandage. *"You look half-dead, Elisha, what has happened to you?"*

"I had the plague."

She gasped aloud, then swallowed, darting him a look,

her eyes glossy with unshed tears. "*Sweet Mary, my angel, how? When?*"

"*I had to, in order to know it, and maybe to cure it.*" The wash of his emotions heated their contact.

"*Jude gave it to you.*" Her touch sizzled with anger.

"*Because I asked him to. Believe me, that was the last thing he wanted to do.*"

"*You survived it, yet you still can't cure it,*" she said with bitter finality.

"*Perhaps one by one, but I cannot stop it. I had to know for certain.*"

A flash of chill steel strengthened Katherine's back, bringing up her shoulders. "*Would it help to kill him? I know you'd hate that, as would I, but if he is the carrier, then surely—*"

"*No, Katherine.*" He reeled at the thought, nearly snatching back his hand. "*There are too many others, too many small ways it spreads. Killing him would stop nothing but his chance to become the master of his own life for once.*"

"*Forgive me. Clearly, you know much more than I.*"

They knelt a long moment, as stone on stone, no emotion shared between them save this frosty silence.

At last, she told him, "*Harald followed a mancer here, Lord Nicolas of Orleans. Harald believed there was more going on than simply a courtier paying a call to the papal city, so he has not yet killed the man, but instead got himself hired as a papal guard—there have been many openings of late. Then, of course, he spotted Renart from your drawing, and asked for me. When I finished my business, I came. It was nothing to do with you.*"

The fact that she withheld her emotions displayed her hurt more than any contact might have done. Had he been too angry? If her suggestion to kill Jude had had merit, would he still have rejected it? "*Thank you for carrying out your duties with such diligence.*" He sent a slight apology, but she offered no response to that.

"*What brought you here?*" she asked. "*Renart, I assume.*"

"*They need the Pope, or at least, enough of the papal authority to destroy the Church, too. Do you know if the Pope has been influenced?*"

"*He's met with Renart, of course, but he meets with many cardinals, when his physician allows him to meet with anyone.*"

"*Guy de Chauliac?*" Interesting. What if the doctor himself had been influenced, and his direction to his esteemed patient was a marker of their control.

"*That priest you asked after, Pierre Roger? I heard some of the nuns talking. Bandits strung a net across the river where the priest was sailing. Apparently, it caused the boat to crash, and he was injured, along with some of the Jews, but they were able to fight off the bandits and bring him here.*"

At their backs, one of the guards cleared his throat significantly. "We must return."

Elisha withdrew his hand, holding his palms lightly together, then crossing himself. "Forgive the disruption, Madame," he murmured to Katherine as he stood.

She gazed up at him, her eyes once again gone moist. "As I said, there is nothing to forgive. Peace be with you."

"And also with you."

Harald fell in beside him on the walk back to the blockhouse, hand on his sword-hilt. They crossed a triangular plaza fronted by palaces, and a low wall surrounding a garden where a few people sat or stood, listening to a woman singing about the miracles of the Virgin. Two of the company gave off the sinister vacancy of mancers. Between them, not screaming, nor struggling, nor bound, clad in fine velvet with a cap on his shaven head, sat Jude.

Chapter 29

❖❖❖

One of the guards noticed as well, giving a snort. "Seems your ward's found a better guardian, eh?" He thrust his chin in the direction of the well-dressed family in their lovely garden, surrounded by the blossoms of springtime.

Elisha's heart ached along with his hands. He longed to break from his guard and dash across the plaza, catching Jude in his arms, asking what happened, begging him to return.

"I shall address him, sir," said Harald. "It was my task to find him for you, and in that I have failed. Let us at least be sure of his circumstances." Not waiting for a reply, Harald strode across the plaza, but the singer finished, and her audience stood, applauding, and filing back into the house. "Hey!" Harald lengthened his stride. "Jude, stop!"

The boy hesitated upon the steps, glancing back.

Elisha raised his hand in greeting, his awareness racing between them, building from his knowledge of the boy. Before he gained more than the briefest sense of his warmth and distance, Jude turned and followed the others inside.

"Yes? May I help you?" asked one of the women.

Harald glanced back, apparently looking for some

confirmation of how to proceed, then said, "That boy who was with you, who is he?"

"An orphan who came to my attention. I understand his former guardian stands accused of dreadful crimes. In times like this, soldier, we have more need of charity than ever." She smiled down at him. "He did wish to send a gift to his guardian." She reached into a pouch at her side and produced a small object, which she placed in Harald's grasp. "Perhaps you might deliver it?"

"Thank you, Madame." He gave a stiff bow, and marched back to join them, tight-lipped, free hand resting on his sword-hilt, the other holding out a small sachet stitched with a cross.

Elisha accepted it, smelling the herbs it contained, and feeling the sting of Jude's panic and pain. The lock of hair his father had torn from his head was inside. "When I am free, I shall return," Elisha murmured, but it seemed hopeless: Having succeeded in his mission for Elisha, Jude had returned to the familiar company of mancers. His silence now was merely another sort of screaming, the defense that provided safety, keeping Elisha safe from him—or was Jude choosing the status that came with power unabashedly abused? What child would not wish to be well-fed, unafraid of violence or death, clad in velvets instead of rags? A child should not have to choose between comfort and trust, but Elisha had a sinking dread that, if he did return to talk with Jude, it would be Elisha who provoked Jude's shrieking terror. The scar at his side, where Jude had cut him, throbbed in time with his palms as they walked back to the blockhouse.

In the morning, Elisha picked at his food, waiting for the moment they would reveal his burns and declare his guilt or innocence. Madness, really, this sort of justice. Thanks to Jude and his father sharing the plague, Elisha knew the body more deeply than ever, all the tiny things that must happen within, whether to spread a sickness, or to heal a burn. If any one of those little things went wrong, even the most innocent man could be infected. God knew Elisha had seen it happen often enough on the battlefield or in the hospital. He felt vaguely guilty, as if he should do a penance for his ability to escape that danger while so many others must face it. Even so, his innocence depended not on his level of healing, but on his inquisitor's interpretation of it.

A rapping on the door startled him, and the familiar guards stood outside, opening the door for his exit. In the courtroom, a smaller crowd gathered, including Father Osbert, Cardinals Renart and Colonna, Guy de Chauliac, and the young barber who had applied the bandages. Brigit was nowhere in sight, making Elisha both grateful and nervous.

The barber stepped up to inspect his hands before unwrapping them. "Aye, these are my knots, untouched."

The bandages showed a bit of blood at the edges, along with the crumbs and stains of the last few days. With a sharp pair of scissors, the barber snipped through the top layers and unwrapped the rest, revealing Elisha's palms. The blackened boundaries of the burns set off the redness within, and a few deeper burns where blisters had formed and receded. Elisha held his breath while Guy and the inquisitor examined the wounds for themselves.

"The healing is relatively advanced," the physician remarked.

"But not unduly so," said the inquisitor, "do you think? Would a revenant display such damage and healing?"

"There is no such thing as a revenant," Cardinal Colonna said. "When the flesh has failed, the soul passes on for judgment. If he is adequately healed, then the Lord has shown the way, and we must release him."

"Very well." Guy spread his hands and stepped back.

"It is a matter for the church, not for medicine, to determine." He stared hard at Elisha.

Father Osbert straightened, holding the book of his records. "So, Elisha of London, we find you innocent by means of the trial by ordeal. Go forth, and sin no more."

Cardinal Renart's jaw twitched, his glare blazing at the inquisitor's back, but he said nothing. They had agreed to the ordeal, and now the court must abide by its justice.

Elisha finally released his breath, and bowed. "Thank you, Father." Exposed to the air, his hands stung and throbbed all over again. "May I ask the return of my medical kit and the relics I carried? I should like to speed my healing as best I can."

"Master, may we have your permission to go to the papal infirmary for oils and simples?" asked the barber, causing Guy to break his stare. "The apothecaries in town have little of use, those that remain."

"Very well."

"And Father Pierre, how is he?" Elisha asked.

"Little changed. But I cannot stop you seeing him." Guy stalked away.

Cardinal Renart stood up. "Then we are done here. As you have said, Father, we all have more important duties than this. Myself, I must attend the Holy Father." He, too, swept from the room.

The weight of his cold presence lifted from Elisha's awareness, and he looked to the other two clerics. "How can a man gain an audience with the Pope?"

Father Osbert shook his head. "In spite of your innocence, sir, you are hardly in a position to ask such a thing. You must prepare a petition and have it presented to the papal nuncio, and he shall decide if your request is worthy. Even then, it may take months. Monarchs, bishops, lords, abbots, so many have precedence."

"A petition to the papal nuncio."

"Yes, generally proffered by your own bishop or arch-bishop. Who is inconveniently deceased." Father Osbert's eyes crinkled as if he recognized this irony.

"I'm already in Avignon, there must be another way."

"You could, of course, approach the nuncio yourself to inquire." Father Osbert tapped the book in his hands. "But he has recently passed on due to the pestilence. In the absence of such an official, it is the duty of one of the cardinals to serve as the Holy Father's gatekeeper, as it were. Alas, that man is Cardinal Renart."

Elisha absorbed this last blow with a sigh. Did that explain how the mancers influenced the Pope, not by getting him to do their bidding, but rather by controlling his access to everyone else?

A soldier returned from the blockhouse, holding out Elisha's medical pouch. "Couldn't find no relics, sir."

Elisha checked inside and found his basic tools—tweezers, tooth key, scalpels, needles—and a few packets of herbs, but nothing else. Sometime in the last week, the mancers confiscated his relics, anything that might give him access to their churches and their crimes. Even these small movements sent shafts of pain up from his hands. "When may we go to the infirmary?"

"Oh, right away, sir. I'll take you, then I've patients to see, myself." The barber set off at a brisk pace. "Rounds of the houses, anyhow, seeing who's gone since yesterday."

The scent of sickness permeated even the high walls of the papal palace, and the shifting currents of death moved around them. Few shades lingered in this palace; it was barely older than Elisha himself, and had seen nothing of war. Beyond one wall, eerie wails broke the sounds of the subdued city, and the barber chuckled. "Peacocks and wildcats, sir. The Pope's got a garden for 'em, over yonder."

Like the royal menagerie back in London, where he had killed a lion to save a traitor's life.

Thomas's ring fit too snugly on his finger, but he'd be

damned if he removed it. Up a set of stairs opposite the
tallest square tower, the barber led him to a high corridor.
"Hospital Saint Benezet is just outside the wall here, near
the bridge. Used to be just a dozen patients, and now it's
filled up." He pointed out a window as they passed, then
his hand fell. "Or maybe empty again, at this rate."

"It's carried by fleas," Elisha said. "You've got to
watch out for the bedding, anything made of cloth. Try
oil of rosemary to get them out."

"Fleas?" The man wrinkled his nose. "That's not what
Master de Chauliac says. He's got the Pope standing, sitting, and sleeping between burning braziers to ward off
the miasma."

Elisha wished he could catch the man's arm and use
his magic to wrench away his veils and show him the
truth without terrifying and alienating him. "Trust me,"
he said, adding a sense of honesty and urgency to his
words, but he did not believe anything would come of it.
There were so many theories of the origin of the pestilence, who would put any stock in what Elisha claimed?
The disease originated not in the punishment of God,
nor the power of the stars, nor the imbalance of humors
carried in the miasma of the world, but tiny, ubiquitous
fleas? What power did they have to influence the body?
All the power they needed, once they made contact between a carrier of the plague, and a body that had none.

They passed through a low door into a chamber that
looked like Salerno in miniature, with charts on every
wall, stacks of books and racks of bottled herbs and oils.
Two people looked up at their entrance: Brigit and
Gretchen, the former looking blank and returning to her
work, a quill in hand. The latter met Elisha's glance and
lifted her chin, her eyes flashing and her presence heating with power as if she expected him to attack.

"Good day, ladies." The barber bowed to both, smiling. "Found everything have you?"

"Our studies are progressing well," Gretchen told him, sparing a smile for him, but a fleeting one that vanished again as quickly.

"What do you study, madam?" Elisha asked.

"Medicine." Gretchen reached for a book and flopped it open.

The barber flinched and shrugged. "Usually she's so kind. Guess we interrupted."

"Or she found something that doesn't agree with her." He had not seen her for months, since she escorted Brigit away from the vale of springtime where the baby had been born. Brigit studying medicine and growing close with the Pope's physician—what could that mean? Nothing good, certainly not for the Pope.

The barber cleared a little space on a counter and started fetching out the ingredients for a poultice, starting with oil of turpentine. Elisha nudged that aside with one finger. "Try oil of roses instead, and a bit of egg."

"I don't see how that's advisable."

"Turpentine burns—surely that suggests that using it to take the heat out of my skin would hardly be effective."

The fellow shook his head and found the other ingredients Elisha asked for, mixing them to his patient's specifications, but with his shoulders hunched and his face set the whole time. Still, Elisha needed someone with two good hands to do the compounding and the wrapping, at least until he could perform his own little miracle and heal his palms with magic. Had he looked like that in his arrogant early years as a barber, forced to do the bidding of the surgeons and physicians?

As the barber applied the poultice and started wrapping, Elisha asked, "Can you read?"

"Some. A lot, really." The young man kept his gaze averted. "Sometimes read in here, when I've got the time." That flash of a nervous smile, caught out in something he was likely not allowed to do.

"When this plague is over, go to medical school," Elisha told him. "I'll bet you know better than the doctors how to heal most things, but they get all the money and all the respect that should be your due."

The barber gave his knot a careful twist, then looked up. "You really think so?"

"Oh, aye. I've been where you are. There's nothing harder than having to take orders from fools."

"Master Guy is no fool." The barber caught up his supplies and rattled them back into their places, then hesitated. "But some of the others." He shook his head, then returned to Elisha's side. "Fleas, you say?" He started toward the door. "You asked after Father Pierre Roger. He's down here. Still barely breathing." He gave Elisha entry to the room, then a wave of his hand as he exited.

The narrow chamber had a sloping roof, and a peaked window that looked into the palace yards below. Father Pierre lay on his side on a pallet, looking pale, his breath hitching. His gaze travelled the room, rising up to Elisha's face, with a flicker of recognition. A long bruise marked his cheek.

Elisha knelt beside him. "Father, I was so sorry to hear you were injured."

"The Jews . . . safe," the priest managed on his shallow breaths.

"You did well."

"Could go to . . . my rest." His eyes shut on a longer blink, his hand fumbling the sign of the cross then dropping back to the blanket. "Not asking that . . . of God."

"I should hope not. May I examine you?"

A slight nod, and Elisha moved closer. From the ring he wore, his single talisman, Elisha conjured his own healing, encouraging the burns to cool and the skin to knit. He gently lay a hand on Father Pierre's shoulder, using the priest's unblemished hands to create the affinity and heal his own. That done, his fingers moved more easily. "You can't lie on your back?" He guided the coverings away from the priest's bare back and found more bruising in a broad swath across his spine. "Never mind, I see why. You fell when they attacked the boat, and you landed on something, is that right?"

With the most delicate touch of his fingers, Elisha ran his hand along the priest's spine, sending his awareness into the other man's flesh. The priest's back and face ached, and fear washed through his body with every tiny, shallow breath, never to walk, never to preach, never to speak the prayers and blessings of his Lord. Elisha sent him comfort.

In spite of the bruising, there was no obvious sign to explain Father Pierre's breathing distress. And, as the barber had said, Master Guy was no fool, he would have noticed most things. The priest's feet moved restlessly, so it was not as straightforward as a broken back—thank God: that was an injury Elisha could not overcome.

That left the small things. All of those little structures of the body that the plague exploited, things he'd not been aware of before he tracked the course of the plague through his own vessels. Then the sense of wrongness pulsed against his fingers, a tiny cramp in his own spine, so small that, if he had not stretched his attunement to the utmost, he might not have noticed at all. Given the heavy bruising of the priest's body and his distress in breathing, Father Pierre likely hadn't noticed. The pressure of a hand against an injured bone could diagnose a myriad of problems in the patient's reaction, but only if that reaction could be interpreted outside the background of any other pain. This felt so small as to be almost nothing, a pinching or a pressure in the filaments of the spine rather than a break or a pain. Elisha settled his hands, waiting for the next breath, and gave a gentle nudge, using his own spine to guide his magic to relieve the pressure. The bones shifted ever so slightly, releasing the trapped filaments.

Father Pierre gasped, then expelled a long, shaky breath. He gasped again, dragging greedily at the air, his chest rising and falling. His hand making the sign of the cross once more, eyes damp with gratitude. "Father," he whispered.

Drawing back his attunement to Father Pierre's injuries, Elisha found the looming presence of someone, or something, more; a surge of interest that had him spin about, already reaching for the salted blade in his boot.

Flanked by a few soldiers, a fleshy older man stood in the doorway wearing a habit of white so pure it would hurt to gaze upon for too long. A curious hat with golden ridges crowned his head, and Elisha's throat went dry as he met the eyes of the Pope himself.

Chapter 30

◆

For a moment, Elisha froze, then dropped his gaze to the floor, sinking back to his knees.

"So you are the man I've heard so much about—the barber, the doctor, the murderer, the king. Defender of the Jews, offender of the cardinals. I have been told under no circumstances to allow you to come before me, and I have been told, by all means, that I should do so. What under Heaven am I to make of it?" Pope Clement had a deep, rich voice well-suited to singing, and Elisha could not tell if he meant this as a rebuke. "At the very least, my son, I am intrigued." The Pope chuckled.

He stepped nearer, his pearl-stitched slippers peeking from beneath his dazzling robe. Four soldiers in his retinue, hot with the potential for violence, and two clerics, shimmering with devotion, and one mancer. Another soldier? Or a cleric? Until invited to do so by the Holy Father, Elisha dare not look up to find out.

"Pierre, my son, how does the day find you?"

"Much improved, Holy Father," the priest replied. "This man seems to have found the difficulty." He coughed a little, then continued, "By the grace of God, I believe he has healed me of the worst."

"Then you shall shortly be on your feet and able to present your petition. Excellent!"

"Seeing that Pierre is improved, Your Holiness, we should move on. It does not to do linger in hospitals," said the voice of Cardinal Renart.

The Pope stepped back. "Very well." Cloth rustled, though he did not move again, and Elisha guessed he was blessing Father Pierre. "Come with me." He moved away, then said, "Doctor, with me. I am not accustomed to asking twice."

Elisha scrambled to his feet and hurried after as the papal party moved from the chamber. An audience with the Pope, indeed, but with Renart right there—what could he possibly say that would be heard? And how could he determine if the mancers held sway over the Pope as well as the kings? While claiming a kingdom required merely controlling the next heir and removing the monarch, claiming the papacy would require manipulating enough of the cardinals to force their choice of candidate into the Holy See.

"Thank you, Your Holiness," Elisha managed.

Pope Clement laughed again. "Ah, I see he does have a voice, although his Latin is weak."

"Yes, Your Holiness, forgive me."

Clement's neck and figure suggested a man who enjoyed his food and wine, while his clothes showed little sign of austerity—only silk could crinkle like that, and the pearls on his slippers alone must have been costly. At his chest hung a golden cross embellished with jewels that winked as they passed the narrow windows.

"Now that the priest is well, Your Holiness, I hope that you will no longer feel it necessary to pay these visits," Renart said as he led the way down the corridor. "People will talk, even priests, and in the circumstances, it seems more fitting to give them no reason to doubt—"

"To doubt what, my son? My interest in every member of my flock, especially those who are shepherds themselves?" The Pope levelled a hard stare at Renart.

"The Lord knows when a sparrow falls, is it not my duty to raise up those sparrows that I, in my limited wisdom, can reach?" Renart turned toward the stairs, but the Pope kept walking. "I should like to visit the ramparts today. It is so rare that my physician allows me outside; I intend to take full advantage, even if we cannot go hunting."

"If Your Holiness would like to plan for a hunt, I am sure that some accommodation can be made, now that summer is nearly upon us. In the meantime, your physician and your cardinals, not to mention your flock, should prefer if you preserve your health." Renart stood with bowed head, hands clasped together as if in pleading.

"In truth, Cardinal, I suspect some of those same cardinals would just as soon proffer themselves to take my place in the shoes of the fisherman if that health should fail." His round face for the first time lost its air of amusement, his eyes keen.

Renart bowed deeper. "Your Holiness, put that thought far from your mind. We pray for your continued health and leadership in these difficult times, it is only that we do not always find our concerns are openly heard, Your Holiness."

"Very well then, tell me your concerns should I walk the ramparts."

"Master Giovanetti seeks your approval on the sketches for the east wall of the chapel before he proceeds with the frescoes—"

"I have approved all the rest of them, and he has done a fine job. Tell him to proceed." He waved his hand, and Renart made a soft rumble of exasperation. The Pope's lips quirked up. "What else, my son? Ah, yes, the coral tree for tonight's banquet—indeed, it must be installed or how shall we detect poisons? As for the petition of the Bishop of Paris, I am still considering it, and I shall consider it all the better if I am allowed to walk in the sun and enjoy the majesty of the Lord's creation." He gestured toward the unseen sky beyond the vaulted roof.

"Yes, Your Holiness."

Pope Clement continued in the direction he had chosen and Renart started after, but the Pope turned, holding up his hand. "I believe you promised to arrange the hunt, and to communicate with my artist." He pointed toward the stairs.

Renart stood a moment longer, his posture stiff, before he finally spoke. "I am sure another man could carry such messages, Your Holiness."

"Indeed, but I have asked you."

"Yes, Your Holiness." Slowly, as if it pained him, he bent a knee and kissed the Pope's ring before he departed.

The Pope's amusement returned. "Each must serve in his own way. Myself, I serve the Lord and my flock, and I must insist that even a cardinal do likewise." He set out again, one of the other priests hurrying ahead to open a door onto a brilliant day, letting in a rush of sunlight and warmth that nearly swept away the Valley's chill. The other cleric spread a short red cape over the Pope's shoulders, its fur lining as white as his robes. The Pope stepped slowly out as if savoring the moment, his robes all the more dazzling in the sunlight, and Elisha followed him onto the narrow walkway between the crenellated wall and the peaked roof of the palace. They walked along a section of older stone, flecked with bits of lichen, the metal of the roof weathered to a softer gray. The palace comprised two roughly rectangular yards, bordered by vast stone buildings. The far side of the second yard had a number of scaffolds in place around the towers and a hall with elaborate windows which Elisha guessed would be a church. While the windows on this end of the palace pierced plain stone, those on the newer construction featured delicately carved arches to frame them.

They entered another doorway and climbed a stair up and up until they emerged onto a square roof with a peak at the center and a crenellated walkway all around. A pair of archers faced them, bowing deeply when the Pope emerged. He waved his retinue to stay by the door and led Elisha down the walkway. The wind whipped at them and the sound of the windmills hummed into the air. At the far corner, they stopped, the Pope leaning on the wall, drinking in the view. A broad bow of the river partly circled the city of Avignon, with the king's bridge pointing across to a land of green pastures and staked vineyards. A promontory thrust out from the palace, home to the half-dozen windmills Elisha had been hearing, grinding away. Even if the world were ending, people still needed bread.

"Your Holiness." Elisha approached hesitantly, trying to frame what he must say.

"Yes, my son?"

"This pestilence that spreads across the land, it is no accident, nor is it divine in origin."

The Pope frowned at him. "Everything is divine in origin, my son."

Elisha mastered the frustration that rose at this. "But it is manipulated by men, evil sorcerers who want the wealth and power that the deaths and the madness will concentrate. They care nothing for either Heaven or Earth, they don't care how many people die because of them—if half the world is destroyed, that will only make it easier for them to control it."

"You sound like a flagellant." At a loss, Elisha shook his head, and the Pope went on, "Like those preachers in the streets who claim that Revelations is upon us, the rapture. That we are all such sinners we cannot avoid the darkness to come."

"But it doesn't strike just sinners, it takes children, priests, monks, everyone."

The Pope smiled. "You take a rather tight definition of 'sinners,' my son. We are all of us sinners, even myself, even the gracious queen some are claiming for the mother of the new savior."

"You think God wants them to die, even if men are the ones who made it happen?"

"God does not *want* as men want. This is His world, His creation. The choices of man, indeed have sullied it—one need only to consider Eve's apple or Cain's murder to see that. We seek the redemption He offers, and the example He gave us in the Lord Jesus Christ. God is not invested in the flesh and the lives of men, but in their souls."

"So we should simply stand back and let everyone die? How can you do that?"

"Come, Doctor, and see all my domain, all that the Lord entrusts me to oversee." The Pope waved Elisha closer, spanning the horizon with its rich farmlands, fine vineyards and new stone houses, the arms of the windmills swooping through the breeze. "There, do you see? Do you see it all?"

Elisha's divided vision overlaid that landscape of wealth and beauty with a map of pain and dying, the Valley swirling here and there as people died, stalking the fields of France like a thunderstorm. "Yes, Your Holiness, I see it—"

"No! You see nothing." Pope Clement turned on him, pressing his palm to Elisha's breast, a brand of heat and faith that seared into his old scars. "Here is my domain, and no one sees it all except the Lord."

Elisha caught his breath, pinned by the power of the old man's presence. A prince of the church, decadent and rich, enjoying his command of a cardinal and looking forward to the pleasures of the hunt as much as any lord of England, and yet, he radiated his belief, a truth so deeply held that it shone, and drew Elisha toward that certainty, a certainty he had not felt since he was a child. Elisha longed for it. He longed to so believe in something, to so trust it, that he could abandon himself to that faith and rest in that knowledge in even the darkest of days.

The Pope's eyes searched Elisha's face, his hand remaining as if he could likewise search Elisha's heart. "You worry for the flesh, Doctor, as well you might—such is your training that you must try everything to heal a man. So be it. And if you heal him, then it is God's will that it be done. It is not my place to intervene in the problems of the flesh, but of the soul." At last, he drew back, as if withdrawing a crutch from a wounded man to see if he could stand alone.

Elisha felt shaky without his touch, letting the stone at his back and under his feet support him as he remembered how to breathe.

"Father Pierre came to ask for my protection for the Jews. His affliction left him barely able to speak of it, and yet you were able to heal him. The Lord wishes this petition to be heard, and so it shall be, for the sake of the souls of the Jews who have yet to come to the truth, and for the sake of the souls of those who assault them in defiance of the Lord's own commandments." His smile returned, the storm within his eyes retreating behind the brighter day. "Yes, we are sinners all, but we seek to repent and sin no more, not to compound those sins with sins ever greater. Perhaps he came also to ask me to return to Rome—"

Elisha quickened at that, opening his mouth, but the Pope held up a warning finger.

"Now, Doctor, I know that Rome is a danger still, although it is my hope that the Orsini and the Colonna together shall revive the city and make it habitable again. I know there are some of those talking voices Cardinal Renart would have me acknowledge who think it is because the Pope is at Avignon that God visits His creation with plagues. And now, there is you." He gestured up and down, indicating Elisha, his ring winking in the sun. "What would you have me do? How am I to safeguard the souls of my flock from these evil men you say are coming in search of power? I cannot stop a man who grasps for power through the ruin of others, although I can pray for his soul. That is a thing of the air—" He stretched out his fingers drawing in the horizon and the wind. "It is not for me. Kings shall rise and kings shall fall. Some of them will be great men, and some will be vile. But the virtuous man will always turn to the Lord and seek there his direction." He tapped Elisha's chest. "I guide them as best I am able when my flock begins to stray. A few of them may be devoured by the wolves as they wander the wilderness, and I pray that the Lord will show them their way back to the fold."

For a long moment, they stood silent. Then the Pope asked, "And you, my son? Are you also a shepherd, or are you a wolf?"

Chapter 31

❖

"**Y**ou are yourself about to be victim to the wolves, Your Holiness." Elisha took a deep breath. The Pope was no mancer, but a man of deepest faith, nor had he yet succumbed to their influence. He must be warned of the dangers that surrounded him, and if Elisha could win his trust, the Pope's voice would be a powerful tool to calm the spreading madness. "Cardinal Renart is one of them, a sorcerer. The people who want you to go to Rome are either sorcerers as well, or are influenced by them—Count Vertuollo of Rome is one, and Lord Nicolas of Orleans."

"And the poet Petrarch? Is it magic that allows him the gift of words?" The Pope's eyes sparkled like his ring.

"You must hear me, Your Holiness! The sorcerers I speak of are necromancers—they kidnap, torture, and kill people, stripping their skins and making their bones into false relics for their own conjuring."

That drew a look of horror from the Pope. "That would be a devilish witchcraft indeed, but my priests have brought me no such tales. Even the Holy Office of the Inquisition hasn't spoken of it. I do not know these others of whom you speak, but Cardinal Renart is a priest of long standing in the papal court; officious, perhaps, but none has ever besmirched his reputation."

"Because they go to great pains to keep their work secret, preying on those who can't fight back." Elisha continued, "These necromancers have already killed Emperor Ludwig in favor of Emperor Charles. They tried to take England, and I stopped them. They already rule in France."

"Ah!" Pope Clement jabbed a finger at him. "Is that what this is about? You think me a puppet of France because I am French and we are in France? These people you name, they are important, influential, yes. And you tell such extraordinary tales of them. Are you not just one more, trying to drag me into politics to suit your own purposes? You are English, and you wish me to shun the French. The Italians want me to return to Italy, not for the glory of God, but for the money they lose when the cardinals are not there." His red cape flapped with his gestures, as if he would launch himself at Elisha or merely fly off into the sky. "You do not, any of you, understand. It is not you I listen to, it is the Lord. Sometimes words are spoken by men which echo the voice that I hear in my heart. Certes, I must balance the thousand earthly voices to appease the French, the Germans, the English, the Italians—but it is that one strong voice that I must hear beyond all of this."

Elisha's heart fell, and he turned away, leaning on the parapet, staring down into the city. Irregular city blocks and plazas crammed the space between the river's bend and the city wall, with a spill-over of cardinal's palaces beyond, and fresh walls arrested in mid-construction as ever more people moved to be near the Pope and the wealth and power he represented. More of those earthly voices the Pope set aside to listen to God. Overlaying this uneven grid of golden stone settled the webbing of death, the shadowy traces of dying, thicker around the churches and hospitals, a dark miasma hanging along certain streets where small houses and hovels were carved into the yards, clustering in a dense blackness over a block of tall buildings, their inner court roofed over again by the remnants of death. Here and there, the Valley flared open, accepting new souls in transit. Did they move on to something better? The Pope clearly believed so. But did that mean their earthly lives should be discounted, their flesh reviled and readily discarded, along with all the joys and trials of the world? The sky above shone bright with summer's promise while the land suffered in terrible darkness.

What did he want of the Pope after all? What could the Pope do but pray? A party of citizens trudged in the direction of the river, carrying shrouded corpses between them. If he focused his senses, he could hear the bearers crying, coughing, cursing.

After a moment, the Pope, too, looked over the wall, watching the river's flow, and made the sign of blessing toward the distant funeral as the dead were consigned to the river.

As Clement said, he must balance the voices of all of those lords and cities and churchmen—he had no army, no weapon to combat the mancers, nothing but his spiritual power, there at the center of the world, where a thousand, thousand people looked up to him and listened. When the Pope brought his hand down to the stone, Elisha reached out and touched him, sending what he heard from the funeral below, from those who suffered in the city, and those who tried in vain to ease their suffering: the sounds of grief and pain, the sounds of loss and dying. "What about those voices? Don't you hear them?"

The Pope stiffened at his touch, but his attention focused, his mouth drawn down.

"If Petrarch, or Father Pierre can speak words that echo the voice of God, then how much greater must your own voice be, Your Holiness? The Jews are being attacked. The poor and the sick are being ignored. Your flock scatters in fear because their kings cannot defend them, and their faith seems unanswered. From the depths they call to you, why else are they here? They can't hear the Lord as clearly as you do, Your Holiness— that's why they listen to you."

Clement looked down at their hands, side by side on the stone, Elisha's scarred, work-hardened, sun-darkened, and now bandaged in white, in sharp contrast with the long, elegant fingers of the Pope, pale and well-tended, the nails clean, the only calluses those of grasping a quill.

One of the priests approached from the doorway. "Forgive me, Your Holiness," he said, shoulders hunched and bowing. "Cardinal Renart is seeking you, Your Holiness. Shall I tell him . . . are you through here?"

Dark eyes reflected Elisha's thin, worried face, then the Pope said, "I am through," and he turned away, brushing past Elisha, calling, "Follow!"

The Pope's broad wake encompassed Elisha, drawing him down the stairs, into the knot of soldiers and clerics, a knot that grew with each level they descended until the cardinal joined them in a broad and beautifully painted chamber with a ceiling covered in stars. "Your Holiness, I hope that your walk has done you good." Renart smiled, flaring his eyes at Elisha as the Pope passed, clearly expecting him to fall into the crowd as well.

The Pope had heard him, heard the voices of his frightened flock, but showed no sign that he would do or say anything to draw them back together. Elisha had failed, bumping along after the Pope like any other servant until the Holy Father saw fit to dismiss him. Then what? What remained to Elisha but to return to the course of the wolf, slaying the mancers as best he could? His bandaged hands hung empty. Pope Clement would not—could not—help him to defeat the mancers at the highest level. This task remained his and his alone.

"Indeed, I have not lately seen you in such high

spirits, Your Holiness," Renart continued. "Shall we go over the afternoon's—"

"We are called to other duties, Cardinal. Send a runner to inform Father Pierre that his petition has been granted—tell him to draft a bull reiterating our defense of the Jews." Clement summoned one of the other priests and ticked off items on his hand. "We need a censer and a deacon to carry it. The tall processional cross, a basin of holy water. We will need five wooden crosses, and a number of novices or servants."

Renart's jaw clenched then loosened. "If I may be so bold as to ask, Your Holiness, what is it that we are doing?"

"Consecrating a cemetery."

"Right now?" The cardinal reached out to try to stop the priest, but he hurried away, carrying the Pope's urgent commands.

"The Lord moves me, Cardinal, do try to keep up. I will pray in the chapel of Saint John, until the items I require are ready." He kept moving.

The cardinal grabbed two handfuls of his robe and hitched up his skirts to hurry along. "What would you have me do in this service, Your Holiness?" Renart asked, but his facade of righteous concern cracked against his confusion. Elisha had no idea what the Pope had in mind, or why, but if it discomfited Renart, it must be a good thing.

"Do? Why, you must pray. Both of you will join me, doctor and cardinal. Perhaps I will see you reconciled of whatever enmity lies between you. 'Forgive us our trespasses as we forgive those who trespass against us.' This will be a holy day, and we shall share it with our people, beginning with you." His gesture hooked Elisha into the small, square chamber, barely big enough for the three of them. Bright frescoes covered most of the walls and ceiling between the arches that formed the central vault. One wall, and part of another showed only sketched

lines and the artist scrambled to his feet as they entered,
wiping his hands on a paint-spattered smock.

"Your Holiness!" The artist darted a glance at the cardinal and back as he bowed, kissing the Pope's ring. "I
had understood that His Eminence Cardinal Renart had
passed along your permission to work."

"You understood correctly, but for now, I wish to
pray."

The artist slipped away as the soldiers circled the entrance to the little chapel. Inside, the Pope sank to his
knees, crossing himself, and Elisha had no choice but to
follow. A little way off, at the Pope's other side, Renart
settled into a pool of crimson fabric, palms pressed together with a rosary cross between them. He gazed
heavenward as if his eyes could bore holes through the
stone ceiling.

Elisha schooled himself to stillness, attuning himself
to the place and the two people who shared it, the silent
majesty of the Pope and the utter void of the cardinal,
edged by the shadows of those he had slain. Could Elisha show that to the Pope as well? Would the Holy Father believe it, or would he imagine it was Elisha who
was the sorcerer, conjuring ghosts to bend the Pope to
his will? He wished he had a relic cold enough to defend
the Pope against the plague without also making him
vulnerable to the mancers' direct attack. For now, Elisha
would be cautious and show no more than he must, no
more than the Pope was willing to understand. His mind
wandered, and he thought of praying. If he prayed, if
God would hear him, what would he say? He would ask
for mercy for the victims of the plague and for courage
in the battle to come. He would ask God to defend Jude
and help him to heal, and to watch out for Katherine,
Harald, and the rest of his assassins; if God saw all, surely
He saw the righteousness in what they did. He imagined
that, across the Channel, Thomas might be praying, too,

praying for Elisha's life and safety, a thought that pierced him: Thomas praying for Elisha, when he should be praying for himself and all the nation as the plague stalked ever closer.

Outside the palace, the forest of steeples pealed the hours twice before the Pope finally raised his head, crossed himself, and spoke his amen. Elisha's knees ached and only the humming strength of the Valley kept him awake and alert through the long afternoon. On the wall before him, the artist's bright paints depicted John the Baptist, likewise kneeling, and a man with a sword at the saint's neck about to lop off his head. The image lingered in Elisha's eye as he stiffly rose and crossed himself.

The time in contemplation seemed to have both darkened Renart's mood and given him direction. He spared no glance at all for Elisha as they accompanied the Pope out of the chapel, joining his entourage of priests and servants, burdened with all the items the Pope had ordered. Even to Elisha's eye, the procession looked small and ragged, as if people were missing and others uncertain where to stand as a result, shifting their weight uneasily, standing aside or reacting as if those absent might suddenly come to take their places. All these little actions revealed the dead as surely as any glimpse of their shades might do. Nonetheless, the Pope's presence united his followers, and they walked together, the deacon swinging his globe to spread a cloud of incense around them.

In the streets beyond the palace, the silent citizens watched, some of them forgetting to bow or curtsey, their faces haunted, and they joined the procession, stepping carefully around the dead who lay here and there upon the stones. The growing crowd filed through a gate toward the river and the Pope murmured with his servants, sending them out with their crosses as he led the procession onto the broad stone span. Two of the servants hurried ahead, holding the wooden crosses, encountering a group of royal guards near the far side. After some discussion, a guard sprinted for the castle beyond. The Pope took no notice, crossing until they reached the center of the span. Here, he held open his arms and began to speak, opening with a prayer, then calling those around him to draw near.

"My children, I know that you fear. Some among you believe the end times are near, that the heavens shall open to release those fierce angels and their terrible horns. Will the seals be broken and this creation brought to ruin? There are moments it seems it must be so." As the Pope spoke in Latin, other voices translated softly all around them, French, Italian, German, a dozen others Elisha did not know. At the back of the crowd, near the city stood a group of Jews, drawn by the spectacle, curious or fearful. "I say to you that the Lord has given me no sign to cause me to tremble. Rather, all around me, I see the signs of hope. I see that you struggle to be faithful, and yet you succeed. I see that many are stricken and many will fall, and yet others will rise and go on. Are these the end times? Will the seas boil and the sky rain fire? It may be so—but remember, my children, that this fearsome event is also a glorious one, for it will mark the return of Our Savior and the fulfillment of the Lord's promise to us."

He drew a deep breath and continued, "And so I say to you, do not fear but be at peace with the will of the Lord. Pray and make offerings. Give to the poor and minister to the sick. Repent of your sins and be cleansed that you may greet the savior with an open heart, even should years pass before these great events of prophecy arrive.

"You have been asked to bear your dead to the cemeteries for their burial, but I know this is another burden

for your already burdened hearts. And so, the Lord
moves me to create this river as holy ground. From this
day forth, your dead will lie peacefully here and await
the day of judgement. From this day forth, let there be
no bloodshed nor no devilry here to despoil this holy
place." Did his glance stray to Renart? If so, it did not
find him. A cluster of cardinals had joined the procession, but Elisha could not find Renart among them. He
pivoted, searching the crowd, and spotted a tall familiar
figure at the far edge, silver hair dancing in the wind.

Elisha slipped between the guards and clerics, working his way free of the crowd as the Pope continued with
his blessing. He moved fast, his heart thundering—surely
he was mistaken. Vertuollo, here?

Then he heard the count's gravely musical voice,
echoing through the Valley, through his heart. "*Come,
Jude. Let us pay a visit. I think you shall like England, and
your small friends will find so many hearths to warm
them.*"

Vertuollo stood on a little rise, Jude at his side, hand
in hand, his brothers in magic, united at last. And the
count's other hand held a little vial of crystal with silver
fittings, a vial of the earth where Elisha's brother died.
For a sensitive magus like Count Vertuollo, that vial held
a pathway directly to the heart of London, and his traveling companion held the plague.

Chapter 32

❖

"**No!**" Elisha shouted. He snatched himself through the Valley, hoping the crowd remained focused on the Pope, and desperate to stop the threat to England. He stumbled to his knees at the count's feet. Vertuollo stepped back, staring down his nose, the vial already concealed.

The count's stern voice resonated through the Valley, sending a chill to Elisha's heart. "*We spoke of this before, my brother, and you would then have no part of the conversation, as if it mattered not at all what might occur. I suggested that you might go home, but you refused, as petulant then as you are today.*"

"*I did not know as much then as I know now, Brother, please.*"

The count nearly smiled. "*It is too late for 'please.' It is too late for nearly anything. You went to Salerno and would not rest. You came to Rome, and would only antagonize me further, and now this.*" He spread his free hand, his graceful sleeve flaring in the wind like a broad wing about to soar. "*We find you in Avignon, bothering the Pope himself. You are a pebble in the shoe of the great, and we grow weary of stumbling.*"

Slowing his racing heart and finding his strength, Elisha pushed himself to his feet and remembered that he had been a king. He set aside humility and donned instead the mantle of power. "*Of course you do. But I don't think you are being completely honest, Brother, not with me, possibly not with yourself. They have set you this task, the most adept among them, but you came to me first.*"

"*Do not lower yourself to flattery, Brother—and do not think I am doing you a favor, not after all you have done to me.*" Vertuollo's eyes flashed, his robe rippling, and Jude shivered, his glance tracing the tall figure beside him, then cast back to the ground.

Through the contact, a hint of emotion, slippery, as if Vertuollo were, indeed, lying. Curious, if Elisha, playing upon the brotherhood Vertuollo had claimed, had guessed at the truth. The mancers—Renart at their head—needed Vertuollo to confront Elisha. Who else could match his skill with the Valley? But the count strained against the role they assigned him. Because of their brotherhood? Because if Jude were as a younger brother to Elisha, then so was Jude to Vertuollo himself?

"*Certainly not, but you're also a practical man. If you take this child to England to spread the plague, you know that I will never rest until every last one of your kind is destroyed.*" The shepherd or the wolf? Faced with the ruin of England, that was no choice at all. Elisha released a little of his armor and allowed the swelling torrent of the Valley to infuse him with its power until his hair shivered and his skin sparked, his breath coming in clouds of ice that melted into the French sunlight. "*They want you to kill England, to draw me back to save it—but you know better. Why should we both lose, me losing my country, and you, every last one of you, losing this war. You cannot kill me, Brother, you know that. Will the fight make me wish I were dead? You know exactly what that kind of loss feels like. Every martyr I lose will only make me stronger, Brother. You and your kind have to kill them personally in order to suck up their strength, I don't. Every death they cause is making me stronger."*

Strangers gathered near the bridge edged away from the silent confrontation, pulling their shawls tighter, clutching their crosses.

"What would you do then, to save England?" Vertuollo let his shimmer turn warm, almost golden, inviting. *"Are you through trying to save the world?"*

"It cannot be saved," Elisha answered, and the truth of those words filled him with a sorrow deeper than rivers, deeper than death. *"What would you have me do?"*

"You must leave Europe and never return. You must never again step foot out of England, nor pursue any foreigner beyond your borders, nor allow any of your acolytes to do so, nor defend them when they have."

"That's a lot to ask."

Vertuollo briefly displayed the vial, letting it wink in the sunlight. *"In return, you will have everything, and everyone, you have ever loved. Brother."*

The single word conjured memories of his own brother's death, captured in that vial. Vertuollo knew precisely what he held—and was that a note of pity in the count's careful projection? The future of England hung before him, haunted by the faces of those he had already lost: Mordecai, Martin, Rosalyn, Walter, Randall—as well as by the faces of those who remained: Allyson, Sundrop, Alfleda, Helena, his infant son . . . Thomas, his beloved king.

In exchange for the grand ruins of Rome, the royalty of Germany, the rich fields of France, the legion of clerics both faithful and not, the terrified knots of the Jewish communities, Queen Margaret, Isaac and his family, the Pope, and the poet. Katherine, Harald, Jude.

"They will let you make this bargain, all on your own?"

Vertuollo hesitated, another tiny gap in his projection of command. *"They will seek some sort of surety."*

Elisha laughed, a great and terrible mocking laughter. "*Do not tempt me with bargains you cannot keep, Brother, I will need surety as well.*"

The count drew down a breath that he expelled in a roil of mist. "*I will need time to bring them to the proper understanding. And many will want to see for themselves.*"

"*Two days, then I go hunting.*"

"*They have a chapel—*"

"*I've seen it.*" Elisha smiled at Vertuollo's surprise. The Pope's parapet had shown him the map of the city, with that darker hollow where the mancers did their slaying. "*Get them there, every one of them that would be convinced of my word. They must all abide by this agreement, or they, too, will pay the price.*"

The count gave a slight, gracious tip of his head, but Elisha stepped up even as the count retreated. "*One more thing. Jude goes with me.*"

Vertuollo paused, his glance given to the child at his side. "*What if he does not choose to? He has told me how you encourage him to choose. What if he has chosen strength over weakness? Wealth over misery?*"

Elisha, too, looked to the boy. Jude stared back at him, his eyes round and moist, his presence thoroughly deflected. "*I would hope he would choose life, Brother, that no others should suffer the pain that he has known.*" Jude's gaze dropped, and Elisha regarded the count. "*I would wish the same for you.*"

"*Naïve as a child, just as the Salernitan said.*"

"*Was your own son ever so innocent?*"

Vertuollo's pale eyes narrowed, then he said, "*In two days.*"

Elisha matched his slight bow. Then the count and the boy were gone. Elisha put off the raiment of death and found his trembling breath. Had he truly just stood toe to toe with Vertuollo and bargained for the safety of

England? At what cost? Two days until he could reclaim the vial and the boy—if he would come—and finally turn away from the bloody plague and go home. Even as he thought it, he knew it would not be that easy.

The scent of incense swirled in the wind around him, and he turned to find the papal procession regrouping to return to the palace, the guards at the wall stepping aside. Instead of the procession entering, however, a small party raced out, led by Guy de Chauliac, Brigit and Gretchen behind him, and the young barber as well.

"Your Holiness!" Guy shouted. "What can you be thinking, to walk out in the city without so much as a kerchief for your face or a pair of torches to ward off the pestilence?"

"I was thinking of the health of my flock, more than my own." Clement's chin rose as he found Elisha on the hillside just beyond. Guy and his party followed the look, the doctor's face a furious red. "It has elevated their souls to witness this act, and to participate in the blessing. In the face of sickness and despair, it is the torch of faith that we require, and that flame burns strong in Avignon."

A cheer rose around him, people pressing close, hands waving as they sought his blessing and his touch. Elisha had reminded the Pope that his voice could wield this power, and Clement had taken up his strength. Already, his flock grew stronger as well. Cardinal Renart's shuttered gaze followed Elisha as he made his way past the crowd. Katherine lurked at the periphery, Harald among the soldiers.

Elisha walked quickly, ignoring the cardinal, cutting through the soldiers with a muttered, "Perdone," catching Harald's eye. He stumbled and let Harald's hand balance him. "*The synagogue, tonight,*" he sent, registering Harald's surprise. "*Bring Katherine.*" Then he went to find his first good meal in weeks. Even a wolf must be sustained.

*   *   *

The jittery strength of the Valley would not let him settle, and Elisha paced the streets of the city, noticing the mancers who noticed him, strangers, but clearly aware. The Valley whispered constantly with their movements; Vertuollo had been busy. The mancers claimed that England could be defended from the plague, but what it needed, what the world needed, was to be defended from them, and Elisha was the only person who might be able to do that. Restless, he walked until evening brought him to the synagogue, where he explained his need to the local Jews, with the help of Menahem, the leader of the Roman Jews recently arrived. Many had heard of him from their relatives and trading partners in Germany and Italy, but their furtive glances and hesitant speech suggested they had heard, too, about the killings in those places. Elisha produced the letters he had from the rabbi of Heidelberg and finally won their permission to meet there, in the one place he could be sure there were no relics.

"A synagogue? Am I even allowed inside?" Katherine peeked around the door frame.

"The mancers can't get in," Elisha said as she stepped through and lowered the hood that hid her face. A hint of blush in her cheeks heightened her beauty, and Elisha armored himself against what he must do, and armored his heart against her reaction. "And there's no need to enter the sanctuary, there's a study chamber over here. Where's—"

Harald slid through from the other direction. "There's a curfew for the Jews, given all the recent violence. We'll need to be out by full nightfall, unless we travel the other road."

"I'd rather not; that would only attract the mancers' attention." The hundred-year-old building radiated a calm that felt absent in the rest of the city, and Elisha felt grateful all over again for the Jews allowing him inside. While the churches outside the Jewish quarter teemed with the sick and the dying, those desperate to log their prayers with God, the Jews apparently had no expectation of that kind of intervention. Instead, they cleaned their houses and closed their doors. In the study, Elisha lit a pair of candles, illuminating scrolls and books inscribed with strange characters, and paintings both beautiful and foreign.

Katherine eyed the room, edging around the lectern and taking a seat where a large book rested open. "It is still hard to overcome all that I've heard about the Jews and think these books are not demonic, and their keepers are not murderers."

Harald and Elisha exchanged a glance. They were both of them murderers, and Katherine a necromancer. The idea of dangerous books and deadly scholars almost brought a return of that half-mad laughter, but Elisha held it in check. "I have made a bargain with the mancers, a bargain to save England."

"What? I don't understand," said Katherine, but Harald grew still, listening as Elisha explained about the count and the vial. Before he had even stopped speaking, she came to her feet, fury swelling in her presence.

"So you will abandon all of us, and all of the people we're fighting to save?"

"What would you have me do?" He opened his hands, inviting any other option. "You've seen what I have seen, you know what I know. Most of it anyhow. When I accepted the plague into my own body, I saw precisely how quickly it spreads and how insidious are its messengers. I can't save the world."

"Instead, you'll let it burn, and us along with it."

He shook his head. "I bought us two days, Katherine. Go back to Germany and warn them, everyone you can. Tell them how the plague spreads, how to watch out for it. If you can, give them talismans cold enough to fend it off—one by one, it should work."

She cut the air with a gesture, as if she could cut off his words, and he caught her shoulders, forcing her to look at him. "Warn them, Katherine, then get yourself to England and be safe."

"You're running away, and you want me to run, too. I won't have it. After the things I've done and the things I've seen, how can I turn coward now?"

Harald spoke up for the first time. "Think of it as withdrawing to the keep. The mancers have placed this world under siege, we can at least hold the line somewhere. England is small, it's an island. The water and the salt will aid in its defense."

Katherine drew herself up, regaining control. "What makes you think you can trust them?"

"Nothing at all. It's why I need you gone. All of you." He cut his gaze toward Harald. "I will give them a show of power they'll not soon forget, but it's risky. If they get frightened or angry, they'll strike back, and I don't want you in danger." He softened his voice. "If I could, I'd send the Pope and the Jews as well."

"As it is, I'll be exhausted—even to pass twice through the Valley in a day is a lot for me, and I'll need to visit Heidelberg, Bad Stollhein, and a few other places as well." Katherine blinked back tears. "Even without taking anyone along, it would be a trial."

"Don't worry over me, Margravine," Harald offered. "I'll make my own way. It may be useful to have eyes and ears here in France for a time, especially if you two must be gone."

Elisha offered a grateful glance. "Thank you, Harald."

Katherine sniffled and wiped at her eyes. "Then what, you'll come to England when you get the vial?"

"And Jude. I'm not leaving without him."

"The boy betrayed you, Elisha—he told them about

the vial, he gave them exactly what they need to entrap you!"

He jerked away from her. "He certainly did not!" Even as the words flew, Elisha wondered if they were true. Why had Jude gone to the mancers? Did he even want Elisha to reclaim him? If he had simply run away and been seized, then surely he would have fought them, screaming and struggling as he always did. Instead, he listened to music in a garden, and stood calmly at Vertu-ollo's side—why? Because the count spoke Hungarian?

"It is worth considering how they knew," Harald said calmly. "Did Gretchen know?"

"She knew it was important to me, but not why." Elisha rubbed his temple. "Although I did take her to England once, she's a sensitive, she might have guessed how we traveled. I'm not convinced she trusts the mancers well enough to betray another magus, even me. She's not a part of the mancer cause, she's only here as hand-maiden to Brigit."

"You told us about the vial at the abbey in Heidel-berg: the Margravine, Isaac, Gilles, and myself."

"It certainly wasn't me," Katherine protested imme-diately, looking wounded simply to be on the list. "Where is Gilles, by the way? What's happened to him?"

"The plague. He caught it at Salerno."

"Before or after he met Jude?"

Harald cleared his throat and said, "Ironic, to fall ill at a medical school."

"Sadly common to get sick in hospital—I've always said those places are deadly." Elisha looked away, his own eyes stinging. He learned what to do too late to save Gilles, the foolish and faithful. Or was he? Elisha consid-ered the events surrounding Gilles's death in a new light. "I took Gilles to die in Rome, at San Giovanni. Shortly after we arrived, Jude ran from me"—he shot a dark look at Katherine to forestall any further recriminations against the boy—"and Danek seized him. I followed to get him back, and when I returned, I found out Gilles had had a visitor in my absence, Count Vertuollo. Vertuollo wanted me to come to him, to talk with him, but Gilles may have welcomed the contact. He may well have told the count how to draw me out."

"Why should Gilles, of all people, betray you? He venerated you." Katherine stalked the far side of the room, glaring at him, then at the Jewish books all around her.

"Because he believed I would rise up in glory to vanquish my enemies. He was talking about it right to the end." Elisha swallowed. "He might have said something to ensure that would happen. How could I defeat those I did not confront?"

"And now you are running from them again."

"If you have a better plan, I am open to it." He flung wide his hands, his palms aching. "Look, Katherine, we've just agreed I cannot save the world. This plague is too much, even for me. If I can stop it somewhere, anywhere, it will be better than nothing, better than letting them run every nation into madness."

Katherine gave a cry of frustration or fury. She stood a moment, chest heaving with emotion, then her head hung, and finally she said, "I will warn the others. How am I to get to England when I'm done? And my sons are coming, too, of course."

"Of course they are." Her acquiescence, however grudging, lightened his heart. "Look for the relics of Saint Louis. The French gave one to the heir to the throne of England, at the behest of the mancers. It's still in the royal chapel."

She let out a breath of laughter. "You would deliver me directly into the chapel of the king?"

"King Thomas is my supporter, as is his servant Pernel and many others at the Tower. They are the ones who need to understand about the plague, and they will bring you to the magi."

"But Thomas is king, why should he listen to me?"

"Because you and he both know me in ways that no one else can."

Her eyes locked to his, brow slightly furrowed, then lifting, her lips parting as she knew the truth. She flung up her hood to hide her face and shoved past them to the door, but not before he saw the sheen of tears.

Chapter 33

❧

For a moment, both men stood silent, as if Katherine's departure had deflated them, then Harald turned to Elisha, a graceful pivot, as if in a dance. "That was nicely done, a perfectly laid trap for a woman who loves you. How better to defeat her than to force her to go to the man you love." Harald folded his arms. "Now, tell me the real plan."

For a moment, Elisha thought of denying it, but Harald's sharp eyes and the grim set of his mouth suggested he knew exactly what Elisha was thinking. Still, his throat felt dry, his chest too tight as he sank into a chair, ceding the higher ground and articulating the truth for the first time. "I can't save England; the plague spreads too quickly, in too many ways. The disease'll take a little longer to cross the water, and it might not survive well in the north, but it will get there. I hope the mancers don't know that I know it." He let out a shuddering breath, staring at a page of the open book, the Hebrew letters dark and strong as engravings in a frame the shape of a gravestone.

"You're letting the mancers think that you believe you can save England—why?"

"So they think they have me. Which they do, really." He ran a finger lightly over his bandaged palm, picturing the scar that pierced him, just there. "I can't save my country or my friends from the plague. I can't save the world from it, but it's not the only problem, it's not even the real problem—it's just a sickness, terrible as it is, and we have faced sickness before. It's the mancers that are the real threat. I can't save the world, but I may be able to cure it. To undertake a surgical solution and excise the corruption before it spreads any further."

Harald hooked a chair with his foot and slid it closer, sitting opposite Elisha, elbows on knees, leaning in. "How?"

"By making contact with as many mancers as possible, and killing them all."

"They'd never allow it."

Elisha said, "They might—contact moves in both directions. If I have contact with them, they'll have it with me. They'll believe they can control me."

"Couldn't they? Surely, if so many of them could reach you at once, they'd kill you."

"That's the very temptation they can't resist. I'll have to fend them off until the last possible moment before I strike back. It'll take a very powerful magic, and I'll need them to be very close by, to get as many as I can."

His dark eyes narrowed. "How can you get that kind of power, Elisha? I know you're strong, but to slay them all, wouldn't you have to—" Harald's fingertips pressed together. "You'd have to kill someone. Even then, it would have to be someone very close to you, am I right? The closer the better."

Elisha stared at his hands, imagining what might be running through Harald's mind. Would he kill Jude? Harald himself? Was that why Elisha had sent Katherine away, so he wouldn't be tempted to kill her? Was it better for Harald to know the full truth, or, like Katherine, to storm away in fury at Elisha's cowardice? He wished there could be another way, that they could make another plan, but every hour he delayed only helped the mancers solidify their power and grind their victims yet further into misery. The plague would spread on its own, to be sure, but it would spread further and faster with the mancers' gleeful deployment, and its impact would be far worse with the mancers there to take advantage of the chaos. There was only one possible solution, perhaps there had always been. Only one possible victim could give him the power he needed.

The Jews believed he was holy; the English peasantry wanted him for a saint, while the Salernitans believed he was a demon. Gilles had called him an angel *and* a daemon: one who stood between the worldly and the divine. Soon enough, it would be up to God to sort that out. For a moment, he could feel the pressure of the Pope's hand over his heart. Did God truly see all? Did He know what lay in Elisha's heart, where fear coiled against his conviction? Only a handful of sinners were guaranteed to go to Hell, without the chance for redemption: traitors, heretics, suicides like his brother. Like himself.

He did not want to be alone. He did not want them all to think the worst of him, until they learned the truth of what he would do, and yet he could not afford to have them close.

"You wouldn't do that. I can no more believe you a murderer than I believed that you would abandon the fight. What, then, Elisha?" But Harald's voice sank to a whisper as he spoke. Elisha heard his breathing and sensed the beating of his heart. "Holy Mary. Have I ever been so blind." Then the warmth of Harald's hand penetrated Elisha's numbness, Harald's fingers gripping his shoulder, drawing him closer so that their heads rested together. "You don't want me to stop you," Harald breathed, his fingers tightening, as if he could hold Elisha right there.

"If you stop me, they win. The most powerful magic

comes from the death of the magus himself—there is no other way."

"By God, I wish I could find you one."

Their breath mingled, Harald's hand steady, even in sorrow. He might well be the only person Elisha would wish to have beside him, the one person he could trust to understand what must be done.

"Why aren't you going to England, then? One last time."

"I'd never come back." Elisha pressed the heels of his hands into his eyes. "If I had to face Thomas again, to look into his eyes, and make this choice, I couldn't do it." He almost laughed, a strained breath of nerves and regret. "As it is, I've given myself too much time to reconsider, or worse, to signal my intentions. I had to give Katherine enough time to get herself and her sons to safety as well as warning the others. But if the mancers figure out what I'm planning, they won't let me get close."

"They won't learn it from me." Harald did laugh, then, a light chuckle. "And the Pope's offered you a distraction: he's invited you to take a chamber in the palace, to dine with him tomorrow and celebrate the mass. It's an all-day affair for some saint or another. I offered to bring you the message."

"Mass with the Pope? Christ."

"Yes, exactly." Then both men were laughing, tears stinging Elisha's eyes, his shoulders shaking, until he had to sit back or risk knocking their heads together. Harald blinked back at him, shaking his head.

Elisha wiped his eyes, gasping for breath. Then he finally said, "After everything else I've been through, I did not expect to be afraid."

"You may be closer to death than any man alive, but you are still human." Harald steepled his fingers and regarded Elisha more coolly. "Are you certain you can carry this off?"

"Dying? I need to choose it, to be prepared for it, in order to bend the magic to my will, but yes. Some days I haven't been sure how to go on living, now all I need to do is to accept my own death." Saying it out loud, meeting Harald's level gaze, made the decision solid and clear, like stamping the king's seal to a freshly inked writ.

"What do you need of me?"

"I need you to keep anyone else away. If Katherine returns, send her off, do something, anything to keep her away. I don't want anyone else caught in this magic, understood?" At Harald's nod, Elisha continued, "And I need you to take Jude, to bring him to safety. He may be able to use the Valley—he's a sensitive, and he's been with me when I opened it, but if this works, the Valley may be sealed, at least for a time. Like an avalanche in the mountains. Whatever purpose it has beyond what the mancers do, it will be reborn, but most of them will be gone. It'll take them a long time to rebuild to their current strength, and they may never be so organized again." He smiled briefly. "They are not a trusting lot, even of each other. It's only the crimes they commit that bind them together."

"I know a thing or two about that." Harald let his hands fall open. "Speaking of trust, are you certain it was not Jude who betrayed you?"

"If he has, then I'm lost—they'll know I had the plague and recovered. As it is, they'll have to assume that Jude shared some of his experience with me. That's why his father was so eager to get him away from me, so I couldn't find out enough to understand the mechanisms of transmission. He was afraid that I would find a cure. He may not have realized what a perfect creation is his pestilence."

"I'll do my best," Harald said, then rose. "There is still that curfew to remember."

"Then it's a good thing I have an escort from the papal guard."

Harald put out his hand and Elisha clasped it, pulling to his feet, and maintaining the contact a little longer, sending his gratitude. Harald said, "At least you'll have a fine bed tonight and a busy day ahead."

By the time they reached the papal palace, Elisha had recovered his composure, casting his deflection dark and deep, accepting the comfort of a soft bed in a chamber painted with such richness that it shocked the eye with garish color, a pattern of vines concealing a multitude of animals. At least the curtains over the bed interrupted the intent black gaze of all those creatures. There would be enough eyes on him tomorrow as it was. But as he lay in the dark, it was Thomas's eyes he remembered, sharp, blue, haunted. On Elisha's brief visit to London before the birth of Brigit's child, Thomas told him he feared Elisha would die overseas, and Thomas without even a grave to visit. Elisha apologized to the darkness, then he brought up the power of death, that oblivion he would soon embrace, and armored himself with cold, the expectant ice of an early winter.

Chapter 34

❖

Elisha allowed that cold to carry him through the next day, admiring the Pope's gilded palace and rich meals, kneeling when he was to kneel and standing when he was to stand. And when he must pray, for the sake of the mancers all around him, he prayed for England. Cardinal Renart loomed near in his awareness, in his sumptuous robes of red, the image of stern piety. If his glance flicked to Elisha a tad too often, that might be blamed on Elisha's unusual status in the palace, neither clergy nor nobility. Guy de Chauliac watched him in a similar way, trailed by the saintly presence of Brigit and her handmaid, Gretchen, the pale beauty and the dark, both remote as the painted angels on the chapel walls. At the morning meal, two other mancers lurked among the clergy, but by the evening Mass, the number swelled to nine: clergy, servants, that French lord Harald followed to Avignon, all performing their roles with no apparent interest in the others.

When the Pope's rolling Latin died away in the church of Saint John, Elisha lined up with the others—far back in the procession of cardinals and lords set to accept communion and the blessing of the Pope's own hand. Cardinal Renart stood beside the Pope, holding the monstrance that had been elevated to the Lord. Clement's gaze met Elisha's as he offered a wafer. "Corpus Christi," he intoned, with the slightest smile of encouragement.

The wafer came from the same monstrance as all the others, and no other member of the congregation showed any ill effect, in spite of Renart's presence. Elisha took it on his tongue, the wafer dry and slightly bitter, its taste familiar, but unlike the wafers of England. Even this ritual should make him long for home, on the eve of the moment he must lose it forever. He had taken communion at Easter in Saint Bartholomew's the year before, behind his brother Nathaniel, and Nathaniel's pregnant wife, not knowing the baby and its father would soon be dead. A year and a half, and he was a father himself, and he would have felt their deaths coming, and he would have felt the swelling strength of their dying, just as he did now, when plague stalked every nation and death hovered so close to his own heart.

Elisha bowed his head to the Pope, rose and walked down the aisle, out into the street. For a moment, he resisted, thinking to walk away, to visit the bridge over the consecrated river, or the church of Saint Agricol, where a poet believed he had seen an angel. But there was no profit in delay, not tonight. Instead, he sought a place to attune himself, and prepare for what he must do. A church, a bridge, a plaza or a palace—all might serve for another man. Elisha followed the twisting, narrow channels of streets to a place where a half-built palace loomed in the growing darkness, its open courtyards filled with hovels, small houses built against the walls, half-halls carved into homes for a dozen families. A few voices rose here in prayer, in song, in weeping, and the bodies of the unburied dead lay along the outer wall, faces covered, given all the dignity these people could afford. There, in the most desperate place in all the city, Elisha knelt among the dead. His furred cloak could not defend him from the cold that rose within, the echoing Valley penetrating, permeating him.

Stilling his fears, his pain already deadened, Elisha attuned himself to Death. He sorted every bit of knowledge he possessed: the quiet deaths of the old and the thrashing agony of a soldier slashed to the bone, the creeping understanding of death that grew in Friar Gilles and how it had grown in Elisha himself when he accepted the plague and learned what it had to offer. He thought of Martin's sacrifice, dousing the flames that might have devoured London, and the final grief of Randall, living long enough to see his daughter avenged by the man he thought had killed her. He recalled the sharp defeat of every patient he had lost and the loss in the faces of mothers told that their children had gone. Last of all, he thought of Nathaniel's quiet despair, believing all his family were dead, believing himself responsible. That memory nearly shattered Elisha's careful work, his layering of death and dying, weaving his knowledge with his power as the Valley swelled with the plague victims. He must be inured to the certainty of death if he would claim its gift tonight. Even his brother's death must hold only knowledge severed from emotion. Fitting, that the moment which had propelled him to this dark discovery of magic, should mirror the moment that ended it.

When he had gathered what strength he could, Elisha bound his knowledge deep and forged his projection, hope and fear in equal measure, his desire to save England, his willingness to do whatever must be done, to sacrifice the world if only his homeland might be safe.

Elisha armored himself with these layers, the projection of hope and fear that his enemies would sense wrapping the knowledge of his own intentions that he would conceal until it was much too late. He rose again to face the night. He walked steadily across the broad plaza before the palace, and down the street toward the block of buildings where death lay thick and dark against his vision. For all of the allies he had gathered, this walk he must take alone. The Valley rippled with mancers shifting, moving, approaching. They need not reveal themselves on the street; clearly their temple held enough relics to serve as the crossroads for a hundred highways of death. And he came there as a highwayman, to steal the tainted fortune they hoped to reap from the downtrodden world they had created.

In the narrow way between two tall houses, a door of old wood bore the chipped image of two knights mounted on a single horse, sign of the Knights Templar, the order destroyed by another Pope forty years ago. The mark of a great betrayal, and of a perfect place for the mancers to carry out their killings. The other mancer lairs he entered stood far from people, in forests, barrows, coal mines, and vineyards, places where the victims might scream to the unhearing night, where blood and flies and the inevitable reek of death were readily concealed or ignored. The mancers of Avignon were reckless or arrogant, to do their killing in the heart of the Pope's own city. Their victims must be gagged, or drugged. It gave Elisha a moment's pause. Here he stood, about to make himself an offering. Could they indeed defeat him, all of them at once?

He drew a deep breath, and sucked down death. They could not. What defeat could he face but death itself, and death was what he'd come here for. If they slew him early, they would only trigger the power he held in store for them. A wolf indeed. Beyond the door, a hundred other wolves lay waiting, imagining they might ambush him, not knowing he had marked them out as sheep.

The familiar warmth of Harald drew near, and Elisha acknowledged him with a tip of his head.

"It got late enough, I hoped you'd found another way." The darkness picked out the gleam of his eyes, and

Elisha shook his head, briefly touching the assassin's shoulder. *"Jude, and the vial."*

"I'll get them," Harald answered. *"God be with you, whatever comes next."*

Elisha rapped on the door, a hollow sound that resonated like the belly of a harp, its strings humming in expectation. The door swung open and Gretchen stared back at him. "I am only here as escort to my lady," she said. "I am not—with them." She retreated, drawing the door open and ushering them in. She dodged Elisha's glance as he passed her into the octagonal space. A series of peaked arches elevated on columns marked the perimeter of the temple, with flickering torches in sconces all around, lighting the place like a pit of Hell. This image framed the crowd of mancers dense with the shades they carried, a shifting mass almost as thick as the flickering chaos of the Valley itself. If he focused his vision, he could see the connections among them, the webbing of deaths they shared, linking the French lord to a German merchant to a Roman peasant. A chainmail conspiracy, gathered here before him. The crackle of power rose on all sides, the focus of awareness on him, against him, wary defenses conjured.

The door closed behind him, Harald following to one side, Gretchen further back.

At the center of the temple a pair of stone sarcophagi dominated the space in a slight clearing where Cardinal Renart and Count Vertuollo stood waiting, framing one of the waist-high tombs where Jude sat between them, his hands pressed between his knees. He alone gave no acknowledgment of Elisha's entrance, his head bowed and shoulders trembling.

"We began to think you would not come," Renart said as Elisha approached. The other mancers shifted back from him, some of them wearing hoods and long robes as if concealing their faces might preserve them from his notice. "Your henchman can stay outside, or I cannot guarantee his safety." He aimed his stare at Harald.

"He is here to ensure you live by your side of the bargain. When he goes, the boy and the vial go with him."

"The count said you demanded surety. The surety we use among ourselves is to be joined to our purpose through relics, like any other order." He stepped back to reveal a pair of knives on the tomb at his side, a curved flensing blade for stripping the skin, and another, a butcher's knife, for severing joints and cutting through meat.

"By killing someone," Elisha supplied. He stood near enough now that he could see the stains of old blood on the carved stone of the tombs and catch the flicker of Jude's lashes as the boy glanced up.

Renart sighed. "I thought you said he had some manners, Vertuollo."

"Some," the count agreed mildly. "The boy is the clear candidate, and for this purpose, he is willing. It would be his choice." He held the last word, meeting Elisha gaze.

"You told us Jude would go free, that the ceremony was only to seal the bargain," Gretchen said suddenly. "You called the boy your brother."

Just as he had called Elisha, his brother in the bond of sensitivity. Was Gretchen then his sister as well?

"The barber will wish to be sure the threat cannot so easily be brought to England."

"I will ensure that in my own fashion," Elisha stepped between the tombs, Jude seated before him, suddenly looking up, eyes wide. "He doesn't have to die."

Jude jabbed his finger against Elisha's chest. "*This is my choice*," he said through the contact, a splinter of anger and desperation.

"*I can't let you choose death, not when you've known so little of living*," Elisha answered, his own choice too near the surface.

"*I'm choosing your life, and everyone you love.*"

"*Not everyone*," Elisha whispered back. Jude snatched back his hand as if the thought burned him.

"I did say it was only the most obvious choice," Vertuollo remarked. "I presume you have another proposal?"

"Blood relics. If every mancer among you is marked, I will know when you're coming."

"Marked—with your blood?" Vertuollo tipped his head.

"So that you have contact at will? Not likely." Renart drew back stiffly, and a few others murmured around him. The Valley shifted and stirred as one of the mancers fled rather than accept.

"As would you, contact is mutual. My mark will warn me if you've broken the bargain, it will also warn you if I have."

"We might not choose to carry it," said Renart.

Elisha spread his hands and let his power flow, shifting the edges of his cloak and lighting his eyes with the Valley's mad swirl. "Anyone who chooses not to carry the mark may travel to England at will—but I am not bound to ignore them. If you come to England, do you think I'll miss you? Remember what happened last time you came." He conjured the image of Smithfield, outside London, where they tried to conquer the barons with the vision of the angel's death, Brigit's magic turning it back against those who bore witness and forcing them to feel the pain—until Elisha broke their circle and slew every mancer who had not immediately fled for their lives. Renart had been among those who left, and the tightening of his features showed how narrow an escape that had been.

"I remember," said a new voice. One of the hooded mancers stepped forward. "He killed two dozen of your friends at a whim," she continued. "He crushed my mind and barely saved my body." Brigit slipped back the hood that concealed her face, glowing now with the truth of her testimony, her eyes bright and hands clasped in pleading. "He is the most powerful magus that ever was, just as my mother foresaw, and to defy him is to die."

Their eyes met. She claimed that she remembered—was it true? Had her old life returned to her in these past months since she awakened? Her presence felt familiar still, and startlingly, untainted by the void of the necromancer, as if she had preserved herself, refusing the power they must have offered.

"You remember?" Gretchen hurried toward Brigit, catching her hand.

"I remember love and loss and darkness. I remember waking to the wonder of the light, lying upon the verge of death, only to rejoin the living." Brigit smiled with some of that grace she once possessed, and Elisha's heart pricked with fear, but he forced it back again. Even if she remembered everything and longed for some vengeance upon him, her vengeance would be his own.

"If you've remembered, your majesty, then we should go," Gretchen urged, but Brigit gently shook her head.

"I am not through here, Gretchen. You may go if you like." Brigit dismissed her regally. Gretchen glanced at the mancers all around them and remained.

"Shall we continue, then?" said Vertuollo. "It is all very touching, but I, at least, have my own concerns to attend to when this business is done."

"Indeed." Renart glanced at the mancers all around them, then plucked a silk kerchief from his sleeve. "Will this do?"

Elisha sat upon the other sarcophagus. "Give the vial to my man." He flung back his cloak and began rolling up his left sleeve. Bleeding, the most common operation of the barber, and one he had performed hundreds of times, mostly, truth be told, upon others.

"Then what guarantee do we have that you'll actually go through with it—go away, and leave us to our business?" Renart said.

Count Vertuollo settled his hand on Jude's shoulder. "The vial is merely a doorway, the passage by which our strength might flow to England. It is not the only one." He smiled faintly.

Here and there among the gathering, a sense of excitement escaped the careful deflections and projections. They thought they had Elisha now, a willing sacrifice to their blood-lust, making a promise that could not be kept to hold back the plague from the threshold of England. Renart acted a good role, suspicious of Elisha at every turn, challenging his word, his own smug defiance resting in the slightest crinkle of his eyes. The mancers believed they had won, defeating him at last, by pretending to concede England. The wolves stalked ever nearer to Elisha's trap. Now, he need only be sure that Jude and Harald were well free before he sprang it. The two larger blades lay waiting at the end of the stone where Elisha sat, but he ignored them. From his medical kit, Elisha drew a scalpel and a strap, tying off the strap at his biceps, holding his blade at the ready, the pulse at his inner elbow throbbing against the pressure. "The vial, or I do not cut."

Count Vertuollo revealed it, and Harald stepped up to slip it from his grasp. He briefly pressed it into Elisha's hand. "Is this it?"

"Aye," Elisha told him, feeling the trapped and familiar dread of his brother's death, and Harald drew back, winding the chain into his hand, clutching it tight.

"What of your henchmen, the killers you have sent against us?" Renart demanded.

"They have already been warned." He shot a glance to Harald who gave a nod. "If they strike you after tonight, they know I won't defend them."

"Very well then." Renart held out the kerchief between two fingers, almost lady-like.

Elisha nicked the vein, the slightest prick of pain, then

his blood trickled down as he faced the mancers. "By this blood, I swear that, after this night, I will no longer hunt you in your homes, nor encourage any of my followers to do so. And anyone who accepts this blood agrees never to set foot in England."

Elisha took the square of silk from Renart and dabbed its corner in his blood, then offered it back, sending the warning of his strength. "Who's next?" A grinning man stepped up, already pulsing with glee at Elisha's offering, letting the blood mark his leather purse. As he walked away, giving ground to the next one, Elisha felt the jab of the mancer's awareness probing him, reaching back, and Elisha answered with a snarl of power that made the mancer withdraw into the web of murders all around as more and more and more of them came up to be marked by the blood that would kill them.

Chapter 35

❖

The mancers pushed close, more a mob than a line, shoving their kerchiefs, shoes, thongs of leather and scraps of wool into the thin stream of Elisha's blood. He endured their glee and their greed though his pulse felt jumpy, his arm trembling already. He had lost much more blood than this before and been all right; he had to trust himself to manage it—the shaky effect might simply be a result of the restless power that lurked deep within, waiting his moment. Elisha divided his attention, concealing his true intent as he warded off the mancers' awareness, prodding his defenses, reveling in the sense of his vulnerability. With each approaching mancer, who then receded with his or her prize, Jude grew more restless, shifting under Vertuollo's grasp, whimpering. The count's determined expression suggested he was trying to coax the boy to stillness, but finally Jude could be still no longer, he howled and thrashed.

Vertuollo addressed him in Hungarian, sharply, but to no avail, forced to grab the boy with both hands, wrapping him tight, just the sort of messy interaction the count normally avoided.

"Madame, will you tame this creature?" Vertuollo demanded, and Gretchen ran over from Brigit's side, adding her hands to his, her eyes pleading with Jude and her presence urgent.

Writhing between them, Jude landed a solid kick in Gretchen's face. She stumbled back, pressing a hand to her nose to stop the spurt of blood. Vertuollo's presence shifted to ice as Jude broke free and launched himself across the gap to Elisha. The line of waiting mancers pressed close, some already drawing their flensing blades, anticipating the slaughter. Vertuollo parted them with his chill, sharp fury, shades gathering at his hand, and the others pressed after him. Some in the back protested their distance from the victim as others howled and chanted for blood. Jude danced upon the stone, evading the hands in his desperation to reach Elisha.

"Stop now—he lives, or I'm through," Elisha shouted at them. He jerked back his arm, encouraging the pulse to slow—still, it took longer than it should, and an ache started at the back of his throat. He could not afford to lose control now, not of his emotions, not of his own blood. Had he marked enough of them to forge the contact he needed, through the webs that bound them together? But if he were to spring his trap, he had to get Jude out of there.

Elisha thrust out his hand and caught Jude's arm. "*Hush, stop. You have to stop.*"

"*It should be me. I should die. I should die for what I am!*"

"*No!*" Elisha said, mustering whatever comfort he could, rushing to conceal his plans, even from Jude's sensitive touch. Jude crumpled against his chest, gasping for breath, sweaty and shaking.

"*I'm evil, I left you, I let them hurt you.*" Images flashed through the boy's flesh: Elisha's trial, the burning of his hands, the anger on Katherine's face and the despair in Harald's touch, the soothing chill of Vertuollo's agreement that he could die. Then, so softly, *"If I die, I can kill them, too. The greatest power, you said. If I die."*

Jesus, that was too close. *"I can't let you,"* Elisha said again. He pulled back his awareness, smothering his response even as he tried to comfort the boy. Barely tutored and not yet come into his own, there was no way Jude could control that kind of power, that he was willing to try both impressed and horrified Elisha.

Gretchen lowered her hands to Jude's trembling back. *"Nobody has to die. That's why he's doing this,"* she said as the boy buried himself in Elisha's arms. *"He is making it so, Jude, so that nobody else has to die."* Her words were quiet, strong, full of conviction, in spite of the damp fear that lit her eyes.

For a moment, Jude drew back, eyes round, then he started screaming into Elisha's flesh. *"You're lying. You're no better than he was!"*

Gretchen's eyes flashed up to meet Elisha's gaze, her touch sending inquiry, then surety. Damnation—Jude and Gretchen both, how long before one of the mancers worked it out?

"Get out of here, both of you—you have to go!" Elisha pushed Jude away, repelling his attachment, rejecting him.

Across the tomb, Harald reached out and caught the boy around the middle, prying him back in spite of his flailing. Please, God, the mancers wouldn't know what Jude meant. He had to act now, with as much contact as he already possessed.

Jude snatched at Elisha's left hand, hauling him across the stone as Harald dragged the boy backward. *"Me, me, me—I was to die."* Forcing contact, drawing magic from the talisman he carried, Jude strengthened his grip as if it were stone, the magic binding them together even as Elisha conjured the surge of his own power. It had to be done, immediately—now. But what could he do with the child still clinging to him, his wild sorcery desperate to hold Elisha by any means? Jude's first deliberate sorcery, achieved with Elisha's teaching, and it could well be his last. Would he now let Jude die, too, just for not letting go?

Harald's strength was no match for Jude's panic-driven power. Though he grappled and tugged, he could not force Jude to release his grasp on Elisha's hand. Gretchen joined the struggle, beseeching through the contact, her own magic rising, but unable to break the bond.

Over the boy's head, Elisha met Harald's stricken gaze, then Elisha snatched up the butcher's knife and slammed it down through his wrist. Perfectly honed, prepared for butchery, the blade sliced through skin and muscle, crunched into bone, then carved into cartilage and finally grated against the stone below. Images from medical texts overlaid the reality of what he had done, precise drawings in fine black ink, to be followed by instructions for bandaging the stump. His severed arm splashed blood.

Jude froze, his magic shattering. He gasped as he dropped the hand, then his wails of fear transformed to a high-pitched scream of sheer terror. Elisha's stomach clenched, and he tried to fend off the sight of his own hand tumbling like a fallen bird.

"*Get them out of here, open the door*," he ordered Gretchen, sending her a thrust of death that roiled from the spilling of his blood. She stumbled after Harald, then burst into a run.

Elisha sprawled to his back, gaping at the distant ceiling, at the mancers who clustered all around him: Vertuollo's towering fury aimed at Renart, Renart's confidence dancing in his features as he faced down the count, the others pressing close. He felt too weak already, his pain numbed by death, and more. Willow bark. A bitter-tasting pain-reliever, that caused blood to flow free. Christ, they had been a step ahead of him. That's what he tasted on the wafer, not poison but medicine, one that wouldn't sicken any member of the congregation, but only spur his own weakness as they maneuvered him into offering his own blood. Vertuollo hadn't known that part of Renart's plan when he made his bargain, else Jude would have felt the lie beneath the promise of his death. No wonder the count was furious: he bargained in good faith, believing Elisha would simply move on to become the master of England, while Renart dug Elisha's grave.

Distantly, he heard the door slam and Harald's presence retreated to safety, taking Jude and Gretchen with him.

Staring at the peak of the arches high above, Elisha mastered his stomach, and opened himself to the Valley. It rushed through him as a flood when the dam had broken, chilling him from fingertips to toes.

Elisha drew deep into himself and broke the seals he had laid upon his knowledge of death. If ever he had had an affinity for death, let it take him now, him and every person marked by his blood—their willow bark only made it strike all the faster, his life's blood streaming from his severed wrist. He sent his presence out, leaping to every spatter and stain.

"Now! Take him down! We can be faster, we are stronger," Renart cried above the growing chaos. "If he reaches for you, send him back. Trapped in the flesh."

"Trapped in the flesh!" others shouted, first in Latin, then Italian, French, German, a handful of other languages too mixed to be recognized.

Outside the temple, others died, the plague sending on a constant stream of shades, hurting, sickened, terrified, and Elisha swept them up into his own knowledge, an ever-expanding wave of death. He lay upon the knight's tomb, spread there bleeding on the boundary between life and death, between temple and Valley, gathering the power of the dead to his command and blasting it back down the webs that joined the mancers each to each.

Mancers screamed and cursed around him. Some fled into the Valley, only to find he was already there. As the chill spread, other mancers sprang upon him, yanking on his limbs, stretching him across the stone as they had held so many others, perhaps thinking, if they worked fast enough, they could avoid the magic he prepared for them. His left wrist throbbed with every heartbeat, the memory of pain that would be paralyzing when the shock wore off: no dose of willow bark could ward off the pain of such an injury forever. But there was one thing that could. Knives bit into him, tearing his clothes and carving into his skin. Already, the cold gripped him, a river of ice flowing to every touch, his vision feathering with frost, and his breath clouding the air obscuring the leering faces of the mancers all around. Panic surged before him as he sent his hunting hounds among these reapers of the dead.

"Don't kill him," Vertuollo thundered through both Valley and air. "Can you not feel what will happen if he dies?"

"If he plans to die, how the fuck do we stop him?" Renart shouted back, and Elisha's spirit soared with cold power and deadly knowledge. They could not stop him, not when murder was all they knew, and Death was so much more.

Overhead, the Valley blazed with brilliant light, as if he gazed into the heart of Hell—or could that be Heaven?—in spite of his death, in spite of his willing this to happen? As it had once before, the Valley spread with welcome, and Elisha felt the spirits of all those who had gone before, as if they joined hands to hold back the horrors and take him home. As the knives slashed at his flesh and stabbed for his throat, desperate to control the power of his dying, Elisha turned from the flesh, already sloughing away that corruption, preparing to slip from knowledge to mystery, to that place beyond the Valley, leaving all fear, all pain, all suffering behind.

Then a hand caught his face, cupping his cheek, cradling the memory of the angel's touch. It turned his frosted gaze away from Heaven with unexpected heat. "*Elisha*," Brigit said into his flesh.

He sent her the lashing cold of Death, embracing it, opening his heart to the fate he had so long denied. The brilliant glow of the Valley encompassed them all, open with madness, with comfort, and with fear.

Brigit cried out, but she did not release her grip. So be it—she would be among the first to die.

Even as he thought it, she pushed back, as firmly and naturally as if she stitched up his wounds with an expert needle, as if she could guide the very nature of the death-magic he hurled against them. Somewhere nearby, the shock of his assault broke a mancer's mind and a shriek died to nothing.

"*You would embrace your death and wield it now.*" Brigit's touch tingled, as if she sought to reach deeper, perhaps to do to him what he had once done to her, chasing down the paths of magic and searing away his soul. For so long, she had coveted the power he could wield, the power born of both his knowledge of death and his service to life.

She knew too late, she remembered too late to save herself, or any of them, for Elisha reached out and bound them all, every mancer he touched with his blood, and every mancer their webs of murder joined. In England, he slew them when they merged their power to attack him, but here, they need not even try—their killings joined them, their hundreds of victims linking each to each with links of power. Elisha's own torture, the knives that carved his body now and spilled his blood all the faster forged an affinity with every one of those deaths, and he took them for his own, the spreading wave of his power conjuring them all, awakening their horror and joining them with his own. He felt as if he rose up, flying, upon an explosion of magic, welling like a fountain that spread through his fingers, through his very flesh and bone and every drop of blood they shed in their eagerness for him to die.

"You want to kill us all with your death, Elisha." Brigit's calm penetrated the delirious rush of dying. *"There is only one problem. You do not wish to die."*

He laughed. All pain, all fear had departed, leaving him open to the all-consuming presence of Death itself. He did not wish to die? He had wished it a thousand times, only to force himself to soldier on, to face the foes that could not be defeated. If she believed that, she knew nothing at all.

"You want to see England again," she continued, tenderly cupping his face. *"You want to walk the streets of London, crowded with the people you've saved, and have hot cross buns at Easter. You want to set a child's broken arm, and see the smile of that baby your brother's wife adopted—oh, Elisha, it's a beautiful smile. You'd like to know if Pernel has recovered from Walter's death, and Allyson from Randall's. You want to see Alfleda grow from a child to a princess worthy of the word, and watch her married, and be certain her husband is worthy of her, for if he is not worthy, you want to be there to warn him away."*

Her words washed over him, every name conjuring the image of someone he cared for, Pernel's loyalty, Allyson's resolve, Alfleda's eagerness. The taste of hot cross buns floated on his tongue, fresh from a baker's oven, the sugar stinging his lips, and he could feel the sheltering houses of London leaning around him, channeling the sky into swaths of glowing gray with their peaked roofs and leaning plastered walls.

"What about our son, Elisha? Will he favor you, or me? Will he have blue eyes or green? What might be his

*first words, and where will he take his first steps? Can you
imagine watching him grow, stumbling toward you, his
hands outstretched, wanting nothing more than your
touch to draw him close?"*

Elisha's breath caught in his ruined throat. Mancers'
blades carved into him, slicing between his muscles, digging into his joints. He only had to let go, to release the
magical storm he carried, the knowledge so hard won, so
hurtful, so deep. To let go of life and embrace his own
death, and he could slay them all.

*"You want to know if the laws you passed as king will
change the ways of justice, and if your victory over France
will last. You want to know if the king will stand on behalf
of all witches as he has stood for you, Elisha."*

Elisha's will trembled, and he tried to avoid her touch,
to fend away what would come next, what she must say,
what he could not bear to hear. He deadened his flesh to
her touch, but they had known each other too long for
that and his very weaving of the webs that joined him to
the mancer had left him vulnerable on the stone before
her, the hot breeze of her breath touching his raw flesh
and racing in to warm his heart.

"And Thomas himself," she murmured, her words
sinking deep. *"Could you really give up and die, without
once more seeing his face, without hearing him call your
name, without looking once more in his eyes?"*

It was hard to work magic without consent, moving
the flesh in the ways that it willed, in full harmony with
its own nature. The flesh was meant to die, to decay and
dissolve back to the earth from which it was born. All
that Elisha needed to do was to let go and consent to his
death. It would be the most natural thing in the world, to
die at last after all he had been through, all that he had
done. More than ever before, he waited on the threshold
between life and death, finally ready to make the other
choice. She stood over him, stroking his cheek and re-

minding him of the world, of all that he had lived for, longed for, fought for—of every reason he had to live. With every speck of blood and strip of muscle, with every scrap of skin and shard of bone, Elisha fought the battle within himself, the same one he had always fought, vanquishing death on behalf of life. Her words and the world that they conjured left him utterly undone, his power unraveling with every cut of a mancer's knife.

To slay the mancers, Elisha must claim Death, and he could not. With all of his heart, he wanted to live.

Chapter 36

❖

"**What are you doing, my lady?**" Renart asked, his voice edged with fear. The torches had blown out in the panic.

"You wanted relics, yes, Your Eminence?" Brigit replied. "You wanted ways to make the world small enough to submit to our will. The law of contagion makes it all possible, but he showed you before, time and again, what you did not wish to see: that life is stronger than death, that the bonds it forges are more powerful even than murder. A talisman of death cold enough to repel the pestilence cannot defend you against death itself—how about a talisman of life? The relic of a saint still living?"

"Can you—" For a moment, Renart's voice failed in the darkness. "Is that even possible?"

"Not for any ordinary magus, but for a man who fought death his entire life, fought it with his entire being? Oh, Your Eminence, what might not be possible with such a man?" Her voice rang in stillness, echoing in Elisha's skull as in the temple all around. "I shall need a light."

A torch flared, illuminating a small circle of eager faces, Renart's eyes gleaming, Brigit's face bright with the flame, Vertuollo still and solemn, a dozen other mancers clustering about, firelight illuminating their shaky grins and shifting blades. Tears glazed Elisha's vision, distorting their features into demons and monsters. He couldn't breathe, and it didn't matter. He couldn't bleed, and it did not matter. He could not die, and he could not even scream as the pain seeped back, the willow bark wearing off. Streaks of agony marked his arms and chest. Unwilling and unbidden, he began to catalog his injuries: severed wrist, severe blood loss, arms partially flayed, multiple stab-wounds to the chest and throat, vocal chords cut. He should be dead already. And yet already his body was trying to heal, nerves and vessels twitching to come together, muscles shivering with the urgency to knit, his barren wrist still reaching for his missing hand. As Brigit encouraged his need to be whole, to heal and survive, his flesh obeyed, her magic binding with this most urgent need.

"Don't just hack him into pieces, we must be very deliberate if we're not to trigger his power. Here." Brigit's voice grew stronger, more commanding, then she brought out a bundle with her off-hand, leaving her other palm cupping Elisha's face. Something clattered onto the stone beside his head, then she lifted a scalpel into the light. "We must balance the urgency for life with his will for death—the perfect balance of opposites. There, spread out that diagram. You—place tourniquets at every limb, at least until we can catch the blood."

Renart chuckled. "My lady, I did not know you were a surgeon."

"I have become what I had to be," she said. "I have learned from the masters—Elisha not least of all. And my title is 'Your Majesty.'"

He laughed again, the sound moving from that slight panic into a relaxed sound of approval. "Tell me how to assist in the operation, Your Majesty, and I am at your will."

"We need to call upon his knowledge of healing, to create an affinity, so that everything we undertake from this point forward will be a surgery, not a slaughter. If we push him too far, I don't know that even I could convince him to go on living."

"Do not underestimate yourself, Your Majesty. You are very persuasive."

"Then you will slay him in the guise of healing?" Vertuollo, his Latin resonant and precise.

Brigit's humor insinuated itself into Elisha's skin. "On the contrary. If we do this right, he shall never die. And anyone with access to one of his relics and the wit to invoke his affinity will live forever."

"What will remain of his awareness?" the count asked. "His sensitivity?"

"Once the cardinal's wafer wears off, I can't imagine that he will have the strength to think on much besides the pain. His essence will be dispersed among the talismans we take. They say that soldiers who have lost a limb will go on feeling it. This will be much the same, if on a greater scale. Pass me those hooks, will you?"

"How will you share, Your Majesty? And with how many?" asked a man's harsh voice in hesitant Latin.

She stroked her fingers down Elisha's face and lifted them at last, pressing his right hand open. "His hands belong to me, and the skin of his right cheek. The rest will be shared."

Elisha tried to turn his head to follow her movement, but the wounds at his throat gaped and pain shot through him so he pressed his head back into the stone. His fur-lined cape lay beneath him, but the fur grew sticky with blood, soft no longer.

Someone cinched a strap around his left arm, cutting off the trickle of blood, then another slid over his right wrist.

"I should have thought you would claim his heart," Vertuollo remarked.

"I've had it before—it's just like any other. It is his hands where his talent lies."

A healing man who carries death in his hands, her mother Rowena had said. When he underwent trepanation and nearly died, Elisha imagined he had seen Rowena, his angel, reaching back for him from the fire, ready to lead him onward, away from this life of pain.

"I will have his witching eyes," said Renart, flaring his own. "We will need vessels to receive our relics. Paolo, to the workshop."

"But I don't want to miss—" protested the harsh voice.

"Did you not hear the queen? You won't miss a thing. If you are quick to return with as many vessels as you find, you may even make your own choice."

"Thank you, Your Eminence."

The Valley fluttered through Elisha's skin with a tingling sense of the man's departure. He could not die and pass beyond it, to whatever might lie there, yet if he survived, if Brigit's surgery proved successful, his mind would be so fragmented, so pierced with pain, he could do nothing to prevent them using him in whatever way they would, taking talismans of him and making themselves immortal, with the whole world laid at their feet, ripe for the slaughter. He remembered the scene at Salerno, lascivious women, drunken men, dancing and debauching one another, stripping each other of dignity and honor while a mancer orchestrated their madness and reaped the power of his reward.

The passage of the Valley pulsed like a second heartbeat as the mancers who had fled now returned, bringing more, and once—there!—the shrill terror of Jude's passage through the Valley, with Gretchen at his side, accompanied by the familiar sorrow of Nathaniel's death. To England then, where he had told them they would be safe. Jude was right: Elisha was a liar, no less than Danek had been. There was no safety. There could be none in a world where plague and mancers both roamed free.

"Shh, shh," Brigit crooned as she worked, her cold steel expertly carving between the bones of his wrist, probing and retreating, working methodically, just as he might have amputated a hand. Guy and his resources had taught her well: She was becoming what she needed. She could not master Death herself, not unless she understood Life as well, and so she undertook the study of surgery and healing, the knowledge Elisha had already possessed when he discovered the mystery of magic. She had wanted him, wanted his power, wanted his worship, wanted his secrets for her own. And now she had him utterly at her command.

His feet grew suddenly cold as someone stripped off his boots and hose, then gave a cry. "Here, Your Majesty, one of those foul blades!"

"Hush! I need to focus." Brigit's blade went awry and jabbed Elisha's palm so that his fingers twitched as if to snatch the scalpel from her.

"The blades that cut magic," said Vertuollo in a hushed tone. "Interesting." He leaned over, briefly visible in Elisha's narrowed view, and took the slender salted knife that glittered in the torchlight. "Can we not sever his own magic with it?"

"She works in opposites," Renart answered, moving beside the count so they might share contact, and whatever was said next, Elisha did not hear.

There must be a way—he could not simply be defeated, not by his mere desire to live. What weapons remained to him? They had taken the salted blade, not that he had a way to use it, and they had already disarmed his affinity with death. The Valley thrummed and pain streaked his limbs. Every time he thought he came close to a solution, the knives dug deeper and the connections flew apart in splintered agony. The mancers around him moved in and back in a terrible dance, filling vials with blood, catching his tears, carving slivers of his skin, sliding through the Valley as if they slid their hands upon him, unstoppable and sickening. Elisha drew himself deep, his awareness retreating from his skin and flesh and bone. Yet the further he withdrew, the louder grew the humming of the Valley. He reached for it again. Now—let him die now!

"Hold him!" Brigit cried aloud and through his broken body. "Everyone with a talisman, conjure him back, hold him here."

Elisha gasped without sound or breath, his spine gone rigid with the strain. For a moment, he imagined he could reach England or Heidelberg or anyplace but this terrible here.

Knocking reverberated through the temple. An icy anger swept the gathered mancers and many of them tugged down their hoods, glancing about uncertainly. Beyond the door, Elisha sensed Harald's return—along with dozens of others. Praise God, he was saved!

Chapter 37

❖

"**I**t's the papal guard," one of the mancers whispered. "We can't afford to be recognized, not if we're to claim benevolence. There aren't enough of us to rule by force."

"I will not allow them stop us now," Renart said, his voice so hard Elisha's brief hope fled.

"We haven't time for a battle." Brigit gripped her scalpel, "but your temple is compromised."

"We have another place to go," Vertuollo said. "The way of the dead."

"But how long can we stay there?" Brigit demanded. "Besides, he'll be closer to his affinity there than anywhere else."

"No, it is ideal. They'll break in the door of an empty room." Renart stared at her. "Although I do appreciate your artistry, Your Majesty, you shall have to work more quickly. If you cannot—"

"I can."

Renart reached out through the Valley. Then he cradled Elisha's head, almost gently, and carried him in to that place between. The maelstrom overwhelmed Elisha, throwing down his defenses, pouring in a cataract of dancing chaos. Shades flickered around him—shades he remembered but could not name, and the clinging dead that marked his captors soared around them, swooping like carrion birds delighted by the scent of fresh meat. The howling escalated in his ears, as if the shades were maddened by the presence of such a company of the living, and a growing company it was.

The Valley lacked direction and definition, except by the ties that linked the killers with the slain, and joined the outspread network of relics they had forged from those they killed. These trails tangled about the mancers, the only solid things in that space of chaos. Yet Elisha's right eye showed a different path. He lay in the grip of the mancers, Brigit readying her blade, and saw that second web in strands of light that penetrated the shadows, even there, in the Valley. He had seen those golden strands before, but never understood them. The mancers prided themselves on their relationships with the dead, but the dead were not all that joined them, not to each other, and not to the world outside. Outside the Valley, Elisha saw the webs of death, but within the Valley, he saw the web of life itself.

"*Hurry! We must hurry,*" Renart spoke through the Valley, in words that echoed from death to death. "*Come and share the queen's bounty.*" As he spoke, those dark strands of death that joined them tightened, and the mancers came. Count Vertuollo slipped through like a lord upon the dance floor, between the couples.

The French lord, the Italian merchant, the Hungarian child, the German maid, the German lady, and the English king. What on earth was happening? The Valley's thrum bewildered his senses, but he felt them still as those other, familiar presences entered the Valley. So many mancers, so few magi, and just one man, *desolati*, and desperate: Thomas, here, in the one place Elisha had sworn he should never see. His friends, too, had come, entering the Valley for what—for a vain attempt to save him?

Elisha screamed. In the air, in the world, they had cut

out his voice, but in the Valley that cut his heart, he spoke for multitudes. The shades in their eternal torment echoed his cry.

"*Attack. Do not let them reach the queen*," Renart ordered calmly.

Brigit sank her blade into Elisha's cheek, carving deep so that the blade chinked against his teeth. "*Go on, kill us now,*" she said into his flesh. "*The dead give voice to your pain, but they can't help you, and they cannot save your friends.*"

Then Renart gripped his chin, anchoring him in this place without form, and shoved a knife into his eye socket, twisting his head aside.

Jude fought in absolute silence, flinging stone after stone, tainted with his own dread knowledge. Gretchen fought beside him, but growing further away, the sinuous streaks of her magic repelling a mancer, only to be faced again with a half-dozen more.

Before blood claimed his vision, Elisha saw an arrow fly, streaking through the shadows and thrusting into a mancer's side, the arrow tipped with glittering salt. Katherine's guidance, Thomas's shot. She stood beside the king, holding him, keeping them both in the Valley, though her presence flickered with exhaustion. Thomas stood braced beside her, a longbow in his hands, launching arrow after arrow as the mancers plunged toward them, and more rose up behind. Pale strands connected them, Elisha and Thomas, Elisha and Katherine, the strands of their shared lives and united memories. Elisha whispered of danger, warning them of a mancer's approach. Katherine heard, sweeping out a long blade of her own, slashing behind them to the mancers who thought to attack from behind. Even then, she did not free her other hand from Thomas's waist.

The mancers surged toward them, and Jude howled,

his presence flaring with a fury that seemed too great for his slight form. Gretchen moved grimly beside him as he flung himself into the mancers, flailing as wildly as ever, and every one he touched crumpled, vomiting, their faces slick with sudden fever. Jude's little friends might not bite a mancer, marked with death, but Jude himself had no such distraction. His affinity with the disease he had so long harbored gave it potency. Jude struck and Gretchen amplified his power, but every blow caused a flicker in their presence, weakened by the struggle of merely remaining in the Valley, of intruding there in Life rather than in Death.

Katherine's presence faltered and she gave a moan. A distraction—their assault could never have been anything more. And if she fell, then Thomas remained, trapped and lost forever. Elisha almost cursed Harald's name—Harald who had sworn to keep his friends away—but the assassin was no magus, never mind a mancer. He would not have felt Renart's call to all the mancers as Katherine would, nor could he act to stop them. He was, in the end, as powerless as Elisha.

Thomas swung about, Katherine following, and nocked a salt-tipped arrow, drawing down on the knot of mancers surrounding Elisha. Their eyes met across that misty space, Thomas's hard and determined, only the pressure of his lips revealing all the fears he stifled. Brigit had her back to him. Without the anatomical drawing, her cutting slowed in spite of Renart's urging. The tip of that salt arrow aimed at her spine.

"*No, Your Majesty—she anchors his life*," Katherine breathed into the contact she shared with Thomas, the contact that touched Elisha even at that distance. Anchored in life, indeed.

Renart shoved at Elisha, shifting their little party, but too late. Thomas's arrow streaked through the seething

Valley and slammed into Renart's skull. He dropped from Elisha's back, his magic snuffed into nothing, even his death diffused like smoke at a breath of wind.

Falling with him, Elisha briefly slipped Brigit's grasp, his blood smoothing his passage. No matter, two dozen hands reached for him already, ringing him with their power, reinforcing the strength of Brigit's binding as she dropped beside him, grinding her fingers between the bones of his arm, pinning him.

Katherine's presence, so deliberate for so long, tremored against his awareness like a captured sparrow, too weak to survive.

Elisha dredged up the shreds of his power and focused on the channels that linked him with his friends, all of those who thought to save him, who did not know they had already failed. Through the tenuous links between them, he rejected them, pushing hard, his body flaring with the pain, then shuddering as he pushed them away. Katherine cried out, and Thomas jerked as she pulled him back, the Valley snapping open to a distant night.

"No!" Thomas shouted, then they were gone.

Chapter 38

◈

Vertuollo slipped into the circle of mancers, their cheers blending with the madness of the Valley. Some of the mancers vanished, retreating as their power failed, others replaced them, rising and falling in waves.

"*What for you, my lord? An ear? An arm?*" Brigit asked.

"*If you will not have it,*" said Vertuollo calmly, "*then I shall have his heart. It seems to me a worthy prize.*"

"*Act fast, my lord—not all of our people have the strength to stay here long.*"

Vertuollo tore back Elisha's shirt, exposing his scarred chest as if preparing him for an operation. He placed a hand over Elisha's heart, and a hand upon his own chest. "*I swore my own heart had been torn out when my son died. The power of death came easily to me, yet I was not prepared for that, to feel the loss of his life.*" His touch was so cold, Elisha's heart slowed, their two frigid hearts beating a slow and terrible unison, their sensitivities focused in that instant upon each other as Vertuollo's power spread between them. Before, Vertuollo used the Valley within, thrusting a shaft of sorcery that nearly slew Elisha. Now, he crafted something much more precise. With this intimate contact, Vertuollo forged an affinity between Elisha's flesh and his own, between Elisha's life, and his own.

"*I called you 'brother.' And you showed me what death meant to the living.*" His pale eyes lingered on Elisha's face. "*You showed me what life meant. No man should live forever by the death of his brother.*"

A shot of cold, like a lance of ice, drove into Vertuollo's chest, centered just beneath his own palm, his touch still joining them, the entire force of his magic directed within. His sorcery united them in that affinity, heart to heart, as he made the choice that Elisha could not and gave him the death of a magus.

The count's eyes rolled back, his head pitching as he collapsed in a pool of silk and silence.

His gift of power rushed Elisha's veins, his healing instincts activated in an instant. His nerves and vessels clasped, his muscles twitching as that dark gift turned from death to life. With an effort, Elisha forced the healing to slow, but the power defied him, that overwhelming strength of the magus in his final moment.

The black storm of Vertuollo's death swirled over him, and the mancers summoned up the shadows. They wreathed themselves in those they murdered, armoring themselves against Death, their webs grown strong in expectation of attack.

Elisha lashed out, Vertuollo's strength doubling his own, and cold lightning streaked the Valley, illuminating the mancers, their faces for a moment glowing pale, then once again flickering with shadow. For that instant, they seemed frozen, convinced that his assault would defeat them, but Elisha's own flesh, the blood talismans they carried blazed with sudden heat.

"*Thomas's face, Elisha. White bread and fresh cheese. Our child's first steps.*" Brigit whispered into him, snaring him in the magic of Life, reminding him of every reason to live in a succession of images so sharp he could taste them, see them, smell them. Even if he had the focus to force the point, Brigit's conjuring, her working of life and death together, anchored Elisha to the life he so longed for. He could not spend Vertuollo's death-magic as if it were his own.

And Vertuollo gave him not only death but his accursed sensitivity. Elisha's awareness stretched among the hundred mancers who carried his mark, showing him the murders they called up, his own tortured body echoing the pain of every one of those: Katherine's daughter, skinned in a forest; an old man slain by his son; a woman torn in an orgy of slaughter. When he called upon his affinity with death, all of these deaths taunted him, his sensitivity so acute he could no longer bind them to his will—each stood alone, a singular tragedy, like the death of Vertuollo's son, showing the master of Rome that the pain was not only for the dead, but for those who must go on living.

Elisha sobbed. His right hand felt loose, and he rocked, twisting himself around the pain, kicking away Brigit's knife and tearing himself free of her grip. He crept, rose, staggered on damaged feet, his arms held tight, his chest still aching with the terrible cold. He swallowed over and over, tasting only blood. For a moment, Brigit herself was gone, fleeing the Valley to find her strength, leaving him to her followers. The greedy dead reached toward him, shadows rising and falling, moaning with the breath of their thousands as the mancers closed in. He lay across Vertuollo's body, already grown thin and disintegrating, the flesh unnatural in this place of shades and nightmares. A slender well of darkness marked the crumpling corpse: the salt blade Harald had given him so very far from here. Elisha reached for it, his fingers barely responding.

"*And what would you do then*?" Brigit demanded as the Valley roiled around her, her entry framing her for a moment with the living world, the temple, the torches. "*You cannot die—and I have claimed your life.*"

Life. A bitter claim indeed. When they first met, when she first recognized him and showed him what he was, Brigit told him, "*You defend the border of life and death, and your choice at any moment might tip the balance.*" And yet he now had no choice at all. She had forced him to live. Vertuollo's sensitivity, added to his own, only made it all the harder to fight back, and even then, he could not strike at them with that core of Death he had created, they had armored themselves against it. Brigit would resume her cutting, making of him the greatest weapon the mancers ever held.

What else did he have? How else could he tip the balance? He had Vertuollo's sensitivity. He had the salted blade, and his attachment to life—if he could only see how to sever it.

"*Roll him over,*" Brigit commanded, and the mancers obeyed, the queer, shifting nature of the Valley pressing up into his pierced throat and creeping into the wounds that gaped in his chest and stomach.

Brigit's fingers pressed along his neck, then, "*Just below the skull,*" she muttered. "*Any pressure to the spine may result in paralysis.*"

It would take only a single cut, short, sharp, and accurate. And in that moment, Elisha knew what to do.

In spite of his agony, in spite of his war, Elisha let go of Death. He surrendered himself to Life, letting her words and images wash over him as she prepared to make that cut. His awareness, heightened by Vertuollo's sensitivity, flowed in the Valley, avoiding the dark webs of murder, streaking instead along the those thin, bright strands of life that tethered the mancers to the world beyond. They who delighted in Death still counted among the living. Brigit's magic made him the center of this binding, death and life in a terrible balance. The mancers held him here in the Valley. It flowed around him, but also through him, its pathways of death and its webbing of life like the veins of a body and he lay now at its heart. Contact he had, and affinity he named.

The next time Brigit's blade pierced his skin, Elisha used the law of affinity to reflect that severing thrust. He turned it from his own weak flesh to the vessels of the Valley itself, and sent it out through every channel of life, every trace of those who dealt in death and ignored its opposite. In an instant, cut from the bonds of worldly life, they crumpled. Each cold presence flared into nothing. The Valley shivered and briefly stilled, its every shade suspended, silence resounding in the misty space. The mancers tumbled and dropped, like so many dolls cast out, like so many corpses died of plague with too few gravediggers to care for the bodies.

Vertuollo's form collapsed into nothing, his fine features dissolving as the skin shredded, the skull beneath fracturing into tiny shards that shivered into dust. All around them, the wind sighed and swelled once more, ruffling the clothing of the dead mancers, its sharp current rising by the moment, sloughing off their skin and swirling them away to nothing. All of the mancers, all of those who willfully spread the plague and reveled in its brutality, who stood to gain by its slaughter, every single one of them—gone.

The Valley bent once more, cracked and spilled him into the temple, its torches still flickering, the fall knocking free the scalpel that probed his spine and allowing the rush of pain that overflowed his senses, until her touch brought him back. "What have you done?"

The brief thrill of victory fled him and tears stung Elisha's aching eyes. Brigit had bound them so closely together that the strands of life and death for her, as for himself, became too tangled to scparate. Elisha sprawled on the tomb he had left, atop his ruined cape, and Brigit still loomed over him. She gripped his severed left hand in hers, and in the other, that scrap of skin she had stolen from his cheek, taking back the touch Rowena had given him all those years ago, when she used the power of her own death-magic to transform into an angel as she burned.

"Elisha? Dear God, can it be?" Harald's voice echoed in the empty chamber.

Brigit's confusion turned to wonder. "I live," she said through the scrap of his flesh she carried, then she did what she had for so long desired: she conjured death from Elisha's severed hand.

The chill power flowed through him and Elisha felt its rush as it leapt to her command. "*Don't touch her,*" he cried without a voice, without even the echo of the dead to carry his words.

In one hand, she carried Death, in the captive form of Elisha's own power. In the other, she carried the scrap of him that held the angel's touch, the memory that linked her with her mother. Demon and angel, so very alike, and so very different. Affinity. Knowledge. Contact. She held it all.

Elisha marshalled the last of the sensitivity Vertuollo had forced upon him, both vulnerability and strength, and he conjured the memory of her mother's death, sending it sharp and clear as she sucked down the black river of death she craved.

With the last strand of power he yet held, Elisha conjured one thing for himself. From the salt blade pressed in his tortured hand, he conjured the affinity to cut magic itself, to sever the connection she had forged between them as he touched off the vision of her mother's death, like the spark that lit a bombard's explosion. With the salt blade, Elisha cut himself free of her binding and left her to die.

Brigit screamed as the spells she carried became one, the death she longed to deliver and the memory of her own mother's death captured in Elisha's flesh. The affinity of Brigit's own presence bound the two spells into one, and, just as her mother had done, she burst into flames. Somewhere beyond her, Harald cried an oath.

The fire billowed up, bursting free of the roof overhead in a shower of ash and timbers that scattered all around. Her death lit up the sky above, the light so intense it felt blinding, but Elisha could not shut the wounded lids of his eyes and so he watched, as he had watched her mother's final agony and dread release.

Elisha lay in silence on the tomb, the air transformed in a moment from terrible heat and thunder to this stillness, the peace of the dead below him. Above him, the peace of Heaven, the brightness of stars.

Chapter 39

❖

Elisha waited for days to rise from the grave. He considered rising at three, but the Biblical significance, if, by chance, he were seen would be far too great to ignore. As it was, he lay still for a long time, his senses turned inward to understand the damage done to his body. He began the painstaking labor of knitting himself back together again, remembering how to be whole, or nearly so: Brigit had taken his left hand with her beyond the grave.

Where before he felt open to the Valley, the tug of it somewhere near his heart, now he touched it, the contact subtle and constant, any shift in its movement, as a ripple in a stream, as if in forging the affinity between his tortured body and the Valley's flows, Elisha remained forever at its heart, its pulses as familiar as his own.

Allowing his awareness to spread from his tortured flesh, Elisha found another corpse laid out not far off, still intact. It showed him the way, serving as a model to guide his healing. Sometime later, Elisha opened his eyes to the darkness. Carefully, he moved his toes, then the fingers of his right hand. Stiff they were, and numb, but they obeyed well enough. The stump of his left wrist healed, the skin smooth over the abrupt knobs of bone. With much prodding and wriggling, he managed to unwrap the top of his winding sheet, tearing it away from his face and shoulders.

Reaching out, Elisha explored his surroundings in all ways, finding the smooth surface of wood a few inches over his face. His awareness roved around him: bodies, old and new, many touched with the particular vibration of holy relics. He lay in a crypt. Had he been buried at Avignon?

Elisha pushed hard against the wood, testing its strength, and it sprang open. The coffin lid clattered to the floor and he flinched at the sound. Lamplight gave a soft glow to the air above although it reeked of death and incense.

Slowly Elisha sat up, dislodging something that lay upon his chest, and looked down. The wooden lid of his coffin lay askew against the wall. It had not been nailed shut.

Another, more subtle fragrance reached him then, and Elisha frowned. He glanced down to find a sprinkling of dried roses on the marble floor below, along with oranges and lemons, cloves and cinnamon, and a hundred tokens—some of metal and some of wood—bearing the sign of Saint Barber. London. Harald had brought him home.

This in itself brought an ache to his throat, his eyes tracing the familiar pale stone of England which he had never expected to see again. Then Elisha turned his attention to the thing he found in his coffin, a folded parchment, unsealed. He bent his sore back and groaned. Every part of him ached, from the tips of his new-healed fingers to the soles of his feet. The flesh of his chest and throat and arms still twitched with the slashes of the mancers' knives. He sat still for a time, then held up the page to let some light fall upon the words.

"My dear Elisha,

"It is only a fool's hope that leads me to imagine you

reading these words, and I further hope that you will forgive me if the ink occasionally runs with tears. I came there to save you, Elisha, and yet I came too late, and I shall repent of it for the rest of my days. I hoped as well that my love, or the promise of it, would be enough to keep you here, even as reason tells me that you had to go.

"Your son is well; your brother's widow treats him as her own. And Alfleda is home with me, but you must know how she grieves, even as she is some solace to my own. The priests would have me believe that you are in a better place. To be true, not a few of them think you are in a place much worse, but neither voice can sway me. They speak more often of Hell now, for so many of them witnessed it body and soul. But none of them, I wager, know it so intimately as you. On the night you fell, a pillar of fire rose over the palace of the Pope himself, and many have taken it for a sign of evil. And yet, this foul pestilence that roams among us is lessened since that day, and I dare pray again that we shall be free of it, as it runs its course without the influence of demons.

"I work to find a place here for your friends, that speechless child whom only Alfleda can convince to leave your side, that soldier-courtier who carried you home, that lady—well, some at court have found her more than pleasing, imagining, for all that we have been so close already, that I have brought her here to wed. It is a thought not unworthy of consideration, and yet . . . my spirit lingers here, entombed.

"Were it in my power, I would have you laid to rest on featherbeds and satin. Did I not know how you would curse me for it, I would lay myself down at your feet. We will be a long time in repairing the damage of these times, and I know that you would have me here to see it done. By the blood of Christ, I swear to you, Elisha, that the sight of you has almost undone me. And yet it seems your wounds are not for love to heal.

*"Go with God, if that be your will, but know that I
envy Him your company. I do not know what lies beyond
your valley, but I may yet hope that even such deep shadows may be pierced by love."*

The page trembled from Elisha's grasp, then slid back
to his lap. His throat ached, and a shaky hand covered his
eyes. Too dry to be true to the beating of his heart.

"Elisha."

He jerked at the sound of the voice and tried to turn,
but succeeded only in spilling the coffin and himself with
it, landing on the pile of tokens, the scent of citrus and
roses brightening the air.

"Don't, don't," Thomas breathed, running. He spilled
his candlestick and left it behind to fall to his knees at
Elisha's side, hands outstretched as if to a fire.

Wincing at the image, Elisha turned his face aside.

Thomas's hand gently turned him back, his fingers lingering upon the scar that Brigit had made of an angel's
touch. Elisha gazed up at him, Thomas's bright eyes still
rimmed by darkness.

"Oh, my king," he sighed, "have you seen no rest?"

At that, Thomas gave the faintest smile. "I have not
been here every night, if that's what you fear. But we do
keep watch over you."

Elisha slowly sat up, and Thomas's hand fell away.
"We?"

"Your friends. Madoc, Robert, Katherine, myself, that
wild boy who must be convinced to do anything but sit
by you. I prayed that I would be the one here, if it happened." His hands clung together in his lap. "If you rose."

Holding up the letter, Elisha said, "You seemed confident of that."

Light brown hair shielded Thomas's down-turned
eyes. "I am a man of faith; you know that. For my own
sake, I had to believe." He blew out a sigh. "I was less
confident that you would stay."

Tracing the edge of the letter, Elisha murmured, "Truth be told, I do not know myself."

Their breathing was the only sound to part the silence, then Thomas asked, "Where were you?"

Elisha shrugged. He had not the strength to speak of the Valley and the madness there, or the darker madness of the days he lingered in the ruined temple, watching his own shade killing Brigit's with that final touch, before he drew himself back to the flesh. He blinked back the visions and focused on the parchment, touching it gently. "I guess I returned for this, to know how it all came out, who had lived and who had not—what victory remained at the battle's end."

Looking sharply away, Thomas made no reply, and Elisha knew it was not the answer he hoped for. Elisha squeezed shut his eyes, tucking the stump of his left wrist under his right arm. "Oh, Thomas, you know as well as I that there's no hope for us—better, in fact."

"Hope of what?" Thomas shot back, and Elisha flinched. "Do you even know what I hope for? It is enough for me to know you're safe, better still to know that you might be happy. God knows I wish that it could be with me."

"But you're the king," said Elisha softly, creeping forward over the flowers and tokens that surrounded his coffin. "You're the king, and I . . ." but he no longer knew what to say, what, exactly, he was, and so he fell silent, Thomas so near that his presence brought warmth to Elisha's face.

The king pointed to a sack beside the plinth where Elisha's coffin had rested. "You'll find clothes in there, and food—we've changed it out every day, just in case—and the key to the lodge, not that you would go there if you mean to avoid me, but you're still welcome. I moved your horse to the livery by Saint Bart's and paid her board." His hand dropped back, trembling, until he clenched it into a fist. "I dreamed of us running off to-gether, fleeing to Capri, perhaps, someplace where it's no sin to love each other." His shoulders slumped, and the blue spark of his eye glanced back to Elisha's face. "But someone has to stay behind. Someone must lead the na-tion out of this darkness. If and when we have recovered from the pestilence, then someone must change the laws, and work to convince the Church, and find a way to make your people safe."

Elisha gave a slight chuckle. "That's what Brigit wanted, too, but she would not have settled for mere equality."

"Some fear witches more than ever, after her temple at Smithfield broke, and they don't even know the truth about the plague. But the cult of Saint Barber grows ev-ery day as well." Then Thomas, too, laughed. "How you must hate that."

"If it does some good."

"Everyone needs something to believe in." He straightened, still staring toward the wall. "Your battle may be over, but ours is just begun."

The cold floor and the pervasive air of death began to seep into Elisha's weary bones. He reached out and drew the sack toward him, hearing the chink of coins. How like Thomas to think of everything. He let the weight of that consideration rest upon his lap, the heels of boots settling against his thigh, the corner of a good wool cape poking out of the sack.

"Elisha, please don't go." Thomas's voice echoed from the stone and the silent statues of the dead. "Please."

"How can I stay without endangering all you would work for?"

"Was it the letter? Did I not say enough?" Then, more softly, "Did I say too much?"

"No," said Elisha. "It's a good letter—the best I've ever had, although that says little for a man who couldn't read until a year ago."

"Then why?"

Elisha, too, gazed at the wall, his breathing unconsciously falling in rhythm with his king's. "Because there has been too much dying, too much pain. I just—I need to find some peace, and I don't know that I can find it here."

"Peace." Thomas nodded. "I could use that, too, but if all this has shown me nothing else it is that some things are worth fighting for." He turned to Elisha, blue eyes sparkling. "You've known too much of dying, my friend. But what do you know about living?"

"They cannot be separated—life and death exist in balance, one is but the shadow of the other." Elisha tried to smile. "Without the darkness, would we know to love the day?"

"Then come," said Thomas, and he lifted his hand. "Come with me and stand in the light. For as long as it lasts, for whatever may come—we have faced the worst that God's world has to offer—can we not still hope for the best?"

In the gentle light of the single lamp, Elisha studied Thomas's face, serious, lean, and handsome. He knew that he should leave, for all the reasons he claimed and more, and yet ... sometimes knowledge was the least part of sorcery.

Elisha reached out and took his hand. Strength flowed between them, and a heat so intense that Elisha forgot he had ever been cold. He laughed aloud then, and Thomas grinned in return. Affinity, he thought. Contact. Thomas pulled him close to his heart, and Elisha accepted the blessing of the king's embrace.

ACKNOWLEDGMENTS

Here we are, at the end of Elisha's story—or at least, at the point where he and Thomas can finally go for a pint. As you read these thanks, please imagine them raising a pint to each and every one of you—and quite possibly getting rather drunk, given the number of people who deserve my gratitude.

First of all, my agent Cameron, editors Josh and Betsy, and the entire crew at DAW who helped to bring this work to your eyes. Without their assistance, the books might never have hit the shelves, and they assuredly would not be as strong as they are. Any faults are my own. Also Cliff Nielsen, the amazing cover artist who offered a glimpse of Elisha's world.

To my beta readers, Ken H., Ken S., Heather A.—and earlier readers Alex, Sarah, Steve, and Brett. With a special shout-out to beta reader and medical advisor, D. T. Friedman. Without you, Elisha might have been lost in the woods for a good long while. I will mention Sherry Peters here, as well, the writing coach who guided me through some rough patches in the midst of the muddle.

My supportive friends and family deserve a longer note for letting me go to conferences like the International Medieval Congress in Kalamazoo, and sometimes for letting me stay home in my office; for not calling a psychiatrist or the police when I suddenly announce, "I've found the perfect way to kill a priest!", and for generally respecting my writing time. Thank you so much, Mom and Dad, Laurel and Gabriel, and especially Ed! (along with cheerleader Stacy, sister Michelle, and writing buddies Robin, Rob, John, and Iain).

Richard, longtime friend and reader, and now also a writing buddy, whose questions always make me dig deeper.

The scholars of Kzoo, especially members of Societas Magica, MEARCSTAPA, Tales After Tolkien, Medica, and AVISTA, whose papers and conversation inspired my own research and sparked so many ideas.

Last, but certainly not least (could somebody bring Elisha and Thomas another round of cider? Thanks!), for the readers who have followed us this far. Writers need readers to complete the journey, and I have been grateful to meet so many of you along the way. Some of you, like Carol and Kris, were there at the start, and some of you, like Ed and Clinton, reached out across the distance. Your enthusiasm has often carried me on the long road back to London.

Many others, readers and writers, fans and friends, who have contributed in their own way. Thank you all, so very much. I hope to meet you all on another adventure someday soon!

Deborah J. Ross
The Seven-Petaled Shield

An all-new high fantasy trilogy of magic, myth, and war—from a co-author of the Darkover novels!

THE SEVEN-PETALED SHIELD
978-0-7564-0621-9

SHANNIVAR
978-0-7564-0920-3

THE HEIR OF KHORED
978-0-7564-0921-0

To Order Call: 1-800-788-6262
www.dawbooks.com

DAW 166

Jacey Bedford
The Rowankind Series

"A finely crafted and well-researched plunge into swashbuckling, sorcery, shape-shifting, and the Fae!"
—Elizabeth Ann Scarborough,
author of *The Healer's War*

"Bedford crafts emotionally complex relationships and interesting secondary characters while carefully building an innovative yet familiar world."
—*RT Reviews*

"Swashbuckling adventure collides with mystical mayhem on land and at sea in this rousing historical fantasy series...set in a magic-infused England in 1800." —*Publishers Weekly*

Winterwood
978-0-7564-1015-5

Silverwolf
978-0-7564-1191-6

To Order Call: 1-800-788-6262
www.dawbooks.com

DAW 199

Saladin Ahmed

Throne of the Crescent Moon

978-0-7564-0778-0

"An arresting, sumptuous and thoroughly satisfying debut."
— *Kirkus* (starred)

"Set in a quasi–Middle Eastern city and populated with the supernatural creatures of Arab folklore, this long-awaited debut by a finalist for the Nebula and Campbell awards brings *The Arabian Nights* to sensuous life. The maturity and wisdom of Ahmed's older protagonists are a delightful contrast to the brave impulsiveness of their younger companions. This trilogy launch will delight fantasy lovers who enjoy flawed but honorable protagonists and a touch of the exotic."   — *Library Journal* (starred)

"Ahmed's debut masterfully paints a world both bright and terrible. Unobtrusive hints of backstory contribute to the sense that this novel is part of a larger ongoing tale, and the Arab-influenced setting is full of vibrant description, characters, and religious expressions that will delight readers weary of pseudo-European epics."
— *Publishers Weekly* (starred)

To Order Call: 1-800-788-6262
www.dawbooks.com